The two men were talking in whispers . . .

"They've found out about Little. They may send someone after him."

"So what?" asked the younger man. "What are they going to make out of that crazy yarn? The Little man doesn't know the truth."

"They could put things together."

"I doubt it, sir."

"Don't doubt it. They could, I say. And something very disagreeable could happen to him."

"No, no. We'll keep an eye on him."

The older man shook his head. "They can get to him. And Little does know the whole thing. The time, the place, the whole thing. But he doesn't know he knows it all. He doesn't know what he knows. And that makes him even more dangerous. He wouldn't even know if he were telling it. They have ways." He shuddered. And thought of J Little walking around with the deadly secret that could be the end of him . . . and of everyone else, too.

CHARLOTTE ARMSTRONG

Seven Seats to the Moon

A FAWCETT CREST BOOK
Fawcett Publications, Inc., Greenwich, Conn.

CHAPTER 1

Saturday Afternoon

The pink curtain hung within inches of his cheek. J could imagine sly little fox ears, sharpening, the other side of the flimsy cloth where another human being could, if he chose, listen to every word. There was no help for it. J didn't find it appropriate to whisper all the way from Chicago to southern California.

"Sophia?" (He tried to sound like himself in spite of his sense of an eavesdropper.) "Listen, don't meet the plane. I'm not going to be on it."

His wife began to wail, and he interrupted. "I'm in the damn hospital."

Sophia's voice changed immediately. "What's the matter?" she demanded.

"Not a darned thing. Ridiculous! But I'm kinda trapped. They won't let me out till tomorrow."

"J, what *happened* to you?" Sophia's concern sounded like anger. It often did.

"All it was," he told her, "I *almost* got hit by a car, and do mean almost. Skinned my knee. Big deal! Seems the old biddy who was driving the car is pretty much in the chips, and she's got me hemmed in by her doctors and her lawyers. *She* doesn't want to get sued. So here I . . ."

"J, shall I come?" He could hear Sophia's mind checking off her chores. Empty the refrigerator. Call off the Neebys.

"No, no," he said. "They've already gone over me, up and down and sideways. I'd have one heck of a time developing a nice expensive injury now. I'm supposed to settle. Listen, I'm having the hotel change my reservation to the same flight tomorrow."

"J, are you sure?"

"Sure I'm sure." J relaxed because he could tell that she

5

was relaxing. "Now, they insist they've got to take pictures of every bone in my head, and it's a damned nuisance, but it's anyhow for free. Thing is, I can't get out of here till the doctors say so."

He considered explaining that he didn't know where they had hidden his torn trousers, but he felt too classically helpless, sitting on the edge of the high bed with his bare, furry legs dangling. Nobody had to see this picture in her mind's eye.

Sophia was demanding the whole story.

"Well, I was crossing the street around nine o'clock this morning, and with the light, too. She just didn't happen to stop, that's all. So I did some pret-ty fast footwork. Put my hand on her hood and kinda vaulted. All that happened was—she didn't hit me, and neither did anybody else, but—I fell. So right away there was a traffic jam you wouldn't believe and cops and the whole uproar. How about meeting the plane tomorrow?"

"I will," said Sophia. "Or somebody will. All the kids are coming for Sunday night supper. Now, J, don't you get on any airplane if you're feeling the slightest bit . . . How do you feel? Were you knocked out or what?"

"No, no," he said. "Skinned my knee and tore the pants to my blue suit. Well, I was shook up, naturally. But I feel fine now. They've put every antibiotic known to man in my bloodstream. So don't worry about infection. It wouldn't dare!"

"Are you going to settle?" Sophia was believing him now. He could hear some slight mischief creeping into her voice. He had a feeling that she could see him—not pitiably languishing, but perched, half-naked, with his thinning hair on end.

"Right now I'd settle for getting out of here," he growled and looked behind him. The hospital gown didn't quite meet in the back, and he could feel eye-beams like a draft on his skin. Two women had come into the room, one a nurse, the other an aide. They had a wheelchair.

"Listen, Sophia," he said, across two-thirds of the continent, "I think they're after me for some damn thing. If it's too much trouble, I can take the bus as far as Hollywood."

"No, no," said his wife. "Don't you do that. Where are you? What hospital?" He told her. "I'll call you back tonight," he announced firmly.

"Hey . . ."

"What?"

"Don't forget to call off the Neebys."

"I won't, J. Take care, dear."

J hung up and looked sourly at the wheelchair. "Boy," he said, "you people must need customers pretty bad."

"Mr. Little," said the nurse in a stern fashion, "you are wanted for X rays. As a matter of fact," she added grimly, "this hospital is full to absolute capacity, and we could use *your* bed, you know."

J took this kindly. It was rather reassuring.

When they brought him back to the room, the pink curtain had been pushed into a column against the wall, and J met his room-mate, who turned out to be a man about his own vintage with a salt-sprinkled, red head and a plump, discontented face. He was an old hand at hospitals.

"They put you in the hospital," he proclaimed. "This is great, for *them*. Best of care and hang the expense, although there's insurance, but this they don't mention. Oh, *they're* doing the right thing, *they* are. Now, they got visiting hours to protect them. Oh, you bet, that's what visiting hours are for, in case you don't realize. Now, all *they* got to do is show up once a day. Once is enough. See, *I* might get tired."

J guessed the man was promised no visitors today and felt miffed.

"Meantime, who gets to lie here and take the wholesale treatment? They run us like an assembly line. Wake us up, feed us, wash us, according to *their* convenience. The rest of the time we get to wait. Routine is not for us, you realize that? It's for *them*. Oh, they don't call us patients for nothing."

J knew at once that this last had been said at least a thousand times. Too lazy to sort out all those pronouns and not disposed to entangle himself in a conversation, J advised the man that he intended to doze. So the man turned on the television set that hung high on the opposite wall and wrapped himself in the earphones.

While the pictured people capered and mouthed, J contemplated his situation, which he had to admit was ludicrous. He simply was not the kind of man who could have said to all those authorities, "I'm all right. Just let me be." The fact was he had thought he was a goner, down on the pavement among the screaming wheels, and afterward he had been easily persuaded to be "wise." He had even thought, in his innocence, that people were being very good to him. Oh, well, he could always clown it up, make a funny story. "Dine out on it" was the phrase his father used. He might work up a little imitation of the old dowager with her diamonds flashing and her bosoms heaving.

Nevertheless, he was in for a dismal siege. The hospital food was too bland, the sheet was so tight it burned, the blanket was *not* cozy. He wasn't going to get his cocktail before dinner. He felt very sorry for himself, incarcerated thus and cruelly kept from home.

But J set himself to improve his own attitude. After all, what was he missing? One Saturday night bridge game with the usual neighborhood couple. He would be in his office on Monday according to schedule, and this adventure wasn't costing him anything in money. He would have to sign a release of some kind, he realized. The lawyers had already made that clear in their oblique but firm fashion. Well, he might put up a bit of a fight for some nuisance money, but he wasn't going to fight so hard that he couldn't get out of here tomorrow. He was not a greedy man.

He was a lucky man—not to have been killed! What? Stone-dead in Chicago, aged forty-nine? An obituary composed itself in his head, and J said aloud, "Oh, God!"

After a while he realized that it was late for J Middleton Little to be setting up a dialogue with God. Oh, he had pondered the big questions when young, but in later years he had been going about his mundane business pretty sure that there must be Something, but not so sure He wanted J to be "good," or if so, what He meant by that. If J had been dispatched this Saturday morning to be judged (some say) by Truth itself, he would have had to go just as he was. J reflected that, on the whole, he had probably been neither a good man nor a bad man, but somewhere in the middle. How true!

When his room-mate turned off the TV, J left off brooding, braced himself, and was glad to see his suitcase arriving in the moment. The hotel had sent it around with a note that confirmed J's plane seat for tomorrow at 2 P.M. Chicago time. He hopped out of bed, fished in his wallet for a tip, slung his suitcase on the bed, and opened it. The sight of his own things was comforting.

"Say," said his room-mate feebly, "as long as you're up, d'you mind going and hollering for a nurse? Slobs, never answer *my* light."

So J got quickly into his own pajamas and his own robe and soft foldable slippers, placed his own toilet kit within the tiny lavatory, and then he left the room. After he had given the message, which was received stoically at the nurses' post, J found himself continuing to stroll. Why not? He was okay. And damned if he was going to sit still in that bed all afternoon, all evening, and all night, too. His knee might stiffen. At all costs, he kidded himself, peering about him with mild interest, we must not stiffen!

In Burbank, California, Sophia Thomas Little called off the Neebys, letting Susie Neeby make do with the bare facts that J couldn't make his plane. Sophia didn't feel like going into J's story. It had disconcerted her somewhat. Besides, it was J's to tell.

But she had called her son's house and told his wife, Marion, who said all the right things. "What a shame! But don't worry, Mother. I'm sure Dad's all right if he says so." Marion then offered Win's services to meet the plane tomorrow. But Sophia said quickly that she would do that herself. "But could you pick up my mother, do you think, dear? Marietta's back at the Wimple."

"Oh, is she?" said Marion sympathetically. "Well, of course. We'll call for her."

Marion then told Sophia how the Little grandkids were and, again, not to worry.

Sophia hung up and sighed deeply. She wasn't exactly worrying. She didn't like having her anticipations canceled. She liked to make a plan and operate within it. She didn't fancy a lonely evening for which she had not been prepared. Her youngest daughter, Nancy Jo, who at the age of sixteen would have thought herself disgraced not to have a date on a Saturday night, couldn't be asked to cancel that and stay home with her *mother*. This was unthinkable. Besides, it wasn't Nanjo that Sophia wanted around.

She just wished that J were coming home.

In Chicago her husband, J Middleton Little, feeling a whole lot better in his own garments, wandered the corridors. He winced now and then to see through an open door a sight that really should not have been exposed to a stranger's eyes. Unclothed, disheveled people, lying down and suffering pain—J couldn't help feeling that it would have been more decent if he had not been able to peer in upon them in their helplessness, since he was humanly unable to refrain. What, *persons!* Stripped of their own garments, unable to project any images! (Which was a human right of sorts, after all.)

He spent quite a while mooning through some glass doors to watch those who were inspecting the new babies, and finally, having worn out the better part of the afternoon and knowing that supper would be gruesomely early, J made his way back to Room 817. The door was closed, and he opened it very gently. He didn't know what ailed his room-mate. He would probably find out, he thought with resignation.

In the far bed, near the window, the man was lying flat, well covered up, seemingly asleep. So J hushed even his breathing and tiptoed in his soft footgear to the lavatory and managed the door soundlessly. Inside the tiny cubicle he felt along the doorjamb for the light switch. His own face leaped to his eye in the mirror. Wait a minute!

Had he misremembered the number and come sneaking into the wrong room? No, there was his own toilet kit on the shelf. But the head on the pillow in the far bed had, in the course of the afternoon, somehow turned pure white.

J frowned at himself and leaned closer to the glass to examine what just might be a small bruise on his cheekbone, thinking on two levels at once. Hah, if all those sophisticated tests had missed an obvious surface injury—phooey on modern science! And it was a trick of the light, of course. Hair didn't turn white in an hour or two, in spite of old wives' tales.

Then he heard a man's voice say, "Close the door."

Another man's voice said, "How are you feeling, sir?"

"Lousy," said the first voice, "from here on out. You know that."

"Bad luck, sir. I don't mind saying . . ."

"Crank me up, will you? We're alone. That's lucky."

J could hear the creaking of the bed's mechanism. He was feeling pretty foolish. They didn't know he was in here! He had better flush the toilet. He hadn't intended to become an eavesdropper.

"Any questions? Quickly," said the first voice.

Before J could move, the visitor began to ask the dog-gonedest questions J had ever heard in his life. He couldn't make head nor tail of whatever jargon was being spoken. It seemed to be English, but J didn't seem to know a whole lot of these words. He began to catch a few clues. Oh, well, science. And damn it, here he was eavesdropping. Maybe he could sneak out later on. J felt hideously embarrassed.

The visitor spoke suddenly in the clear. "That checks, then. I also wanted to say I'm honored to be your replacement. Sorry you can't make it yourself, sir. Of all people, you deserve to go."

"One of the elite, eh?" said the patient. "Top, so they say. Don't cry for me, Bryce. I'm sorry enough for myself, to be just missing what may be the very top. Poonacootamoowa." He spoke the strange sounds in a lingering way.

"If it turns out to be so," said the visitor, "the human race is going to have a fine string of syllables to get used to. Poonacootamoowa."

"If the race survives," said the patient in a voice that had edges.

"Pain, sir?" the visitor was quick.

"You bet," snapped the patient.

"Can't they do something to ease that?"

"I won't have it," said the patient. "A week is only seven days. And what's a day?"

"Can't they at least give you a private room, sir?" said the visitor in some distress.

"This is it," said the patient. "My friend, whoever he is, leaves tomorrow. Then they'll batten down the hatches, and I can scream all I want. No," he added, as if the visitor had grimaced disagreement, "I will not have drugs. Too damned dangerous."

"Oh, I don't think . . ."

"*I* think. And I will not be the one to blow it. A fine crown to my career that would be. Now, now, don't think of me as any heroic martyr. It's a form of vanity, like everything else. What a piece of work is man, eh?"

"He'll survive," said the visitor softly.

"You must have a seat to the moon," said the patient savagely, "to be so sure of that." He moaned, and then he seemed to rally. "You should remember," he said, "that antique mankind had to put up with any and all pain. No anesthesia, no dainty white pills, no kindly needles, no blessed sleep to knit up the raveled sleeve. . . ."

"Oh, I don't know," said his visitor. "Ingenious little creature, man. Could be he has always scrounged around for a drop of something to ease the way."

"It may be so," said the patient with good humor.

"Well, I'll get along, sir. Do my best."

"Naturally," said the patient, suddenly cross again. "But it's a mean thing when a man comes as close as this . . . Get out of here, Bryce. Give my regards to 'Mr. Smith.' " His voice drawled on the name, putting it in quotation marks.

"I'll do that, Doctor."

"And tell him . . . No, never mind."

"Anything you say," said the visitor lightly.

"Tell him that if I can't take it, I'll shuffle off this mortal coil by the nearest exit." The visitor made a hissing sound. "You're going to argue?" said the patient. "Don't you realize that I may be especially watched? And don't meowl about the moral of it, either. When the better part of at least one continent is swarming with children gone mad, it behooves grown men with brains in their heads to use them. I hope I'm smart enough to know that when my brain goes, there go I. So get along."

"Well, good-bye," said the visitor after a moment.

"I expect He will be," said the patient, "no less and no more than He ever was."

"If you could rest. . . ."

"On my laurels, eh?" said the patient. "Mind, now. Mind, now. There's danger. I've said so. Take care."

"So help us God, eh?" said the visitor awkwardly.

"Good-bye," said the patient gently.

Then J could hear feet walking, and he seemed to hear the sigh of the door. There came a slapping sound, as if some palm caught the door's swing. A woman's voice said, "Are you comfortable, Mr. Barkis?"

"Not at all," said the patient wearily.

J flashed around where he was and flushed the toilet. Quickly he opened the door of the lavatory and stepped into the room, already wishing that he had not flushed the toilet because, with luck, the patient might not have noticed from whence he had come.

"Oh, there you are, Mr. Little," said the nurse brightly. "Hop in, now. You fellows had better get yourselves ready for your supper trays. The rumor is the food's not bad to-night." She fussed a few moments, making adjustments of the bed machinery and motherly smoothings of the coverings.

When she had gone, J, sitting high, turned his face to his new room-mate and put on a smile. "Hi. My name is J Middleton Little," he said politely. "Glad to know you, sir."

The new room-mate, who was perhaps in his late sixties, had a lean old face, very clean. His skin was drawn, shallowing the wrinkles. He had dark eyes, and they were fierce. He said nothing. J felt like an idiot. "That's just the initial J," he babbled. "My family didn't bother ... Say, what happened to the other man? Did he vanish?"

"Maybe he died," said the man in the other bed bitterly, and he looked away.

"Well," said J in a moment, "all I can say is I wish to the Lord I had a double martini." He stared straight ahead.

He heard a throaty sound. "I'm sorry, Mr. Little," his roommate said. "My name is John Barkis, and the fact is, so do I."

J looked, and the man was smiling at him. J couldn't help feeling an impact. For some reason there was power here. And it had charm.

CHAPTER 2

Saturday Night

The trays came, the meal was eaten, the trays went away. All the while J bore in mind the idea that this man was in a desperate state of health and had seemed to have been in pain. But J had no chance to arrange or even affirm any other recollections of the peculiar conversation he had overheard. His room-mate was betraying no sign of pain and no sign of suspicion, either. On the contrary, he kept asking the usual kindly questions, and J found himself delivering his autobiography in the usual sketchy manner. He did so gladly. It took him off the hook.

"What I do is, I manage an office," he told this Barkis. "That is, I'm the assistant, but it is a very, very big firm of CPA's, and second banana there is bigger than a lot of top bananas elsewhere—as bigness goes."

"Oh, sure, *I* find the job interesting."

"Well ... I had four years of liberal arts and then graduate work. School of Business. That was after the service."

"You bet. Fought the war at my desk in San Francisco. Never flinched," J clowned. But the other man's smile was fleeting. He asked another question.

"No, in Southern California. I'm only here since Thursday. I was supposed to fly home today, but the darnedest thing. . . ."

J went into the tale of his near-accident and warmed up to the task of making it amusing. His audience gave him perfect attention, but J could not make the man laugh aloud. Instead, his room-mate asked where in Southern California J lived.

"Burbank. Suburban Los Angeles, you could say. Nice place to raise a family."

"You have a family, then?"

"I sure do. Three kids, boy and two girls. Our youngest daughter is still in high school. The others are married. Three grandchildren, now. Girl and two boys. Makes a nice balance, so far."

"Indeed. And your wife is ... with you?"

"You bet. Same old wife I started with."

"You have not—seen much of the world, I take it?"

"Every once in a while," said J solemnly, "I go half a mile over the border to Mexico and drink a glass of beer. No, I never got around to travel," he continued as this fell flat. "I just keep slogging along in the same old rut. Nice place, my rut, you know. All the comforts of home. Who needs foreign intrigue?"

J reflected that he would be hard put to dig up anything bizarre or exciting in that sense that had ever happened to him. "You know," he burst out, "I was thinking to myself this morning that I may be smack dab in the middle of this whole society. You tend to stop and think when you've nearly got yourself ..."

He was going to say "dead," but J caught the word before

it fell out of his mouth. "Well, I'll tell you," he recovered smoothly. "Turn over in your mind the name I've had all my life. Middleton was my mother's family name. So here I am, J Middleton Little. And, by golly, it suits me. I'm middleclass. Middle-income. (Of course, I like to think it's *high* middle.) And middlebrow, for sure. I just might *be* the Average Reasonable Man in the Street, for all I know."

"J Middleton Little," the other man murmured, and J seemed to hear a note of pity.

J wasn't asking for pity. He said, "I enjoy it, Mr. Barkis. Neither the top nor the bottom, that's for me." (Whoops! "Top" was a word he had overheard.)

"What you say is very interesting," said his room-mate dreamily.

No, it's not, thought J, trying to corner another wisp of memory. Hadn't that visitor called this man Doctor? J didn't want to ask. He wasn't going to turn the tables and start a series of questions now, however polite that might be. If his room-mate didn't know about the eavesdropping or, knowing, was choosing to ignore it, J was more than willing to skip the whole thing himself.

"After all," Barkis was saying, "the economy, at least, bases on you, does it not? On your conscientious industry day in and day out, on you and all the others like you, who go your rounds and pay your bills and ask for nothing more."

The phone rang, and J was glad of it. (Nuts to this turn of the talk. His sense of self had begun to bristle at that "nothing more"!) He picked up the phone. "Excuse me. This will be my wife."

"Long suffering . . . in quiet desperation . . . gallant enough to say that you enjoy . . . Perhaps you do," the old man kept mumbling.

Sophia said into J's ear in her accusing way, "How are you now?"

"Just fine. A-okay. How's everything there?"

Sophia began to tell him that everything there was fine, but J watched (out of his eye corner, with some surprise) his room-mate begin to struggle out of the other bed and totter to his feet. (Should he be doing that? J wondered.)

He began to give Sophia a list of the kinds of tests he had undergone, but at the same time he kept ready to spring to assist while the thin old body, arrayed in rather elegant pajamas, staggered perilously across to the lavatory door. When that door closed, J sighed into the phone.

"What?" said Sophia at once.

"Nothing, honey. I guess I don't like it much being stuck here another night."

"I don't like it, either," she said promptly. "Are you surely getting home tomorrow?"

"That I am. All I've got to do is get past the lawyers. I'm getting out of this bed as early in the morning as I can. Believe me, I'd rather be sitting in the airport."

"Oh, J, it must be miserable!"

"I don't know," he said. "It's been interesting in a way. Tell you all about it when I get there."

"Well, you be sure and get here," she said in her scolding voice. "But you do feel perfectly all right?"

"Not only that, I've got the word of modern science on it. Only things wrong with me come from hanging around for darned near fifty years."

Sophia laughed. They said goodnight.

J settled back. His room-mate came out of the lavatory. He went to his bed rather more briskly than he had left it. He lay, breathing fast, for a moment. Then he said, "I am trying to remember exactly what you must have heard."

Why the old fox! J thought. He dragged himself in there just to test it out!

"Listen, I never meant to hide in there. I'm very sorry. It just got too embarrassing. I'd like to apologize. I honestly . . ."

His room-mate said quietly, "Are you a lover of mankind, Mr. Little?"

J was jolted. "I gather there was some top secret stuff being mentioned, but you don't have to worry about *me*, Mr. Barkis." He was going to add that he hadn't understood a thing, but Barkis interrupted.

"I wonder, Mr. Little, if you would mind getting out of bed and closing the door very firmly? Please?"

J got out of bed and closed the door to the corridor. He firmed it with exaggerated care. He got back under his covers, feeling frightened for some reason. "I don't want you to tell me anything I'm not supposed to know," he said. "I promise you that I won't mention a word that was said. Listen, I never took a science course in my life without kicking and screaming all the way. All I know is right out of science fiction. That's about the extent. . . ."

J subsided. His room-mate was rigid. He seemed to be screaming silently. Was he in pain?

In a while Barkis turned his face. "I'll ask you not only to make that promise," he said, giving J a cold lick of his eye, "but promise not even to mention me. Let it be assumed that your original companion lasted out the night."

"All right," said J uncomfortably.

"But it won't be easy, will it? For you to refrain from telling your wife and your grown children something of this very strange adventure?"

There it was again, that pitying distance. J began to say that even if he told, his people were trustworthy, but he didn't get beyond two words into his sentence.

"I am asking you to promise not to speak of this to one living soul." Now the older man's eyes were fierce. "Mr. Little, I am what they call a terminal case. I am going to die quite soon. You overheard that, surely? Nevertheless, I ought to have known that you were there. My . . . friend simply assumed that I would know. It's not his fault. It's not your fault. The fault is mine."

"But if I promise you . . ."

"I have resolved," Barkis swept on bleakly, "to let them give me no pain-killers whatsoever, lest in some drugged state my tongue went out of control, and I said too much. I had resolved to deny this miserable body any dominion and use my will. Then I blew it, after all."

J said promptly, "No, you didn't. Whatever was said won't go out of this room with me."

"It *will* go out of this room with you," said Barkis, "and sit, bursting in your memory, all the way to California."

"*What* will?" J snapped impatiently. "You don't understand. Listen, I couldn't make head nor tail of one damned thing the two of you did say. Gibberish! Poonacootamoowa to the moon! How can I tell a top secret that I don't *know?*"

"You wouldn't *know* you were telling it," said Barkis flatly. "In my judgment you had better know."

J sank against his pillows, feeling annoyed.

"And for your promise," said his room-mate with a high overtone like a subtle screech, "to obliterate the consequences of my stupidity, *I* can promise *you* seven seats to the moon."

Oh? Well! J winced away from this knowledge. He had long ago concluded that this man was a scientist of some kind, and probably top, at that. But now he knew that the finest mind can deteriorate. This seemed very sad to J.

"So you read science fiction, Mr. Little?" Barkis broke the silence rather sweetly.

"Some," said J shortly. "Not much."

"What do you think of it?"

"It can be good or bad, I guess," said J sulkily.

"Implausible, of course?"

"Oh, sure," said J. "Although I guess we've learned not to be quite so sure." He was squirming. The fact was, J thought, such stories were too often only good old Westerns in space helmets. Furthermore, he tended to resent authors who could give the good guys or the bad guys any old kind of imagined magic, at any time, so that the reader never even knew the rules.

"I suppose, then, you'd repeat an old nut's dying fantasies? Surely, they are only a form of fiction."

J was hit. He said stiffly, "I have already told you that I won't repeat a word I heard you say."

"Ah, yes," said Barkis, "but such a promise is subject to revision. For instance, if you revise your notion of the circumstances under which it was given? As the mental state of him to whom you gave it?"

"It *is*?" said J tightly.

"And subject, also, to *your* faith in the integrity of some other. Your wife, for instance. A secret is not much fun to keep alone."

"Why don't you," said J angrily, "stop having so much fun, then?"

They were silent. J felt shame. That hadn't been a very nice thing to say. "It wasn't your fault," he murmured. "Don't worry . . ."

"I have no children nor grandchildren," the man said.

J glanced at him. Now what?

"Even so, I should be sorry to see the human race vanish from the universe. I can assume you feel that, too?"

J didn't even bother to answer.

"There are things," said Barkis slowly, "that some men can do, *now,* that most men cannot imagine ever being done. There are things known, and the Average Reasonable Man knows not that they are known."

"You speak as one of the elite, I guess," said J, stung.

"Why, I suppose so," said Barkis. His smile did pleasant things to his wrinkles. "If I tell you that it is quite possible—today, tonight, tomorrow—for men to colonize the moon, will you believe it?"

"I have no way to assess or judge your knowledge," said J, "have I?"

Barkis sighed. "Aye, there's the rub." He raised on his elbow. "But you do know it is possible that this planet could be made uninhabitable—never mind in how many ways?"

"I've heard rumors to that effect," said J stiffly. "We live with that these days."

"There is a . . . what shall I call it? . . . a group of people who know that, and live with it, but who do not intend to be present on the occasion of the extinction of the species. They are of all so-called races and nationalities, and they watch, all over the world, in very sensitive spots." The man was speaking in flat tones as if he droned a report. "The moment it becomes apparent to them that such desolation is upon us, they intend to remove themselves and a few well-chosen thousands to the moon. And shelter there. When this earth is clean, in time, they will return and be the seed. And so the species can try again."

"Who's choosing the chosen people?" said J promptly. "Who elected the elite?" he asked. (He didn't believe a word of this nonsense, but he was beginning to enjoy it.)

"That's shrewd," said Barkis. His clean old face now sparkled. "That's very shrewd. But what can the elite be, today, but the brainy ones? Who else could make this project work? Still it has recently occurred to me that the group may be somewhat top-heavy. It may need at least one Average Reasonable Man. And perhaps his Average Family? I can't go, as you see. But since I wear some laurels in the sight of that company, I have the disposition of seven seats. They are now yours, Mr. Little. As a reward if you like. Or a bribe. Whichever."

"Oh, boy," sighed J. Even his toes were wiggling in outrage. "This is all very interesting, as a bedtime story. But I *said* I won't talk, and I *won't* talk, and that should be enough without an elaborate snow job."

"And, of course, you never promised not to repeat a silly bedtime story. What harm, eh?" The man was bitter.

J was getting angry. "Okay. *What* harm?" he snapped. "Explain to me."

"Do you see resigned millions letting the chosen go?" said Barkis wearily.

"So you've got to bribe anybody who gets to know? But you haven't got enough bribes for everybody?"

"Efforts continue," said Barkis, "to save everybody. This Ark may never have to be set afloat. The reason for secrecy," he said in a louder voice, "is a well-considered decision not to risk bringing on the catastrophe we still hope to avert."

"Well, I'm certainly glad to hear that efforts continue," said J sarcastically. "Is the President brainy enough to get to go? What's the government's position?"

"I don't see it along nationalist lines," said Barkis. "I see the human family. You are a father. Would you—"

"Don't preach to me, *please*," barked J. "For one thing, I'm the father of three human children, not mankind."

His room-mate began to nibble on his pale lips. J licked his own. This argument was weird.

"To answer your question," Barkis said in a minute, "governments know; none can officially know. So don't go running to our government for confirmation. Not every one in government knows what the government knows."

J blinked at him.

"Don't you see it can't be public? Tell me, Mr. Little, do you conceive of the common people of many nations as becoming, in an instant, a harmony of thoughtful minds, all dedicated to the long view and the salvation of the seed of man?"

J, feeling slightly chilled (within the story), said, "I imagine there'd be some questions raised—How come your guys got more seats than our guys?—and so on."

Barkis rolled his head. "And some mad children on this earth with power to destroy more than they recognize to be in being."

"Okay, okay," said J. "I've given you my word."

There was silence.

"Tell me this," said J in a moment. "Why can't you just take a promise? Isn't your little group of top brains going to have to believe what you promise one another? You'll never get to the moon, let alone back again, if you don't."

"You speak of a principle," said Barkis softly. "That eases me."

"I'm glad," said J grimly. "So now don't give it another thought."

He seemed to know that Barkis was in pain, although the man made no moan. The spasms seemed to come and go.

"We are agreed," his room-mate said. "But there's one thing more. You are going to California tomorrow?"

"You bet I am."

"Then I must arrange for you to receive the ticket."

"What ticket?"

"Seven seats to the moon." Barkis raised on his elbow again. "*My* word is good, Mr. Little. I'll have it registered in your name and delivered to you. Six seats to fill as you like, but you must sit in the seventh. Write down your address."

J didn't protest. If the old man was really loopy, too much argument couldn't be good for him. J wrote down his name and address.

Barkis received the piece of paper and put it into his pajama pocket (whence J expected it would probably go to the laundry). "The carrier," said the old man musingly, "will have to identify himself. You might, by chance, be approached by the wrong people, who may be watching *me*, especially."

(Ah, J thought, poor old cracked head! What needless suffering!)

"Let the password be anything to do with Noah or his Ark."

"That seems appropriate," said J genially. "Well, thanks very much, sir." Now that he was going along with the gag J began to feel quite some affection for the poor old kook, who must have been quite a fellow in his day.

"I suppose I'll get an early warning?" he puzzled aloud. "When do you expect ... Or don't you, really? This is just in case, I guess."

"My foreboding," said Barkis, "is that the flood *will* come. My guess is—within the year."

"As much margin as that?" said J, surprised and wondering what was surprising him.

"A year," droned Barkis, "is only fifty-two weeks. A week is only seven days."

"And what's a day?" supplied J cheerfully, quoting (now that he remembered). "But there's got to be a gathering place. I mean when you stop to think, it's going to be mighty tricky."

"The mechanics will be explained to you," said Barkis in an exhausted voice. He turned off his lamp abruptly.

J felt sorry that he had pressed unreason with reasonable inquiries. He said in a moment, "Say, why don't I crank down your bed? You can't get comfortable sitting up so high."

He slipped his feet to the floor, moved, and performed the small service. The old man watched him with hooded eyes. His thanks were faint; his voice was feeble.

J climbed back into bed and, in silence, began to try to remember all of the conversation he had overheard. It was pretty mixed up now with this fantastic yarn. He *had* remembered the word "elite." And, yes, something about a seat to the moon, by golly! And then he remembered with a lurch of his heart what seemed to have been, there at the last, a discussion of suicide.

J began to think that Barkis believed all this stuff. (Well, he must be crazy!) But who had the visitor been? Had *he* believed it? No, no, must have been some friend, well-aware of a pitiable obsession, a delusion fallen on a fine mind in its latter days. He must have been playing along in affectionate kindness. J could figure that. A replacement, the visitor had called himself. A scientist of some kind, from his vocabulary. Couldn't have been faking that, could he? Did *he* have a seat to the moon?

Ah, come on! The whole thing had to be phony baloney. For all J knew the old man beside him was some kind of two-bit scientist who was dreaming all this up as his ego's final gasp, just because he had never got anywhere near the top. Grandeur, sure. Thinking he was "watched especially," for instance.

J began to feel very tense in the muscles. If the other man—mad or not—was falling mercifully asleep, J didn't want to thresh and turn. But he couldn't lie still. So he slipped out of the bed and got into his robe. It was still early. In fact, the evening visiting hour must be still in effect. J said very softly, "Just going for a stroll on the premises. Don't worry."

His room-mate neither stirred nor replied.

So J went softly out of the room into the brighter corridors, among the sounds of voices, the bustle of people in their grotesque variety. Yet, in the big hospital's population of visitors, one element was missing. There were no child visitors. J caught himself thinking, The Little kids must go. That's three seats taken.

He chided himself for this at once. But the trouble was J was in the middle. *He didn't know enough.* Had, for instance, no notion by what means or brainy struggle human life could be sustained for years on what he understood to be a barren hunk of rock and dust, hanging in space.

Yet, on the other hand, *he knew too much.* J wasn't one who would have laughed when Galileo sat down to his telescope. Or yelled, "Get a horse." J was a pretty civilized fellow. He was supposed to keep his mind open and so balance along the tight wire of uncertainty, taking care at all times never to be absolutely sure of anything.

J thought wistfully that to be a furious savage, righteous in ignorance, with all his glands pumping away to some single purpose—though that be perilous—would sure be an easier way to live.

When the door to 817 had closed, a thin old hand reached for the telephone.

"Mr. Smith here."

"Willing."

"And ready. Go ahead."

"There's some trouble. Could be serious."

"How serious?"

"Abort. Reschedule."

"What's to do?"

"Send somebody."

"Bryce?"

"No, somebody practical."

"When?"

"Tomorrow. Not too early."

"Will do, Doctor."

When J sneaked back three-quarters of an hour later, the room was still, the air fresh. All had been neatened, the window opened. Some nurse had been in.

He crept into the lavatory, brushed his teeth, and otherwise prepared himself for sleep. As he climbed into the bed, his room-mate spoke softly. "Good night, Mr. Little. I hope I won't disturb you."

"That's all right," said J. "Goodnight," and added, "sir."

"This is a burden for a man like you," said Barkis suddenly. "I'm sorry." And then he said, as if he didn't realize he was making sounds, "Oh, God, I'm so tired ... so tired ... All my fellows?"

"Try to rest," said J.

His room-mate murmured something. "The rest is silence," J thought he said.

All night J could only doze. He was terribly conscious of the older man. He could tell at times that there was pain, and he did not think that this was fantasy. But J lay very low. He dared not call a nurse: How could he, J Middleton Little, from Burbank, California, give orders that this man be sedated against his will? And how suggest that he ought to be in a room that had bars on its window?

J didn't know enough. He knew too much. He might hang onto the old chap's pajama tails for one night. But J was going home tomorrow. Surely authorities knew the man's condition. Didn't they? J hoped. J feared. He was miserable all night long while, in the small breeze, the curtains on this eighth-floor open window moved hypnotically.

When the dusk of the room began to brighten and voices and clatterings began to be heard, Barkis was sound asleep, but J M. Little was feeling pretty darned exhausted.

CHAPTER 3

Sunday

A nurse came and pulled the pink curtain to make a token wall. A doctor came and disappeared behind it. J popped out of bed and trotted off to take his shower down the hall. He wasn't going to eavesdrop anymore if he could help it.

When he returned, the curtain was out of the way. Barkis was sitting up and looking fairly spry. They exchanged no more than genial good mornings. Breakfast came. J wondered if his elder had already forgotten last evening's conversation.

He was half-dressed and packing his suitcase when a man's high-pitched voice said, "Well, well, well! Doctor Livingstone, I presume. Hello there, sir! Now, what's all this?"

It wasn't a visiting hour. Maybe this was another doctor. But whoever he was, as the stranger came bounding into the room, making for the other bed, J loathed him on sight. He was the very image of the extrovert. His florid face was arranged in a permanent smile, revealing a set of very large teeth. He had writhing brows the dark color of his stiff, abundant hair, and ice-cold, pale brown eyes.

"What are *you* doing here?" said J's room-mate dourly.

"I'm having a baby. Heh, heh," said the stranger. "Well, I mean my sister is." He sat down on the foot of J's bed, as J couldn't help feeling he ought not to have done.

"Anything serious?" the man inquired of Barkis.

"Not very," said Barkis coldly. "Mr. Little, this is Barry Goodrick. Don't trust him an inch."

"Bygones, bygones," the stranger chided. "How are you, Mr. Little? Glad to see you!"

(He wasn't. How could he be?) J muttered something.

"How have you been, Barry?" said Barkis to the rescue.

"Oh, fair. Fair," said Goodrick. "You leaving us, Mr. Little?" His glance was licking instrusively over the open suitcase and J's dirty underwear.

"I sure am," said J. "Excuse me." He went to fetch his things from the lavatory. He tied his tie.

"Well, I'm certainly sorry," Goodrick was saying to Barkis, "to find you under the weather, sir. Something sudden, was it?"

"Not very," said Barkis in the same cold way. "I don't think you are supposed to be in here."

"Oh, what they don't know won't hurt them," said the stranger, lounging back on his elbow which, to J, was somehow infuriating. That bed was still J's bed, and even temporary sheets are personal! "Passed any miracles lately? Heh. Heh. How are things going?"

Barkis didn't answer. His eyes had taken on that fierce light. J, who thought this Goodrick was a real pain in the neck, hated to leave the old man at his mercy, but his suitcase was closed. He picked up his jacket.

"Say . . . uh . . . I've got a plane to catch," he said, "and I sure don't want to miss it this time."

"When's it leave?" said Goodrick immediately.

"Two o'clock this afternoon," said J, deadpan. Goodrick narrowed his eyes. "Well," said J to his friend, "I'll say good-bye, sir."

He moved around the beds to the window side, and the old man gave him his hand. It was very thin and dry. The clasp was firm, and J seemed to feel a second pressure, which was as if to say, "Remember?" He wished this damned other man wasn't here.

"Nice to have known you," he said to Barkis, "and I guess we'll let the Sweet Prince of Denmark have the last word. Okay? Good luck, sir. Good-bye."

"Good-bye," said Barkis bleakly, sadly, without a smile.

J nodded to Goodrick, whose eyes were much narrowed now, although his smile was as wide as ever. J picked up his bag and left the room, feeling that he had just been rather clever. Waiting for the elevator he preened himself to have remembered that Barkis had quoted the works of William Shakespeare several times in his hearing and had even quoted the very line to which J had just so cleverly referred. He felt that the reassuring message had been given and received right under the snooping nose of that snoop-nosed Goodrick, whoever *he* was.

He rode down, and lo, in the lobby, one of Mrs. Evangeline Burns' lawyers was waiting with the papers. So J negotiated for his departure at the desk, and then he sat down to sign whatever he'd have to sign to get free and go home.

Up in Room 817 Goodrick said, "What was *that* all about?"

Barkis said, "What?"

"Something's, by any chance, rotten in Denmark? Heh. Heh."

Barkis said testily, "We had a literary sort of chat last night. You wouldn't understand."

"That so? Who is the man?"

"I haven't the faintest idea," said Barkis with bad temper. "Some half-educated bourgeois bore. I'm supposed to have peace and quiet in this place, by the way, and I don't feel like company."

"Nervous?"

"I can have you put out," said Barkis. "Don't tempt me."

"You shouldn't carry a grudge, Doctor."

"I wouldn't call my intense aversion to your personality a grudge, exactly."

"I'm just wondering," said Goodrick, paying no attention to insults but putting his left thumb to his mouth and chewing (between words) on the flesh around the nail, "if there was something in the lab went a little bit whacky? And made you sick? Eh?"

Barkis looked out the window.

"I can't help it," said Goodrick, "if I'm imaginative. For instance, *what does he know*, the Little bourgeois?"

Barkis said thoughtfully, "It's not so much that I dislike you. Your kind of mind doesn't interest me." Then he winced.

"Don't feel so good, Doctor?" said Goodrick alertly.

An orderly, a scrubwoman, and an aide appeared in the doorway. "Excuse us," said the orderly sternly. He and the aide grasped J's bed, preparing to move it out the door. Goodrick got up. It was as if they'd dumped him. The scrubwoman put down her pail and readied her mop. A nurse put her head in. "Excuse me," she trumpeted. "Sir, visitors are not permitted in a patient's room at this hour."

"Well, since I'm outnumbered," said Goodrick, "I'll see you later, Doctor."

"I sincerely hope not," said Barkis firmly.

Downstairs J saw Goodrick come out of an elevator and go over to the desk. He saw the woman there point with her pencil in his (J's) direction. But Goodrick neither turned to look nor did he approach. Instead he walked away toward a row of phone booths. J was glad. He had not liked that man.

The session with the lawyer didn't take long; J was extremely agreeable to suggestions this morning.

As the cab bore him through the bustle of the noisy city, J reckoned up the hours he would have to wait at O'Hare. Well, he didn't care. He figured to ensconce himself in the Ambassador Club and read the papers.

But once settled down there, he found the newsprint fading in his sight. J couldn't help thinking about the dying man he had left behind, the mad plot, the whole bizarre experience. What would he do, he wondered, if somebody did show up one day, give the password, and hand J Middleton Little seven seats to the moon?

Just for the heck of it, who would go?

Well, the three Little kids first, naturally, and then Grosvenor Winthrop Little V, J's only son and the children's father. Win was twenty-seven; he must go. And Amy Alice Little Gardner, aged twenty-three? Of course, Amy! J couldn't bear to think of Amy, destroyed. And Nancy Jo Little,˙ aged sixteen, the apple of J's eye? *She* must go, surely. Was that six already? J, himself, must sit in the seventh seat.

But what about Sophia? Or Marion, his son's wife? Or Avery, his daughter's husband?

Only *mine?* he wondered. Me and mine, my own, my blood, my seed?

He felt so depressed and horrified that he forced his attention to the sports page.

In the hospital a young man with a snubbed brown nose on a tanned face was bending over the only bed in Room 817.

"I've got all that," he said. "We'll fix. I don't think there's too much to worry . . ."

"You know Barry Goodrick, Tony?"

"I've met him. Heard some rumors."

"Somebody got on to my collapse, I suppose, and sent him sniffing around. He saw and he heard this man Little. And I don't know, Tony, I don't know. It depends." The old man threshed.

The young man straightened and said, "Suppose Goodrick does take a notion to worm himself into the Little man's confidence? What's he going to make out of that crazy yarn? The Little man doesn't know the truth."

"They could put things together."

"I doubt it, sir."

"Don't doubt it. They could, I say!"

"All right, if you say so." The young man smiled at his elder and thought to himself, Pretty tough if all you've got left to do now is *worry,* after what you've done in a lifetime. "What kind of man is this Little chap from"—Tony looked at the slip of paper in his hand—"Burbank, California? You say he promised? How reliably, do you think?"

"Oh, he's a middling kind of man. Middle-class, middle-income, middlebrow, he said. Bit of a clown. Middling intelligent. Disposed to be honest, I imagine. How strong to keep silent if he was *not* gulled, I'm not sure. And if he *was* gulled, he can be gulled again." The patient groaned.

"Sounds like a type who'd believe almost anything modern science tells him," said Tony good-humoredly, trying to lighten the tone of the talk. "You gave him quite a pill to swallow, Doctor."

"Ten members of his immediate family," said the patient in a patient, weary way. "I counted. So I said six seats besides his own, to occupy his mind, you see? He'd feel, I thought, concerned and, I suppose, torn."

Tony whistled softly. It might pass for admiration.

"And I was not even middling intelligent, was I?" said the old man calmly. "Tony, have I already come to the point where I only think I'm thinking?"

"I wouldn't say so, sir," the young man soothed. He thought, although I almost could.

"Something disagreeable could happen to that Little man, as well as to all . . ." The old man's eyes had grown wide and wild.

"No, no. We'll keep an eye on . . ."

The old man's hand grasped for Tony's jacket. "Tell the Little man the truth. I should have."

"Oh, I don't know, sir. He must be nicely muddled. With a nasty problem for his middle-class conscience to resolve. Ought to keep him busy long enough. It's only another . . ."

"Don't *say* the time!" said Barkis violently. "Oh, God, he has got the whole thing! He has got the time *and* the place. And he doesn't know it! He doesn't *know* what he knows."

"Time and place, but not *what*," said Tony sharply. "Or so you just told me."

"No, no, but *they* know what," said Barkis. "Somebody got hold of Etting in that hospital. I'm sure of it. That's why I . . . I don't trust that confounded Goodrick. Don't you realize . . . Tell Smith we have to call it off."

"I really think you are unnecessarily upsetting yourself, sir," said Tony. "What you ultimately fear has very little chance of happening."

"It is definitely under consideration by somebody. I *know* that—will you then tell me, with your brain, that there is no chance?"

Tony said gently, "If the voice on the phone two weeks ago was whose you thought it was, and if the message meant what you thought it meant, and if they do find out what you are afraid they might, then there would be a *small* chance. Very iffy."

"Brains," said the old man. "My whole life has been my faith in the human brain. Can't you see why I, of all people, can't bear to think——"

"I suggest that you simply try not to think about it anymore," said Tony quietly. "Your brain must tell you that it is out of your hands now. That others have just as much concern. You should be resting, sir."

"So I should," said the patient. "To eke out my body's strength to the last syllable. But when my brain goes, *I* go tumbling after. I'll say no more. Except good-bye."

When the young man had gone, the old man had a few more words in him. "Good-bye, Mr. J Middleton Little," he said to the ceiling. "God be with you, sir."

The jet took off, and J, peering out, reflected that the earth was a darned big place and might not be so easy to render all-over uninhabitable as some folks supposed. Of course, what did *he* know? And how would the earth look to a few thousand chosen people waiting on the moon, homesick in Babylon? *Terrible* idea! Impossible, of course. But so sad!

J was very tired after his miserable night and his long wait in the airport. He advised himself to cut this out and relax. So he composed his limbs for a nap, with a flash of an old feeling. If one went to sleep on one of these contraptions, the plane might crash. One was obliged to will these things to stay up in the air, although, of course, one never said so. But today seemed different. The big bird, born of the restless ingenuity of man, mated with his deep desire, slipped easily along the sky, and any man (or feeble old crone for that matter) could fly today. All it took was money. So much for wonders.

And didn't man keep chewing off another and then another piece of the unknown, digesting it, fearing it no more, only needing to fear what man might do with his knowledge? Yet God kept letting man in on more and more of his secrets, so (J thought) all this must be okay with God.

Here, now. J had thought about God on two days in a row. Well, like they say, no atheists in foxholes. J suddenly skipped all the way back, whizzing past college, the Army, adolescence. He began to repeat aloud, although not loudly, "Now I lay me down to sleep. I pray the Lord my soul to keep. And if I die before I wake, I pray the Lord my soul to take." As he closed his eyes, he was smiling—to remember that he had once been a child—never mind how long ago.

The man in the next seat got up. He looked nervously down at J's face, just an ordinary face, a longish jaw, a curly kind of mouth, a straight nose that nevertheless did not draw its straight line quite in the center. Eyelids down over the not very blue, but not quite gray, eyes. One visible, pink, jug-handled ear, silvering hair, neither all gray nor all brown. Pleasant enough looking fellow. Not handsome, not ugly.

The passenger said to the stewardess, "Say, who is he? Some kind of nut or something?"

"Well, well, well!" J's elbow was jogged; the high-pitched voice was in his very ear. He woke, blinking, and there in the seat beside him was none other than the obnoxious Goodrick.

"How are you, Mr. Little? Long time no see! Heh, heh. What a coincidence, eh?"

"Oh! Hi," said J weakly. "Excuse me. I must have really conked out."

"Sorry if I woke you," said the man, showing those large teeth in which he was almost certainly lying. "Just now spotted you. California, here we come, eh?"

Befogged and bewildered, J looked out the window, but the cloud floor told him nothing about where he was. He looked at his watch. "We must be pretty close to the border, at that."

"We'll be starting down around about San Berdoo," said his neighbor. "Fantastic, isn't it?"

"Oh, you get used to it," J muttered, running his hands over his face and head.

"In the hospital long, Mr. Little?"

"No, no," said J. He didn't feel like going over his story again, not to *this* man. A thought came to him. What if Goodrick were to mention Noah's Ark? J turned to look at him. "Are you a Californian, Mr. Goodrick?" he asked, turning the tables, becoming the inquirer.

"Oh, I dunno," said Goodrick. "You are, eh?" No table had turned.

"How's the baby?" said J suddenly.

"Pardon me?"

J kept still and watched the other man's wits scramble for

reference. "Oh, oh," he said. "Heh, heh. I didn't know for a minute . . . Not *my* baby, you see. Oh, fine. Eight pounds."

"Boy or girl?"

"Oh, a boy, naturally. I put in my order with the Man Upstairs for a nephew. Heh, heh."

(If God has any sense at all, fumed J, He wouldn't take orders from this bumptious idiot!)

"Enjoy yourself with your bedfellow? Heh, heh," said Goodrick. "Your roomfellow, I should say."

"Your friend, you mean? Very pleasant company."

"You a literary man?"

"What?"

"I understand you had a literary discussion with my friend."

"Although I was brought up in a literate household," said J stuffily, "I'm not a literary man."

"Well, *he* said you were a bit of a bourgeois bore," said Goodrick, "but I thought the way you referred to that quotation was pretty cute."

J feared he was turning red. He said, staccato, "You've just lost me, Mr. Goodrick."

"Oh, now, come on, Mr. Little. You've got to realize that I know who that was. Barkis? Heh, heh. Why, I've known Doctor Ambrose Willing for years. Used to work under him at one time. Fact is, he fired me. Heh, heh."

J turned his face toward the window.

"Surprisingly literary, wouldn't you say, for what he is?" said Goodrick, disagreeably close to J's ear.

But the phrase that pounded through J's head was "Barkis is willin'. Barkis is willin'."

"And he'd be interested, you thought, in the word 'silence'?" said Goodrick, and J's heart jumped.

He covered this by shrinking away with an offended arching of his neck and saying, "Do you mind not shouting in my ear? There is nothing the matter with my hearing."

"Went to school, myself," said Goodrick calmly. "The rest is silence?"

J simply stared at him.

"Last word of Sweet Prince Hamlet, wasn't it? *Silence,* eh?"

The only thing J felt was fury. This man had no right to sit there and needle J Little and be so right about J Little's miserable ineptitude. He said huffily, "Are you sure you want to conduct a conversation with a bourgeois bore like me?"

"Oh, now," said Goodrick, flashing his teeth, "the great man may have felt grumpy because he'd been indiscreet. He told *me*, of course. Fabulous, eh? What he's been up to?"

But J saw the trap. "No point trying to tell *me* what he's been up to. I never got more than a C-minus in a science course in my life." He shrugged and looked out the window.

"You must have understood some of it," said Goodrick coaxingly in a moment.

"Some of *what?*" said J impatiently. "I can't seem to follow you, Mr. Goodrick. I'd appreciate it if you'd clue me in a little better."

"Maybe I should," said Goodrick. "Normally I prefer to work undercover, that being my job."

"I don't believe it!" burst J.

"Why not?"

"Because you're so *obviously* nosey. And pretty crude about it if I may say so."

"That's right," said Goodrick, who was nibbling at his thumb from time to time. "That's the way I operate. I found out long ago that if you ask a blunt question, you're going to get an answer . . . even if not a word is said." His grin was infuriating.

"For whom," J said coldly, "if you don't mind a blunt question, do you work undercover?"

"Government," said Goodrick. "Ours, naturally. U.S.A."

J simply did not believe this. He didn't want to, for one thing. But he said, "Okay, what do you want to know from me?"

"It's a security problem," said Goodrick. "Doctor Ambrose Willing has got a head full of secrets. So the point is how sick is he? Did he seem rational? What did you talk about?"

"I am no diagnostician to know how sick he is," J said. "I *deduced* that he was in the hospital because he wasn't well. Listen," J was very angry, "it so happens that hospitals have this buddy system. So he and I happened to get put in together. So we happened to get onto the works of William Shakespeare. Is that all right with you? And the U.S.A.?"

"Not a literary man, you say?" said Goodrick, who had a maddening way of paying no attention to insults. "What *is* your field?"

"I'm in office management," snapped J. "Business. And if you don't mind, I'd prefer to mind my business. I don't know a damned thing about science, or medicine, either. You woke me up, and I'm tired."

"Bad night?" said Goodrick quickly.

J shut his eyes.

"By the way," said Goodrick slyly, "how come you mention science? Did *I* say that?"

J, by a mighty effort, kept his mouth shut.

A voice said gruffly, "My seat, d'ya mind? We're losing altitude." J opened his eyes, and there stood his former seatmate in the aisle.

"Oh, oh," said Goodrick. "This your seat? Sorry, fella. Well, I'll be seeing you, Mr. Little. Maybe in Burbank. Nice to talk to you." He flashed his teeth and scrambled away.

J leaned back, fuming. Some coincidence! Pretty damn fishy! But how could Goodrick have managed to get on this plane deliberately? Well, he had spoken of J at the hospital desk, as J recalled. Could have got J's full name and so forth there. How else could he know Burbank? And J, himself, had told his departure time. What if Goodrick had called a lot of airlines (in that phone booth?) and so found out which flight? Would they have told him? Sure, they would have told him, one way or another, if he'd lied in his big fat teeth and said he was J M. Little. Oh, he could have found out, all right.

J was feeling terrible now about his attempt at being cryptic. Goofed that up pretty good, he had. Now, now. Was he believing that all this was important enough for Goodrick to have gone to all that trouble?

He began to try on for size serious belief in the tale of the voyage of the chosen few. But some knowledge of his own rose up. J did understand something about money, after all, and to build ... or even to learn how to build ... such an Ark would cost more money than there was.

Then the old man was loopy, and the government might well be worried that he had a room-mate, even for one night. True, the old man had told J not to trust this Goodrick, but if the old man was loopy ... J didn't want to obstruct the providence of his government, of course, and just because he found this Goodrick so obnoxious. ...

He could see the so-and-so standing in the aisle talking to the stewardess. Goodrick's head was half-turned; J saw him in profile. Now what was that glimpse, something foreign and yet familiar? A certain flattening? J couldn't believe that so flamboyant a character could be an *undercover* man!

He was going in circles; a disbelief in the one man kept kicking him around to a disbelief in the other when suddenly he found his foot upon a rock.

J, himself, had given his word. Okay. He had not told one syllable he had overheard, and he would not, simply because he had said he would not. And that was that. Whew! J stretched and looked out the window.

A suspicion crept softly into his mind. What if the old man hadn't been crazy, but a projected voyage of an Ark to the moon was *not* the secret? Well, if so, J would have to keep the secret, just the same. Although no Noah, he. Now Noah had been a good man, he mused, whatever that was. Noah had taken his family, his own, his seed. It was all just a myth, of course. J understood that you mustn't take those old tales for literal history. Yet you must, at the same time, consider them to be profound truths of some sort.

The clouds shredded suddenly. J could see through to the earth. He could see a cluster of buildings down there on the land, looking like a bug, with tentacles of roads reaching out. Once upon a time, myth said, the Lord had sent a flood. Maybe the Lord was beginning to think of man as a disease on his beautiful earth. A parasite, cells multiplying, spreading destruction, spoiling, and growing faster and faster the more it grew—until one day the earth might die of its cancer, man. *A cancer always suicides.* J shivered.

He fastened his seat belt and watched as they lumbered in on a long slant toward the enormous sore of the metropolis. A really bad patch of scale it made, spreading, spreading, pulling down the mountains, dirtying the air and sea.

J squeezed his eyes shut; when he opened them, his perspective had shifted.

He had always enjoyed flying into Los Angeles at night. He liked to spot some tract of dwellings with its streetlamps contained in its own tight design, like a pearl brooch on the dark, the kind he remembered on his grandmother's gowns. Even by day, as now, he liked to watch the car-corpuscles moving in the city's veins. And see backyards with their lids off. Sometimes the blue-green flecks of swimming pools, like a burst of broken plaster chips, thrown down among a fuzz of trees. Sometimes rows of tiny pens that walled in trash. The parking lots in their flat and ugly symmetry. And here · and there a thrusting up of shining buildings.

CHAPTER 4

Sunday Afternoon

Having shuffled off the plane, J soon picked out from the crowd the familiar flip of Sophia's hand. He was very glad to see her, but he did not embrace her with as much shameless affection as he felt because he could see that Goodrick was watching them.

He had a flash of retrospective recognition; well, J thought indignantly, if Goodrick has got any yellow blood mixed in, he must be the most damned scrutable Oriental spy that ever was!

"You look all right," said his wife accusingly. "How do you feel?"

"Augh," J shrugged, meaning not bad, not good. They began to walk.

"Do you want to go straight to Doctor Lodge, J? Even on Sunday I'm sure . . ."

"No, no. Why should I give him time and a half to tell me the same thing? You by yourself?"

"The girls are kindly getting supper for the multitude," said Sophia. "Win's riding herd on the Little kids. My mother is there."

"Oh?" He guided her step and stepped beside her on the moving stairs.

"I wanted to see how you were," said Sophia. "And anyhow, I like airports."

J was feeling something of a brand on his brow—a man with secrets he must not tell, followed by a spy. But worse . . . a man very much afraid of his own wife. He had better not even think about it; Sophia could read his slightest shift of mood.

But the angle of his own vision was somehow changed. He was seeing Mr. and Mrs. J M. Little through the eyes of a spying stranger. A whole series of overlapping images from other years went fading out; he saw Sophia as she was.

In the latter stretch of her forties Sophia was rather handsome. She was tall with good legs and ankles. Her waist was not as slim as a girl's waist, but she was full-breasted and held herself high, and her figure was not dumpy. Her soft black hair was well-threaded with gray, and she wore it folded over itself in some mysterious way at the back and puffed up on top. Her best feature was the manner in which her large brown eyes were set into her face, where the skin around them had crumpled in a way that J personally found very attractive.

"Now, I want to know," she said, taking his arm as they set out down the tiled tunnel, "exactly what happened to you."

So he began to tell her all over again, putting in details, as the state of the weather, the make of the car, the name of the woman (Evangeline Burns), and what she had been wearing at the time. To all of this Sophia listened like a Desdemona. J did not say too much about the hospital except that he was sure glad to be out of that dump.

"But, J," she said, frowning a little as the door to the luggage place opened magically before them, "if they couldn't find anything wrong, why did they make you stay there all night?"

"For observation," said J gloomily. "Although as far as I know (and I should know), nobody so much as peeked in at the door. So much for observation."

"Was it a private room?"

"No, no," said J. He reached into his pocket for the check he had almost forgotten. "So this morning I settled for a little something. Here."

Sophia read it and frowned. "Seven hundred and fifty dollars?" (J was trying to spot that Goodrick. He wasn't around. No luggage, eh? Hah!) "It doesn't seem like very much," his wife was saying.

"Oh, well, price of a suit and a little extra. What does it matter?"

"J, you seem . . . You're not worried about anything, are you?"

He rubbed his face. "No, no. I'm just kind of beat. Didn't sleep worth a darn." (He beat down his memory of the reason.)

"Then I'm sorry the mob is there."

"No, no. Be glad to see them." J pretended that he had seen his suitcase in the mass. (He was going to have to take hold of himself. He couldn't afford to be stabbed by the shocking thought that Sophia would have no seat to the moon. Aw, come on, knock it off! There's nothing *in* it.)

When he had found his bag and turned back to her, she was holding out the check. "Tell you what," said J impulsively, "why don't you spend it?"

"Does it count as income? Is it taxable?" Sophia was the household budgeteer. She understood about money, too, on her own scale.

"I don't think so. Not worth worrying about. Go ahead. Blow it in."

"Humph," said Sophia gravely. It was an old family custom to pronounce "humph" as spelled. She tucked the check into her handbag without saying thank you. The family often did not. Thanks were usually given by a display of pleasure in the gift. All of them were used to assuming that the giver had wished to please.

They went outside, and there was Goodrick, just getting into a taxi. He waved, teeth gleaming.

"Who's that?" said Sophia.

"Fellow on the plane," said J so gloomily that she asked no more. They crossed to the parking lot. He tossed his bag into the back of his Oldsmobile. He was feeling shaky now that the spy was gone. "Want to drive?" he said to her.

"I will," she said so quickly that he knew she had not expected to drive going home. Sophia drove well, a little tensely, perhaps. She maneuvered out of the lot, wended the way to the San Diego Freeway going north. Once on it, she slipped into the pace smoothly.

J gazed at the cars, the cars, the cars, tearing along at 68 miles per hour and in phase as if they had rehearsed this like a water ballet. At the tons of expensive machinery, running on millions of dollars' worth of road and carrying so few human persons that the whole lot of them could have walked sedately on a three-foot sidewalk and not jostled an elbow. It was absurd. Absurd? Well, what was it but man paring down space with the knife of speed?

Sophia said, "How was the trip, by the way, businesswise?"

And J thought; it was *absurd*.

Sophia was feeling pretty sure that poor J must have had a bad scare. She had immediately sensed the air of anxious gloom about him. Well, J wasn't getting any younger, and for all his boasting about his physical prowess in the crisis she could imagine him fallen in the street and lying there, helpless and terrified. For which terror she certainly did not blame him. But, of course, in female wisdom she would not press him to admit this. Sophia resolved not only to understand, but to do it quietly.

The trouble was she could also imagine poor J's frightened leap. The angles of his bones would have strained the cloth of his trousers with a most ungazellelike effect, and before the mirth got any higher in her throat (the crude but almost irresistible comedy of the banana peel, or dignity overthrown), Sophia had changed the subject.

J was speaking, "Oh, the trip was okay, businesswise. I was just a chip, you know. They threw me into the pot so they could see their next cards. Too many fancy clubs like that turn out to be run by the wrong people. So they threw me in just to keep one toe on the ground floor." (J was often a reckless mixer of metaphors.) "In case *that* outfit *is* going anywhere. All I had to do," he said, "was be there, sit quietly, and not fidget. In which endeavor I succeeded brilliantly."

"That's good." Why so gloomy, Sophia was thinking.

No, it wasn't, J thought. It was pseudowisdom, phony and absurd. For what did man make his marvelous machines? So that J could go, sit in Chicago on an expense account, take notes, and not fidget?

Now the San Fernando Valley was spread below to receive them into its soft haze, and the car became a drop in the stream pouring down. Sophia concentrated on getting through the maze of the interchange.

When they became a drop in the stream flowing east on the Ventura Freeway, Sophia said, "J, are you sure you feel perfectly all right?"

J roused himself from too long a silence.

"I would have been scared green," added Sophia, the female, applauding male courage.

"You bet you would," said J. "If you'd seen and heard old Evangeline, flinging out orders far and wide, with her diamonds heaving and her bosoms flashing. Enough to make your blood run cold."

Sophia's mouth tucked in at the corner. "Wait and tell it for the kids," she said, recognizing a vaudeville turn in the making.

J said belatedly, "What's up, anyhow? How *is* everything?"

"Sure you're strong enough to find out?" Sophia said solemnly.

"I've got to know sometime," said J in the same spirit.

"Well, let's see. The dishwasher is on the blink. Naturally, since we have ten for supper, counting the Little kids. Cal, the gardener, says the Chinese elm has a fungus, and this is dire. That publisher is after your father again. He's been calling; your father has, that is. My mother's back at the Wimple with only twenty dollars left for the rest of the month. Her O.G.A. told her to give all the rest away, and then auras clashed, and she's moved out of her boardinghouse until some evil spirit's month there is up. Meanwhile Avery needs new glasses (so says our Amy) and must have them like last week. Nanjo has set her heart and soul on a dress at I. Magnin's that costs three hundred and fifty dollars. Without it she *might* not be chosen, which is unthinkable. And Mrs. Arriola has announced that the house is haunted."

"How the hell can it be *haunted?*" exploded J, reeling with the onslaught of the facts of his life. "It's only eight years old!"

In the house which lay high on the long slope to the Verdugo hills and looked south and westward over the valley, the telephone was ringing.

Nancy Jo Little, aged sixteen, couldn't hear the phone from where she sat in Cary Bruce's sports car out on the street, under the pepper tree.

Grosvenor Winthrop Little V, aged twenty-seven, was entangled with his three small fry on the back lawn, where Mrs. Marietta Thomas, aged seventy-one, was imprisoned at the hips by a garden chair.

Mrs. Grosvenor Winthrop Little V (nee Marion Coons), aged twenty-six, was in the kitchen, and her hands were dusty with flour. She lifted them to indicate her helplessness and said in her sweet voice, "Amy, could you get that?"

Amy Alice Little Gardner, aged twenty-three, who was slouched to the back of her neck on one of the dinette benches, with slim trousered legs higher than her head, did not leap up gladly. She unfolded one token leg.

It was Avery Gardner, aged twenty-nine, lankly and lonesomely pacing the living room, who now regarded the instrument glumly for the space of four rings and then picked it up as if it might bite him.

"Mr. J Middleton Little, please?"

"He's not here."

"When do you expect him?"

"I don't know," said Avery, who could have guessed an hour if he had tried but felt disinclined to try.

"May I leave a message?" said the high-pitched voice that was possibly male. "With whom am I speaking? Is this a member of his family?"

"Son-in-law," said Avery grudgingly.

"I see. Will you take down this number, please, and ask Mr. Little to call it at his very first opportunity?"

The voice gave a number. Avery began to write, but the downstroke of a seven began to interest him, and he continued it, ceasing to listen very hard.

"Tell him this is a messenger from Doctor Willing. Doctor Ambrose Willing. Have you got that?"

"Got that," said Avery with the sudden relish of a snapping crocodile.

"Thanks, very much."

"Not at all," said Avery. He hung up and licked his lips. A vision was gathering in his head. Could one paint a telephone? Only its meaning, of course. Its impudence, its stridency, its power. Paint imperative sound, and the pain in it?

When he saw his wife's dark head come around the doorframe, he glared at her to ward her off. Avery made for the bathroom. He was always seeking sanctuary in some bathroom or other, because all people (even Amy sometimes) were careless about interrupting the vulnerable, invisible, but so precious first glimpse and seed of the work. Avery took off his glasses, soaked a cloth in cold water, held it over his eyes, and watched his painting becoming more or less solid at the bottom and to the left, at least.

Marion was in the dining room inspecting the elongated table. "That looks rather nice, I think," she said. "Who was on the phone?"

Amy gamboled toward the table and snitched a black olive. "I don't know," she said. "Avery hung up."

Marion looked at her gravely. "I hope it wasn't important."

"How could it be?" said Amy, grinning around the olive.

In his hotel room near the airport Goodrick, having brought nothing with him but money, had no unpacking to do. So he settled down to wait for this man Little to ring him back. The first few words might tell him, for sure, whether there was anything in this fragile lead. Goodrick already knew that his employer would like very much to find out anything at all that Dr. Ambrose Willing might want kept *silent*.

Sophia took the "off" ramp neatly. Now that they were on a surface street J could feel her relief. "It's a poltergiest according to Mrs. Arriola," she explained. "That's how come Aunt Geraldine's cut-glass pitcher fell off the buffet, you see. Oh, it didn't break. But what I'm afraid of . . ." Sophia went on, "suppose Marietta finds out? Are we going to have to be exorcised, do you think?"

"Oh, no," groaned J. Everything Sophia said was clued in for him.

He was seeing a web, like a spider's web, and himself in the middle of it. He had threads spun out to all the persons and things that Sophia had mentioned and to more besides. There were also threads spun between, connecting some of them with one another, because of him. J had the right to expect that one day death's plucking finger would remove his central figure. But there should remain many other webs, around other spinning creatures, even if his own were to fold up like a web on a broom.

The whole thing, *everything* on earth, was intertwined somewhere! There was this airy lace . . . elastic, but tough. And if some giant broom were to brush it all away in one great sweep, J didn't think he wanted to survive. What should he do on the moon without Sophia or Avery or Marion or his father or (for that matter) his mother-in-law or the neighbors or the office—all his fellows?

CHAPTER 5

Sunday Evening

J sat in "his" chair in the family room with the Little kids swarming over him. Mary, aged six and a half, was screaming into his left ear. "What did you bring me, Grandad?" Grove, aged four and a half, was shouting, "Bring me? Bring me?" and even the baby, Donald, who was only two and a half, pounded on J's kneecap with a tablespoon babbling, "Bing? Bing?"

He made his arms hard and held them off. "Nothing," he said.

There was a sudden hush and the hovering possibility of howls. Then Marion, the children's mother, was there making soothing noises. "Grandad is very tired. Poor Grandad has had a long, long trip."

Sophia began to explain to the adults in low tones that J had had a nasty shock, and no wonder that, this once, he had forgotten. Marion began to promise television, which the children immediately preferred to a giftless grandfather who was in no mood for play. J couldn't blame them for reading his mood. Off they went, hippety-hop, behind their mother into the den, where the crackling noises and jolly cries soon arose. The children's father sighed and thanked aloud the powers-that-be for the baby-sitting aspects of the tube, destructive though it might be to their little minds. "Don't give it another thought, Dad," he said to his father and began to mix the before-supper drinks.

J found himself silent and knew that his silence was assumed to be evidence of a more or less broken heart over his unprecedented forgetfulness. So the tides of custom were flowing to obliterate such uncharacteristic behavior. Well, J *had* had a nasty experience. Oh, yes, he had been shocked, all right, although not altogether as they thought. One trouble was his heart had felt as if it were going to break as the car had turned into his driveway and Sophia had taken it into the double garage. It was that broken brick on the right that set him off, the one J always saw as he came in, always resolved to replace and had not replaced yet. Then it was the ivy on the fence, and it was the junk hanging on the garage walls. It was the very smell of his own garage. His heart had seemed to crack (twanging) from love of this earth the way it was.

Then Nanjo had come prancing across the front lawn to embrace him. She had her hair caught up high and away from her face, and J experienced the same old stab of pleasure in the sight. He had never liked the now declining fashion during which period a girl's long hair hung straight down all around, so that she must peer between lank locks. He liked to be able to see the crisp purity of Nanjo's small nose, the adorable tininess of her mouth and chin. He also knew that Nanjo knew as much and had wished to please him today. Oh, well, a father always knows these things.

His daughter-in-law, Marion, was at the front door, a pleasant-looking young woman, a little shorter and a little rounder than his own two lean girls. Marion had brushed his cheek with cool lips and murmured graceful welcome. And J's heart had winced because he'd had to leave her *out*. (Oh, should he?)

Then Amy, his middle child, and her light smack. "Hi, Pops! So you made it, huh?" Very slim Amy in tight black pants and a tight black sweater, his mysterious one. J didn't understand her and was a little afraid of her if the truth were told.

He had hauled his bag into the house, through the pleasant living room into the bedroom wing, down the hall into the huge square bedroom that pushed three sides out into the back garden. He'd washed his face in his and Sophia's bathroom and had tried to pull himself together.

Then, from the glass-walled room across the back (in which the family really lived) he could see the garden and the small, bright, moving bodies out there. His mother-in-law, Marietta, had come waddling to touch cheeks with him, to beam upon him, with the familiar, quick, and easy moisture making her blue eyes shiny. "Home safe, dear J. Oh, yes—I asked my Own Good Angel to watch over you."

J endured this without visible wincing. It was the sort of thing Marietta was always saying. She was, J thought, one of the most purely embarrassing conversationalists he had ever known in his life.

Then his son, Win, had come through the glass wall with his brood.

And here sat J with his own, his own, his seed all around him, and his wife, and his daughter-in-law, and his mother-in-law besides.

Win handed him his drink and said, "What's all this about a hospital? On *Saturday* night! Sure you weren't out on the town with some babe, Dad?"

Every one of J's senses was somehow raw. He felt his son would never have said such a thing had he believed it to be *possible*.

Then Marion. "You weren't really hurt, were you, Dad? You're looking marvelous."

(He wasn't.)

Nanjo said, "Oh, pooh! He's tough!"

(Which J was not.)

But he knew, with great sadness, that it was time for his vaudeville act. So he obliged. He did the dowager. He did the put-upon harangue of his first room-mate. He sacrificed and made them a picture of himself in a trouserless state, and they laughed. The deeper he sank into personal gloom the more he was credited with an artful deadpan delivery.

The time came for a fluttering of females, charmingly disputing over who should sit still and who serve the meal. Nanjo glided off at the end of the pack (as usual, J noted) a little late. Only Amy did not even pretend to join. She sighed and sat down on the floor.

Now Win, sitting with one ankle on the other knee and one hand on the ankle, drink in the other hand, his eyes in his handsome face wearing their accustomed optimistic but knowing twinkle, leaned forward and said, "I guess Mother told you about this slight—uh—financial bind, did she?"

"No," said J, his poor heart fainting in his breast. "No, she did not."

"Oh?" said Win. "Well, how would you like to take over the second mortgage on my house? Only five grand, with fierce high interest, by the way. I'm a little bit behind, and things are getting on the sticky side. Thirty days would do it."

"I see," said J listlessly. He saw, for one thing, that in Sophia's judgment this news had not been suitable for the freeway. For another, he had a vision of the tightrope Win walked, by choice, into his credit-based economy. More than once already J had been his balance pole. But what matter?

Before J could speak again, Avery Gardner came drifting into the room. He had not been missed. Avery was a drifter; he came and he went; there was no pinning him down. "Oh, hi," he said and turned his back to mix himself something at the bamboo bar.

"Hi, Avery," said J absentmindedly. He was adding up sums of money. If he had not given Sophia the seven hundred and fifty dollars, that would have covered Nanjo's expensive dress (about which he would no doubt soon be approached) and leave enough to cover Avery's new eyeglasses which, J felt sure (they being so salient a feature of Avery's personality), would be very expensive indeed. Then, if J eschewed the replacing of his blue suit, as he supposed he could, he might help out Marietta besides. But for the five thousand dollars he must scrounge among his assets for the least of several evils. But what did any of it matter?

"It's secured, Dad," Win was saying earnestly. "The house is worth half again as much as we paid, already, with the pool and all. If Faulkner doesn't sign a week from Tuesday, then we will scale down and start selling, I suppose, here and there. But if he does . . . ho, ho . . . we're in like Flynn!" Win drank deep. "So it's no real risk," he said, believing himself thoroughly.

"I guess we can manage," J said numbly.

"Oh, hey, that's *great*," said Win. "That's wonderful. See, I *could* get them off my back by taking it out of the office, but I've got to meet my payroll. Especially because of George Faulkner showing up. Something happens to the atmosphere if payday's postponed. It gets into the air conditioning."

J wasn't paying attention. He knew what he was doing. He was buying off his conscience because Win couldn't have five out of seven seats to the moon. He'd be getting four, as it was. J looked at Win's wife, Marion, who couldn't go.

She wasn't rejoicing, he noticed at once. Her large gray eyes met his almost hostilely for a second. Then Marion smiled as sweetly as ever and began to praise him softly.

Marietta reappeared from the kitchen, where she had probably been, as usual, enthusiastically in the way.

"What's this about you being at the Wimple?" J asked her.

The Wimple was a shabby little hotel on a back street in Hollywood, whither Marietta tended to gravitate in moments of transition. The charm of the place had always escaped her son-in-law, but it had charm for Marietta, although her resources did not permit her to become a permanent resident there. "And what's all this," J went on, "about only twenty dollars left?"

"Until the first of the month, J dear," said Marietta, putting her ample hips into a chair. She ate, as far as J could tell, like a bird, but whatever she ate seemed to turn magically into rosy flesh. She wore her gray hair in a Dutch bob, and it was not as grotesque as it might have been, at her age, because of the fresh and unlined smoothness of her plump face. Once you got used to it, that is.

"But she had need," said his mother-in-law rapturously, "dear soul, and I was sent to help her. So there was nothing else, of course, that I could do."

Amy put in the links her grandmother was leaving out. "Some character she met in the park, Pops. Wanted to get into some home . . . a cult-type joint, I guess . . . and didn't have the entrance fee."

"A beautiful, beautiful retreat!" beamed Marietta. "She took me to see. Ah, simple and immaculate—and filled with loving kindness. I *knew*, then."

"How much did she get out of her?" said Win to his sister.

"A C-note," said Amy, disentangling the pronouns with ease.

"Ow!" said Win.

"All right," said J patiently to Marietta. "But what's this got to do with your leaving your own room and moving into the Wimple? You are paid up, aren't you, with Mrs. Dickson?"

"Oh, J," said Marietta in a low voice, "an evil force has entered that house." Marietta, who never lived by bread alone, did not like to speak of some things, so she spoke softly as if she hoped Nothing would hear this blasphemy. "Oh, I have prayed, but it will not be overcome, just yet. My Own Good Angel advised me to go away from there until in good time . . ."

"I see," said J, who was used to her. "The evil force moves out in three weeks, eh? So you need the price of three weeks someplace else. How much does it come to at the Wimple?"

Marietta's expression, normally radiant with her insistence that all—all—was roses, changed to the blank look she put on at the mention of arithmetic. "I think Sophia understands all that, J dear. Doesn't she?"

Sophia, who had come in, said, "We won't worry about it now, Mother. Come on to supper, everybody."

"But I *never* worry," said Marietta in a scandalized tone as she wiggled herself out of the chair. "That is a sin, you know."

J, trailing with the rest into the dining room, thought to himself that Marietta might already be on a moon of her own. He wished *he* knew the trick of never worrying.

The meal was much like all family meetings at table. Much the same things were served and eaten. J found himself not very hungry and disinclined to speak. He felt apart. He knew that Sophia's eye was on him and suspected that signals flew over his head. He was assumed to be tired. And he was! He was!

Here, in the middle of his web, where J had his tethers to the earth, he knew that those ties had been rudely strained. In the first place he might have been ripped untimely all the way away. Shock enough! In the second place strands from some foreign web had come tangling in. It would have been an enormous relief had J been able to tell them all about Barkis. But that relief he could not have.

Eight seats at this table. (Seven seats to the moon!) And that wasn't counting the Little kids.

J glanced at Avery Gardner. (No seat for him.)

Avery, as usual, made no remarks at all but devoted himself to his heaping plate of food, which he devoured as if he had not been fed for days. His table manners were deplorable. The family looked the other way. Avery was a young man too tall for his width, with eyeglassed eyes magnified to be too big for his face. If Avery had been painfully shy, one might have pitied him, but he was the exact opposite. He simply had no wish to converse with any of them since he assumed (and always had assumed) that none of them could possibly say anything of importance. He came here to eat, so far as J could determine. Or perhaps he ate so ravenously in default of anything here that seemed, to him, better to do. Whenever he came, he seemed to cast off even Amy and count her in with her kin.

J knew very well that he had never liked Amy's husband.

He did not like him now. But J personally had never been in any kind of touch with Avery. How *could* he like him?

Win's wife, Marion, J liked well enough. But under her full armor of gracious manners, which made the surface so easy, J had no idea what might be there. Marion was a kind of straight woman; it was she who always squealed at a dirty word. It was she who always turned someone's self-deprecating statement around and made a compliment to counter it. She was like a little machine! You pushed the button and out came the correct response. This could get dull, J admitted.

Of all J's in-laws Marietta was perhaps the least strange to him for all her outrageous pronouncements and her general attitude of outer fringes. She could at least be relied upon to say the *wrong* thing, socially speaking. But the family had practiced skills in the matter of sliding past Marietta's contributions. She was the family eccentric, waddling recklessly along the earth with one foot in paradise. (She couldn't go to the moon, of course.)

J, picking at the food, which was excellent and perfectly to his taste, began to listen to the voices of his own.

Nanjo spoke in a nasal whine. He had noticed this before, but never quite so sharply. She was wearing a shapeless garment that came about halfway down her thighs, but she managed to twist her healthy young body so that its outline played hide-and-seek with the eye of the beholder. Nanjo did not look like a woman in her face, but the body was womanly. Had he noticed this before? Certainly he had. J suppressed a sigh. He and Sophia had even discussed it. The modern parent bewares the unwisdom of wanting his child to remain a child. But J knew that he *had* wanted that, just the same. He couldn't have it, but he *wanted* it. (Of course, not now.)

Nanjo will need a mate, he thought.

Amy, when she spoke, was abrupt but not forthright. The essence of Amy lay very low, at least when she was in this house. J did not understand her marriage. Of course, he and Sophia simply assumed that Amy was the nearest thing they had to a rebel. The middle child. Quite natural.

But J, himself, had been a middle child, and he reflected now that he had never rebelled very much—at least not *yet*. He couldn't help wishing that Amy had not married Avery. He wished the two of them did not live the way they lived. Of course, a parent, if he is wise, never says such things.

But now, at least half torn and loosened to hang suspended as he was, J thought to himself, But that's absurd. Why shouldn't a parent, having lived, speak up about a way of life? Or about a marriage, the single most important choice one's child can make? Why must he not speak? J remembered that there had seemed to have been a reason; he couldn't remember, at the moment, what the reason was.

Then there was Win, careening along, going the ways of his generation. Oh, Win was honest. To loan him money was not to give it away. J knew that the "fierce high" interest would be paid, but probably not in a regular pattern. Win would pay back the principal when he could; but none could say ... Win could not say ... when that would be. So J would lose *his* right of timing. And J preferred his income and his outgo to be in orderly relation to each other. It wasn't risk he minded. It was disorder.

By coffee time, as J was beginning to wonder if he had kept himself a secret from his children, the phone rang. Nanjo rushed to answer. Avery muttered something about a call for J. Nanjo came saying it was for Daddy. It was grandfather.

So J went to take up the phone in the entrance area, which was not a room but divided from the living room by what was frankly called a room divider. J, who was so strangely out from under the spell of nomenclature, thought it was (in fact) quite silly.

Grosvenor Winthrop Little III was calling his only surviving son from his lonely apartment in Santa Monica. At the sound of his dry voice the skin on J's shoulders began to crawl. (No seat ... no seat for him!)

"Ah, back, I see, J?"

"Yep. I finally got here. How are you, Father?"

"Very well, thank you. J, Mr. Pudney was here yesterday morning."

"Oh, was he?"

"It seems that they are very much interested in my manuscript. They foresee quite a demand. Libraries, he tells me, will almost certainly be compelled to keep it on their shelves, which gives it quite an advantage over a mere piece of fiction."

J rocked on his heels, silently groaning.

"Now he has made," his father went on, "a most interest-

ing suggestion. In fact, I think it may be the solution. I would
like very much to talk it over with you."

"I'll try to come by so you can tell me about it."

"When may I expect you? I thought you were due home
yesterday." His father sounded as if he had been deceived.

"There was a little delay."

"I see. I see." (But he hadn't waited, even to hear.) "I
would appreciate your making a definite appointment," his
father said, "as soon as possible, although I know, of course,
how busy you young people think you are."

Grosvenor Winthrop Little III would have been welcome at
the clan gathering, but J's father came to the house no
oftener than every Christmas. He could not, he said abide
confusion. He was a man of seventy-five, who did not live in
the roaring world, and perhaps never had, but nested cozily
within his own imagination, mated now to an obsession, his
one continuing passion. What he could not abide was contact
with other people who might be thinking about something
else. This confused him.

J said, "I'll come as soon as I can."

"Tomorrow?"

"Maybe so. I'll try, Father. I'll call you in the morning."

"And with that I must be content," his father said and
hung up.

Now J heard the raucous bleating of an auto horn out in
the street. Nanjo brushed by. She opened the front door and
signaled with her arm. The horn desisted. Some swain
bleating out there? J rather expected Nanjo to plead an
urgency and vanish, since boyfriends came first, but tonight
she turned back into the house. Oh, yes, he thought, that's
right. Nanjo wants something, too.

He fled into the family room and into the bosom of his
own now gathered there.

J sat down in the middle. He, the spider, in the middle of
his web. (Something wrong with the pronoun? Never mind.
He—she, the hell with that. J fancied the image.) Spinning
endlessly to support and supply (according to J's notion of
the function of a spider) and in the middle, in the middle.

J felt very low, very low. How come I got elected, he
thought, to be in the middle and hold up the whole shebang?
I could have been stone-cold-dead in Chicago! And then
what?

But at the bottom of his despression was something he

knew now and seemed to have known for quite a while. Barkis-Willing had given him a snow job, all right. But not in madness. Rather in contempt. So he, J Middleton Little, not only held up the whole damned thing but was despised for his pains. He did not even know what it was that he must not reveal; he had not been trusted to know.

So the smart ones thought he was stupid. No doubt the stupid ones thought he thought he was pretty smart. But J was neither smart nor stupid. He was good and goddamned tired! That's what *he* was!

CHAPTER 6

Sunday Night

The dishes had been stacked pending Mrs. Arriola's Monday and also the repair of the dishwasher. The children had been disposed of; the baby was sound asleep in Marietta's ample lap, and the other two drooped in the den over still more television. Amy and Avery were sitting on the floor side by side, their long thin legs stretched out before them as if they were rag dolls that some giant child had propped in the angle of the floor and wall.

Nanjo was fluttering at J's shoulder. "Daddy, there's a book I want to show you. I want you to see the cover. It's the neatest thing!"

"Not now, Nanjo," said Sophia quietly. Nanjo sighed and sat down.

J could feel himself the focus of attention. (Spin, old spider!) A notion struck him. It wasn't that he didn't want to give these few everything he had. He was tired. But tired of trying to figure out what he could afford. Didn't he always manage? So why didn't he just *do it*, now. Settle all their problems right away. Would anything be lost? On the contrary something might be saved. Time, for instance. An exhilaration took him. Fast, free, and easy while the world lasted; that was the way!

"Marietta," he said, "why don't you stay at the Wimple until your next check comes and send me the bill? You like it there."

"Why, J . . ." Marietta beamed on him mostly.

"Three weeks there comes to almost her whole monthly check," said Sophia calmly, "not even counting food."

"I know," said J recklessly. "It doesn't matter. Now, Win, the best thing for me to do is take the five thousand dollars out of the Savings and Loan. How do you want it? And will that cover?"

"Can I meet you there, Dad?" said Win quickly.

"Fine. Ten, tomorrow? May as well take care of it first thing."

Sophia had become very still.

"Now Amy, how much will Avery's glasses cost, do you think? And the examination, of course."

Amy said, "I don't know, Pops. Last time it was nearly a hundred and fifty dollars before he got through."

"All right," said J cheerfully. "A hundred and fifty dollars. And Nanjo?"

"Daddy, I already put down fifty dollars that Uncle Tobias gave me for Christmas and my birthday, and maybe you could take the rest out of my allowance? The thing is, the dress just happens to be exactly the very same dress that's on the *book*, and . . ."

"Why don't you charge it to our account?" said J.

"Oh, Dad-deee!" Nanjo flew to him. Her bare arms went around his head. Her smacking kiss was loud in his eardrum. J guessed this was worth three hundred dollars. He wondered wryly if the dress was suitable for traveling.

"Just a minute," said Sophia. "Nanjo, be quiet. J, are you planning to pay that Vanity Press to publish your father's book?"

"I think so," said J easily. "Let him have that pleasure."

There should be pleasure. If J had the power to give it, why shouldn't he enjoy his power?

"How much?" his wife was demanding.

"To publish Father's book? Last I heard it was a thousand dollars. They may have come down."

"Why wasn't I consulted about all this, may I ask?"

Silence fell with a bang. The two black rag dolls on the

floor simply stared. Win and Marion tilted their heads politely, but they didn't like this. Nanjo held down her own
rejoicing. Marietta mooned over the sleeping child, choosing
(as usual) not to notice strife.

Sophia had a temper, as J well knew. She was not permitting herself to blast him, yet. She had always struggled for
control. Sophia's mother was irresponsible enough for one
family, but her father, although responsible, had been a
Welshman, and in Sophia there were banked fires. J knew that
he had let himself be carried away, and he ought to have
known better.

"It won't break us," he said. "I'm still earning." (Spinning!) "So if they need it . . ." Even his voice was tired now.

"If you had asked me," said Sophia coldly, "I would have
said that I don't fancy sending them *our* bills when we are
old."

"Ah, why not, Ma?" said Win lightly. "That's fair enough."

"Could be," said J, rousing himself. He wasn't a man who
liked to sound dreary. J had a quaint notion that this was
discourteous. "You're bucking to be the most important man
in this society, Win, just like me."

"What's all this?" said Win genially.

"Well, now, this was called to my attention." (Sure it was,
thought J. By the brilliant brain of Barkis, who was just
trying to butter me up, but, by golly, he didn't mention the
half of it!) "By my conscientious industry," he announced,
"day in and day out, *I* hold up the economy. Not only do I
consume, like everybody else. *I* pay my bills, thus holding
up agriculture and so forth, and all the repairmen, besides. I
also pay the taxes. So who bears the costs of government and
the military and all their gadgets? Who pays for *any* mistake
that *anybody* makes? Board and room for criminals, cops to
catch them, courts to let them go? Who pays for schools,
roads, parks, charity, and buys the soup and the vino for all
the bums on skid row? Takes care of the unemployed, the
insane, the aged, *and* the orphan? Listen, I'm even buying for
the elite, the great brains—their time to *think*. *I'm* picking up
the check for going to the moon, you know. Why, *I* pay the
damages for the acts of God even, fire and flood. And I also
provide the hay and the peanuts for all the animals in the
zoo."

If he was clowning, his act wasn't getting off the ground. J
realized they were waiting for the punch line. He didn't have

one! "This is known as quiet desperation," he said in desperation, "but that's absurd. It's power, see? Power! Of course, I ought to be organized. Dream me up a catchy slogan, Win."

His son did not answer.

His wife said dryly, "How about 'Things are tough all over'?" Everyone seemed stunned.

"Don't you think, J," she went on, "you have enough expense without buying your sixteen-year-old daughter a dress that costs three hundred and fifty dollars to be worn once? What part of the economy does that hold up? I say it's out of scale, and Nanjo *needs* no such thing."

"Mo-*ther!*" wailed Nanjo.

"And it is a fact that Marietta can't afford to live at the Wimple. She happens to have a perfectly comfortable room, already paid for, and her board besides. I say she can either go back to it, or move in here and sleep in Nanjo's other bed for the duration."

J felt shocked. Marietta's Own Good Angel, once having spoken, was the law *and* the prophets. *She* wouldn't go back to her room. Also, Sophia did not enjoy having her mother as a houseguest. Sophia would be sorry. "Well, she's welcome," he said weakly, seeing Nanjo's face dismayed.

Marietta said tearfully, "Such dear good hearts—"

But Sophia was developing a theme now. She shut her mother up with one look. "I'll grant you that Avery, of all people, had better take care of his eyes. If neither he nor his wife" (Amy was looking alert and listening intently) "can afford the price, then we'll have to do it. I, however, can very easily buy the glasses out of the seven hundred and fifty dollars *you* gave *me* to fritter away." (She was glaring at J. He was guilty for his *gift?*) "Your father is your business," Sophia went on, "but if he didn't have some nonsensical scruples, he could buy his own book. Win's loan may be necessary, but he ought to retract—"

"Wait a minute," said Win. "Whoa, Ma. Dad, I'm not going to let you take that money out of your Savings and Loan account. I wish I'd realized how you were feeling with everything on your neck. I see what you mean. In my business there are risks you never took, and why should you take them now? It's a different world. You should do things your way. Ma's right. You should hang onto your security."

Marion's eyes were round. "Of course she is right," she said quite spunkily.

But Amy said in her blunt way, "Maybe Pops picked up some loot in Chicago. Maybe he's filthy rich all of a sudden. He's not usually that casual with a nickel, you know. So come on, Pops. Where did you get it?"

J, wounded to calm in the middle of the storm, only shook his head.

Marietta said, "J has always been one of the sweetest and most generous souls . . ."

Sophia turned ferociously on her mother and took out some temper in that direction. "It's one thing to be generous. It's another thing to be forced to give some perfect stranger in a park one hundred dollars, whether you want to or not. Why can't you see, Mother. that when you give money away, somebody else just has to pay *your* bills?"

J rused himself. This was getting too thick, too bad. He'd have to stop it.

"Now, now," he said, "everybody calm down. Don't take it so serious. I was wrong not to talk it over. Okay, I'll just crawl right back into the groove . . ."

He had let slip some bitterness. They were all silent. But they didn't know what he was bitter about! J no sooner had this thought than it began to be verified.

Amy said, "Oh, gosh, it must be a drag. Poor old Pops. Never mind about the glasses. Money's not *that* important. I can earn the price. I bet it's not all that hard."

Nanjo said in a little girl whine, "Daddy, I knew the dress was out of scale. I just had this dream, that's all. Never mind. Honestly. They'll give me the fifty dollars back. And I can buy myself something that'll be okay." She got up and patted him on the head. "I guess we give you a bad time, sometimes. Could I be excused now, Mother?"

"Who's out there?" said Sophia crossly.

"Just Cary Bruce. We're just going over to Debby's. Goodnight, Daddy. Thanks a lot, anyway." She kissed his crown and went away. Her feet, so often light, seemed to trudge.

Sophia got up. "J, you are just exhausted. I think you ought to go to bed early and definitely see Doctor Lodge in the morning. This is no time to make decisions."

Yes, it is, thought J. It always is. And *you* blew your top, didn't you? He couldn't help a middle-grade glare at her.

Win rose, murmuring that J mustn't worry about a thing, and they'd better get the kids home. "I'm so sorry, Dad," said

Marion softly as she glided toward the den to gather her young.

J knew that signals were flying over his bowed head. He sat and let them fly.

Avery got up as if he were one of the children being roused, and Amy seized his hand and sprang up. "Come on, Marietta," she said, "we'll cart you back to the Wimple for the night at least. Okay, Mom?"

"I'll get her out of hock tomorrow," said Sophia gloomily. "She'll have to come here, of course. Thanks, Amy."

They disentangled Marietta from the sleeping child. It seemed to J that the room was a-twitter with a flock of birds, but he couldn't speak—so to speak—bird language.

Amy smacked his brow. "Hey, Pops," she said, "if you did rob some bank, why don't you send the money back in the mail? Who needs it, anyway?" Her eyes slipped sideways in a winking sort of way.

"I'll do that," said J heavily. "Anonymously, eh?"

Amy winced and turned abruptly, and J felt terrible. He *never* quarreled with his children. He wasn't a quarrelsome man.

Marion said sweetly, "Dad, I hope you'll be feeling better and your old self again in the morning." And J thought, What is that?

Sophia went off with them to the front door to wave them away into the night, no doubt with comforting pats and what other assurances he knew not. *He* didn't get to go and see them off. He wasn't feeling well enough. Now what the devil had he done, that they were insisting he wasn't feeling well?

Damn it, I would have loaned Win the money and bought every one of them what they said they needed. Don't they know that? True, I would have done it only after long solemn balancing of pros and cons and talking it over, which only means going around and around and coming out where you came in, dead on the original impulse. But finally I would have handed out the money, the same money, with neat little lectures pinned on. Make a show of taking it out of Nanjo's allowance to teach her values—which we would forget all about in a month or two. Compromise on Marietta's board and room, pay for it somewhere, *not* the Wimple, and she'd have to be grateful just the same. What kind of generosity have we got here?

Sophia came back. "Ah, J," she said gently, "now tell me. What's the matter?"

"I wish I knew," said J, his spirit backing away, "what's the matter with all of *you*. So I got to thinking. So I thought it was funny. What with everybody rebelling nowadays . . . I thought what if *I* took a notion to rebel? I'm not going to *do it*."

Sophia pretended to think that he was only clowning now; perhaps he was. She sighed and sat down.

"It might be a good idea if you did rebel," she said. "The other way around. It won't hurt a single one of them if they have to pull up their socks and do without Santa Claus J Little, you know. The way Amy and Avery operate is ridiculous. I'm sure they're frugal, but I don't see why *you* have got to go on paying for any slightest extra. And Win is old enough to go ahead and take his risks, for pity's sake. And if he's overextended, let him retract. That house . . ."

Win and Marion lived in a long, low ultramodern house on a hillside in Encino, with a newly built swimming pool and as much service as was convenient or possible. They both drove late-model cars. Marion had a full-length mink. Little Mary went to a private school.

"People have been known to lose a house and survive," said Sophia. "If we never lost any of ours, that's because we never overextended ourselves for show or status."

She'd never said a thing like this before. Also, it wasn't true.

"Oh, come on," said J wearily. "Sure we did. Everybody does to some degree. It's the American way." The easiest gamble to forget is the one you took and *won,* he thought. "Way, way behind the times to use your own money."

"That's because very few have got any." Sophia was beginning to smoke around the edges. "J, I *don't* understand what got into you. You didn't even listen to any details. You worked darned hard for what we've got, and you can't afford . . ."

"I guess you're right," said J sadly. "I did so well that I can't afford a simple, kindly impulse."

Sophia burst into flame. "No," she cried, "you can't! And it may not be so simple or so darned kind, either. And you should know that! And how come *you* get to play simple kindly old Santa Claus, and *I* get to play the part of the mean old battleax?" she said, hitting the bull's-eye of her personal distress. "And I'm going to bed," she went right on, "before I completely blow my top. This is *not* a conversation." She was white. She had a war on within herself, fighting her own temper.

Let her win, J thought, as he rubbed his hand over his eyes. But, being human, he couldn't help saying, "Okay, I was temporarily insane. So now we'll talk it over—and take all the fun out of doing the very same thing four days later, when time's a-wasting—"

"Good night," she said in another voice. He lifted his head. Sophia was wearing a strange look.

"What's the matter?" he said quickly.

"I'm sorry, J," she said rather coldly, "if there is something you don't want to tell me. I hope someday you'll decide you can. Just don't sit up too late, dear."

She kissed the top of his head, and, holding herself stiffly, she went away.

So there sat J Middleton Little, all by himself, and nobody loved him anymore. Oh, come on, they were only protecting him. From what? J realized that he didn't really want his children or his female wife protecting him from anything, at least not yet. He didn't even want to see them wiggle out completely from under *his* protection. He wasn't that unselfish. He would have felt warm and proud and hedged those favors all around with pseudowisdom only to disguise . . . what? His own pleasure?

But why shouldn't he please himself? It might not be wise or even kind, but why wasn't it simple?

Sophia got into her bed, although it was too early for sleeping. She was very much frightened. Her heart was thudding, and she could not make it slow down. Oh, what's happened to him? Oh, what *is* it? she kept wondering. He surely was in that hospital. I called him there. But that's such a silly yarn about the rich old woman and the car. J doesn't lie. But I don't know. I don't know. There's the check from the lawyers. It must be true. Could there be more to it? Was he in some way humiliated? Did they laugh at him? Did he do something foolish for somebody—for a woman maybe— and was he misunderstood? *Why* isn't he telling me?

Thus she came back around to the sudden thought that had scared her so much. Oh, did they find out in that hospital that J has got something horrible, one of those awful slow hopeless . . . Oh, did J find out that he is going to die?

When the phone rang, alarm assailed J at once. Police, injury, crisis? It was not late; yet it was late for the telephone. That damn Cary Bruce and his sports car! He hurried around the wall to the entrance area and said a brave, gruff "Hello?"

"Mr. J Middleton Little?" The voice was faint, far away, almost a whisper.

"Speaking."

"I'm speaking for Doctor Willing."

But J had heard the extension click as it was lifted in the bedroom. "Sophia," he yelled, *"get off the phone!"*

Sophia hung up the extension with a punishing wham.

"Excuse me," said J into the phone, gathering his wits. "I couldn't hear. What did you say?" (He had heard the name Willing, but nothing, yet, about Noah or his Ark.)

"Is everything all right?" said the whisperer.

"I don't understand. Who is this? Whom are you calling?"

"J Middleton Little?" the voice whispered. "I am a friend. Doctor Willing sent me."

"If you could speak up," J kept stalling.

The voice said out loud, "I was sent by Doctor Ambrose Willing."

J didn't believe it. Oh, ho, no! He knew who this was now. "I'm not sure I know anybody by that name," he said. "What was it you wanted, Mr. Goodrick?"

"Very good, Mr. Little," said Goodrick as himself. "Just testing. Happy to see that you are being careful. Have you told your wife by the way?"

J didn't know what to answer. Couldn't say "No." "Yes" wasn't appropriate, either. *Did you beat her, as usual?* J began to laugh.

"What say?" said Goodrick sharply.

"Excuse me," said J, "but you are one of the weirdest characters I ever met in my life. Why don't you break down and tell me what this is all about?"

"Excellent," said Goodrick. "And you were very wise to make sure nobody listened in on the extension, weren't you?" He hung up softly.

J stood there. He was *furious!* He thought, If that man doesn't stop nagging me, I'll ... Uh, huh, he'd *what?*

J went over to the bookshelves and took down the fat red volume of *Who's Who*. He carried it into the family room, sat down, and under "Willing, Ambrose" skimmed a long column of mysterious combinations of initial letters that must stand for honors and credits and memberships and prizes. When he had finished, he knew that Dr. Ambrose Willing was indeed tops. That his field was chemistry. That he had, indeed, no family. That he was sixty-nine years old and at the height of his powers, the harvesttime of his working years. Oh, yes, he did, indeed, deserve to go to the moon and be saved.

As J sank deeper into the chair, feeling terribly depressed, the silence of the house was split at last. Sophia, who was sitting upright in her own bed, had been waiting long enough. She let her voice blast. "Am I not supposed to know who that was, *ever?*"

"Business," shouted J, almost savagely. "My business."

"*Forgive* me for having so stupidly thought that *I* was entitled to answer the telephone in *my own house!*"

J couldn't bear this; her rage was justified. But he couldn't explain. He began to tremble. "Listen, honey, I'm sorry I yelled at you. I'm sorry. I was just startled."

(Oh, please, help me, Sophia? Don't *you* be against me!)

In a moment his wife called in a totally different tone, "All right, J. Never mind. I'm sorry, too."

"It was that idiot from the plane," J called in desperation. "I don't *know* what he wanted. I think he's nuts!"

"All right," she said.

In the bedroom as Sophia lay back, she discovered herself to be trembling. She had heard the voice on the phone say "Doctor" Somebody. What secret business could J have with a *doctor?* He'll tell me, she thought. *He'll have to!* So do him the courtesy of being patient. Let him work himself up to it. If J has a fight on inside himself to keep some—dignity, oh, let him win.

She lay as still as she could.

J, in his chair, was awash in a flood of self-pity. His plight was miserable and unfair. He was an innocent victim. But this is no world for a victim. He only gets it in the neck again. Oh, J was in the middle now, all right. On one side the crude and persistent prying of that Goodrick. On the other the anxious, loving prying of his own wife, which, J knew, he was in for.

Would there be a day when he *could* explain?

J was sensitive to ridicule, perhaps especially so. He had

suspected that therein lay the reason for his assumption of
the role of the clown so often. (He didn't mind laughter
when he had asked for it.) Now he projected scene and
dialogue on the day when people would find out about those
ridiculous seven seats to the moon. "Oh, no!" they would cry.
"You took such nonsense seriously! You *didn't!* Oh, poor
gullible old J." And if he said he knew it was nonsense, but it
haunted his mind, they'd pity him and smile.

J began to feel afloat in a high and chilly region. And if
they asked him what he figured to do with those seven seats?
Yet how could he say there was a different secret? He didn't
know, and would probably never know, what it was. And if
he said that he had stood on a principle, that would only send
the smiling pity underground. He thought, I can never explain. Well, he must now (he saw clearly) climb very deliberately and warily back into his harness, his habits, his own
garments. He must not cause any more surprises or alarms.
He must just be the same old J.

And the silken threads are made of steel, he thought
(mixing metaphors wildly). So it's back to the mines, old
spider! There'll be no strike tonight! They'd forget about this
evening, wouldn't they?

Would Sophia?

Oh, boy, J thought, my name must be Rumplestiltskin. No,
no, that wasn't the right character. He was thinking of some
old-fashioned kid's story. Wasn't there some poor schmo (in
more than one tale) who stuck out his neck and said something reckless, made a big gesture or a boast or some such
thing, and then found himself in a jam with his bluff being
called?

Wasn't there always a fairy godmother, or a little gnome
in the forest, or a frog, or some damn thing, who came along
to save him from the consequence, the shame, and the humili-
ation of being human? And wasn't the human reader always
on the side of the schmo? And wasn't he, J Middleton Little,
human being, on the side of *himself* in this matter?

All right, he had made a bold and careless gesture of
casual generosity. Hadn't even asked for details. (What did
they matter on the scale of the earth and the moon and the
fate of mankind?) But ho-ho-ho, how his gesture had
bounced back and told J a thing or two!

All to do with money, he mused. And how *they* thought *he*
thought about money. Win seemed to think that J, the

security-minded, had tried to be too brave for his own temperament. As if J believed in such a thing as total financial security. What J would really like to do was to take all that he had, split it three ways, and hand it over, *now*. J could start again at the bottom, yes, and take care of Sophia, too. He knew how to do that. He had *done* it. Once upon a time he had *been* at the economic bottom, young and penniless. Once upon a time he had had a young wife, a baby coming, and no security whatsoever. Was he not, then, the last man to be afraid? How come his son, Win, believed just the opposite?

Amy had evidently always thought J was very fond of money and had needed to be told that it was not *that* important. How come Amy didn't know what J thought *was* important? Had he never told her?

What did Nanjo think? J feared she thought that he (who neither dreamed nor remembered having dreamed) agreed that a dream, *costing money,* had best be forgotten. Did Nanjo think he had never dreamed of anything else?

Sophia thought he must be something like out of his mind. "Poor J." "So tired." "Not well." Only Marietta thought he'd simply had a generous impulse—old fool that *she* was!

But why in hell had he spilled out all that rigmarole about being in the middle? Oh, worse than laughter, now they pitied him.

Well, J would just have to sit it out, although Sophia, with deadly intuition, now knew he had a secret, and Goodrick probably thought so more than ever.

J sure wished some fairy godmother, or little gnome, or frog, or some damn thing, would come along and get him off *this* spot.

The moon had risen. A band of soft light fell across the terrace just outside. Illusion, J thought wearily. Reflected light. And I'm fixing to be moonshine, going to settle for *my* reflection, and be what's expected of me. Hey, by golly. No. Shine direct! Hey, I am damn well *going* to have an identity crisis! And there's a little gnome for you. A nice modern little gnome, too, and it may serve.

Marion Little had finally got the weary, whining Little kids to their beds. She left the boys' room, shutting the door on its perfection. Everything two little boys could possibly need was in there. *They* didn't appreciate it. As she moved on the soft carpet to the great living room with its wide windows from which the view was a marvel, Marion knew she wasn't appreciating, either. She could not force herself to do it.

Win was standing, hands in his pockets, looking out. She didn't speak, but he spoke as if she had. "Don't worry. I'm not going to ask *your* father."

Marion felt hurt; she adored her father. (No modern daughter dares admit this.)

"Only confirm his original estimate," said Win bitterly. "I'm devilish worldly, and I'll come to no good end."

Papa might be right, thought Marion but didn't say so.

Win heard her just the same. "He might be right, eh?"

"Oh, *your* father will probably talk your mother around," said Marion. She sat down on the huge curving sofa.

"Dad was in a funny mood tonight," said Win. "Ma's pretty much got her feet on the ground." (Win adored his mother. Naughty, naughty! Never tell.)

His father's mood had made Win sad. How was it to be finished, to have done about as much as you are ever going to do? Lacking the forward plunge, the vorlage, the very hazards? To be safe and nothing more? *I'd* feel tired, too, Win thought. *I'd* feel like throwing it away, and the hell with it!

"I told them I wouldn't take it," he said aloud.

"What are you going to do, then?" Marion said.

Win didn't answer.

"I can always take the kids and go home," his wife said. "That would save money."

"If that's the way you want it." He didn't look around at her. What the devil did she want, anyhow? "Do you mind very much waiting until after the Faulkners have been for supper next Sunday?"

"Oh, not at all," said Marion coolly. "And then, after a delightful social evening in the sprawling, modern hillside home of that brilliant young advertising executive Win Little, Mr. Faulkner will come drooling into the office on Tuesday aweek and sign the contract."

"You don't think so?" said Win without passion.

"And after that, of course," she said, "you and I will live happily ever after." She put her head back and closed her eyes. She was miserable.

Win looked out over the sparkling valley. He began to think of his small but spry agency—G. W. Little and Associates—

and of the brilliant presentation (damn it, it *was* brilliant) he'd made to Faulkner. And of the gate that would swing open toward bigger and better things, in spite of the fact that his bread-and-butter account had quit on him. Stodgy. Who needed it? Faulkner was *exciting!*

Win knew he was turning to where the fun was. "Game" was not so inept a word. Damn it, why can't a wife see what's bound to happen when it gets to be no fun at home? If it weren't for the Little kids, Win didn't know that he'd mind so much if Marion did go home. Yah, home! She used that word for whatever parsonage the Reverend Coons happened to be in at the moment. Never for *this* house.

And so to bed, Win thought, and three kids for fruit, and ups and downs and thicks and thins enough, already. She *still* wants me to be just like her Reverend Papa, *which I'll never*.

"I'm sure," he said cuttingly, "the Faulkners will sense the generous warmth of a totally fulfilled woman."

"Oh, shut up, damn you!" said the minister's daughter. (He's always pushing me to be like Sophia, she thought, *but I am not!*)

A Mr. Smith said into a telephone in Chicago, "I think you'd better get on out there yourself."

Tony Thees, on the other end of the line said, "Will do, sir."

At ten thirty o'clock Nanjo Little extracted herself from the farewell embraces of her escort. Cary wasn't really trying, but she hated the conventional struggle. Oh, Nanjo knew how to pretend when the kids got talking, but for hard and selfish reasons *she* wasn't going to mess around. Nanjo had an ambition. "Love" would stand in its way.

She also knew that Cary Bruce, who never really tried, was just as glad to skim along where only the surface gestures were required and yet acquire status by dating one who was as "popular" as she. While Nanjo acquired merit of another sort by being broad-minded enough to date a boy without a background. (Of course, he had this car.)

Oh, Nanjo knew how to balance things off, the pros and the cons, and get about what Nanjo wanted.

Some light was on in the family room; the house seemed very still. She came around the corner and saw her father there alone, just sitting in his chair, not even reading.

"Daddy? Where's Mother?"

"Gone to bed." He roused himself. Nanjo was sure he was going to say his usual "Have a good time?" but J said, "Where were you, Nanjo?"

"We went over to Debby's, but she had a history paper to write, so we just rode around and then went to the hamburger hut." J looked at his watch. "And then we just rode around some more. It's not late," said Nanjo defensively.

"Later than you think," he muttered.

She took a few steps. "Daddy, do you want anything? Is there anything I can do for you?"

He said, "Why yes, there is. You can stop just riding around with Cary Bruce."

Nanjo was so shocked she staggered. "What did you say?"

"You'd be better off," he said dreamily, "in a jungle with only lions and tigers."

"But, Daddy," she gasped. "I'm not doing anything you have to *worry* about. All the kids ride around. And he's just a date, you know. I mean, honestly, we're not going steady or anything. I know he's from the wrong side of the tracks."

"What tracks are these?" her father said, looking at her without the light of worship in his eye. "Money?"

"It isn't *his* fault," said Nanjo, confused. "Don't *worry*, Daddy," she added impatiently. "I know what I'm doing."

"I'll worry on my own time," said J.

"But I can't just stay home," said his bewildered daughter.

"Well, now," said J, putting his head back and looking at the lamp, "that is just exactly what I would really like. Say, I'd like it fine if you'd stay right here in the castle, like one of those princesses your mother used to read about aloud. I'd be the king, you know, and in good time I'd line up before you a whole row of suitors—well-seeded characters. (Seeded by *me*, of course.) And from that group of the . . . the elite, you could choose a bridegroom. I wonder if things were ever like that? Just one of those human dreams, I suppose, that human fathers sometimes dream."

Nanjo was beginning to feel scared.

"It sounds kinda gruesome," she faltered, hoping he was clowning.

"Oh, nowadays everything's turned around the other way," said J. He rubbed his eyes. "That's a funny thing, though, Nanjo. I was taught that the human child takes longer to mature because there's so much more to him that has to grow up. I thought that was a sign of a superior potential. But nowadays children are supposed to know what they're doing better than you, on the day they're born." J had his eyes squeezed shut. "It kinda knocks out," he said, "one reason for trying to learn anything, don't you think?"

Nanjo said timidly, in her littlest voice, "Daddy, why don't you go to bed?"

"And in the morning," said her father, "I'll see the sense of it all?" He smiled and touched her hand.

Nanjo's hand jumped.

"I order you," said J mischievously, "not to worry about me."

Nanjo didn't know what to answer. He wasn't acting like himself *at all*. "But I *do* worry," she wailed. "I don't want you to feel so low, Daddy. Everything's all right. Honestly."

"You must have a ticket ... to somewhere else," said J sadly, "to be so sure of that."

"Daddy," burst Nanjo in a moment, "if I promise not to date Cary anymore, will that make you feel better?"

J lifted his head. "No," he said. "No, I don't think it would."

"Daddy, I don't *understand* you."

"Oh, well, neither do I. But honest people shouldn't go around making too many promises. Run along, baby." He pulled himself higher. "Good luck with the universe."

"Goodnight." Nanjo kissed his brow and slid away. She wished she knew what was the *matter* with her father! This was awful!

J sighed and turned off the last lamp. The glass wall became transparent, and he could see, under the mild moon, his "small portion." What did I say just now? he asked himself. Some philosopher! Quoting Victorian sundials. Old fogey, bemoaning the good old days (that never were) and wishing *he* had the running of the universe. "Ah, love, could you and I with Him conspire. . . ."

J laughed, although not aloud. He got up and went to bed. Sophia was either asleep or playing possum. J was glad and possumed himself. It was only somewhat comforting to think about God for a moment, Who, if indeed He had made everything that is made, must, in all logic, have a sense of humor, mustn't He?

CHAPTER 7

Monday Morning

On a plane that left Chicago very early on Monday morning there was by no means a full contingent of passengers. When they had been airborne awhile, a tanned young man with a snub nose crossed the aisle, leaving his lonely bank of three seats, to sit down next to the young woman by herself at her window. Nobody sat immediately before or behind them.

"What the devil are you doing here?" she said. "I thought I was supposed to handle this."

He said, "You don't know everything, sweetheart."

"God forbid!" She rolled her large eyes that had been carefully framed in assorted colors of paint. "Something more I ought to know?"

"Maybe," he said. "See, it was just a question of a follow-up until our beloved leader found out that somebody went to the trouble of scrambling onto the same plane with our Little man, yesterday."

"Somebody we'd rather he hadn't?"

"You know a man name of Barry Goodrick? Tell me true."

"Never heard of him."

"Then I'd better tell you what he looks like," said Tony Thees, "in case you cross his track." He made her a picture briefly and added, "Don't give him the time of day."

"So you're going to do something about him, eh?"

"If he's hanging around our Little man," said Tony, "all I can say is we had better know it."

"Say no more." The girl was well-shaped in the body; her face was thin, almost hollow-cheeked. Her hair was so pale as to seem silver; cut short and artfully uneven, it thatched her round skull. She seemed lively, confident, and full of mischief this morning. "Mine not to know the inside of the inside," she said flippantly.

"I'm turning it in my mind," said Tony gloomily, "to call you off and send you home. I'm not so sure you're a good idea."

"Oh, I don't know," she drawled. "Isn't our pigeon one of those dull family men, getting a bit long in the tooth?"

"He's forty-nine years old."

The girl smiled. "Ah, the dangerous age. Our leader knows life!"

But Tony wasn't amused. "It's not too funny, anymore," he said. "It's really not too funny." He gave her a sharp look. "I thought the old man was more or less having a fit of nerves. Damn sick, he was. But the more I think the more I wonder, especially now."

The girl seemed to be thinking hard. She changed her voice to soft pleading. "Could you tell me again, Tony darling, exactly what I'm supposed to accomplish?"

Tony was silent for a while. (Darling! he thought. Hardy har har!) Then he said quietly, "The Little man has promised not to repeat some things he heard in the hospital room. The old man was pretty sure he meant to keep his word. But he can't be much of an actor, can he? And he's not trained in our business. Where you come in is, first, you're going to be his chum, in on the deal, and he can *talk* to *you*. Second, you're going to take the lightning off, in case he acts *as if* he's got a secret."

"Yes," she said, grave and sweet, all mischief gone, "I understand. I'll *be* the secret. And that crazy ticket and all, that's for openers?"

"Right. Don't bother about it, by the way. I'll fix it today. Think you can take his mind off?"

"Oh, I should imagine so," she drawled. "Mysterioso cum sexy, who could ask for anything more?" She moved her mouth. It softened and moistened.

Tony looked away and said, "If Goodrick's been put off and has gone elsewhere, that'll be fine."

"How will you know whether Goodrick's elsewhere?"

"I don't care where he is," said Tony, "if he's not dogging our Little man. So *I* dog our Little man. Elementary? Just the same, the first thing you do, sweetheart, is find out whether Goodrick did approach him and, if so, exactly what was said.

"My mind shall be as your tape recorder, master."

He twitched. Then he smiled. "Make like a pickup. Smile at me, sweetheart."

She smiled and looked at him flirtatiously. (Only yesterday she had said she wouldn't marry him.) "Suicide," she said, "gives me the damnedest goose bumps. I hate to even think . . ."

"I get goose bumps, too," said Tony. And shut her out of his thoughts with a slam of will.

That old man didn't jump for fear of pain, he thought. I don't believe it. So shall I go the easy route and say to myself for-get it, *all* suicides are crazy. Hm. Maybe I brushed off Dr. Ambrose Willing a little too soon. Would a man like that be scared for *no* reason? Would he try to call off his whole life's dream—like some kid who can't go to the party and therefore wants the party wrecked for all the rest? I don't believe it. If I get sure they know the time and place, Smith will absolutely have to call it off.

He yearned for their arrival.

The girl took out her compact and studied her face, coolly inspecting a work of art.

Later on the same morning, in a shabby booth of a third-class restaurant in Los Angeles, Goodrick was listening to the purring voice of a small, slim, round-faced man who was too immaculately and expensively clad for these surroundings.

"Obviously Halliwell Bryce inherits the project," he was saying.

"Question: What's the project?" said Goodrick with his jack-o'-lantern smile.

"I have decided that you should know my thoughts," purred the other man. "Scientists are a strange breed, you know. Barry. Highly disciplined, within limits—outside of which they are the worst of wild-eyed dreamers." He sipped his late breakfast tea and made a grimace of distaste.

"Smith's no scientist," said Goodrick. "Who is he hired out to?"

His companion's shrug was minimal. "Smith has been trotting around the world for some time, talking confidentially only to men at the very top in what I may as well call weaponry. That includes more than hardware, of course. In deepest secrecy," the man wiped a faint smile from his lips with his own handkerchief, "he has been working up an international—no, an extranational conference—at which these great brains will sit down and reason together. Transcending political allegiances as well as race, creed, and color," the voice was mocking, "they will discuss with pitiful solemnity the future of the entire world. Although with typical hypocrisy they are not *really* including all races, creeds, colors, or ideologies. . . ."

Goodrick cut in. "So what you want is an ear in? Pick up secrets cheap, eh?"

"No, no. I doubt they'll exchange anything practical in the way of secrets. It will be fears and hopes and noble resolutions. Poor innocents, they dream they can meet as individuals at a private party."

"Sure ought to be a swinging party. Heh, heh." Goodrick poured himself more coffee. "Why not break the secret to the press? *They'd* cover it for you."

"No, no," said the man. "They'd kill it. If the press began to spout off, imagine the uproar, traitors, everyone! Political consequences! There would be no meeting. All *I* want," he said more softly than ever, "is the rendezvous."

"They can't possibly keep that a secret," said Goodrick bluntly.

"Not forever," his companion agreed. "There'll be transportation laid on, routes converging from all around the globe. But although I have eyes, I cannot afford them everywhere. Nor am I in possession of a precise list of those who will be going. I may run into the problem of false trails, co-incidental journeys, even decoys. The true meeting place may not emerge from the pattern soon enough for my purposes."

Goodrick asked no questions. He was gnawing on his thumb.

"You see," said his companion, *"I* am a private party in this instance." He settled back and spoke dreamily. "If the meeting is to be on a ship, for instance, which would seem a fairly convenient device, there would be no difficulty in arranging a marine disaster of some mysterious sort. If they choose a remote and isolated spot on land, some individual 'madman' or other could be found to fly over, just once, and once would do. Afterwards all governments would prefer a mystery."

Goodrick took sugar. "Be a little harder," he said, "if they pick some big city. But, say they want secrecy, any city crawls with newshawks." He stirred his coffee vigorously. His companion seemed to be watching his hand. Goodrick took the spoon out of the cup and said, narrowing his eyes, "You drop that thing on a city, nothing's going to keep it any mystery. *Shoop. Shoop.*" Goodrick's lips opened and pursed on this strange sound. It seemed to indicate disapproval, as if a robot were saying, "It does not compute."

"One thing I am sure of," said the man coldly. "Doctor Ambrose Willing was deeply involved. If the rendezvous has been set, he knew it."

"Oh, oh," said Goodrick. "I wish I'd known what I was after."

"Yes, I may have sent you too blindly. That's why I tell you all this now. You tell me, Barry ... you have a strong proportion of the blood. Why will these people suicide? Why did Doctor Willing end his life last evening? Personal despair, his career being over? Fear of suffering? A sentimental guilt, perhaps? Do they feel shame?"

Goodrick shrugged. "Why don't you find out the rendezvous the same place you found out about the project?"

"Aren't you clever?" said the other man nastily. "There happened to be one of these so-called brains—a Doctor Etting—dying in a hospital the other side of the world a few weeks ago. And in attendance a young nephew of mine. Oh, indeed, I sent him back to get the rendezvous. But it had not yet been set—at that time." He sighed.

"And the great brain. Where is he now?"

"As dead as Doctor Willing," snapped his companion. "But unfortunately my nephew had once studied under Willing, and he took it into his stupid head, once he—uh—became aware of my thoughts, to warn his old mentor *not to go.*"

"Well, well, well," said Goodrick. "So Doctor Willing could have had an idea what your thoughts are?"

"I have arranged a strict watch on Halliwell Bryce, of course, but it seems wise," said the other man, ignoring the question, "to explore the local situation very thoroughly. They are fanatics, you know," he said, suddenly angry.

Goodrick was staring at him. "I'd say this man Little is keeping quiet about something," he said. "I doubt it's about this. That's not likely."

"It wasn't likely, was it?" purred the other. "Tell me, Barry, have you ever heard of a Tony Thees?"

"Sure. Know him by sight, in fact."

"Good. Did you know that he has been working very closely with Mr. Smith?" Goodrick shook his head.

"Do you know that Tony Thees landed in Los Angeles this morning? Why is that, do you imagine? Can anything in these parts be worrying Mr. Smith?"

"Well, well," Goodrick widened his grin.

The other man rapped on the tabletop. "Now, if Tony Thees seems to be in any way watching over this man Little, would it not then seem that we have struck a vein here?" He was looking sly.

"Excuse me," said Goodrick flatly. "I've got blood to tell me this. If Willing, knowing your thoughts, did let slip the rendezvous, he would simply have said so. They'd call the meeting off."

"Did he say so? Necessarily? The great Doctor Ambrose Willing, caught blabbing to a nonentity, carelessly spilling this sacred secret? He'd feel *no* reluctance to confess his final idiocy? No shame?"

Goodrick sipped and licked his lips. "He might have just run out on the embarrassment, eh? After all, he had to die, anyway. Maybe Tony Thees doesn't know what the man Little might know, either. How about taking a crack at opening up Tony Thees? Better bet, wouldn't it be?"

"Would it?" purred his companion. "Shall we have a go at a man, trained to resist interrogation, who in all probability is only blindly following orders and could not tell us? Now the man Little is a different case. Just some ordinary American citizen, isn't he? Shouldn't be much trouble to open *him* up. Appeal to his deepest core. Let him tell all for the sake of mother, flag, and apple pie. Or bribe him. He must be greedy. They all are. Threaten him. He'll have no stamina. Actually, it would take no more than three minutes to break him the direct way if we chose to do that. I prefer a method less extreme, of course, for the sake of quiet. I want the rendezvous kept secret so that it will be *kept,* do you understand? I, myself, simply want to know *what it is.*"

"And nobody is talking?" said Goodrick skeptically. "How many men, all over the globe, aren't talking?"

"I told you they were fanatics," said the other impatiently. "Some chord has been struck with those men. The conceit that they have! And, of course, it's unwise to seize and seclude one of *them*. That would cancel the meeting. I don't—"

"What about money?" Goodrick broke in.

"Do you mean your fee?" said the other man drawing back coldly. "It will be generous." Then he cast his torso forward and began to speak with no purr whatsoever, rising toward rant.

"Are you stupid? Don't you know that the only realistic hope for humanity lies in *our* domination? Will you press for more American dollars for your individual self—when you must understand how the loss of the top brains of much of the rest of the world would give *our* brains precious time? Don't you see, as I see, the opportunity here?"

Goodrick said, cold-eyed and unruffled, "I wanted to know how much money I am authorized to offer the man Little. For myself, I'll take the usual generous fee, since this won't be much of a chore."

His companion studied him suspiciously, but Goodrick showed no particular emotion. At last the other man resumed his purr. "Ah, the cool professional! Very good. What sum would impress him?"

"Not too much," said Goodrick. "He'll be scared to death of the tax man. Heh, heh. Say fifty thousand maximum? I'll start with less."

"I'll see that you get it. Naturally we'll be trying pressures wherever else seems possible. But it seems to me that we may have here the weakest link of all. Check him out, will you?"

"Okay," said Goodrick. "Where can I reach you?"

The man said, "At the Biltmore Hotel. You may ask for John Jones. *Mr. Jones,*" he added and giggled in a high squeal, looking for a moment like a mad child.

CHAPTER 8

Monday Morning Continued

The blinds were drawn; the room was dim and quiet. The telephone had awakened him. J sat on the edge of his bed, scratching at his waistline for quite some time. Then he picked up the phone, although it was not ringing anymore.

"Thank you so much, Mr. Bringgold," Sophia was saying out in the living room. "I didn't feel that I ought to wake him. I'm so glad you understand."

"Well, you take good care of him, Mrs. Little. We can't have old J down sick, you know."

"I'm hoping that I can get him to our own doctor today. I want to be absolutely sure."

"Well, you just *be* sure, and let me know how he is. We can't get along down here without old J; you know that."

"Well, I certainly hope that you can't, Mr. Bringgold," said Sophia coyly. When they began to thank each other with the usual idiotic profusion, J slipped the phone back.

"Humph!" he said out loud.

It was almost ten in the morning. He ought to have been at the office long ago.

"They can get along without me very well," sang J to himself. Oh, they'd have a few problems breaking Tom Pollack into the full load, but they wouldn't have those problems very long. They'd get somebody else.

Humph. He bathed and dressed very slowly, deliberately dawdling. He felt, if not quite angry, at least miffed. He didn't like his wife and his boss "handling" him. He wasn't going to go to the damn doctor.

Mrs. Arriola was wielding the vacuum cleaner in the family room. She was a spidery little woman, with dark wisps of hair hanging out of a head scarf, and she wore her normal expression of woe and foreboding. "Oh, Mr. Little, how are you feeling?" Her eyes raked him up and down for signs of distress.

"Fine," he said. "Fine. How are you, Mrs. Arriola?"

"Oh, Mr. Little, that was a terrible thing nearly happened. I knew something was wrong. I didn't feel right all day Saturday. I couldn't help thinking of a plane crash, but they didn't say anything on the six o'clock news."

"My plane didn't crash," said J patiently. "I'm okay," he added, knowing very well that she wasn't going to accept this.

"Oh, Mr. Little, you want to watch out for them internal injuries. Them doctors, they don't always catch everything. Them things can kick back on you, and you wouldn't know what hit you. Oh, Mr. Little!"

"We must hope for the best," said J feebly, and he got away.

Sophia was in the kitchen. They said to each other, very carefully, what they always said to each other. "Hi. Do you want an egg?"

"Hi," he said. "I guess so."

"How many?"

"Oh, a couple." J slid into one of the plastic benches in the corner of the kitchen and looked out at his backyard, which slept in light.

"That," said Sophia, who had heard the extension click, "was Mr. Bringgold on the phone. I told him about your accident."

"I know," said J. So it was his property? Like *his* operation? Or *his* cold? He was in a word-sensitive mood.

"You slept," said Sophia, as if he had just denied it. She poured his juice.

"Fine," he said absently.

"J, I wish you would stop by Doctor Lodge's office. I called, and they think they can work you in."

J grunted. This was the same as saying, "I don't want to do that." Sophia didn't press. She concentrated on his eggs. J did not open the newspaper that lay at his hand. He felt afloat; the gears of Monday were not engaged at all.

"I'll let you read the paper in peace," hinted Sophia as she slid his perfectly fried eggs before him. He had everything at his hand, the toaster, the percolator. "I hope the coffee's not too muddy. Shall I make fresh, dear?"

"No, no," he said, not looking at her.

Sophia went softly out of the kitchen.

J ate his breakfast without unfolding the paper at all. He didn't need the Monday's harvest of the weekend's horrors. Mrs. Arriola kept peeking in to see whether he had yet been stricken, and Sophia kept coaxing her away.

At last J got himself ready to leave the house, and Sophia followed him to the passage that was a link from kitchen to garage. "J, will you stop at the doctor's?"

"No." he said. "No, I don't think so. No point in it. I'm going to the office."

"I wish you wouldn't. Mr. Bringgold doesn't expect you."

J braced himself. Since he must now, in a way, lie to Sophia, he had better look sharp about it. He said, "I'll tell you what's the matter." He was looking over her head. "I might have been stone-cold-dead in Chicago. Well, I wasn't, but it sure as hell made me stop and think."

"Oh, don't. . . ." Sophia grabbed for him. J was trembling slightly, and he knew she could tell as much. He held her off.

"I guess it just caught up with me, you know, the good old question." He looked down at her slyly. "I don't know who I am."

"Oh, J," said Sophia. Half relief, half concern in her voice came out not unlike stifled laughter. J knew the drill as well as she. Now she must tell him that he mustn't *mind* being not very much really, because he was beloved.

J crinkled the skin under his eyes just slightly, to warn her off that stuff. Sophia caught the warning.

"I want to know if you are okay to drive," she said. *"That* is the question."

"Oh, I'll make it. See—I guess this is just one of those things. But I've got a notion it's not the kind that if you lie down it will go away. Maybe I'll get a clue in the office." He kissed her lightly on the cheek. "Don't worry."

He knew she didn't like any part of this and was worried.

"I won't, J," she lied.

Sophia was the wise wife; she wouldn't nag. She let him go.

J went out and got into his car. The garage gave him a pang. How strange! Why shouldn't she nag? he thought to himself. How come we've got all these modern rules, that everybody has to be let do what he wants to do, whether you think it is dangerous or not? Is it because if you don't think he ought to do it and *say so,* then he won't love you anymore? So let him go have a crash on the freeway as the lesser of two evils? This didn't seem to make any sense at all.

J felt somewhat lighter of heart, however, to be alone. He breezed along the freeway, which was a delight at this hour. He paid no attention to a blue Ford that changed lanes, behind him, exactly as he did.

He was very late. All the girls looked up with curiosity. Hah, old dependable goofed for once! thought J rather gleefully. His assistant, Tom Pollack, came fussing nervously. J went to his desk, sat down in his chair, and thought, *Here I am—in the middle.* He was assistant to Herman Bringgold, who was the office manager. J also had an assistant.

Mr. Bringgold was a somewhat maddening superior, one of those who veered, who often contradicted his own didactically given instructions, and was always very much surprised that they had not been understood to have been tentative in the first place. J's assistant was an unfortunate young man who died a thousand deaths whenever he was contradicted in the slightest.

Between his boss's insensitivity and his assistant's thin and quivering skin, J usually slid in skillful tension.

But today he sat. I am neither capital nor labor, he mused. I am neither dispensable nor indispensable.

Then Bringgold came roaring like a little lion out of his office (which, naturally, was larger and handsomer and on the corner). "Ah, J! Good to see you. Excuse me. The printers want your notes."

Bringgold was a plump, short man with black hair combed sideways and glasses on his meaty little nose. He exuded an air of "hurry-hurry."

J surrendered his notes on the meetings he had been sent to attend in Chicago. He had long ago learned to take legible, orderly, and complete notes, because Bringgold almost never permitted his assistant to catch even a glimpse of the high and the mighty, the Partners, the "really big" bosses.

Hah, Bringgold's in the middle, too, J reflected, as his boss hurried away on small feet that twinkled in shining shoes. But over Bringgold's shoulder the man now cast, and J accepted, an invitation to lunch.

J, brushing off Tom Pollack as if he had been a mosquito, sat at his desk for a full hour and did absolutely nothing. The enlightening thing was that this seemed to make no difference whatsoever to the universe or mankind. And God, as usual, chose not to tell J Little what *He* thought of it.

Lunchtime came. J had just (he felt) eaten breakfast. He accepted, however, the offered cocktail. Uneasily, it sat upon the eggs.

Bringgold had taken some time to settle in the restaurant chair. He had acquaintances to nod to, the waitress to patronize, the napkin to unfold. the water glass to shift, the silver to realign. When he had at last come to rest like a hummingbird upon a twig. the table and chair still seemed to sway (like the twig) in an aftermath of his bustle.

The boss demanded to know all about what happened in Chicago.

J bestirred himself to do a moderately humorous sketch of his accident, but it went very flat, and Bringgold's glasses shone upon him suspiciously.

"You'd better get a checkup from your own man," Bringgold advised. "I told your good wife that we can't have you out of the office with some damn thing. Pollack tries, you know, J."

"I know."

Bringgold sighed. "He's got the old college try, but not the old college spirit. Don't you poop out on me," chided the boss. "After all, we wear the old school tie."

J put one shrimp into his mouth and chewed it slowly. "Did we ever see each other on campus in our lives?" he said thoughtfully.

Bringgold goggled at him.

"What the hell does it mean," asked J, "if, coincidentally, we were sent to the same huge university? You were a junior when I was a frosh. You were fairly large on campus," (Bringgold bridled), "and studying didn't bother you I'll bet. You went for background, and you got background." (Bringgold visibly stiffened.) "Whereas I went because my highly educated family assumed that I would lap up knowledge thirstily and cry for more. I was slow at the books, though. I had a terrible time just getting through. I never played any games or held any offices or joined any fun groups. As a matter of fact, I didn't *have* much fun."

"Here, here, that's no way to talk!" Bringgold took his glasses off and began to clean them. His face, without them, looked like the face of another man.

He said, "I think you've had a shocking experience, old

boy, maybe worse than you admit. Right? Tell you, why don't you take off the rest of the week? We can stagger along with Pollack that long, I suppose. All work and no play makes Jack, ha, ha, I always say. But you want to watch your health, you know that."

"There is nothing physically wrong—" J began and stopped, because he could see Bringgold continuing the sentence with a "but."

"Take a few days, why don't you?" his boss said when J dried up, "and get yourself a little recreation."

J said, "Recreation?"

"Sure. Get out on the golf course a couple of hours a day."

"And I will be created anew?"

Bringgold popped his glasses on and stared.

J thought, I'm scaring the liver out of him. The notion tickled him. The boss was not (as J well knew) a word person; playfulness with a word was not within his ken.

Bringgold said rather coldly, "You brought in a good report. Thanks very much. But you could have sent it in by messenger. I think you should go home and stay there until you're perfectly all right."

He thinks I am "emotionally upset," J reflected, and he doesn't know what else to do about it but order it to go away. He smiled and said, "All right, Herman." He almost never used the first name. "I won't go back, then. Something I said I'd do this afternoon. Okay?"

"Fine, fine," said the boss, grabbing the check in a fast, wide gesture that announced to anyone who might have been watching that he was grabbing it. "Do that, J. This—uh—trouble in Chicago," his eyeglasses shone, "whatever it takes to get you over it and back on the ball, you take," he said severely. "Your wife is a fine woman."

By the time J followed him out of the restaurant he knew that Bringgold's notion of emotional upset was tied to one human function only, and that Bringgold no longer believed that he had been told the truth about what had happened in Chicago. (What happened in Boston, Willy?)

J ambled to his car, wondering what the devil he thought he was doing. Maybe it was time he had some recreation. If trying to find out who-he-was involved blatting out what-he-thought whenever he felt like it, J perceived that what-he-thought was no neat package of firmly held convictions, consistently developed, hanging together, well arrived at, the sum of an examined life, ripened into a philosophy. It seemed, instead, to be a series of rambling speculations that did not hang together at all and were going to offend or alarm almost everybody. (Poor Nanjo!)

Well, he'd take this occasion to go see his father, but pretty soon he had better begin to speak the boss's language (a pidgin English, used in trade, which J *could* speak, of course). For the wheels of business would roll on. Oh, they would roll, those deep and dark-blue wheels! And if J fell out of his place as a useful, although not irreplaceable cog, he would have to go to the trouble of meshing back in again.

He crept out of the parking lot and meshed into traffic.

A green Chevrolet pulled away from the curb and fell in behind him. A blue Ford fell in behind the Chevvy. A few traffic lights farther, Tony Thees on J's tail in the Chevvy began to try to shake off Barry Goodrick in the Ford. So while they did tricky lane shifts, fast turns and do-si-dos around some blocks, J, unaware, lost them both. He found an "on" ramp to the Harbor, changed over to the Santa Monica, and went his way.

CHAPTER 9

Monday Afternoon

At about one o'clock Win Little phoned his mother. "Hi, Ma. How's Dad?"

"He seemed to have a good night," said Sophia. "He slept late. I didn't want him to go to the office at all, but nothing would do—off he went. How are *you*, dear?" She didn't wait for him to answer. "Win, you know I didn't mean to sound like such a miserly old witch last night. If your father wants to loan you the money, I shouldn't—"

"No, no," said Win quickly. "You didn't, Ma. I just

thought I'd tell you that everything's going to be all right. So forget it."

"Oh, good. How did you manage?"

"Oh, I'm about to sweet-talk the bank. It'll be okay. I certainly don't want . . . Ma, is Dad all right? I couldn't quite figure out what he was . . . well . . . you know, driving at."

"I don't know, dear," said Sophia, her heart swooping. "I wanted him to go to the doctor's this morning."

"Oh, any particular reason?"

"Well, I don't *know,* dear." Sophia wasn't going to betray J's half confidence of the morning. "I would just rather have Doctor Lodge's opinion. I mean, for my own sake."

"He *looked* okay, I thought. It wasn't that."

"No," she said on a long note. "No." Then she said briskly, "I imagine it was the shock. After all, to be fallen down in the street, and then the fuss they made afterward. That would be upsetting, too."

"It sure would," said Win heartily to reassure her. "You should get him to the doctor, though, Ma. Shall we all gang up on him?"

"No, no. I'll get him there," said Sophia grimly. "How's Marion? And the Little kids?"

Win hung up finally, feeling not quite sure what his mother was afraid of, but knowing that she was afraid. He had been calling from a downtown bank lobby. He walked out into the busy place, reaching for his keycase. He went up to the window for safe-deposit boxes and tapped lightly on the counter with his neat fingernails.

Sophia, listening for the whereabouts of Mrs. Arriola, ducked into the kitchen. She spent her Mondays and Wednesdays avoiding her cleaning woman, who would rather talk than work, naturally. The dishwasher repairman had gone, so Sophia sat down lonesomely in the breakfast nook and looked out at her garden.

All things had changed subtly. Some era was threatening to end. Sophia wondered whether J should retire. The prospect had often made them both shudder, and they had a thing against shuffleboard. No, it wasn't time. Not yet. But if J had been shocked into searching backward for something lost along the way, what then? Sophia didn't kid herself that things hadn't been lost.

What if he decided to quit his job, change his work, do

something else? Sophia remembered the tale of the man who had taken off for the South Seas to paint, ruthlessly leaving his family behind. *The Moon and Sixpence,* wasn't it? She couldn't remember the man's name. *Sophia* did not want to go to the South Seas. She couldn't imagine anything that would suit her less. But she didn't want to stay here if J went anywhere else.

Oh, stop your nonsense, Sophia scolded herself. J had never shown the slightest sign of yearning to be any kind of artist.

But maybe, she thought, we *should* take a long trip, somewhere different, to Europe, or around the world. It would be expensive and would cut into their security. But maybe not. Maybe just the oppsoite. She began to brood on far places. At the same time she could feel the house around her threatened. Abandoned without care, it would burn down or something. It would crumble, decay. Who would water the lawn? All her plants would die. Sophia was a caretaking kind of person. It was her pride to keep and take care.

The fear returned. Maybe he was trying to give me a gentle sort of hint, she thought—all that about dead in Chicago. *Maybe it's true! J is going to die!* Sophia clasped her hands. Her neck was stiff. She was *furious* with him! Damn it, she thought, am I such an old woman that I have to be *spared?*

Amy came tearing up the stairs and burst into the apartment. "P.S. I got the job," she cried. "Starts on Wednesday."

Her husband was cross-legged on the floor. He clapped his hands to his ears and groaned.

"Oh, gosh," she said. "Headache? I'm sorry. But listen. . . ." She knelt and began to stroke the back of his neck and speak softly. "The money is amazing! Just call me Philistina, why don't you?"

Avery kept holding his head.

"How long since you took an aspirin?" Amy canceled out her own affairs. Avery only swayed.

"What color is it?" she asked softly, in a moment.

"The color of bruises," he said, "the sound of tin pans."

Marion said into the phone, "Well, that's wonderful! It was all right to do, was it?"

"Of course it was all right to do," said Win testily. "I

called him up and asked him. He'll never touch them. They were always going to be mine."

"Well, then," she sagged, "I'm glad."

"How about squab for Sunday? With wild rice?"

"That's a dollar a grain," said Marion, sounding more cheerful. "And a nuisance to fix."

"Yes, but you fix it so *good,*" said Win. "We can tell the Faulkners that we get it for free from an old Indian chief who's a friend of the family."

"I'll think about it," Marion said. But what she thought was, Why does he want to have something very expensive and then pretend it cost nothing?

Win thought he could read her mind. "But that," he said, "would be dishonest, and we wouldn't get to heaven, would we?"

Marion said nothing. What was there to say?

When he had hung up, Win thought, Oh, God, we have got to get straightened around. As soon as we're all set. *Got* to get things in the clear. He didn't know how they were going to do that, really.

"Listen, you'll prolly win," said Cary Bruce. His longish hair whipped back and forth. He squinted against the sun and steered furiously. Somebody honked him off a lane straddle. The honker was an old-timer of twenty-nine. Cary, who was eighteen and who despised as the walking dead anybody over twenty-one, ripped diagonally across two and a half lanes, flipping the tail of his low car under the snub nose of a truck driven by an ancient of thirty-two with quick reflexes.

Nanjo, who had just missed at least mutilation by eighteen inches, paid no attention to that. She was back on the subject that haunted her mind. "But it's so weird. It just plain *is* the dress on the book cover. If Daddy hadn't said that he would buy it . . . Til my Mom had to get chintzy. . . ."

"What's it to him?" said her escort. "Peanuts, I'll bet."

"Of course, I never got to even talk to Daddy. He doesn't know why it's so important. Sandra said today that the talent scout is going to come for sure. Her father works in the studio. And I mean when you think of all the money people make in the movies, it does seem like peanuts. Three hundred mere dollars."

"Prolly the scout is going to pick you, anyway," said Cary.

"But if I had that perfect, perfect dress! Oh, well . . . Let's not talk about it anymore." Nanjo settled to a sad patience that forbade any other topic to raise its head.

Cary Bruce, flying along the freeway at 70 miles per hour, hated people like Nanjo's father, who had money all the time. Everything Cary could earn at odd jobs or wangle out of his parents or otherwise acquire was in his car. The car was bone of his bone, flesh of his flesh. In it was all the power that he had. In a way he could understand, all right, how Nanjo Little felt about this dress.

"Yah, peanuts," he said. "I might know where there's peanuts like three hundred dollars."

Nanjo said, "Hey, I've got to be back for French Circle."

Cary immediately swooped for an "off" ramp, almost chasing some old crate up on the shoulder. Waiting to cross traffic below, he made the car snort and then took a fast swing-around under the freeway to roar up the ramp on the other side. "Hey," he cried, delighted with himself, "how about that?"

Nanjo was glad he had forgotten to tell her where the three hundred dollars might be. She both knew and refused to know where some of the money he put into his car had come from. A lot of kids . . . well . . . snitched stuff once in a while. In a way they had to. Nanjo could understand how Cary felt about his car.

CHAPTER 10

Monday Afternoon Continued

"I have more or less given up on Edmund," said Grosvenor Winthrop Little III. "I shall not, of course, fall back on the variations common to Elizabethan spelling or the prevalence of clerical error. I shall simply note some alternate possibility. All we know is that there died in London, in 1607, an Edmund Shakespeare, aged twenty-seven, a player. And someone paid for a toll of the great bell of Southwark

Cathedral. Yet, might not an apprenticed boy have taken the name of his patron? Or, if I am right about the Poet, *this* Edmund might have been his son. Baseborn, perhaps."

J listened to his father's light voice trip along familiar paths.

"There is, and can be, no proof," his father said. "I find it amusing to read 'doubtless' when there must be doubt, and 'evidently' when there is no evidence, and 'certainly' when the point is that we cannot be certain. I try to avoid such chicanery with the language."

J's father sat at his narrow desk, thin old hands nimble among many papers. His narrow skull with its cap of white hair was backgrounded by shelves of books. The chair J sat in was small and uncomfortable. So were all the chairs in this small apartment. It was as if his father had no need of easy chairs. He was a lean old gentleman, immaculate; everything about him seemed very dry. J could not remember him otherwise.

"The coat of arms," his father continued, "is a far more complex problem. I have my theory, as you know, but even supposing that I am right, there remains the designation 'Gent' on the Brend leases."

"Is that so?" murmured J.

"I must, in all fairness, raise that question, even though I am only an amateur theorist and no authority."

When does an amateur become an authority? J wondered. When he makes a buck? No, that marks the professional.

"Why aren't you an authority?" he dared to say. "You've been studying for—how many years?"

The old gentleman looked frostily severe. "I have not had access to original documents." He sighed, a dry whispery sound. "Winnie would have had access."

But J kept wondering why his father had not become a professor of literature, or of history, or of both. Supposing his father had not been born to wealth, would he then have turned at least pro? J's older brother, Grosvenor Winthrop Little IV (whom the family called Winnie), had been, at an early age, a full professor. Poor Winnie. Before he came to his fortieth year, this brother had suicided. The rumor was that in view of his health, he had taken a tough-minded and courageous decision. J felt a bit of a pang. He wished now that he could have understood Winnie. If Winnie had not turned pro and gone into the soul-searing business of teaching the young, meantime resisting pressures of all kinds from the inevitable Old Guard, could he have survived? Winnie may have been not tough, but too tender.

J could remember the days of his youth and life in a well-regulated New England household which, although never ostentatious, still had not lacked creature comforts. His mother had been, or had seemed to be, a placid woman. J remembered her as having moved always to some stately measure. She had spun out all her days without (as far as he knew) drama until the outrageous agony of her final suffering. She had been dead before Winnie's death and before the death of William James Little, J's younger brother, in the war. Willy, full of physical vitality, a hunter, a fisherman, a football player, a soldier, had gone off laughing. Yet Willy, so tough, had died in some vaguely ignoble manner. The details were blurred.

J sighed for his lost brothers, neither of whom he had really known.

His father, the other survivor, had successfully transferred himself to the West Coast, to this decent little apartment, in this equable climate, and had adjusted (if that was the right word) to the loss of a wife and two out of three sons and furthermore the bulk of the family fortune, very well. He lived according to his own taste, frugally but not in want. His one extravagance was to buy books now and again.

"I must be prepared for controversy," his father was saying. "Stratfordians will and must scoff. Other theorists will be piqued. The Baconians are, for the most part, lunatics. The Oxfordians, in the ascendancy, are not, in my opinion, much sounder. The Rutlandians are in possession of one or two points, such as *Laelia*, but the rest of what they say is rather silly. I can state, without any personal doubt, that it was *not* some great earl who wrote immortal literature with the back of his hand."

J marveled at his father's passion, dry though it be.

"The proponents of the Great Nobleman theories are forever pointing out," said his father indignantly, "that Shakespeare knew so much about the life at court and the behavior of monarchs that he must (they say) have been a courtier. But what they forget is, *we* know almost nothing about the life at court in Tudor days or the behavior of monarchs, and, furthermore, what we *think* we know, we have gained from one source only. The imaginative works of William Shake-speare."

The old gentleman grinned like a wolf.

"And now to business," he said.

J winced within. He had always been somewhat dubious about the prospect of paying to have the book printed. So far, in the course of his father's interviews with this Mr. Pudney, J had listened and hedged and played wise, and his father had seemed well satisfied with the game of hesitation, the suspension of decision, with, in fact, the dreaming. He kept saying that he had not quite finished the work.

Many times J had asked himself whether the old gentle-man ought not to have so harmless a pleasure. But his doubts would resume. J feared there might be no distribution of the book and his father would receive only a sense of dreary failure. Even more important, would he not lose his only occupation?

"As you know, J," his father said, "I have yet to find the name, complete. The first syllable I know. The second contin-ues to elude me. Now, Mr. Pudney and I discussed this on Friday last, and he suggests the following procedure. Let us bring out a book, using only the first dozen chapters, where I cover the entire analysis, the signatures, the dwelling places, the portraits, my thoughts about the Blackfriars Purchase, Ben Jonson, the will, the monument, and the First Folio. I shall make my points. But I shall withhold the later sections to do with the true name of the Poet, only suggesting that I have clues. Later on, we shall issue the chapters to do with the name in a slim little companion volume. Mr. Pudney thought it a very good solution, enabling me to go on with the research, of course, and providing . . . He had some term. Oh, yes, what he called a cliff-hanger?"

J groaned to himself. Good old Pudney. So he had figured out how to leave the old gentleman with his occupation still, and also how he might just rook his victim twice.

"What do you think?" his father was asking. "Of course, in view of the fact that he may expect to get *two* books, the terms have altered rather favorably. See here."

J barely glanced at the neatly typed proposal of an agree-ment. "I don't think I ought to do this for you, Father," he said.

"You would not lose by it," his father said patiently.

"You would receive a fair share of the profits as a return on your investment."

J sighed. "What profits?"

"Do you mean to say the book will not succeed?"

"I don't mean that, exactly. There will be profit—for Mr. Pudney."

"Do you mean to imply that the man is dishonest?"

"No, no, I suppose—not quite. Aren't you a little inconsistent?" J suggested as gently as he could. "If there is to be this demand by libraries, then why not a regular publisher of reference books?"

"I believe I have just stated that I am not an authority." His father was stiff.

"Then *why* *must* you be on the reference shelves?" said J not without pain. "You don't expect it to be a popular best seller. You have told me you've made no concessions in your style."

"Certainly not," his father said. His dry, pink wattles shook. "I fail to understand your position, J."

"I can't afford to give *Pudney* that much money."

"That," said his father crisply, "is unfortunate, isn't it? Mr. Pudney cannot hold this offer open indefinitely."

"Oh, yes he can and will," said J wearily, "as long as he sees *his* chance of profit."

"I have long been aware, J," said his father, "that you have never had any particular sympathy for my work. If Winnie had lived, he could have discussed it knowledgeably. Even your brother Willy," his father was not looking at him, "might have been loyal...." The voice died out.

J knew that this was only disappointment speaking and tried not to feel hurt. But, he thought, Winnie knew too much. He'd pick holes in your theories. Willy had no truck with books at all. But I, the middle one, being neither ignorant nor knowledgeable, have listened at least politely.

He said, "Whatever they might have done, Father, I don't quite see my way."

But J felt chilled and afloat. Now he was thinking that an old man with so little future, not even present in the present, deserved no seat to the moon. So should he perish? But to contemplate the past was not an evil occupation. Why should not *some men* keep in mind what man had once done in a golden age? Why did every living soul have to be all the time so damned modern? J was flooded with an old familiar affection for his father.

He said suddenly, "All right. I'll do it."

But his father put on a thin smile and rose. "I think not, thank you," he said serenely. (J wondered if he felt relief that his work would not go to the test yet.) "I hadn't realized it would seem so large a sum to you. You must think no more about it," he went on in a kindly fashion. "Thanks very much, J, for coming down."

J got up. His father's mouth began to writhe, presaging humor. "Do you know, J, I wonder why you have never asked me the inevitable question? What difference does it make who wrote Shakespeare?" Evidently his father considered the question to be entertainingly stupid.

"All right," said J, "I'll admit I have wondered. What's the answer?"

His father lifted a bony finger. "Ha," he pounced, "what difference will it make when we get to the moon? How can we know the difference *until we get there?* Can you answer that question?"

He seemed to think he had triumphed. J had been, indeed, hit. He felt crushed. He slunk away.

J usually thought of himself as "all his father had." But as he drove off, he let himself notice, for comfort, that his father could have "had" J's entire family, the children and the children's children, the whole tribe. But the only one *he* tolerated at all was his namesake. Grosvenor Winthrop Little, V, who was sometimes his errand boy, fetching papers from the bank for the old gentleman to sign and delivering them whither they should go.

J's father, perhaps with some uncanny knowledge of who he was, had always chosen his associates without regard for the feelings of anyone he chose not to choose.

Yet he had given his children attention. In fact, his second son had had all the attention he had either needed or desired, and mercifully *no more.* This had suited J very well, as he could remember. He wondered why it is that moderns carry on so about fathers paying attention to sons when, as he recalled, the day dawns quite early in a boy's life when he only and devoutly hopes that by good luck (and some clever management on the part of the boy) father (and mother, too) will just stay out of the boy's own fascinating business and let him lead his private life without the nuisance of having to cope with antiquated notions not pertinent to the scene.

A wall dissolved between two compartments of J's mind. Ah, yes, Nanjo. Win. Amy. Yes, he could see the generations marching and the whole world shifting under their feet. No use to teach his children to fear and avoid what had used to frighten J. What they ought to fear and avoid, J had probably never heard of. They had no time to bring him up-to-date.

And so much for attention.

But when had his father left off brooding to see the moon ahead of man? J, not having expected surprise, was twice surprised.

Goodrick said into the telephone, "You were right. Tony Thees is definitely around."

"Ah," purred Mr. Jones. "Very encouraging. Find out why."

Tony Thees said into the long distance telephone, "Goodrick is hanging around, all right. Must mean he hasn't got what he's after. Yet."

"Get sure of that," said Mr. Smith, "and make it fast. I don't like what I hear about his boss."

CHAPTER 11

Monday Afternoon Continued

When J drove into the garage, Sophia's smart little car was out, and he was just as glad. The serviceable old Chevvy that Nanjo used for transportation whenever she wasn't the guest of some boy stood under the grapefruit tree. This did not necessarily mean that Nanjo was at home.

J let himself in through the kitchen, feeling deeply depressed and confused. The house was shining from the ministrations of Mrs. Arriola (who had departed). J stood within its orderly comfort, breathing the scent of his own place, deciding that he ought to sit down and *think* quietly, when the phone rang.

J went to answer.

"Is Nancy Jo there, please?"

"Afraid I don't know. I just came in. I'll see."

"Mr. Little, sir? This is Bobby James."

"Oh, yes, Bobby. Hang on, and I'll look around."

"Thanks a lot, sir."

J crossed the living room to the bedroom wing, where all the doors stood open and nobody was to be seen. By habit he thought, Poor Bobby. Young James was, from Nanjo's point of view, an old man. He was just out of college, starting at the bottom in a bank, a sober and industrious young fellow with what is called a good background, who had fallen helplessly in love with Nanjo, aged sixteen. She treated him with great cruelty.

For one thing they had not met in a manner approved by Nanjo's peers. Bobby James was the son of a woman with whom Sophia had gone to school, who had one day descended *en famille* to visit her old acquaintance. One look, and poor Bobby had been a goner. Nanjo, however, thought of him as a joke and treated him as if he were an ancient sugar daddy, sometimes permitting him to take her to expensive places. Poor Bobby did not know that he had no chance. No chance.

J prowled through to the family room to look out into the yard. Nanjo might be out there somewhere. Cal, the gardener, was out there. He had a small wire rake in his powerful hands, and he was briskly brushing the soil under the azaleas, as Sophia had begged him never to do.

J slid back the door and then the screen and said to him, "Cal, would you mind not raking there? Mrs. Little says the plants won't like it."

"Yes, sir, Mr. Little. I's only cleaning up. Excuse me." The big man sounded aflutter.

I wonder what he does on the Mondays that I'm not around? thought J with a flash of natural suspicion.

Then he saw, to his right, near the bricked barbecue platform, well behind the garage, his daughter, lying on the grass, bent over a book, her bright hair pouring down over her cheeks, and her flesh, gleaming with oil in the lowering western sun, looking as if it were made of dark gold.

When he called her, she started, tossed back the hair, pulled the big beach towel up as she rose, and wearing it like a serape, she ran on her pretty bare feet into the house, wafting under J's nose the slightly oily perfume that rose from her baked skin.

J stepped out into the yard. "What's this about the elm?" he asked the gardener.

Cal had a speech impediment of some sort, a touch of stutter, a touch of lisp. He was difficult to understand. J stood gazing at the elm and absorbing the news that it must be very drastically pruned and that Cal would do it, but it would take him time, and if Mr. Little didn't want the mowing and clipping let go for a week, then Cal would have to do it on an extra half day, which he happened to have free on Wednesday. (And which will cost me extra money, J concluded. It figures.)

He kept receiving the impression that Cal was speaking faster and even less intelligibly than usual, that he was for some reason nervous. Well, of course, it was Sophia who usually gave him his instructions. Perhaps he came of a class habitually awed by the man of the house. (If such a class *existed* in the U.S.A.)

J didn't know much about the fellow except that he was a big brute, with a crop of bushy blond hair and thick lips that mumbled over bad teeth. He had powerful legs and enormous feet in heavy boots that would have been serviceable in a jungle but which seemed unnecessary among the garden flowers and on the grass.

J didn't want to think about the Chinese elm, so he said that he would think about it. Susie Neeby hailed him over the fence. The Neebys' house was next door on the corner, and the husband and wife were best friends to the Littles—in that whenever it was more fun to be four instead of two, they played games or went places together.

"Hey, hey, J!" cried Susie. "How come *you're* playing hookey?"

"Well," said J, "I said to myself, 'Why not?' How you been?"

"Sophia says you had a wild time in Chicago. What happened? She wouldn't tell me."

"It's a long, sad story," said J. "When are we picking up the rain check?"

"Friday."

"Okay," said J. "I'll tell you the whole thing, words and music, when Glad's around to hear my rendition."

"The suspense will be terrible," said Susie, "but don't forget, we're going to clobber them. Right, partner?"

J brushed off this exchange from where it had lit, with butterfly feet, on the very skin of his mind, and went indoors, where he simply sat down in "his" chair, because he felt so discouraged and so sad.

Very soon Nanjo, with her hair pulled tightly away from her face and a blue muumuu concealing her bathing suit, sunsuit, bikini (or whatever the two scraps of cloth were being called this season), came gliding on her bare feet and curled herself on the floor. She had a book in her hands. "You're in the doghouse, Daddy," she told him with a twinkling partisanship. "Mom's gone to get Marietta."

"I suppose I could have picked her up at the Wimple," said J feebly. "I forgot all about her."

But Nanjo chattily explained that he was not to be reproached for this. His sin was to have left his office for parts unknown when Sophia wanted to ask him how he felt. She had called all over town, Nanjo said, and had finally reached his father and received news of him.

J wasn't paying much attention to her words but was reflecting that Nanjo didn't often stay beside him and simply chat. Oh, she would chat at table, rather impatiently, and then be off about her fascinating private life, he supposed. He watched her face and her head as it bobbed and turned, and he knew, in his detachment, that here was a female setting about to manipulate a male. When Nanjo pushed the wide neckline of the muumuu off one shoulder and said she'd been trying to get rid of strap marks, J admired her technical skill at leading into the subject she wished to discuss.

"Daddy, you never *did* let me tell you about that dress."

It seemed that there was to be a parade of the Prom Princesses in what Nanjo called formals when the kids would vote for the Queen. J supposed that Nanjo wanted to be the Queen. Well, he wanted her to be the Queen, too, he guessed.

But now, with her knees tenting the garment she wore, her bare feet demurely side by side, Nanjo began to tell him about her ambition. It seemed there was a best-selling novel about a teen-ager. She put the book into his hand. The story was going to become a motion picture. The producers were reported to be looking for an unknown young girl to play the leading role. A scout was *known* to be coming to the parade of the princesses in Nanjo's high school. So there was this exciting chance. And there was this fabulous *dress!*

"Look, Daddy." J looked. The book jacket seemed garish to him. It said to him, "Don't be afraid to read this book. It is cheap and superficial and guaranteed to be no strain upon your mind. It will shock you without *any* effort on your part."

"That's the very same identical dress," cried Nanjo, "and I *found* it! And besides, do you see what I see and all the kids see, too? Don't I look like her? Don't I, Daddy?"

J troubled by the cartoonlike sketch of a very young girl whose breasts were bursting from a formal, looked at Nanjo and *was* shocked. Her face, so young and dear to him, did have the same exaggerated features. Her eyes were too big, her forehead too broad, her whole face pinched too quickly into a chin that was much too small Her mouth was a weak, and yet somehow vicious, little doll's mouth. J felt a terrible pang. Nanjo passed for a pretty girl this year; but styles change.

He said distantly, "It takes more than a certain dress or a certain face, Nanjo."

He saw her eager eyes deaden, the patience seep in as Nanjo prepared to endure the same old stuff. Hard work. Yah. Yah.

J said more sharply, "If I had known what this was all about, I never would have said you could buy the dress." He looked at her steadily. "That's a cheap nasty book, and the picture will be a cheap nasty exploitation picture, and that role would plague you for the rest of your life. You may not like my knowing that, but I do know it."

Nanjo didn't blink. "I know it, too," she said, "but I would make an awful lot of money on a one-shot deal and afterward who'd care?"

Something had fallen and smashed as it fell. Somebody's image?

A car horn now honked twice in the driveway. It was the family signal. (Hey, I'm home!) J rose with relief to go deal with Marietta's baggage.

Nanjo had turned her head to a cringing angle. "Does Grandmother *have* to be in my room?" she said nasally.

"If you don't want her there, tell her so," said J.

"I can't do that," said Nanjo in her whine. (You know we've got to wear these masks.)

"And if you want that dress," said J, "talk your mother into it. It doesn't worry me. You'd be *out* of the picture the minute you opened your mouth and said something through your nose."

His daughter looked at him as if he had gone mad.

Marietta and her disorderly possessions made a natural buffer between J and his wife, who inquired for his health, kindly, and did not reproach him for anything. While Marietta invaded Nanjo's room, whither Nanjo had gone to defend her fortress in what small measure she could, Sophia said to her husband, "By the way, Win called. He got that loan."

"That's good!" J said heavily.

(It didn't enter his mind that having called his office, Sophia must have heard that he was taking time off, must be wondering why, but was not asking.)

"And Amy called to see how you were," his wife went on, "and she's got a job. A real one, it seems to be."

"Good, I guess," said J.

"And how was your father?"

"All right," said J. "I think he's given up about his book for the time being."

"Good," said Sophia, "and you have the first appointment tomorrow with Doctor Lodge."

"All right," said J. He was pulling himself into a shell. He wanted to think, but nobody would let him think. J knotted himself around himself and went into the kitchen for some ice cubes.

When he returned and went to the bar to mix a highball, Sophia said, with disapproval and alarm both battened down under an air of mild puzzlement, "Isn't it a little early?"

"It is neither early nor late," he replied with pain and a ridiculous pomposity. He saw Sophia draw herself into herself warily.

CHAPTER 12

Monday Evening

Sophia served an early dinner. Afterward Nanjo vanished to lie on the floor in the living room, waving first one leg and then the other up and down for the purpose of firming her thighs, while she talked to her cronies on the telephone.

In the family room Sophia, all her feminine antennae aquiver, had gone underground. She was sitting there, playing the game of nothing's-the-matter while her hands kept busy with a ribbon-knit costume she had been working on for weeks. J, who knew very well that she was watching him like a fox, was miserable.

Marietta Thomas billowed in a third chair. She was beaming upon all and speaking with her insufferable ecstasy. "So lovely a home! Such precious warmth! I don't mean the material comforts" (she never did) "but the generosity of spirit, the love in this house!" Her eyes were moistening. She was carrying herself away, as usual.

But J looked at her and thought with a jolt, Old lady, are you crazy? Blind, deaf, crazy?

Hadn't she heard the resentment in Nanjo's whining voice, in every word of Nanjo's since Marietta had entered this house? Didn't she know that her own daughter welcomed her, but with an exasperated combination of pity and obligation that could not quite be called a generosity of spirit? Hadn't she noticed his own faintly insulting patience, for which J felt ashamed (although he couldn't help it) because it, too, was something less than love or generosity?

And didn't Marietta sense the atmosphere right here in the room, where J sat helplessly suffering within and Sophia lay low, hiding anxiety in order to be "wise"? Where both of them were glad of Marietta's presence only because it meant they couldn't really talk to each other right now when it was "wiser" not to?

"So relaxed. So restful," Marietta proclaimed.

Then J, in tension, received on his stretched nerves the information that Marietta was neither relaxed nor resting but pushing very hard (J began to mix metaphors in his mind)— plastering over any and all rifts in the lute, weaving an iron curtain of covering bliss, *selecting* heaven on earth, and denying with all her might any evidence to the contrary. It was the first time he had perceived his mother-in-law's force.

Nanjo must have left the telephone for at least one second, because it rang. J waited for her to snatch it up, but she did not, so he went.

"Mr. Little?" said a male voice.

"Speaking."

"This is Tony Thees. Haven't seen *you* since Noah built the Ark! Remember?"

"Oh. Yes. I guess that's right." J was completely flustered. He pressed the instrument to his ear so hard that it hurt.

"I'm the friend of a friend that you expected. Call me Tony."

"Yes, I . . . uh . . . How are you, Tony?"

"The point is, how are you, sir?"

"Oh, I'm fine."

"Good. No problems?"

"No, no."

"I've been trying to get you."

"Oh well, we've got a teen-ager in this house."

"I see. I tried at your office this afternoon."

"Well, I didn't happen to go back after lunch," said J, as if he had to apologize. "I had to go see my father. I . . . uh . . ."

"Sorry I missed you," said Tony. "Now, sir, no later than tomorrow someone will contact you. Not at your home if you don't mind. And will bring, as our friend suggested . . ." the voice began to space out words, "the-little-antique-paper-weight-you-found-in-the-funny-old-shop."

"Oh. Well. Fine. Listen, I wish you'd tell our mutual friend . . . uh . . . thank you. How is he?" J was seeing Barkis in his mind's eye.

The wire buzzed by itself for a few seconds. Then Tony said, "You haven't heard? Well, since you're bound to see the papers, and I doubt the names will confuse you . . ."

"What's this?"

"I had better tell you, and I'm sorry. Doctor Willing, our mutual friend, has passed away."

"What?"

"I wouldn't mention that it signifies. You never met him."

"No, no. But gosh, I'm sorry to hear . . . he . . . he was . . ." (Barkis, thought J. Gone?)

"He was a very sick man," said Tony. "We are all sorry. You won't, and haven't, mentioned anything he said?"

"No, no."

"To *anyone?*"

"Not a soul," bristled J. "What do you think? . . ."

"Careful," said Tony. "Thank you. Just keep on that way."

"As I *said* . . ."

"Very good. By the way, you met me, Tony Thees, casually in Chicago. You forgot the little package. Left it in a restaurant. I kindly brought it out for you and left it in your office. Got that?"

"Yes. I guess so. Sure."

"It is not in your office, of course, but you will receive it. Say 'Thank you, Tony.' "

"Thank you very much, Tony," said J.

"Good man." Tony hung up.

J stood stunned, in the entrance area until Sophia called, "Who was that, dear?"

"Oh," called J, "some fellow—says I met him in Chicago. Seems I mislaid a little package. He says he took it to my office."

"Well," called Sophia, "that was nice of him. What's in the package, J?" Her voice was playing the game secrets-are-fun.

"Just something silly," said J. (*A ticket to the moon!*) He made for his den.

He switched on the set, zipping past old movies and new games until he found a newscaster. J sat down, and he was trembling.

Out in the family room Sophia's head was high. Her ears were straining.

The news ran through the wars and woes, the crimes and clashes. It took a long time before the newscaster changed his voice to the low funereal dragging that heralded an obituary.

"Ladies and gentlemen, this country has lost one of its very great men. Doctor Ambrose Willing, the man who . . ."

J sat through the eulogy doggedly.

"Doctor Willing," the voice picked up briskness, "died last night, Sunday, in a fall from the eighth story of a Chicago hospital. It is believed that he was under sedation, unsteady, and confused. His death was an accident. The Los Angeles Dodgers . . ."

J sat all the way through the sportscasting.

Oh, he should have made sure—should have checked and made sure—that somebody knew the old man's notions. Should have been sure that authority *knew*. Poor old man, shouldn't have been left all alone in pain and confusion. Somebody should have taken care.

J sat on into a comedy half hour.

Since J was not addicted to TV, and they had a houseguest, inevitably Sophia came to see why he was being so rude.

He gave her a look of desperate pleading. (Let me alone, please?) He couldn't tell her that he was guilty, or even that he mourned. Her hand was suddenly on his forehead, testing for fever in her well-worn way. "J, you *don't* feel right. There is something the matter. Now we are absolutely going to see the doctor in the morning. And I'm putting you to bed right smack now, and don't you dare say No."

"I do feel kinda awful." J knew that his eyes were still beggars. (But don't abandon me?)

"Is there pain, anywhere?" she demanded fiercely.

"No, no, I just feel so damned low, Sophia." J could have bawled.

"Well," she soothed, "it isn't easy to get over the shock you had. But Doctor Lodge knows you so well. He'll fix. Now get into your pajamas. I'll fix you a hot drink. Go on, now. Scoot."

J got up and began to walk feebly toward their bedroom. He was a hundred years old. Or a thousand. Or man, not old, not young. A few million years.

Marietta's bulk loomed in the door to the family room. "Ah, you cannot feel depressed, dear J. So blessed. . . ."

Sophia gave J a push at the shoulder. She said to her mother, "This is J's house. He can feel whatever he *feels* like feeling!" Marietta was blown away in the storm.

But J was bundled into bed with special pillows, as if he were one of the children and Sophia his mother . . . coddling-severe, in charge of him, commanding him into a position for peace and rest. And J went falling, with exquisite relief. He would have blurted out all he knew, as if in sanctuary, but Sophia would permit no such thing. She gave him his hot drink, that powerful symbol. (He didn't need a hot drink; he needed what it meant.) She tucked him in and kissed his cheek. She soothed his brow; she opened the window; she dimmed the light; and let him alone, but not abandoned.

Well, J had all along known that he was sometimes Sophia's child, as she was sometimes his. And when she was mother, he could afford to rest. He thought drowsily that he could make Win play the part of the ticket holder. Who would know the difference? Then Sophia could go! Even if it was all nonsense (Oh, poor old man! Poor crazy . . .), yet the thought that he might, after all, save Sophia made J feel better. Never mind brains. The race *must have*, from time to time, its brow soothed.

In the other room Marietta said, "Pray, Sophia. And do not be afraid. J is good."

"J is no angel, Mother," said Sophia tartly. And the Lord had better not cart him off to heaven under any such delusion, she thought grimly. (Oh, J, with half your natural teeth long gone and your hair all moth-eaten, and you can be so maddening . . . But don't. . . .)

It was going to be a long night and long breakfast time, a long wait in the doctor's waiting room tomorrow.

Sophia could wait. Maybe it was only psychological.

CHAPTER 13

Tuesday Morning

By dint of having been first on the list J got out of the doctor's clutches by a little after 10 A.M. He and Sophia had come in two cars. They walked to the curb together.

J had suffered patiently through the tedious tests and examinations. The doctor had summoned Sophia to his private office to hear his verdict. There didn't seem to be much the matter with J (pending some test results, of course). The *doctor* was not worried. Sophia really should have realized that the city of Chicago was, after all, a civilized part of the world. Now, what was this accident, exactly?

So J had done his bit about the dowager and had been pleased to notice that the act was crystallizing; he had the story properly timed and rolling. The doctor had laughed in all the right places.

He knew, however, that Sophia, who ought to have been satisfied, was on the contrary holding in her temper. She seemed to be good and mad at him. J possumed; he kissed her in the customary manner and told her that since he could take the day or any part of it off, he thought he'd run on down to Amy's with the hundred and fifty dollars, which had been promised, agreed upon between her parents, but since forgotten. He'd make her take it.

"Of course, dear," Sophia said too sweetly.

J pulled away from the curb, leaving Sophia standing beside her own vehicle, ready to bawl with a confusing combination of relief and rage. So J *wasn't* going to die from natural causes, at least no sooner than anybody else. But Sophia had *not* been foolish to wonder. She had had cause! And it wasn't very nice of J not even to notice the suffering to which his behavior had put her or the noble restraint with which she had endured it. Laugh, clown, laugh. Hah!

From the curb just behind her a black Mercury pulled away. It would have darted off on J's heels, but a station wagon came barging into the street from an alley and clipped its front fender with a dainty metallic crunch. J had gone on. But Sophia, whose own way was now blocked, stood where she was, thinking, Oh, nuts! I'm a witness.

The wagon reversed, pulled back from the entanglement, which did not seem serious, took a sharp cut into the street, and roared away. Oh, oh! Hit and run! The driver of the Mercury got out, leaving the car's door open, and made directly for Sophia. By now people had popped out of the pavements, as if they were angleworms after a rain. But Sophia, the only person who had already been here, braced herself.

"Excuse me," the man said. "You saw that, ma'am?"

"Yes, I did," she said stoically.

"His fault?"

"As far as I could tell, yes." (Oh, the nuisance of being a witness, but it was her duty. Besides, she didn't see how she could get out of it.)

"Get a look at the driver? Wait a minute!" The man bent close. "Aren't you Mrs. Little?"

"Yes," said Sophia, realizing at the same time that she had seen his face before.

"So it *was* J M. Little just came out of this building?"

"Yes."

"My name is Goodrick," said the man, whose wide array of large white teeth were now displayed. "Been to see a doctor, has he? How is he? What's the trouble?"

But Sophia was not the wife to hash over her husband's health with a stranger. "You know my name," she said. "Do you want my address? I did *not* get a look at the driver."

But the man seemed to have forgotten all about the fact that she was a witness to his innocence in the matter of the small collision.

He said, "Wasn't that a terrible thing happened in Chicago?" His cold eyes watched her.

Sophia was at once invaded by several emotions. Alarm, resistance to curiosity, and a violent curiosity of her own. She said, "Didn't I see you at the airport? Weren't you on the plane with my husband?"

Goodrick said, "Of course. Of course. What did he have to *say* about his room-mate?"

"Room-mate?" said Sophia, bewildered.

"In the hospital."

"Why, nothing much," she said, astonished.

"Come, come. Surely your husband tells *you* everything."

Sophia bristled. What kind of remark was this!

"Didn't he tell you his room-mate jumped out the window?" said Goodrick. "Didn't do him any good, believe me, from the eighth floor."

The shock was brutal. Sophia staggered.

"Mr. Little told you, didn't he, what his room-mate *said* to him?"

Sophia didn't like his voice in her ear. She pulled herself up. "I haven't heard anything about this," she said coolly. "If you want me for a witness, you can find my phone number."

"He didn't tell you!" said Goodrick. "Oh, come on now, Mrs. Little, that's hard to believe."

Sophia got into her car and began to slide across the front

seat. The man leaned in at the window. "Mrs. Little, could I call on you and discuss . . ."

"I'm afraid not," said Sophia. "You see it is very hard for me to believe what *you* say, and in fact I *don't* believe a word of it. I did not, by the way, get the license of that station wagon. I doubt that I can help you."

She drove away, maneuvering around the stalled Mercury with swift skill, watching her rearview mirror, half afraid he would follow her. But cops had come. Goodrick seemed to be standing there with his left thumb to his mouth.

Sophia made for home, her anger drowned temporarily in a surge of pity. Oh, poor J if that's what it was! How awful to see a man do such a thing! No wonder he's been acting so peculiarly. Okay (anger surfaced), but why in the world didn't he tell *me*, at least, all about it? And the children, too. It isn't pleasant. It wouldn't have made any of us happy. But to have seen such a thing, had *that* happen, and not tell us. . . .

What is wrong? Oh, does J think he ought not to have let it happen? Did he try to stop the poor man and fail? He must have been full of it, to tell that unpleasant stranger on the plane.

But what was the stranger doing outside Dr. Lodge's office? Why had he called the house, as J said he had. Who *was* he?

Then she began to hear J doing his vaudeville turn, imitating the trivial complaints, aping a funny old sourpuss, dubbing him his room-mate. Wait a minute! That performance did not go with what she had just heard. No, it jarred. It clashed.

But if that Goodrick had been lying to her, why? Why was it his business, anyhow? And why, thought Sophia angrily, isn't it mine?

Amy and Avery lived in an old frame house, not a block from the water, which someone had split up into apartments long ago. The street floor was abandoned; J suspected it of harboring rats. The old stairs came up into a long hall that bisected the place and led, at the far end, to a fire escape of sorts. The whole building was rickety and worn; the remodeling needed remodeling.

Sophia didn't like to come here. It distressed her. J had always overcompensated, telling himself that this was Bohemia. But today, having taken it into his head to see how his middle child was faring, he let the effect hit him as it would.

Amy opened the door and showed surprise but welcome. Her apartment was strange enough without the added strangeness of its furnishings. J stepped in to what he supposed to be the living room, a large, high-ceilinged, almost square space, with two old-fashioned sash windows that overlooked not the ocean but a gas station. Here, since Amy kept the dark-green shades, their sharp edges unblurred by any drapery, drawn to the sills, there was very little light. The old floor was bare, except for half a dozen enormous pillows in sad, neutral colors. The walls bore in thick array many unframed canvases in a jumbled variety of sizes. The paintings were all by Avery, and J had never been able to figure out a single one of them. There was a fireplace, and there were two rather tall iron candelabra that stood on the floor. There were books piled in teetering columns in the corners. Usually J tried to imagine the place by night. With a fire going, the candle lit, and young bodies sprawled on those cushions, there might be some coziness or even glamour here. By day it was simply gloomy, but the gloom was not even serenely austere, because of the colors writhing in the half dark on the walls.

Amy was in her usual outfit, the tight trousers and the tight jersey top; her black hair was tousled. She had a book in her hand, her finger marking her place. Where can she see to read? J wondered.

Drawn toward light, he peered into what he supposed had been a dining room but was now Avery's studio. Avery was out walking, Amy said. He had a bit of a headache and wanted the air. The studio was smelly and messy, but light did come harshly through the big, bare bay window that also overlooked the gas station.

"Sit down, Pops," said Amy, throwing her book on the floor to signify the turn of her attention to him exclusively. "How come you're not at the office?"

J said he was taking the day off, and he asked to use the bathroom. This was located unhandily; the living room must be crossed by any customers from the bedroom. It was clean enough, perhaps just barely clean enough, but full of clutter. The antique tub stood on legs; the wash-basin faucets dripped upon yellow stains; the toilet flushed with a horrendous noise. J came forth, reminding himself that this was all there was except the kitchen, very old and shabby and inconvenient, and the bedroom, which lay at the front of the building overlooking the street, where (he knew from other inspections) there was item: one double bed without headboard or spread; and item: three old wooden benches along one wall, on which all the clothing lay in heaps, the soiled beside the laundered.

He had always tried to take a liberal view. After all, there was no law that clothing must be kept in a certain order or even in any.

"When are *you* going to be going to the office?" he asked this daughter. "Your mother says you've got a job."

"Starts tomorrow," she said. "The worst of it is I've got to wear skirts and nylons. Ick!" She was piling three of the huge pillows to make a stack of them, thoughtful of his antique knees. J sat down, feeling ridiculously sultanic. "How about some elevenses?" she said mischievously. "A spot of wine?"

"Fine," said J heartily. Amy covered her slight surprise at this quick acceptance and scuttled away.

"Staying on here, are you?" he said when she returned from the kitchen with a bottle and two unmatching glasses.

"The rent's about as cheap as there is," she said carelessly.

"What have you got against chairs?" her father inquired.

"Not necessary." She gave him his filled glass and sank down herself with such limber grace that he got her point. "What are you up to, anyhow, Pops?" she asked impudently.

So he told her about going to the doctor's at her mother's insistence, knowing that Amy's fine eyes were probing to discover what might be behind his visit now. J was a little afraid of her. She had remarkable eyes. Her features were not stylishly pretty, but J realized suddenly that they would never be out of style. Amy, who didn't ask to be thought beautiful, was, in fact, a classic beauty.

"The doctor said you were all right, did he?" she was asking.

"Fine. Fine," said J, feeling shame. Had her own father been unable to see the real article without a label? Amy did not do the things a girl does which say, "SEE ... THE ... GIRL? ... IS ... SHE ... NOT ... ATTRACTIVE? ... OH ... ADMIRE ... THE ... PRETTY ... GIRL!"

"Well, I'm glad you went," Amy said in her abrupt way. "Poor Mom probably thought you'd found out you were dying of something loathsome and didn't want to tell us so."

"What?" said J feebly.

"Well, gosh," said Amy, "you did act as if the end was near, so the hell with money."

J pressed his lips grimly together. If it were so that Sophia had thought such a thought, he was sorry, but he was also very much annoyed.

"If you're so healthy," his daughter said, "why aren't you back at the nine to five bit?"

"What's this job you've got?" snapped J. "Nine to four thirty maybe?"

"Oh," said Amy, grinning, "I'm going to interview applicants for jobs. I have to ask them a whole lot of nasty questions and check off the answers and cull out the ones who would make any foreseeable trouble if they did get hired. It doesn't take experience The questions have been mimeographed since the early dawn of Doctor Freud. It just takes a cold heart. But the pay's quite good," she added brightly.

J got out his checkbook.

"Hey!" she said.

"You not only need the money for Avery's eye doctor," said J sternly, "you need some respectable clothing to wear to work. That's called overhead."

"Oh, I borrowed a dress," said Amy. "It'll do."

"It will not," said J. "You don't know anything about offices. This isn't going to be the same as baby-sitting."

Amy had done a lot of baby-sitting, which seemed to include often some actual domestic service. This was how she supported the two of them, hand to mouth, going to some woman's house only when funds were low, never having any trouble finding a house to go to or some woman delighted to find a young and intelligent female willing to do her *this* service.

"It sure isn't," drawled Amy. "Baby-sitting is anyhow human, and your soul's your own."

J was scribbling a check for two hundred and fifty dollars. Now he looked up at the walls. "Is Avery getting anywhere near being able to sell some of his . . . uh . . . work?"

"Oh, Pops," said Amy, "don't talk about it." She gave him a half smile.

"I don't get these pictures, Amy," J blurted. "I never have." He threw the check on the floor between them and slurped from his glass.

"I know, Pops," she said indulgently. "It doesn't matter if you don't understand." She picked up the check. "Humph," she said.

"How do you know I couldn't understand? If you'd take the trouble to clue me?" J growled.

"Because you don't even ask the right questions," she said promptly. "You don't ponder the creativity or the concepts or the self-expression. You want to know will they sell? But you see, Avery's business isn't a buying and selling kind of thing."

"Well, I do my best," said J. "Humph! Avery paints all these pictures. But he isn't interested in selling them. I'm not going too far, am I, if I suppose he has to eat like everybody else? You're not farmers. Food has to be purchased. So who is going to pay for it? You are, eh? For how long? That's all I asked, and I don't see anything wrong about the question." J was vehement and felt huffy.

"Oh, someday," she said, "maybe he'll sell. Maybe after we're dead and gone. Who knows? But that's not . . ." Amy stopped herself and drank deeply. "We'll go ahead and do things our way, you know," she said. "One thing might make you feel better. We're serious, Pops. He's hitting for big insights, big stuff. Avery works very hard. Harder, I imagine, than anybody you ever saw in your whole life." She stared at him over the glass.

"I doubt," J chided, "that you can imagine what I may have seen in my whole life."

"Oh, well," she said, flushing, "I mean roughly speaking. Come on, Pops. Bottoms up! There's more on the vine."

J felt angry and frustrated. He let her pour again. The wine was sweet. Its effect seemed odd at this hour of the day. "Well," he said at last, wishing the three pillows had a back so that he could sag, "I guess I've been given pause. I'm not getting any younger, as the saying goes. Self-expression, you said? That's the on-ly way to live, eh? Of course, I've always thought I was more or less expressing myself. But maybe there's something in it that I've missed."

"There may be," she said very carefully.

"What bothers me, though," said J chummily, "say I do express myself. To whom do I do that?"

Amy closed her eyes.

"All right, let me try to clear that up." J was feeling giddy. "Say I see the light and walk out on my nine to five bit."

Amy's eyes flew open and stared boldly.

"Now then, I'm figuring to express myself," J went on, "but who is going to pay attention?"

"It doesn't matter."

"It *doesn't!*" said J with genuine astonishment. "That's funny. You mean art has no value, at all, except to the artist? Then why is Avery any more important than anybody else? Than *you*, for instance?"

Amy said nothing; her mouth twitched. J thought that if he himself wasn't quite sure whether he was musing aloud or attacking, how could she tell?

"Seems to me, in that case," he rambled on, "I may as well take up building sand castles. Let the tide come in and wipe them out. No matter. I should have expressed myself."

"So you would," she said abruptly. "What do you want art to do, Pops? Make *money?*" She sat on folded legs confronting him.

"Listen," said J, his heart leaping, "I'm not asking art to do anything in particular. There it is, eh?" He was getting a little bit drunk. After all, breakfast had been very light, anticipating the doctor's tests, and a long time ago besides.

"You know what you like, I suppose," Amy said in warm tones, spiced with only a delicate contempt.

"Sure I do," said J, confronting her. "I couldn't tell you what a painting *is*, but I can tell you what it *does* if I like it. It speaks to me. *To me*, understand? Not to the artist. What do I care for him? Why should I go to the trouble of warping my imagination around to try to feel what he feels? The question is, what do *I* feel? Of course, maybe that's the wrong question." J forgot there was no back to his throne and had to catch himself from going over backward.

"You're not looking for the right things in these paintings," Amy said patiently.

"There's no such thing as creativity," said J, surprising himself very much.

"How's Mother?" said Amy sweetly.

"Now, now, wait a minute," said J, shaking his finger at her. "Laws in the universe, don't you think? Say the artist doesn't know what they are until he finds them? Like what's the use of going to the moon?" J had begun to mumble; he braced up. "So what's *creative?* You take invention. Hah, that's only discovery, too. Don't you suppose there was penicillin in the days of Moses? How's about another little drink?"

Amy poured somewhat grimly.

"I might be serious about my problem," J announced with an antic look. "How am *I* going to express myself? You can't do it in business. Everybody knows that. Well, I can't paint," J continued with a wave of his hand. "Can't sculp, either. The art of the dawnce has passed me by. Music? Well, since I can't even carry a tune . . . What shall I do then? Be an actor?"

Amy kept her eyes cast down, not to show pity.

"Write? Hah, anybody can write!"

"No," said Amy, "that's not true."

"Why not? I can put words down on paper. I know a whole lot of words. It doesn't matter, you tell me, whether they mean anything to anybody else. Okay, then, so be it." J reeled where he sat, feeling rather clever.

"It's preferable to have something to say," said Amy tightly.

"Why?" pressed J. "I don't follow. Avery doesn't have to say anything. To anybody else, that is."

"Oh, Pops, you're just being ornery. Of course there's communication in art."

"But only with some small esoteric body of connoisseurs?" said J, being as ornery as he could think how to be. "What is it they connoise, to coin a verb? Say *I* became an artist. Who's going to say that I 'unique' am saying *nothing*? How would they know, except by whether or not I spoke to them?" He didn't know what he was babbling about. His heart seemed to have a pain in it.

"Now *you*," he went on, helplessly carried away, "aren't going to live the way I've lived. You've rebelled against that. So, maybe you are right, and I ought to shuck off my stupid values. And you ought to approve of it if I do." He felt like Pan. His hooves twitched. No, wait, maybe he meant Silenus. J forgot. He'd never been able to sort out those old Greek characters. There had been too many of those old gods and most of them bums, in J's opinion. Unreasonable. Troublemakers.

"Pops, I'm sorry," Amy was saying. "I didn't mean to hurt your feelings. I know how you've slaved and sacrificed to do things for us. I'd never say I don't appreciate . . ."

"Aren't you ever going to have any babies?" J said softly.

She was severely startled. Even in the gloom he could tell by her face. "All right," she wailed, "I can't talk to you *at all*." Her head bent over, knobs rose and dotted the black jersey along her spine.

But J thought to himself sadly, No, I'm afraid we talked this time. But he retreated. "Well," he said aloud, "I didn't come down here to make you cry." He began to scramble to his feet by a process of first resting on all fours, and from this position he said, "It's too late. I fold like a chair."

Amy looked and began to laugh. She rocked where she sat, in a fit of giggles.

J managed to get to his feet; he brushed a hand through his hair, which seemed to have become rumpled and was tending to stand on end. Perhaps it had twisted into horns above his temples. What a clown he was! He gazed down at her through a mist, knowing there was pain the other side of the cloud. "I'll scoot now," he said and then woodenly, "Sorry to have missed Avery."

"I'm sorry he missed you," Amy whooped. "It would have done him good to see how f-funny . . ."

This was cruel. J recognized that she needed to be cruel because of pain. But he couldn't figure how he could unsay what he had said.

"Good luck," he muttered and staggered toward the door. Amy was up, springing to open it for him.

"I'm sorry," she said, rather desperately.

"No, no," J said. "No, no. Listen, I understand this much. You sacrifice . . ."

"No, I don't!" she shouted angrily. "No, I *don't*."

"I see that, too," said J heavily, "because neither did I. All right, Amy."

There was a woman in the hall. She was in the act of opening the door to the other apartment across the way. "Oh, hi," she said.

"Hi, Lily. Good-bye, Pops. Good luck," Amy spoke lightly and shut her door fast.

J staggered and grabbed for the wall. It eluded him. His back fell against it, and his feet began to slide. He realized that he must be a ludicrous sight, middle-aged fellow in a business suit, drunk in the morning, and about to fall down.

The woman said, "Whoopsie," and her strong hand came under his armpit.

"I have looked upon the grape. . . ." he babbled.

"Listen, you don't wanna try and drive right now, mister. How's about me fixing you a cuppa black coffee?"

"Be very kind," said J, who was ready to bawl.

The other side of the door Amy Alice Little Gardner pressed her forehead on the wood and one hand to her mouth. She was sorry she had laughed; she couldn't afford to cry. She loved her father; she wished he hadn't come. All J's bumbling talk had been touching. But she didn't want . . . couldn't afford to be touched. Amy had problems enough.

In a while, however, a certain silence in the building seeped through to her. She skipped into the bedroom, looked out the window, down at her father's car, silently still there at the curb. Amy wiped her face on the first thing that came to hand, a pair of Avery's socks. She braced on her fine lean legs and felt her insides turning over.

Well, if *that* was what was the matter with old Pops, if *that* was his commonplace middle-aged-male-in-a-panic problem, he might at least have had better taste than to buy himself what he needed right across the hall. Trust Lily Eden, though, to glom onto a customer! That old creep! Amy's young skin crawled. Well, if *that* was what he was going to do to express himself. . . . "This is really terribly amusing," said Amy to herself.

But it was Amy's quality to know when she was lying.

CHAPTER 14

Tuesday Afternoon

J was weeping as he had not wept since he was six years old. This place where he was had furniture. He sat in a kitchen chair; his head lay on the kitchen table. The chair was hard. The tabletop was formica, and from time to time he rolled his head to press his throbbing temples to the cold of it.

Oh, what a great soft sinking down was this into the luxury of defeat! "Enough. Enough," he wept, allowing himself to lose the long and futile battle. "No more. I can't do it anymore," he sobbed, "and why should I?" Oh, the struggle of the years, the disciplines, the hazards and the hesitations, the punctuating joys. Yet nobody—*nobody*—knew, or bothered to inquire, what J had thought he'd been doing all that time. He, who had sold his soul for a chair to sit in—clod and slave.

"The middle way," he wept. "You bet! Supposed to be so great, so right, so wise. The Greeks said so, and everybody knows the Greeks knew everything. Yah, the ancient Greeks should be around to see what you get out of the middle way these days.

"You aren't exciting. You're not even *interesting!* Hah, you fall on the big fat hump of the probability curve where, as an individual, you count the least of all. Because your name is legion. Your real name never gets in the paper. Oh, no! But just the same, old Legion J Middle, he gets all the blame.

"Every damn thing that's wrong with the world today is *your* fault, fella. Haven't you heard? Certainly. Poverty, misery, corruption, crime, mental illness, certainly, certainly. All would be roses if it weren't for the cheating way you've gone ahead and gone to the office and taken your wage and paid your bills. Cold heart!

"Why, if you'd had any compassion, you'd have gone forth to bind up the wounds of the leper with your bare, ignorant hands. *You* can't have compassion, sitting in a chair, paying for the doctor. If you wanted reform, you'd go into the street, fight and push and shove and holler and go to jail. That's where you should have gone. You'd just as soon show goodwill to man? Yah, you should have gone to Africa. You can't do it in the office. Go *anywhere* but to your office from nine to five.

"All right. Okay. I give up. I never had a clue. I got no big insights. Oh, you can have big insights in a slum or out in the wood or else in Sweden. But *you* can't have big insights in Burbank, California. You're too comfortable! What do *you* know of blood and pain? It doesn't count if your mother died in agony. The bed was clean. It wasn't society's fault. So why should you feel anything?

"You're just a comfort-loving slave, remember. No heart, no soul. You think you appreciated the ten toes of your normal healthy baby? Or the dew in the morning on some tame rose in your ordinary backyard? Well, you just don't know who you *are,* that's all. The trouble with you, you're not *wild.* You're civilized! And you've had it, old boy. That's where you made your big mistake."

The wine sickness, however, was subsiding. J had begun to listen to himself. He sounded like a very unhappy child. He began to know that the woman was there, sitting across the table, pouring more coffee from time to time, in silence—not touching him or even murmuring. J thought, in sudden peace, what a nice woman she must be. He was very grateful to her. He was grateful for this place. He was grateful for the coffee and for her silence and for this wonderful escape from everyone who knew him and everywhere that he was known.

But how come he was bawling his head off, complaining like a baby, at noon of a Tuesday, before a stranger in a strange place? This was at least middling wild!

He lifted his head, but he couldn't see very well through his swollen eyes. He asked about the bathroom, and she said, "Sure thing."

The bathroom was just like Amy's. J went in, shut the door, used the john, flushed it, took the corner of a more or less clean towel, soaked it, and mopped his face. The face in the mirror suddenly gave him a wink and a grin of pure mischief. J and the face seemed to have a secret between them. Hey, all that sobbing and heaving and flood of hot tears, that whole fit had been . . . well . . . (okay, *we* know this, don't we?) pretty damn phony. "You old bastard," he said to the face, without sound.

He dried his fleshly face. The one in the mirror looked awful. But J felt absolutely wonderful. The word "catharsis" did not come into his mind. (J was pretty much off the Greeks at the moment.)

He came out into the strange woman's living room, feeling serene. There wasn't enough shame *in* him for forming an apology. But he could see her now; he smiled at her.

She was medium tall, somewhat flabby, not young. Her hair was dyed bright yellow. The skin of her face sagged under the makeup. Her eyes were hooded. Their color was black. "Two pitch balls stuck in her face. . . ." Where had J heard that? His father?

But before he could identify or complete the phrase or, with another part of his mind, form a phrase to say, the woman spoke up in a business-like way. "So, okay? You ready?"

J's brain got no message at all from this.

Then Lily Eden decided to find out, in the swiftest, most direct, and practical way possible, the answer to her question. At the touch of her hand J jumped like a scalded cat.

The present truth burst upon him, where he was, with whom, and what was expected of him now. He thought he was going into a fit! An enormous whoop of laughter started in his very gut and ripped up through his body. J M. Little the clown of the world! The clown of the *universe!*

He gulped and choked and struggled to beat down the laughter. It wasn't very nice of him; she might misunderstand. He wasn't laughing at *her*. She'd been very nice to him; J still thought so. (Yah, whether she knew it or not, whoever she was.) He finally was able to speak. "Excuse me ... uh ..." he almost strangled. "What's the—uh—usual fee?"

She said in tones of brass, her black eyes like hard dried raisins in the dough of her flesh, "Fifty dollars."

It was too much. J knew that. He might be a clown—but he wasn't *that* gullible. He got out his wallet. There were two twenties and a single in it. He took out one twenty, glanced at his watch, and said, "Afraid I'm running a little late." His voice kept high and tight against the threat of laughter. "Here's for the coffee and the company. No offense?"

Lily took the money and showed him her upper gums. "Okay," she drawled. "Better luck next time."

Maybe she had a heart of gold. Probably it was neither gold nor dross. What the devil is *dross?* J dared not make another sound; he still felt hysterical. He was afraid he'd begin to laugh (or cry) to the point where he would double up and fall down, after all.

He made it to the hall. There was Amy's door. He shunned it. He went as fast as he could down the dusty old stairs. When he came out to the sidewalk, he became aware that the wine and the strong coffee had not quite finished their war below. He was in no fit condition for the freeways. Better (in middle-aged prudence?) walk off some of these mixed feelings. So he turned to the right, toward the shimmer of sand at the end of the block, and began to take strides.

"So I am neither a prude nor a libertine," he chuckled to himself. His fancy veered to wonder how far he could have beaten down the asking price. J steadied himself and steered away from some ribald wordplay. Well, he hadn't wanted *that* woman at any price. On the other hand, neither had he been compelled to take her in order to prove something or other. Maybe he wasn't normal.

Oh, come on, given another time, another place, another woman, another mood, and not quite so much wine . . . "Humph," J chuckled to himself, "I'll bet I'm neither normal nor abnormal. I must be somewhere in the middle." He knew there was something wrong with the logic of this, but he was in no mood to be logical in so ridiculous a world as this one.

He had gone a few yards, talking to himself, smiling to himself, when he saw Avery Gardner mooching along toward him. J hailed the tall lad.

"Oh, hi," said Avery, drifting to a halt. He must have just come from the beach, but he was not sunburned. J, looking at this chap with eyes refreshed, thought that the sun didn't seem to be interested in Avery. (Neither would the moon be, alas!) The boy didn't look healthy to J. Too white, too skinny, too wispy. Eyes red-rimmed behind thick lenses. Posture poor. Thin neck, too slight a stalk for the heavy blossom of that skull. Poor kid, J thought.

"Wait a minute, Avery," he said briskly, fishing for his checkbook. "How are you by the way?" J made this a true question.

" 'M 'K," said Avery dully.

"Let me use your shoulder," said J, turning him with a gentle shove. "I want to write another little check here, and then I want you to make an appointment with a regular doctor, over and above the eye man. Mind now! And you do what the doctor says."

Resting the checkbook on Avery's shoulder blade, J began to write out a check for the sum of a hundred dollars. Meantime Avery stood with his neck in a violent twist, not seeming to know what J was doing or whether Avery ought not to shy away in animal alarm.

"Okay, thanks," J tore out the check. "This is for you, yourself," he said sternly. "Tell Amy . . ." J had been going to say "I worked very hard for it," but he thought that was pretty smart-alecky. "Tell Amy," he substituted, "that I might take some understanding, too." J winced at what he had said. But better words failed him, and Avery probably wasn't listening anyway. So J gave up, patted the lad's shoulder, and went striding off toward the sea.

Although Avery had heard the words, he had scarcely seen J's face. Numbed by pain-killers, he walked on, went upstairs, in at his own door, and said to Amy, "Look. Your father said he could take some understanding." Avery wasn't in the habit of struggling to figure out (with his brain) why other people did as they did. He sank down, took off his glasses, put his palms over his eyes, and paid not even bewildered heed to what Amy did now.

She took one swift glance at the check in her hand. Her mouth contorted. "Buying, eh?" She snatched the other check out of her book and tore it, with the second one, into little pieces and threw all the pieces at the ceiling.

J found himself leaning, bemused, against a chest-high stone wall, gazing across the sands toward the mirror-bright sea, watching the tiny human creatures frisking along its edge as if an ocean were a plaything invented for their holiday.

Well, he didn't understand what Avery Gardner was up to in this world. But had his daughter Amy never understood what J was up to, *at all?*

Since when is a soul negotiable in the market place? he mused. Who sets out to buy one of those? A man might market his strength, his skill, his knowledge, or even his mere presence in a certain place (from nine to five), but it's his own fault if he gets his soul tangled up in the package. Who needs it? What the devil would Herman Bringgold want with any soul of mine?

J sighed. What a strange conception Amy had of business. As if every business weren't in a state of snafu, 90 per cent of the time, so that the marvel is that anything gets done. What with the unreliability of even those who *intend* to be reliable, the personalities clashing within, not to mention the outside factors, the tides and the winds that flow and blow in history. Shocks and surprises that no man, by selling his soul or anything else, could prevent or often even anticipate. To J the whole raft of seemingly hardheaded occupations subsumed under the word "business" floated in a sea of chance on a mass of emotional jelly.

His image was getting away from him, and someone seemed to have come up beside him and was now leaning on the wall near enough so that he could sense the warmth of the body. This was odd, considering the expanse of leaning space.

A female voice said, "Nice day for Ark launching. Maybe Noah didn't have to launch. Did he? Or just sit and watch the water coming up? What do you think, Mr. Little?"

CHAPTER 15

Tuesday Afternoon Continued

J turned a startled head. She was probably a very pretty girl. She wore all the labels to say so. As young, or younger, than Amy. Her hair a saucy artificial silver. Gray eyes painted around with blues and purples saying, "SEE . . . THE . . . GIRL . . . IS . . . SHE . . . NOT . . . DESIRABLE?"

"I believe Tony Thees told you to expect me," she said. "I have something for you."

J cast a look around at the wide sand, the sea, the sky, and the gray, deserted line of the wall. "How did you know I was here?" he gasped. He had never been *exactly* here in his whole life before.

"Oh, Tony called and told me to rush on down," she said, leaning gracefully, gazing out to sea now. "He said you were calling on your daughter, and it might be a good chance to catch you alone."

J felt caught, all right. He didn't like it. "How did this Tony know?" he demanded.

"Tony keeps his eye on," the girl said. "By the way, Mr. Barry Goodrick was keeping his eye on, so Tony had to bop him one in the fender, outside your doctor's office."

"Wha . . ." said J, staggering. "Listen . . . who *is* everybody?"

"My name is Annette Woods," she said. "I am supposed to help Tony help you. Tony is afraid Goodrick knows his face, but Goodrick doesn't know mine."

"Neither do I," said J.

She turned her head and smiled up at him.

"Did Goodrick try to talk to you on the plane?" she asked.

J reeled again and clutched the wall. He had the disagreeable feeling that he was in the presence of omniscience.

"Uh-huh," he groaned.

"Please tell me the whole conversation."

"How come you don't already know every damn word that was said?" barked J. "Listen, I don't want people keeping an eye on me."

"Oh, please don't think . . ." The girl's crisp outline seemed to blur. Her voice became—what? Wistful? (Full of wist, eh? thought J.) "I'm not suspecting you of talking too much. I know you wouldn't do that. It's just that this Goodrick is an awful tricky man, Tony says."

"I can't stand him," said J. "He said he used to work for Bark . . . for Doctor Willing, but he got fired."

"That's true, I believe." Now she was listening gravely, sweetly.

"And he implied that Bark—Doctor Willing was up to something—scientific, I guess—that *he* knew all about."

"I doubt he does."

"So did I," said J. "The idea was that since I knew, too, we could have a nice chat about it."

"But you didn't?"

"Of course not."

"So then?" she prompted.

"He said he worked undercover for the U.S.A."

"Not true."

"He said it was a security problem. They were scared this Bark—the doctor would say too much."

"You didn't believe *that?*" Her eye was adding slyly, You're too smart, aren't you?"

"I neither believed nor disbelieved," said J stiffly. "I'm lost in the shuffle, believe me."

"And that was all you said, Mr. Little?"

"Well, we discussed Hamlet."

"Hamlet!"

"Well, we didn't exactly discuss Hamlet. Listen," said J, "I wish you'd tell me why I'm standing here answering all your questions? How do I know you're on the right side, whatever that is?"

"I am here to carry out Doctor Willing's wishes," she said. "So I am on your side, sir."

"What is he to you?" snapped J, because she was now a shade too young, too pure, too deferential.

"An older man," she said with innocent eyes, "I admired very, very much."

J looked out to sea.

"This is for you," she said softly. She took a small package out of her handbag, wrapped in newspaper. She put it on the wall before him, and J picked it up. He slid the string off the package, noting the genuine Chicago newspaper, and unwrapped a metal plaque about the size and shape of a playing card. The color was a dull silver. One side was plain. The other side was embossed with a design. It might have been a paperweight.

Then, as he stared, an Arabic seven came out at the upper left and upside down at the lower right. Next to each J could now see a Roman seven, done in delicate long-legged ridges, similarly reversed. Scattered around there were many small bosses, each dimpled in a familiar shape. Oh, yes, J said to himself—*half-moons*.

He gave the girl a glance. She smiled. He began to count. Sure enough, there were fourteen half-moons. "Two doesn't gazinta, eh?" said J, amused. "But, you know, they could have made them full and put the seventh in the middle." He blinked and looked at her.

"I don't know why they didn't," she said calmly, "That's seven in your name."

"Seven what?" he said, testing.

She put her hand on his sleeve and said very softly, "Seven seats to the moon."

"Well, well, this is pretty cute," he said, hefting the object. "Somebody sure went to a lot of trouble."

"No trouble at all," she said. "I'm all the time taking something to somebody."

"Who *are* you?"

"Why, I'm your contact, sir. I am to contact all passengers in this part of the world when the time comes."

"Are you a passenger?"

"Yes, sir. I'll be going with you." This was very, very innocent. Was it?

"Any more seats to be had?" said J, frowning.

"I believe not, sir."

"What are *you?* A brain?" He turned on her.

"No, sir," she replied sweetly. "A certain number of healthy young females are to be available."

J looked to sea to hide his smile. The little object was warming in his hand. (Seven seats to the moon! Could it be? Of course not.) He thought it a pity that this girl had learned to lie so well, so young, but she wasn't perfect. She'd gone a little bit too far just now.

The girl said, "Uncle J?"

"Huh!"

"Have you a sister?"

"Nope."

"A grown-up female cousin, then?"

"I used to have."

"What was her name?"

"Cynthia Hamilton."

"Tell me about her."

"Lived in Columbus, Ohio. Taught high school for thirty years. Never married. Has passed away."

"How long since?"

"Two . . . two and a half years. Why?"

The girl's face was twinkling with mischief now. "Well, for goodness sakes!" she said. "Dear old Miss Hamilton! I was a protégé of hers, as good as her daughter. She *told* me to look you up, Cousin J."

J shifted uneasily away from her. "No, no. I'm not going to get mixed up in a pack of lies and make things worse than they are now. Listen, I said I wouldn't talk, and I won't, and that ain't easy. So that's *all* you're going to get from me."

She said nothing.

"I don't believe a word of it, anyhow," he grumbled.

The girl bent over the wall. "I wish I could explain the whole thing to you better, Mr. Little," she said, becoming wistful once more. "I don't know enough to do that. I just know that it's terribly important. We're kind of in the same Ark, wouldn't you say?"

"In the middle, eh?" he said.

"That's right." She widened her eyes in admiration. "But listen," she went on, putting her small and narrow-fingered hand on his sleeve again, "it's bothering my . . . my bosses that this Goodrick keeps following you."

"He won't get anything out of me," said J. "I can't stand him."

"But there *are* ways, you know."

"What's this?"

"Oh, if you were drugged."

"Lady," said J gently, "fun is fun, but don't push me too far."

She seemed startled.

"I know," she sighed in a moment. "It does sound absolutely fantastic. But—funny things go on. I guess I've promised, too."

"Promised?"

"I'm supposed to help you if I can."

J couldn't help being pleased with her at the moment. Her eyes so respectful, her perfume in his nostrils. He patted her bare right hand. "And you're being a very good girl," he said as if to reassure her. He saw the tiny leap of suspicion in her eye.

"Say," he went on, "I'd like to talk to this Tony fellow or somebody who could give me an extension on my original promise."

"Oh?"

"I think I'd better tell my wife, you see."

"Oh." The girl drew away, her mouth in the O still.

"Are you married?" J asked. She shook her head. "Well, then, let me tell you that if I keep on trying to keep a secret from my wife, I'm heading into trouble."

"I don't have authority."

"But you can get in touch with your bosses. So pass my question on like a good girl? And let me know as soon as you can."

She said in a new voice, low and loaded with awe, "Doctor Willing died. Did you know?"

"Yes, I—"

"He wouldn't risk saying so much as a word, where even one nurse—one common ordinary nurse—might hear it. Just in case. It's that important."

J straightened, feeling his bones creak.

"Of course," she went on mournfully, "I know it must be awfully difficult to keep a secret from your wife."

"But pretty common ordinary, compared with jumping out the window, eh?" said J irritably. "Don't preach to me, *please.*"

He put the ticket into his pocket and stuffed its wrapping into his pocket, too. She seemed to be watching him warily.

"Who does Goodrick work for?" J demanded.

"Tony says he works for"—she squeezed her eyes shut, and then they flew open—"somebody who isn't very bright. Who thinks—well—that half the world could blow up without hurting the other half."

J was startled by an echo here. Hadn't Barkis said something along these lines?

"Well, well," he drawled. "So if I tell Goodrick all I know, then this not very bright fellow is going to blow it, and maybe even us chosen few don't get away. Oh, boy, imagine that." J shook his head. "Little me, with such great power. Mankind in the palm of my hand. All power corrupts. Who said that?"

The girl swayed suddenly toward him. Her forehead came against his chest. J had to hold her. It wasn't an unpleasant chore.

"We don't know enough," she said, voice muffled, "you and I. But I don't want them to force you to talk."

"How come," said J amiably, "you haven't got one of those capsules for me to tuck in the back of my tooth? Just in case?"

She swayed away and looked up with a spark of anger.

"It's okay," soothed J. *"My* name is Legion. Now, they don't ask old Legion, ordinarily, to keep important secrets. Poor old Legion, he usually doesn't know what's going on till somebody exposes it twenty years later. But it's okay. I'm on the side of not letting the world blow up, for what that's worth. Say, can I give you a lift, or have you got a car?"

"I parked behind you," she said tightly.

J turned her with a touch on her arm. She obeyed. They began to walk away from the beach, along the street. They said nothing. J stopped at his car and put his hand on the door handle.

"You can call me, Miss—uh—"

"Cousin Annette," she said. Then, there she was, standing in a certain way. J didn't know how women did it, but this one knew how. A vision of Lily crossed his mind's eye. J grinned. He put his forefinger on the girl's nose and pushed it playfully. "I sure feel safer," he said, "now that you are going to protect me. Good luck with the universe, kitten."

He got in and drove jauntily away.

From the window above, Amy watched the girl (what girl

was this?) get into the other car and leave. She couldn't *understand.*

J went his way, convinced that the girl and this Tony-on-the-telephone had, indeed, come from Barkis and were somehow continuing that man's gambit. So Goodrick must be on another side. But J, who didn't know what the game really was, could not play. (To whom could he usefully tell what?) He was more like a pawn, he guessed. Well, then, his concern was to slide off the board altogether. He had lived long enough to know, for sure, that if you quietly continue the way that you were going, many problems simply vanish into air, thin air.

But she was pretty cute, that girl, in an insulting kind of way.

CHAPTER 16

Tuesday Evening

By the time J had snatched himself a bite to eat and ambled home at last, the afternoon was waning toward the dinner hour. He came in from the garage, braced for questions, but Marietta, standing at the kitchen counter, cutting carrot sticks, hailed him with a joyous cry. "Company's coming! Tobias is in town! Oh, J, isn't that wonderful?"

"What do you know?" drawled J. He looked at Sophia, who was there in the kitchen, very busy, and the moment their eyes met he knew that life had taken one of its mysterious turns for the better. Sophia said, with the skin crinkling around her eyes, that the doctor had called, the tests were fine, the doctor was proud of J.

"That's white of him when he's losing money himself," said J with normal cheer.

Sophia laughed. She then confirmed the news that Tobias, as usual, had telephoned out of the blue. Sophia's brother was a man who made many careful plans, but he hated to let anyone else know what they were.

Marietta began a chant of praise and thanksgiving for the good health of her son-in-law, the devotion of her son, and the remarkable crispness of these particular carrots, but husband and wife were not listening to these tiresome ecstasies. J, for no reason except that he happened to feel like it, touched Sophia on her shoulder, and Sophia bent her head until her cheek brushed briefly the back of his hand. And there it was. They moved apart quickly lest Marietta turn around and begin to bless, with swimming eyes, this casual little miracle.

J, a bit shocked to find himself thinking that some truths were too holy for Marietta, said he had better get cleaned up and go tend bar, and Sophia said she wished he would.

She hadn't asked him where he'd been all day. He hadn't told her. Maybe Amy was right. Now that Sophia knew he wasn't mortally ill, her suspicions had gone. Into thin air. The face in the bathroom mirror looked at J with calm encouragement. "We're home," the mirrored eyes were saying. The dialogue at the beach went glimmering, fading like a dream in the morning.

Sophia, in the kitchen, was thankful that she had cast out the devil of impatience. Oh, J could be wrong and stubborn in the wrong. Oh, J could be maddening! But J would never, until the world should end, leave off, according to his lights, protecting her. Ah, but someday, just the same, he would tell her whatever it was he now kept from her. And the truth was Sophia needn't do a thing about it. The weight of all their years was pressure enough. Why should Sophia soil her soul, in the meantime, when all she had to do was wait, and he would tell her?

Her husband had ambled into the family room to inspect the resources of the bar when Nanjo came dancing out of the bedroom wing, wearing a dress and short jacket of soft green silk and pretty shoes to match.

"Hey, hey," said her father. "What's up?"

"Bobby James is taking me out to dinner." Nanjo didn't sound overjoyed.

"On Tuesday?"

"There's no school tomorrow. Some dumb teachers' convention." Nanjo struck a pose and bent to notice where her skirt came on her left leg. "I look like something out of the gay nineties," she said bitterly.

J understood that Bobby James, being a member of the establishment and well brought up besides, considered it only proper to take a date to some dignified and rather elegant restaurant, where even Nanjo wasn't brash enough to go in the bright, fantastic costumes of her kind.

"You look pretty darned nice to me," said J fatuously.

"Well, after all," Nanjo mocked, "when I'm going out with one of the seeded suitors, I'm supposed to look nice to you."

J winced, but he said steadily, "You'll miss Uncle Tobias."

"And that just breaks my heart," said Nanjo. "Yah," she cried as the doorbell played its little tune. "Set your watch, why don't you, Daddy?" She went dancing away to let in Bobby James, who thought it proper to arrive exactly when he said he would. Nanjo seemed to think this was very dull of him.

J found that he didn't envy Bobby an evening with Nanjo in her present mood.

In a moment his daughter brought her young man into the family room, or perhaps it was vice versa, because there was no convincing Bobby that he need not greet the elders politely and assure them that he would take good care of their precious child. The fact was that both J and Bobby enjoyed a chat. They inhabited the same world. Bobby gave respect to rank, and J enjoyed this and felt benign. After all, here was J Middleton Little in embryo, and who could help feeling well disposed toward oneself, when young, with whatever pity? But Nanjo wasn't having any boring business talk tonight. "Well, are we going or aren't we?" she demanded almost at once, and Bobby jumped to her command.

When they had gone, J couldn't help feeling sorry to see that Nanjo was in the process of throwing this admirable ... well, reliable and steady . . . well, all right, *admirable* suitor out of her life. Bobby, although presently infatuated, was no fool.

J, puttering at the bar, wondered if he had ever explained to her that courtesy was not his generation's whimsical invention, but the discovery of a law. Why, he mused, should so many kids have to discover so many laws all over again, as if they were all Adams and Eves? Of course, maybe J had taken for law what was only a fad of his parents' day, a passing notion, courtesy, out-of-date now. A way to get yourself liked; hypocrisy.

He then sat very still and listened to some angel saying in

his ear, "Don't you buy that dress. Okay," argued this angel, who happened to speak American, "you gave Amy a check for some clothes. Fair is fair, eh? Well, you just put away that old stuff. Don't you buy that dress for Nanjo, and never mind why not."

J, however, knew more than the angel thought he did. He could get his feelings hurt, just like anybody else, and pretty soon, one of these days, he'd be confronting Nanjo.

Nanjo, in Bobby's car, had found out a little more about the practical uses of courtesy than she had just seemed to know. "Oh, Bobby," she said, "I'm sorry. I didn't mean to sound so bossy. I'm kind of feuding with Daddy, that's all. It's nothing to do with you."

"What's the trouble?" said Bobby, instantly concerned.

So she told him. She told him all the way to the restaurant and all the way through the first course. Bobby watched her. He adored her. He hadn't read the book. All he knew, he didn't want her to be picked by any talent scout to become rich and famous and far from him. But he tried so hard to be fair that the only note of common sense he dared sound was a protest on behalf of J's motives.

"But listen, Nanjo, I'm pretty sure your father would do just about anything if he thought it was good for you. Gosh, *I* would."

Nanjo, after all, was having a fine time, since they were discussing her favorite subject (which was Miss Nancy Jo Little). She smiled at Bobby, who swooned inside with delight.

"Oh, Daddy's wonderful!" she said. "He really is. I know that. But see, he thinks of me as a baby. Well, to him I am. But still, if you're going to have a career in motion pictures, you have to start when you're young. And I'll be seventeen in May."

At this, her swain could only moan softly.

"I don't say they have to choose me," Nanjo went on. "I don't even say I have to have *that dress* to make them do it. But it's so *perfect*, and there it is in the store, and I *found* it, and when there's this chance, and it's right in *front* of me. . . ."

"I see what you mean," said Bobby miserably.

"I put down fifty dollars," said Nanjo in a minute, "so

they'd hold it for me. It's only three hundred dollars more."
She looked down at her plate.

Bobby, suddenly depressed, looked down at his. Honorable
young men do not give the girls they are courting sums of
money. Those who had raised Bobby had told him this. They
hadn't said why not, but he had believed them. He had also
heard that nice girls don't ask.

"Oh, well," said Nanjo in another moment, "let's not talk
about it anymore." But a sense of something shifting for the
worse had fallen like a tent over the table.

Tobias Thomas was a dapper man about J's age, who
always seemed, wherever he was, to have just come from
some more glamorous place. Sophia was fonder of him than
she was willing to admit. She took the trouble, for instance, to
put her best culinary foot forward when he was here.

Tobias, who evidently preferred his days to be long in the
land, came dutifully to see his mother whenever he flitted
through Los Angeles. J observed, however, that (as usual)
Tobias had nothing to say to Marietta, and oddly enough
neither had she very much to say to her only son. Marietta
sat as one enthroned, basking silently in his token presence,
while Tobias chatted along with his contemporaries, not
bothering to include her.

(Sooner or later Sophia would take her brother aside, and
they would discuss their mother to each other's satisfaction,
because, after all, they and they alone had known her all
their lives.)

But Tobias, as J knew, was not a possible source of
revenue for his mother in her present emergency. According
to his lights, Tobias was a generous man with money, but he
shied off immediately if asked for any. Long ago he had
Done His Share. This was well understood by all. Once, when
flush, Tobias had bought the annuity upon which Marietta
subsisted.

Twice every year he sent each of his sister's children a
check for twenty-five dollars, once at Christmastime and
again on each child's birthday. So far, he had not extended his
largess to Sophia's grandchildren. He sent his sister perfume
twice every year, and for J, once a year at Christmas, there
always arrived a wallet. The quality of these gifts might vary
somewhat with the state of Tobias' finances, but they always
came.

J appreciated the fact that Tobias, for his sister's sake, had never gone to work to charm any money out of J. Oh, he could have done it! Tobias happened to be a successful and experienced con man. It was his trade, and he seemed in good control of his considerable skill. J suspected that the trick of always appearing to have just come from, or being poised on the brink of just taking off for, some magic place where the money was greener was a part of his working costume. J, listening to him with affection (for who is as charming as a charming rascal?), bethought himself of this expertise and asked Tobias about this Mr. Pudney's possible racket.

Tobias listened to the tale of J's father, his manuscript, the vanity press, and opined that J was most probably correct in his judgments. Just the same, something about Tobias was taking notes. Some fox ears had quivered. Was there anything in this for Tobias? J felt it would be looked into.

He wondered what Tobias would make of a voyage to the moon and caught himself deciding that the doughy mass of the brainiest people might be better off with the leaven of a rascal or two.

Annette, wearing trousers, was lying on a bed in her hotel room with her knees up, one over the other, and the top leg swinging. "He wants to talk to you," she reported. "He wants permission to tell his wife."

Tony Thees, lounging on his elbow on the other bed, said gloomily, "At least he hasn't told her yet. He better not. Mr. Smith's dug up a connection that's making him nervous. Certain exstudent of the old man's happens to be related to Goodrick's boss. So Goodrick and Company may be exactly what the old man was afraid of. Trouble is, if we pick up Goodrick and put him elsewhere, we might as well advertise. Looks like a bind, sweetheart."

"What kind of a wife has he got, I wonder? I could go and see."

"He's all that dominated, and *you* get into the domestic scene, she'll make him tell her."

"I realize you know all about husbands and wives, Tony darling." Annette was trying to be maddening?

"What he'd tell her is the moon biz," said Tony, refusing to be annoyed. "Juicy bit for the Ladies Auxiliary, that."

"He says he doesn't believe a word of that," she said. "Bluster, I guess."

"So it's uppermost in his mind?"

"You bet."

"Well, the ladies could have a fine old panic, and it wouldn't mean much."

"But Goodrick and Company don't belong to the Ladies Auxiliary," said Annette shrewdly and maddeningly.

Tony swore. "I'm afraid Mr. Smith is going to have to change some plans. And that's that." He rolled over. "Dumb luck."

"And when he does, it isn't going to matter if Goodrick beats the secret out of our Little man? Goody!"

"What's the matter with *you?*"

"He wasn't what I expected," she said thoughtfully, and this was maddening, too.

"So go to your hero," said Tony. "So the old lady will put the old man's back up by unjust suspicions, and they can have a fine old fight, which could put Goodrick off and might last long enough? Well, I guess that's no sillier than the moon biz."

"How long is long enough?" she snapped.

He hesitated. Then he said, "Till Sunday night."

The girl said, "I'll see what I can do."

Tony shrugged. He didn't think it mattered much what she did. Why the devil wouldn't she marry him, he wondered. True, he had been somewhat above himself when he'd asked her, but the refusal stung, just the same. She'd said she liked her own pad and didn't want to move her stuff, and what was the matter with the way things were?

"Keep it cool, sweetheart," he said, somewhat sarcastically.

CHAPTER 17

Tuesday Night

After dinner, when Marietta rose and left the group in the family room to toddle off to the bedroom wing, nobody, naturally, inquired *why*.

An auto horn began to blast out in the street and persisted beyond any time required to ask something to get out of its way.

"Would that be somebody for Nanjo?" frowned Sophia at last.

J, too, had begun to recognize not only the tone but the rhythm. He supposed he'd have to go tell Cary Bruce that Nanjo wasn't here.

He excused himself and went out the front door. Yes, there was the low-slung car in its usual place under the pepper tree. Its headlights were bouncing beams off the silver-colored mailbox. As J crossed the lawn, the boy stopped his noise.

"Nanjo's not here, Cary," said J, being simply informative. He could see the face only faintly in light from the dash. He could sense tension and excitement.

The boy said, "Tell her to come out a minute, will you?"

"She isn't here."

"Tell her to come out, man," said Cary. "Do that, why don't you?"

J said sharply, "Didn't you hear me?"

Cary said with enormous confidence, "Oh, she's in there."

It was an impasse. Nothing was getting through from one mind to the other.

To J Cary sounded like some old-time gangster in the movies who never listens but keeps on saying the same thing, adding a loud "I said," thus indicating ruthless power. In J's mind bloomed the imagined pleasure of dragging this impudent brat (who was calling him a liar) out of that car and beating him thoroughly. The trouble was J knew he couldn't do it. Even if it were "wise."

Cary, who had just seen the light go on in Nanjo's room, had no idea that Marietta was in the house and, in fact, had only the vaguest awareness of her existence. Cary thought he had before him the usual "stupid" authoritarian who thought he could push people around.

"I got something to tell her," he said impatiently. "Aw, come on, Nanjo!" Cary leaned on his horn again.

What Cary wanted to tell Nanjo was all about a shortcut to some money. It was, in fact, a way to take some from a place where a man kept it. It would take guts but, he thought proudly, he *had* guts. While thinking of himself with such a fine sense of his own bright courage, Cary had no time for a stupid old man like J, who thought he could stand in the way of progress by telling lies.

And J Middleton Little, on his own front lawn, felt paralyzed vis-à-vis the barbarian, while the maddeningly unreasonable, intrusive, hateful sound of the horn continued to corrupt the evening air. In the moment's terror, he admitted to himself that Nanjo could have handled this, although her father could not.

In the house Sophia, outraged, wanted to call the police, but her brother Tobias strongly advised against this. He had no confidence in the police, he said. They were not, for one thing, very bright. And *they* couldn't stop those kids. There weren't enough of them. Did Sophia want a feud on?

Outside, a car came swooping to the curb, cutting in front of Cary's vehicle. In the continuing noise J turned to look, and there was that girl, that Annette-something, putting her pretty foot upon *his* curbing.

J took steps toward her and grasped her arm. She bent away, and he put his arm around her to pull her near so that she'd hear him speak. "I told you *No,*" he said into her ear. "Go on. Beat it."

At this moment the front door opened. Tobias emerged and then Sophia. Cary, jolted by these arrivals, nevertheless now had his honor (otherwise known as fear of showing up chicken) on the line, so he kept the horn going. Surrounded by sound, the others must pantomime. Sophia stood in the door; Tobias came light-footed across the grass; J let go of the girl with a guilty start; the girl turned and looked, not at Cary, but with deep attention and a sudden cock of her head, at Cary's car.

Tobias, looming up quietly, seemed suddenly alerted. He went down into a squat and peered under the sports car with deep attention.

Cary couldn't *understand* this!

The girl made her mouth into a big O, and she too squatted down.

J couldn't understand this, either.

The two of them, crouched there, had their heads together. Cary couldn't hear what they were saying. The horn's rhythm broke and stuttered. Helplessly curious, the boy let up on the noise.

Tobias said conversationally, "Lot of money been put into this crate, too. What a shame!"

"Major surgery," the girl said. "What was he hollering for? A mechanic?"

Cary was outraged. He felt beside himself. If he knew anything in this world, he knew his car! It was his one hard contact with the laws of the universe. She wouldn't run sweet if she wasn't right. Didn't Cary knock himself out to keep her running sweet? He revved up the motor.

Tobias rose. "Do you need a tow?" he shouted.

The girl rose. "You're in bad shape, buddy," she said. "Trade it in for a stock car, why don't you?"

Cary yanked the lever. He screamed profane instructions at them all and took off, leaving rubber as he screeched around the corner.

"He'll kill himself," gasped J.

"I can't stand those kids," said Tobias cheerfully. "Hit 'em where they live, eh, young lady? Whoever you may be."

"Oh," said Annette, becoming another person, very young, helpless, appealing. "Mr. Little, my name is Annette Woods. You do remember Miss Cynthia Hamilton? She told me to look you up, so I hope you don't mind."

J was stricken dumb. The leery look in Tobias' eye was visible even in the evening. He began to light-foot it (tactfully) across the grass. Sophia's voice called from the housedoor. "Has he gone?"

Annette saw her and darted away from J. "Mrs. Little?" the girl said gushingly. "I'm sorry to come barging in like this, but I don't know anybody else in this whole city. I'm Annette Woods. Miss Hamilton, in Columbus, Ohio? Well, she was my best teacher and my best friend, and she told me all about you."

"You mean J's cousin Cynthia?" said Sophia. "Is anything the matter?" she went on kindly.

The girl said, "I guess I'm a little bit scared. I need to talk to people I can be sure of. I don't think I ought to be all by myself this evening."

"Then come in, of course," said Sophia.

J followed Tobias, who was stepping softly in the rear of the females. In the entrance area Tobias halted and said over his shoulder to his brother-in-law, "Watch it, J."

J, who had bumped into him, grunted.

Tobias, craning around, was grinning. "I'm telling you, watch that dolly. It takes one to know one." He winked and went on.

In the family room there was fluttering and a further exchange of, if not identities, at least labels. Marietta had come back to sit, rosy and fat, in her favorite chair and pour pious syrup over the introductions, during which Annette behaved like a little lady, Sophia behaved like a big lady, and J just sat down.

When the subject turned to Cary Bruce, Marietta (who heard no evil) dropped out.

Tobias began to expound on the subject of those kids. All gut and no wit. Easy enough to outfox such primitives. He winked at Annette, who remained sweetly respectful to an elder. That car was loaded, Tobias went on, and if his folks weren't silly rich, the kid had probably gone in for what Tobias called greasy kid crime. Tobias had no patience with it. Crime for the sake of a mere machine? Or crime for kicks? What, foul up one's record and impede and imperil one's future for a few more miles per hour? Or the passing excitement of a gland or two? Crime, in Tobias' opinion, was *not* a toy!

Having been very entertaining for the space of five minutes, Tobias signaled his sister, and Sophia announced that she would make him a stirrup cup of coffee and Tobias must keep her company. They adjourned to the kitchen for their talk. J shuddered to think of Tobias giving warning right there in the kitchen about this young con woman.

He looked at the young con woman.

She was sparkling. "He's *wonderful!*" she said.

"He tells me it takes one to know one," said J bluntly. J knew that Marietta couldn't follow, but Annette did not, and she glanced at the stout woman warily.

Marietta had caught one clue. She now went into ecstasies over a son's pure and unselfish devotion and her Own Good Angel's approval of dear Tobias. J, not without sly pleasure, watched the girl's face try to put on a mask suitable for listening to this.

The coffee appeared in a very few minutes. (Oh, yes, Tobias must have given his opinion.) That one tossed his beverage off and departed for his hotel, characteristically having told none of them which hotel it was. He was off very soon (he didn't say exactly when) for foreign parts, although he omitted to say just which parts, naturally.

When he had gone, Marietta pronounced a kind of grace upon his visit and went into instant meditation.

In the slightly awkward silence that followed, Sophia said, "Now, my dear, in what way can we help you?"

"You have helped me already," the girl said. "You are all so *good*. It is so wonderful to be where people believe in something."

(Oh, oh, thought J, Marietta's taken her in!)

"You see, I'm all alone," said Annette, "and there is a young man. I . . . well . . . I guess I ran away from him. But you see, he's turned up *here,* so I didn't *get* away, and I'm afraid. . . ."

"What frightens you?" said Sophia.

Annette lowered her lids and murmured, "Myself."

J watched for Sophia's eyebrow to twitch, which it did.

"Aunt Cynthia," the girl said, "told me you have a daughter." She raised her humble gaze.

"An assortment of two," said Sophia pleasantly. "Yes."

(J listened to Sophia's voice. He was lying low. This was a war of some kind. Annette was trying to fool Sophia. Sophia knew it and was trying to be courteous, all the same. J found himself betting on Sophia.)

"If it's yourself you're afraid of," she said now in a kindly calm, "you'll have to take it up with yourself, won't you? How do we come into it?"

"Oh, just to *see* successfully married people! It's hard for my generation. You can't imagine. . . ."

Sophia smiled. "We are old," she said gently. "Of course, we can't imagine."

Annette managed to look hurt. "I never had a family," she said pathetically. "Dad had gone away before I remember. And my Mom died when I was only three and three quarters."

(J did admire that three-quarters!)

"So I had foster homes. Miss Hamilton was the one older person . . . She was so good to me . . . The nearest thing to a mother I ever had."

"She must have been a comfort," said Sophia, sweetly skeptical. (Cynthia had been full of vinegar.)

"I know I'm putting too much on you, of course," Annette said, rising. "It was good of you to let me come in at all. I'm only a stranger to *you*, I know, Mrs. Little. So I'll go back to the hotel. Thank you very, very much."

Rejected again was the name of the act. J lay low, admiring the performance, waiting for Sophia's riposte.

"You have met my husband before, then?" said Sophia smoothly.

Annette looked down. Then she cast a nicely nervous glance at J. "Well," her voice stumbled nicely, too, "I have this job in Chicago, you see, and it so happened I saw his name on the list for the banquet."

So J found himself plop in the middle of the battlefield. Middle, hell! He *was* the disputed ground.

"You looked him up in Chicago, then?" said his wife.

"Well, it was only for a *minute*," said the girl. "But he was so kind, and that's why I thought. . . ."

"I'll tell you what I'll do for you, Cousin Annette," said J briskly. "What's your young man's name again? *Tony*, isn't it?"

Annette licked her lip. "Oh," she said. "I hadn't realized that I'd said."

"Well, you fix it for me to meet him," said J, "and I will give him the news that you, being basically an old-fashioned good girl, have had the good judgment to seek the advice of older and wiser heads than your own. Okay?"

Her face had become a battleground of expressions.

"In fact," said J, "it might be good for *him*, poor benighted chap, if he could have the benefit of actually seeing successfully married people. So why don't you bring him to lunch here tomorrow?"

Sophia's brows had gone as high as they could go, but J had drawn on his clown face. She knew it and lay low.

"Oh, I don't think ..." The girl looked as if she'd like to get out of here.

"Do try," said Sophia graciously. "Will you be all right getting back to your hotel? Should J go with you?"

J said, "I'll take her as far as her car."

So there were farewell speeches, each sweeter than the preceding. This part ended in a draw, J felt.

Then he had the girl by her arm, and they were walking toward the curb.

She said as they went, "I'm sorry. I asked Tony. He said, No, absolutely don't tell her. And he *can't* come here."

"Why not?" J opened the car door. "I want to talk to him."

"Because," she said, "I wouldn't be surprised if Goodrick isn't across the street in that dark parked car right now. He *knows* who Tony is."

"You're sure having a whole lot of fun with us old bodies," said J. "Get in. Get in."

"It's not so funny, Mr. Little."

"Call me Cousin J," said J, "and explain to me why you're stirring up the broth. You're making mountains out of molehills with your own little hatchet. Now, I don't want to threaten anybody, but it could be you'll succeed in making it *impossible* for me to keep my mouth shut."

She said with a gasp, "I'll have to tell you this. Things are happening. If certain things do happen, then it won't matter if you tell. But not yet."

J said gently, "Did you really think Sophia was a fool?"

She said, "*Tell* your wife, then. *Do* that." She was staring at the valley, but she snapped an order just the same.

J said, "Sorry, but what I say to my wife, or anybody else, is *my* business."

She yanked at the car door; J slammed it shut. She drove away at once with an angry spryness. The dark car across the street sprang into life and went pelting after her. J rolled his eyes to heaven.

Then he stood, looking down at the great sparkle of the valley, wherein bright threads of freeways kept their constant double shimmer of relentless motion, the diamonds going one way, the rubies the other, and wide avenues with their neon blues and greens and reds slashed the basic pattern of yellow on black. Well, that was man, interrupting the dark and, with his discoveries, taking a shallow slab of the night away from the stars and the moon.

J felt a snatch at his breath. He—anxious, reckless, defiant, whimsical, touchy, and humanly inconsistent—what might he do, or not do, when he didn't understand?

What he did was turn tail and head for his cave.

Sophia had taken the coffee cups off to the kitchen. Only Marietta was still sitting in the family room. J settled in his chair. Struck by the continuing silence, he looked and saw his mother-in-law's bobbed white head bent and her plump pink hands pressed palm to palm in the classic attitude. J, realizing what she was up to, kept still, thinking two thoughts at once. She was his elder, but when had he paid any attention to her ideas? And what did she think her present effort would accomplish?

When she lifted her head at last, her rosy face enraptured, J blurted, "Say, how does that work?" At once ashamed, he continued, "I'm sorry, Marietta. I didn't mean to make fun."

"Of course you didn't, dear J."

"I got to wondering. You see," he confessed, "I—uh—thought *I* heard an angel, earlier on." He meant to speak lightly in a friendly way.

"Oh J! Of course you have a Good Angel of your very own. I have always known that. And have hoped. . . ." Her large blue eyes reminded J of certain marbles he had cherished when a lad.

"But I don't know if I understand the system," said J. "Now, God runs everything? You'd say so?"

"Of course, dear."

"So what you do is, you ask your O. G. A." J had let slip the family abbreviation. "I mean your angel, to tell God how you'd like things handled?" The blue eyes were blank, so J pursued his logic. "Okay then, supposing I ask my angel to tell God please not to let us, for instance, blow up the world. Does that count?"

"All true prayer is answered," said Marietta easily.

(But then *I'd* be running the universe! thought J with shock.)

"There is nothing to worry about," she was continuing. "All is good, and all is beautiful. If only you can see."

J said softly, "I see." But he did not. He thought he'd dare to state his *wishes* maybe, but he didn't have the crust to assume that if he did, all *his* wishes must come true. He knew darned well that J Middleton Little had better not run any universe.

But Marietta was leaping onward in rising ecstasy. "Oh, J, I am so happy that you, too, understand these wonderful things! And now you have this lovely comfort for your own dear self!"

J didn't have the heart to say that his own dear self, which it was all right (dear to J, that is), still didn't see how the thing worked. He bent his head, smiling to imagine what a hell of a lot of mistakes he'd make. "Ah, love, could you and I with Him conspire. . . ."

But in a moment he realized that he, J Little, not only couldn't run the universe, but right now, in his own chair, he was making a miserable mess of a very small corner of it. Head bent, hands clasped for no reason at all, he was fooling this fond foolish lady as he had not meant to do, and if he disillusioned her now, she would be hurt out of all proportion.

Sophia came in and said calmly, "What's the matter, Mother?"

"All is gloriously well!" cried Marietta. "Good night! Good night!" She waddled away, still tearfully rejoicing.

"Anything special?" Sophia asked.

J, in cowardice, shook his head. How could he explain? He couldn't explain a *thing*. He couldn't, for instance, explain Annette, which he was going to have to do right now. Sophia sat down and said, still calm, "Quite an invasion. Well?"

" 'Well' is right," said J (pronouncing it à la Jack Benny). "And Tobias was right, too."

"*Was* he?" said Sophia thoughtfully. "How much of what she said was true, I wonder." Sophia seemed to be asking herself.

J said, "Not much. Struck me pretty phony." He reached into his pocket. "Here." He tossed her his ticket to the moon.

"Why, it's beautiful!" said Sophia. "What is it, may I ask?"

"Well, it's a kind of weight, I guess," said J, "to—uh—hold things where you want them." (Yah, he thought, exactly so!)

"You mean a paperweight?" said Sophia. He had, and he hadn't. He didn't answer. She looked up at him. "Aren't you going to tell me?"

"No," he said, "because I don't *know*."

"Well," (Sophia, who could ask double questions, could hear double answers), "life is full of little mysteries, I guess. Shall we sit up for Nanjo," she added amiably, "and give her fits about that miserable boy? I don't want Nanjo hurt when he ends up in a ditch."

"Nanjo is going to be hurt," said J.

"What do you mean, dear?" Her voice kept steady.

"I mean sometime. Somehow. Listen, *I* don't know what I mean. I don't know what anything means, or why it has to mean anything. Who am I, that *I* should know?"

Sophia waited for this childish outburst to be overcome, and just as J's "Sorry" had formed in his throat, she said quietly, "There was a little collision this morning when we left the doctor's. One of the drivers called me by name. He said his name was Goodrick. He said you had a room-mate in the hospital, and he jumped out the eighth-floor window. Why didn't you tell me?"

"I wasn't there," J blurted.

"Yes, you were," said Sophia. "I *called* the hospital."

"No, no. I mean I wasn't there when the man jumped. I heard about it. But *I* wasn't there."

"Oh," Sophia was hefting the ticket to the moon thoughtfully. "Then you had two room-mates," she said shrewdly.

"What makes you say . . ."

"Because," said Sophia confidently.

J had the feeling that his skull was made of glass and she could see his thoughts waltzing around in there. "I made a promise," he said. "I made a foolish promise, Sophia."

She listened as if she could hear his thoughts rustling, the other side of his words.

"But I never promised *her* anything. I said I wouldn't tell one living soul something I accidentally overheard in Chicago. That's it. That's all."

His wife's face began to change.

"But that girl," J exploded, "I don't know who the hell she is. She came around and *ordered* me to tell you. But it seems to me that, if I gave my word, it's *my* business whether or not I keep it."

"Well, it certainly *is*," snapped Sophia and burst into tears.

So J went over and sat in the same chair and petted her while she wept. "Oh, J . . . at first I thought you were dying. And then I thought you had seen some terrible thing. But I didn't want ... I tried not to be a snoopy old ... bossy old ... oh...."

So J crooned words to the effect that she had been put upon, yes, she had. She had been very patient withal, and it hadn't been easy, and hush, he knew.

So he fathered her, for she was his child.

But when they heard Nanjo's key in the front door, they scrambled as fast as they could to their bedroom, where very soon they began to behave like a man and a woman.

CHAPTER 18

Wednesday Morning

J decided against going downtown on Wednesday morning. After all, he had the week off, and he wasn't sure but what Annette would turn up, bringing this Tony Thees. J didn't want to miss a chance of getting out of the middle of some mysterious contest between mysterious factions. He also wanted to keep an eye out for Goodrick in case he was lurking. J didn't want him bothering Sophia.

But the house was roaring; J was chased hither and thither; there was no peace.

There was no school. Nanjo was around. Marietta was around. It was a Mrs. Arriola day. She was around. J couldn't even sit out on the terrace. Cal, the gardener, was around, out there pruning the Chinese elm, and would rather talk than *do* it.

Sophia was, of course, around too, and although there was peace between husband and wife, there was developing a touch of strain. It had occurred to J that, after all, he *had* told her, and what if he'd put her in the middle, too? He must, however, bite back warnings and alarms. Sophia had a habit of becoming very aggressively angry instead of afraid.

At the same time, it had occurred to Sophia that he had not, after all, *really* told her, and she was biting back many questions. Little loose ends. If he hadn't gone to the office yesterday, how come he had the paperweight that J said somebody said had been left at the office? And how come J knew the name of the girl's boyfriend? And hadn't Sophia heard him say "Tony" at some *other* time?

Oh, well . . . They shifted around the house, never settling down together.

Marietta, who thought of herself as a superservant, ever-willing, no snob, was "helping" Mrs. Arriola. After a while J, keeping one room ahead of them as best he could, was tickled to take notice of a war between woe and roses. Mrs. Arriola was, as usual, full of portents and intimations of disaster which pressed Marietta to rejoice more effusively than ever. As far as J could tell, woe was winning, at least on a practical level, because Mrs. Arriola was allowing herself to be helped to the point where she gave the instructions and Marietta did all the work.

Nanjo was no help at all. She had heard about Cary's performance with the car horn from her mother at breakfast and had protested that all the kids honked their horns. That was the way it was done in modern times. And Cary drove the way you'd better drive in modern times, and if you asked Nanjo, Bobby James was *dangerously* timid. *She* couldn't help it if Cary hadn't believed what Daddy said.

Later, after one or two phone calls, Nanjo had said to her mother (not to J, although in nasal wails that he could not help but hear) that Cary had seen a light in her room. And if anybody had had any sense at all, they'd have seen it, too. And then if they had explained about her grandmother! Well, of course, Cary knew which room was Nanjo's! Was it supposed to be a big old secret for gosh sakes?

She had then gone to sunbathe, padding past J swiftly without speaking.

Her father thought he'd probably have to spank her pretty soon, but he put it off. There wasn't any private place to do it, with the house so full.

Tony said brusquely, "If, at your not very smart reversal of your instructions, he has taken your advice, we'll have to watch his wife, too."

Annette said, "You don't understand. You weren't there. It was the lesser risk, I'm telling you. We should have let him alone in the first place."

"Alone with Goodrick, eh?" Tony was furious.

"Oh, come on," she said wearily, disdainfully. "Goodrick does know a thing! He followed me last night. Why don't you instruct me to take *his* mind off?"

"Holy cats!" said Tony. "How female can you get? Listen, sweetheart . . ."

"I'd be glad to listen," she snapped, "if you'd speak up, for instance, like a man."

"The time has come for you to take this serious," Tony glowered. He was too angry with her to use the pronoun "we," which would have been proper. "There's a private gathering," he said. "I won't say where, because I don't know where. That's a secret. But this bunch of world-important men will be *together,* and Goodrick and Company think it would be great sport if they were all blown up in one blast. Whoosh! Pow! But since Goodrick and Company have not been able to find out where *is* the gathering place, they can't very well do that, can they?"

"Elementary," she murmured. She licked her lip.

"Now, security is laid on, of course, in as much strength as is possible when the whole thing is theoretically private. But has it ever occurred to you, sweetheart, that some rich fella, if he had a mind to, could just as easily hire himself the help and buy himself what it takes and make himself a nice private little bomb that would do the job, all right? And say he's a fanatic, why couldn't he go ahead and drop the thing without asking anybody's leave?"

"And this rich fanatic is Goodrick's boss?"

"Yep. And I'm telling you, sweetheart, that if he does that, it ain't going to be private no more."

"Really," she said, her intelligence insulted.

"So there go a whole lot of big brains, which is too bad. But still and all, lots of brains in the world, you know. Point is, there's an added feature there. Every damned one of the gathered ones is a hero in his own land, see? And all kinds of countries are going to be good and mad at all kinds of other countries, especially this one. Not only that, but who is going to believe in a *private* fanatic and never have it enter his old cranium that the rich fella maybe acted on *his* country's instructions? So not only do a whole lot of valuable men stand to get killed off in the first explosion, there stand to be plenty more explosions."

(She was looking serious, all right.) "Now," he added, "if

all that stands between this and us is *you,* setting out to lure Goodrick off his job . . ."

"Our Little man knows about this?" she said sternly, condemning nonsense.

Tony hesitated. "What he knows is the time and the place," he said deliberately. "He doesn't know he knows them, or what they mean. He'd been muddled with the moon biz. But let Goodrick and Co. get him under hypnosis, for instance, or anything else (like great pain?) that would give him total recall of what he *definitely did hear,* the! the moon biz shows up for the moonshine it is, and they've got what they didn't ought to have."

"Call off the gathering!" she cried. "Or else get out the Army and the Navy and the Air Force! What good is this gathering supposed to do, anyway?"

"Who knows?" said Tony, who became the calmer the more excited she. *"Nobody* knows what might happen if human brains ever did sit down to hassle things out in cold blood."

"Secretly?" she cried. "What kind of devious mind thought this up?"

"You could say," said Tony, "it was a big brain who didn't want the sensation-mongering press to roil up the common people."

"Why would the common people . . ."

"Grow up," said Tony. "It's only a dream. You never heard of a dream that got to be too wide-open to the sensation-mongering press and too occupied with roiling up the common people (which is to say playing propaganda games) to do a whole lot of *thinking* on behalf of the human race?"

She glared at him for a moment. "Tony, how do you *know* Goodrick and Co. want to blow them up?"

"We had some reason to think it was under consideration to do something," said Tony, "because one of the old man's former pupils called him up one day and said he didn't want to see the old man dead or anything, and he wished the old man wouldn't *go* to the gathering."

"Oof!" said Annette.

"Well, now, seeing as how the chap shouldn't have known there ever was to be such a gathering, we should have guessed things were getting a little out of hand. If we had taken serious what the old man told us, that is."

"You should have called it off then and there," she stormed.

"Doctor Willing thought so," said Tony rather sadly. "But you see, those big brains were willing to risk it on one another's integrity, on the cold-blooded assumption that they *all* thought it would be better if they *all* stayed alive to think some more. And they were right, I guess. They were big about it. None of them knew one ordinary Little man was going to get in on the act."

Annette kept staring at him.

"It's too late, honey child," he said with a sigh. "As of this morning, half of them are already there, and the rest are on the way."

"What's to do?" she said quietly.

"We may have to fix to kidnap our Little man and hide him in a very deep hole."

"Until after Sunday?"

"Right. After that, they couldn't get them *all*."

"But if he's told his wife . . ." She was thoughtful.

"Oh, it's trickier than that. Tell you why. We're pretty sure . . . hell, we *are* sure . . . that Goodrick doesn't know *yet*, and therefore he doesn't know the urgency. Possibly he'll keep on fooling around the outskirts long enough. But if *we* jump, *he* jumps. And deep enough holes are hard to find. Oh, I'm thinking. I'm thinking."

"Tell you what," she said, "while you're thinking . . . which is a better idea than letting Goodrick see *you* fooling around the outskirts . . ."

(Tony shut his eyes. Okay. She was smart. She had caught on to his basic mistake.)

"Why don't I wangle myself into that house?" Annette was saying. "I can butter up his old lady. I understand her type, now. You know, suburban earth-mother. No fool, exactly. But if I'm there, watching in the nighttime, ready to holler "Cops" and so forth, Goodrick can't kidnap our Little man by night. And *my* being there won't tell him a thing. Hey, I'm invited to lunch, and I'm going!"

She jumped up and began to take fresh clothing out of the hotel closet. He didn't try to stop her.

"Tony?"

"Uh, huh?"

"I was just thinking, what if you told our Little man the

whole thing? Wouldn't he agree to vanish? Wouldn't that be
. . . you know . . . easier on everybody?"

"For God's sakes," he burst, "do *not* tell him the whole
thing! Right now, he doesn't even know what he knows. So
there's the chance that, even if they do get him, he'll somehow omit what's important. But if he *knows*. . . ."

"You mean it will then be uppermost in his mind?" she said
slowly.

"Sometimes you're quite bright," Tony said grudgingly.

She opened her mouth but closed it. Silently she began to
change her clothes.

Win Little said on the phone to his wife, "If I come home,
will you fix me a sandwich?"

"We might run to that," Marion said.

"Honey, will you please not take everything I say . . ."

"I'm sorry. I get confused. I don't know whether to feel
rich or poor."

"I'll tell you on Tuesday. Cheer up. Please. You'll jinx the
luck."

"I don't *understand* going on luck, Win. I don't *understand*
borrowing your grandmother's bonds for thirty days. What if
. . ."

"Never mind," he said, "*I* understand it. On second thought
I'm going to some posh place for lunch. For luck, you
know."

But it's not so much for luck, he thought, hanging up. It's
for morale. Oh, he loved Marion, had loved, and loved still
the sweetness of her flesh. He loved the Little kids.

And yet, if Marion could not bear the gambles he must
take, could not enjoy them as he enjoyed them, could not *in
any other way* be with him—well?

Susie Neeby was saying to her late morning caller that J
Middleton Little was, indeed, known to her, and she was glad
to be able to tell the FBI that he was a loyal American, an
upright citizen, with high moral standards, a very dear
friend, who had never been in any trouble that Susie could
remember.

"Excuse me, Mrs. Neeby," said Goodrick, "but wasn't
there a little trouble in Chicago just this last weekend?"

"I don't know," said Susie, round-eyed. "I know that
something happened. I haven't heard the story yet. I get the

idea that it's a funny story. J tells stories awfully well." Her little pink face went into a kind of total pucker. "What kind of trouble?" she demanded.

"Perhaps nothing. Perhaps nothing," Goodrick said soothingly. "Well, thank you very much, Mrs. Neeby."

"I didn't realize," said Susie, "that J was in any kind of business that had to have clearances. *Why* does he?"

"Perhaps he doesn't just now," said Goodrick.

"Is he looking for another job?" gasped Susie.

Goodrick began to show some slight impatience as he evaded answering all these blunt intrusive questions.

J was holed up in his den when Sophia tapped on the door. "Your girlfriend seems to be arriving. No boyfriend in tow."

J started up.

"She's early, isn't she?" said Sophia and withdrew.

J, for reasons unknown to himself, scooped up the ticket to the moon and put it into his top desk drawer.

When he got to the entrance area, Sophia had already let the girl in.

"I should have called, but I just came," Annette was saying girlishly. "I don't have any manners, do I, Cousin J?"

"Oh, well," said J, "manners may be obsolete." But he relented. (J did not enjoy being rude. A matter of taste, perhaps.) "Hi, Cousin Annie."

"Come on back," said Sophia, "and tell us how you are today."

"Oh, I'm *all right*," said Annette dubiously, "but I think I know, now, what I need. Mrs. Little, you did help me. You have no idea how much. And I've got something to ask you . . . ask both of you . . . I know I am being selfish but—"

"Just a minute," J interrupted. "Mrs. Arriola" (for there stood Mrs. Arriola in the door to the kitchen, looking for something terrible to suspect) "do you mind if we entertain in this room?"

"That's okay," said she gloomily. "We's finished in there."

"Could you please," said Sophia, who knew the market value of the cleaning woman and spoke humbly, "rush a bit with the kitchen? We have a guest for lunch," she apologized.

Mrs. Arriola turned and bellowed over her shoulder, "Say,

Miz Thomas, better not start cleaning that oven. Oh, Miz Little, it's going to be in bad shape by Monday."

But Sophia was enjoining the guest to sit down. Mrs. Arriola retreated, muttering.

J chuckled. "I can see by your face," he said to Annette, "that you haven't had to cope with the servant problem in suburbia." He went on (and this was careless of him!) to say to his wife, "Listen, Mrs. Arriola ought to split the fee with your mother. Don't you know what's been going on here all morning?"

At this, J felt the peace between them shatter. *What, Sophia said in silence, makes you think I don't know what's going on here? Obviously you want to talk to your little phony alone. Very well, of course.*

Sophia said aloud, "I think I *am* going to have to deal with matters in the kitchen. If you will excuse me, Annette? I'm sure J will do the honors nicely."

As Sophia tripped off, Annette met J's eyes with a look of urgency. "Did you tell her?"

The phone rang. J, moving his head in the negative, said aloud, "Excuse me, just a minute?" and went to answer the phone.

It was Bringgold. "How're you doing?" he wanted to know rather sourly.

"Fine," said J.

"You didn't think you ought to come in this morning, eh?"

"As I remember, you told me the rest of the week," said J mildly, knowing very well that Bringgold wasn't going to remember this or, if he happened to remember, he wouldn't have quite meant *this*.

Sure enough, Bringgold said, "I couldn't have said anything of the kind. We are in a mess down here that is about to send me off my rocker. *Your* assistant" (his assistant was all J's fault naturally) "has managed to foul things up. . . . Four seniors are snarling at one another right now. The client is having fits, and they're not the only ones. I wish you'd get down here."

"You need me, eh?"

"Damn right."

"Okay," said J, "I'll be in right after lunch." He hung up, feeling rather pleased to be needed. He could see the street from where he stood. There was a car parked out there in front of the Neebys'. J moved to see it better.

Sophia, having reproached both Mrs. Arriola and her mother while still fighting her own temper, left them temporarily allied under the lash and came into the family room to find the guest all alone, sitting on one foot, swinging the other, and gazing raptly out into the yard.

"Don't tell me J has lost his manners, too," Sophia said.

Annette smiled at her and explained that J was on the phone.

Sophia sat down, her back to the glass. "Panic all gone away?" she spoke as to a child. "Don't hesitate to be selfish. Unless you'd feel more comfortable confiding in a man."

Annette controlled herself beautifully. "Mrs. Little," she said solemnly, "I needed to talk to a wise woman. But first, forgive me. . . ." Annette was too young to resist seeming "wiser." "If you *don't* know, I'm sure you *ought* to know. You are a mother. You wouldn't approve of what's going on out there, would you?"

Sophia was stiffening toward stone. No phony little twerp was going to tell Sophia Thomas Little what she *ought* to know. But she turned her head.

CHAPTER 19

Wednesday Noon

The first J heard of the trouble was Nanjo's howling. She was howling in the family room. "What's the matter! What's the *matter* with *Mother?*"

J hurried around the wall. Nanjo, barefoot and a good bit more than half-naked in her sunbathing outfit, stood with the big towel trailing off one shoulder and her face in turmoil, howling at the stranger, who started to speak.

But J looked through the glass and saw Sophia and Cal, the gardener, and he knew by their postures that his wife was in the throes of what J thought of as a white rage. A big one! He hurried out there.

His wife turned a bloodless face; even her voice was white hot. "J, find out what we owe this man, and give it to him. I want him out of this yard as fast as he can go, and I never want him to come back."

Cal had his head down, but he was looking up and muttering, "How come it's my fault? Hell, lady, what do you want?" He seemed to J to be on the verge of an outburst.

"J," Sophia's voice rang out, "do as I say!"

"Just go into the house, Sophia," said J gently, turning her with a firm but gentle hand on her shoulder. She began to walk stiffly. "I think," J said to Cal, the gardener, "there's nothing to be said or done except for me to pay you what we owe you. Mrs. Little no longer wants you working here."

"Yah!" Cal looked after Sophia, who was moving stiffly and slowly away, as if he would like to stab her in the back with his pruning device. "That's okay for you. What do you care? Sit on your fat can and get rich, and *your* kids can do what they damn feel like. But me, I work for a living, and I can go . . ."

As he began to use words that in all prudence J had to ignore, J began to figure out the debt in his own mind.

In the house Annette swung her free foot and said to Nanjo, who was whimpering and shivering, "Honey, you've got to be kidding! With that equipment you mean to say you didn't know a *man* was standing there, practically . . ."

"Well, it's not my fault," howled Nanjo.

"Why give it away, honey?" said Annette with an air of reason. "He was getting a whole lot too much for nothing."

"You're *disgusting!*" screeched Nanjo. (She had been toasting in the sun, dreaming a dream. An audience had been clapping. From all sides had been beaming approval and admiration. How adorable! How adorable she is! Tiny waist. Lovely shoulders. Dear little bosom.)

"Oh, for God's sake," Annette was saying. "You're not talking to your mother, honey, or Queen Victoria, either. Sex, you've heard of? Didn't you know he was there?"

Nanjo had forgotten he was there. So she screamed, "NO."

"Careless," said Annette.

This, being true, was *too much*. "You shut up!" screamed Nanjo.

Outside, Cal said, "For God's sakes, Mr. Little, your wife goes *crazy!* I wasn't going to hurt her. Dontcha know that?"

"I doubt you would have," said J quietly and said no more. He was in the middle, and firmly he stayed there. Cal took the check (his wage, plus some severance pay) ungraciously, slung his long pole over his shoulder, and began to walk toward the path around the garage, muttering and spitting.

(As he backed his truck out and was away, a car went after him. Nobody noticed, although Goodrick dogged him all the way to the nearest tavern.)

"Mother!" howled Nanjo. "You *scared* me! You just about . . . Look, I'm just shaking. . . ."

Sophia was getting a reaction herself. "Go and cover yourself up," she said icily. "Excuse me, too, please?" She bowed rather quaintly to the guest and went off to her own bathroom where she could fight herself until she won—too late.

But Nanjo began to howl at her father as he came in and closed the sliding glass. "Daddy, I'd like to know what I did that was so wrong? If I can't work on my suntan in my own yard, where *can* I work on my suntan? I don't see why Mother had to come out there and yell at me to 'git' as if I were some kind of hound dog. You'd think I was some kind of criminal."

"That was too bad, Nanjo," said J. "Would you get dressed, please? I'd just as soon not present you in that state."

"Well, it's not my fault, the state I'm in. Mother just about scared me to death! And I wasn't doing one darned thing!"

But J was not going to be pushed off his balance in the middle. So his daughter howled, "You just don't want me to do anything, either one of you. If I'm supposed to sit around this darned old castle in some kind of flannel shroud, I might as well be dead. I hate you!"

J said nothing to this. He didn't even wince. Given the incident (which had certainly been too bad), this only followed. But Annette spoke up. "Flannel could be sexier than you think, honey," she drawled. "That outfit is suitable only for the lower classes."

Nanjo choked. Too angry even to howl, she tore out of the room.

"Papa better spank, eh?" said Annette, as one adult to another. "How old is the child?"

"Sixteen," said J. He sat down, thinking, Papa's going to spank *you* in just about another minute. He realized that Annette had been trying to puncture Nanjo's outsize stubbornness, as she had Cary's the other evening. But it is one thing to understand, another to condone.

Annette had already dismissed the incident. "Mr. Little, things are very tense. Either you will have to go into hiding or someone must be here in the house during the night. I thought. . . ."

J truly did not know what she was talking about and said so.

Then Sophia was there, saying calmly, "I apologize for the unseemly ructions, Miss Woods."

"You mustn't be too hard on the poor kid," said the wise young woman. "Of course, I *knew*. . . ."

"Yes, I must thank you for calling it to my attention," said Sophia, causing her husband to shudder within.

But then Marietta was there saying, "Oh, we have company? How lovely you look today! Doesn't she, J? How delightful to have young people around the house."

There were a few confused moments, during which J said he was wanted at the office and perhaps he had better be off, and Annette chimed in to say that Mrs. Little having been so understandably upset, she wouldn't dream of being a bother. But Sophia announced in a voice permitting no arguments that luncheon would be served in fifteen minutes.

So Marietta got to entertain the guest, because Sophia went to the kitchen, and J went quietly out of the room and tapped on Nanjo's door.

She was burrowing under a fat quilt on her bed. "I don't care," she wept stubbornly, "I don't see why I had to be blasted. I don't see why she had to make such a big deal. . . ."

"It wasn't very pleasant for your mother, either," said J patiently (or for Cal, the gardener, he thought. Or for me).

"Mother just made a big *fool* out of me!" Nanjo came up on all fours, her hair hanging down around her face. "What did she think I was going to do, anyway? If I wanted to *do* anything, I wouldn't have to depend on the lower classes. *I know all about sex!*"

At this preposterous remark, J couldn't help feeling a little better momentarily.

Oh, he had heard long since that all they talked about in high school was sex. The girls talked about it to the girls. The boys talked about it to the boys. The girls and boys talked about it to one another. And the teachers talked about it to either or both the boys and the girls. Oh, Nanjo had talked about it a lot—and seen it playacted on the screens, heard it wailed about in songs, and read it written about in book after book all the way from junk to literature.

But surely only a virgin could say what she had just said!

Still J, who did not believe that there was more than one way to *know* even the first thing about sex, found himself soon saddened to think of all the generations who by whisper-whisper or talk-talk-talk had been and would be brought impure to the experience, already prejudiced one way or the other.

"I wish you were Eve," he said sadly, "but it's too late."

Why should he say more? Why should *he* talk? More talk? (But how can a human resist the lure of language?) "As it is," J said in spite of himself, "I guess you'd better go be a sexpot in the movies, Nanjo. That's only pictures. You'd never have to know who's watching. Or what side of the tracks he comes from. You'd never have to know there was anybody out there at all."

Nanjo fell flat with a thump. "You make me sick," she murmured. The quilt billowed. J could see the flush along her cheekbone. He guessed he'd spanked her.

"You may be excused from luncheon," he said.

"I'd throw up!" howled Nanjo, rearing up again. "I can't *stand* that bleached blond character. How come it's okay for *her* to be a sexpot?" She glared; she would be in the right, *somehow*.

"I wish you knew who you were trying to fool," said J.

"I'm *not!* I hate the whole stupid thing! I don't know what you *want*. I'm not trying to fool anybody!"

"Yes, you are," said J, "but it won't be me."

He left her, thinking that if he had to choose a side, he just might find himself on the side of Cal, the gardener!

Luncheon was a very polite affair.

Sophia, under her iron mask, was mortified. She had let her cursed temper explode under the temptation of an outlet for it that had nothing to do with its true cause. Well, she didn't care (anymore) what this Annette thought, and her mother didn't count, and Nanjo she would deal with somehow. But she hated to have made such a fool of herself in J's eyes. He could be so maddening, as for instance when *he* kept his temper. She tried defensively to believe he took this all too casually, but it didn't work. Sophia knew he was upset and much saddened.

Lunch did not take as long as it seemed to take. J said he'd have to go now. Annette sprang up; she must go, too.

"Must you really?" Sophia said, as lightly as she could. "Let me say again that I am sorry for the unpleasantness."

"Oh, don't be on my account," said Annette generously.

Marietta, having tuned out at the very mention of unpleasantness, now started for her room, which was also Nanjo's. J went to his room in preparation for departure.

Sophia saw the guest's eyes change and become fake-shy. "I had meant to get up the nerve," she breathed, "to ask an enormous favor of you, Mrs. Little. I don't know whether I've got the nerve, after all."

"What favor is this?"

"I was wondering if I could possibly dare ask you to let me come and stay and—be a kind of daughter to you for a few days."

"Daughter!" Sophia was startled enough to snap.

"I know that would have been an awfully nervy thing to ask. But you see . . ."

"I'm so glad you didn't," gushed Sophia. "I would have had to say certainly not. J," she turned to him as he reappeared, "she wants to move in here and be our daughter. I've said No. But I'm sorry. I should have talked it over with you, of course." She glittered dangerously.

"Why?" said J. "It's obvious. We can't have that." He gave the girl a steady look. ("Out, out," it said.) "Well, good-bye, Cousin Annie," he said aloud. "See you, Sophia." He did not kiss his wife's cheek. He knew she wouldn't have liked it.

"Good-bye, Mrs. Little," he could hear Annette saying behind him, breathless to get away. "I hope your little girl will be all right."

"I'm sure she will," lied Sophia. "Good-bye."

Annette went out to the car at the curb. J was in the garage getting into his car. Sophia wasn't going anywhere. *She* would have to deal with Nanjo.

And I wouldn't have handled it the way I did at all, she thought, if it hadn't been for that miserable female twerp. Daughter! *Hah!*

CHAPTER 20

Wednesday Afternoon

In Nanjo's room Nanjo was up on all fours again. "No," she screamed at her grandmother. "Oh, for God's sake, Grandmother!"

"But Nanjo, dear," said Marietta, "I don't wish to see you so unhappy. I know how much you wanted that beautiful gown. And I want you to look beautiful, of course I do. Beauty is our right, and such lovely material in the stores. I still have almost twenty dollars."

"I don't *want* any stupid, old, botched-up, homemade dress," howled Nanjo. "I wouldn't be caught *dead* in some crumby old formal *you* made. Oh ... woe...." Nanjo rolled over.

The door of the room flew open so fast it banged the wall. Sophia stood there. Nanjo shut up and quivered as if she had been hit.

"Mother," said Sophia, "just get out of this room and leave this miserable brat to me."

Marietta began to walk backward. She backed out of the room. In the moment Nanjo rose to a sitting position to stare at her mother.

"You are a perfect mess," said Sophia coldly, "and I am bitterly ashamed of you. I am bitterly ashamed of me, too."

The words echoed around the walls.

They could both hear Marietta blathering, "So sweet of you, Mrs. Neeby. Such a good neighbor."

"Well, I heard some commotion in the garden," said Susie, "and I was wondering if there is anything I could *do,* you know?"

Nanjo saw Sophia's chin come slowly up and her mother's face settle into smiling lines and a cool mantle of control come down over her mother's whole person.

"Get up, now," said Sophia to her daughter quietly. "Put on some decent clothes. Wash your face. Make it up. Look civilized."

"Why?" said Nanjo so quietly that she surprised herself.

"Because you and I have a date to go somewhere," said Sophia. "Or so I am about to tell Susie Neeby. All right?"

"All right," said Nanjo, feeling ten years older in a flash.

When Marietta saw *her* daughter coming, she turned and tottered to the kitchen. Mrs. Arriola, having dealt with the debris of luncheon, was retying her head scarf. "Oh, Miz Thomas, I got to go now. But oh, Miz Thomas, there's something bad, bad, going on around here, ain't there?"

"Lovely home," said Marietta. "So warm, so generous to include." Marietta was not being sarcastic. She didn't know how.

"Oh, Miz Thomas, there's some black cloud hanging over *this* house," said Mrs. Arriola. "You remember what I'm saying."

"My Own Good Angel is over this house," said Marietta tearfully.

"Oh, Miz Thomas, I dunno about that," said Mrs. Arriola. "There's angels of darkness, too, don't forget."

"I guess the whole block heard me blowing up and booting out the gardener," Sophia was saying to her best friend.

"What brought this on?" Susie wanted to know.

"Oh, there's probably a straw for every camel's back," said Sophia. "He hasn't been satisfactory for a long time. I just wish I didn't have to get worked up before I can fire anybody." She looked out at the half-pruned tree and the heaps of branches on the ground.

"Spoke too fast, didn't I?" she said. "Should have let him finish the elm. Poor J." (Sophia felt uneasy for that booting out. But done was done. She might have had to do it in any case.)

"Where did J go by the way?" Susie asked.

"To the office. Why?"

"Say, who's the platinum babe?"

"What babe?" Sophia pretended she didn't know.

"The one who stopped her car around the corner in front of my house and honked at J so he stopped, too. They kinda had their heads together for a minute."

"Oh, *that* platinum babe," said Sophia. "She's some kind of cousin. I can never figure out whether it's first cousin twice removed or second cousin once. Pore little thing"—Sophia's eyes assured Susie that this *was* sarcasm—"is in some kind of a state over a boyfriend. Well, you know, old reliable J, the father figure?"

"I guess he's pretty good with girls, that that," said Susie mischievously. "What's all this about J looking for another position?"

"You got me there, pal," said Sophia bluntly.

"Oh, listen, there was this man showed up this morning. He said he was checking J out for clearance, for top secret."

"I'll be darned," said Sophia.

"Listen, I can't help knowing that J hasn't *been* to his office. Sophia, I'll telling you, if they've fired J, they must be crazy."

"If who has fired J?" Sophia drawled. "Oh, darn it, he forgot to endorse that check again. I guess I can charge it. Nanjo?" she called. "Almost ready?" Then she said to Susie, "We're on our way to I. Magnin's. Nanjo saw a dress there she wants for only three fifty. And I might find a little something for myself for say, three ninety-five."

"What do you mean three fifty? Three ninety-five?"

"Say four hundred, then," said Sophia. "That's the dregs of seven fifty, isn't it? J told me to blow it all in."

"Do you mean," said Susie, "seven hundred and fifty *dollars?*"

"That's what I said, didn't I?" said Sophia with a grin.

"Hey, can I come, too?" said Susie. "I love to see money spent. Anybody's money."

"Be my guest," said Sophia carelessly. Thinking, *Damn it!*

The moment he put his foot inside the office door J saw his work cut out for him. So he simply fell to, putting aside his unhappy thoughts about Nanjo and his irritation with Cousin Annette. That one had had no business honking him to a halt and begging him to follow her to a secret conference because great affairs hung in the balance. J had had it with great affairs. He had affairs enough in his own backyard.

He knew very well that somehow or other Annette had

been the spark to a fuse and that there would not have been quite such an explosion in his own backyard had she not been in his house.

So he had looked upon Annette with stern disfavor and had said to her, "Beat it. And don't come around anymore. I've got nothing to confer with you about, and I won't have you upsetting my family. The day you move in! Hah! That'll be the day! Move on."

"But Mr. Little, you'd get to *understand*. You're in danger."

"One danger," J had barked, "I'm getting out of right now is you and your helpful hints to *my daughter*. I understand you don't know any better. But your assumptions are ignorant, and your ignorance is destructive. I can't do a thing about it, since I didn't have the raising of you. But I don't have to put up with it around *my* house. So beat it, like I said."

"But for the sake of so many important people, I have to beg you ... Would you be willing to go into hiding for a while?"

"I would not." (Who the hell does she think is *important?*)

"But you must be careful. This man, Goodrick . . ."

"Go play hide-and-seek with him, why don't you?" J had said, putting his car in "drive." "He's childish, too. Now *I'm* a grown-up. I ... and don't ask me why, because you'd *never* understand ... I have got to go to the office."

He had watched in his rearview mirror, but her car had not moved to follow. Nor had any other car—that he noticed.

The mess at the office was the consequence of indecision; tempers were touchy, feelings had been hurt, progress hung up; something like mutiny was brewing. J wasted no time in making soothing remarks. He simply began to make decisions in an orderly array. After a while, he thought to himself (mixing metaphors as usual) that he had hold of the right threads to thin out the fog and set up the applecart, by golly, and here was something he did know how to do, whoever he was.

He had been at it for about an hour when his phone told him that he had a visitor, "A Mr. Goodrick to see you."

"Tell him I'm busy."

The phone rang again. "He says it is very urgent. He says only three minutes."

"Tell him No."

"He says he'll wait, Mr. Little." J received the sense of the receptionist's cry for help.

"I'm coming out there," he said.

In the reception room, sure enough, there stood Goodrick, flashing his teeth as whitely as ever and playing to be the old backslapping buddy wanting to repair to some inner sanctum, but J would have none of that.

He said, "What do you want? I'm busy."

So Goodrick began to speak in low tones, eyeing the receptionist the while. "I only ask you to do me the favor of coming to my hotel room," he coaxed, "as soon as convenient, for only an hour or so, and repeating to me every word that Doctor Willing said to you. For the sake of your country? I know you'll do it."

J stared glumly.

"Now, I am *willing*," Goodrick sidled closer and leered to see if J had caught his pun, "to give you, for your time and trouble, say, ten thousand dollars? Cash?" If Goodrick had expected J's eyes to light up, he got a fishy stare instead.

"First," said J, "I can't remember every word that Doctor Willing said to me. How about that?"

"If you would allow me to use certain techniques, associative probings and so on, to rouse your latent . . ."

J said, "Second, I wouldn't touch any ten thousand dollars from you."

"Ah, but you could report it as income if you like," said Goodrick soothingly. "There's nothing to be afraid of. I can call it a fee if you would feel safer paying the tax on it."

J said, "Third, I am not inclined to do you any favor in the first place."

"Well," said Goodrick, "I am sorry to hear that. It was a fair offer. There may be other ways. I can't see why you are being so coy." He leered as if J had already told him volumes.

"Who are you?"

"You wouldn't be giving away secrets to *me*," said Goodrick, "*I* know all about it. I told you who I am. I told you what I want to know. Just how far he went. Give you any *dates*, did he? That sort of thing?"

"*I* just thought of another way," said J. "Set up an appointment in some government office, where I can go, *knowing* that I'm doing this for my country. I'll meet you there and nowhere else. But if the United States Government wants to pay me ten thousand dollars for an hour of my time, I betcha I'll have a thing or two to say to *it* about throwing my money around."

"Too much, eh?" said Goodrick. "Who is Annette Woods?"

"What the hell do you care?" J bristled. (Goodrick's phrase "too much" had sounded like an insult.)

"From Chicago?" said Goodrick, slime on his tongue. "Would you want your good wife to hear all about it?"

"My wife just fed her a darned good lunch at our house," said J. "What is it she hasn't heard all about?"

Goodrick stared. "Have you ever heard of a Tony Thees?"

It was J's turn to stare while his brain thumbed through some possible answers, rapidly deciding (as any businessman knows how to do) which answer would both stand up and do J the most good.

He said, "You must mean Cousin Annie's boyfriend, the one that chased her all the way out here. *I* don't know the man. What's all this to you?"

"Thees chased a *girl!*"

J was pleased to see astonishment. "Well, *I* don't know," he said with a dismissing wave of his mind. "The girl's a pseudo-cousin of mine, but I don't figure her love life is my business. I can't stand her, anyway. I've got work. Say, why don't *you* go play Cupid?" He added, with his clown face on, "Just tell the government to charge it to me, as usual."

He left Goodrick chewing his thumb.

J sat down at his desk, thinking he had done okay. He might have just gotten himself out of the middle. Let them chase one another around and tell one another lies.

What had been Noah's line of work, he wondered, while he'd built that Ark on weekends and after-hours? What had that man been doing to earn a living, in the meantime, while the earth lasted?

"That was pretty silly." Sophia sank down on Nanjo's bed beside the two big boxes.

"Mother," said Nanjo, quavering, "I meant it when I said I didn't want it. I don't want it anymore. I really don't."

Sophia, whose head was aching fiercely, leaned back against

Nanjo's headboard and half closed her eyes. "I would agree," she said, "that you look like a high-class little tart in that thing, especially by the way Susie said it was adorable. Just put it away carefully, Nanjo. We can take them both back." She rubbed her brow.

"But why did you buy them?"

"It was an act," said Sophia, "for the benefit of my best friend, who doesn't have to know everything." She began to allow herself to think about Susie's tale of an FBI man. Of J and that Annette with their heads together around the corner.

Nanjo said woefully, "I *didn't* think about Cal, the gardener, being there. I'm sorry. I should have, hm?"

"I know you didn't think about it," said Sophia. "I'm sorry, too. But you're right. You should have." Sophia knew that normally she would have stopped what had been going on in the backyard with poise and the quiet admonition that although this was not anybody's fault exactly, it would not do.

Nanjo was whining, "I was just upset when I yelled at Grandmother. Honestly, I know I shouldn't have done that."

"Um, hum," said Sophia, "and I was upset when I yelled at you. Well, that's the way it goes, sometimes." A certain companionable ease was falling on them.

"Mother, who was that girl who was here?"

"I don't believe I know," said Sophia wearily. But she opened her eyes, drawn to look hard at her daughter and realized that there is such a thing as being *too* chummy in this world with one's child. "There's lots of peace for you to make, Nanjo," she said gently. "Oh, your grandmother will forgive you. Your father already understands. Don't ever think he doesn't. You and I—well—we got rid of the yelling and screaming, anyhow. Peace?"

Nanjo sank down on the bench to her dressing table, where she drooped and seemed disconsolate. Sophia thought, I can't help her now. This is no time for a cozy chat about the war between the men and the women.

She dragged to her feet and picked up the box with her own elegant dress in it, the one she had chosen in order to show off. Show off what? That J had *not* lost his job, *was* prosperous? Was *Sophia's?* She realized wryly that it was no good blaming Susie.

She said, "My head is killing me. That's what you get for blowing your top. It's getting late. I don't know where the dickens your grandmother has got to. Dad will be home soon. I'd better pull myself together. Why don't you do the same?" She touched Nanjo's head lightly. Nanjo smiled wanly.

Sophia left the room. Nanjo sat still, staring at the box wherein lay that dress, the fabulous dress, the one she'd been so excited about, the one that made her look exactly like the girl on the book—a smooth-shouldered, high-busted, big-eyed, small-chinned, stupid-looking, nitwitted, good-for-nothing-but-sex, high-class tart.

Nanjo got up and thrust the box in on her closet floor, kicking it behind the row of shoes. She was chilly. She sat down again, hugging herself. What had Daddy *meant,* it was too late? Sure, she'd had the usual wrestling matches, but that was all. She didn't understand. What had he *meant,* she was fooling somebody? Oh, how could there be peace? Her grandmother was a professional forgiver of everything and everyone, but Nanjo didn't know how she was going to make peace with her father. Or with any male.

CHAPTER 21

Wednesday Evening

At five o'clock, when Marietta came out of the blue-painted door in the stucco wall around what she called the Retreat, Goodrick was still sitting in his rented car.

"How good of you to have waited all this time," cried she.

"Get in," he said, his eyes leery. "Where to now, Mrs. Thomas?"

"But I don't quite know." Standing there, the plump woman with the rosy face, the Dutch bob, and the round blue eyes looked childishly lost.

"I want to talk to you some more," said Goodrick. He'd had his orders. "She's either crazy," he had said to Mr. Jones, "or a liar."

"Ah," Mr. Jones had said. "Pick her up again and find out which."

Marietta got into the car, fumbling for her handkerchief. "I understand the rules," she said. "Of course I do. They *must* have the hundred dollars for the trial week. Perhaps I could wait at the Wimple. No, I don't think—"

Goodrick wasn't bothering to follow very far. "Now," he said, turning in the seat to speak confidentially, but in a businesslike way, "you say that J Little was knocked down by a large automobile, but not hurt?"

"It was a miracle," said Marietta.

"He wasn't hurt, but they took him to the hospital?"

"But they were so kind, you see."

"Tell me again what he says about the other man in his room."

"Oh, it must have been a very funny man," she said, "because everybody was laughing."

"That's what I thought you said. Now, why are you lying to me?"

Marietta simply erased this from her brain. "Everything so clean and simple and filled with the spirit." She yearned toward the blue door in the gray wall. "Surely my Own Good Angel sent me here."

"What was the man's name?" said Goodrick.

"I beg your pardon?"

"The man in the hospital. The funny one." (Dr. Ambrose Willing hadn't been a comic, that Goodrick remembered.)

"I don't . . . Oh, but I'm sure J would be happy to tell you. Perhaps if you drive me back to Sophia's and come in, Mr. Goodrick, we can chat and when J comes home. . . ."

"He's not telling all he knows. He's hiding something, isn't he?"

"You would be so welcome," she said. "So gracious a hospitality there."

"Who is the girl?" said Goodrick. "Annette Woods?"

"Do you mean that pretty thing who came to lunch? Such beautiful manners. . . ."

"She got a boyfriend named Tony Thees?" (Mr. Jones had been extremely skeptical.)

Marietta looked bewildered. Goodrick banged his fist on the back of the front seat. "What did she want with J Little? What does he know that he's not talking about? Somebody spoke to him."

"Oh," said Mairetta, "oh, now I understand. But people don't talk about such things. Dear J, I was happy for him. We have always been very close."

"Is that so?" Goodrick's teeth became wolf's teeth in grandmother's clothing. "Now we're getting somewhere. You tell me what it is he won't talk about, I'll give you one hundred dollars."

Marietta's eyes filled. "Oh, bread," she said, "upon the waters."

"Come on. Come on," said Goodrick. "What's his big secret?"

"Dear J," she said tearfully. "So good. I knew that one day he would hear an angel speak to him in revelation."

Goodrick blinked. "The room-mate in the hospital, he had something to do with this . . . uh . . . revelation?

"Ah," said Marietta, "angels come in so many disguises. You, yourself, have been an angel unaware this very day."

Goodrick bit off a rather large sliver of skin.

"Listen," he said in a moment, "I said I'd give you a hundred dollars, and I will, but first you've got to help me."

"We are all here to help one another."

"Can you just try to listen? I'll give you a phone number. You get J to talk about the hospital and everything that happened there. The man. The room-mate. Call the number, ask for John Jones, and tell *him* whatever you find out. You do that, old lady, and maybe it's worth more than a hundred dollars. Heh. Heh."

"But dear Mr. Goodrick," said Marietta, "why don't you ask J? You see," she quavered, "my Own Good Angel tells me *never* to dwell on thoughts of illness. And I obey."

"Forget it," said Goodrick rather violently. "Forget I ever saw you. Don't mention it. Can you keep a secret?"

"When you give alms, do it in secret," said she.

He started the car. In a few minutes she recognized the route and said, "Of course. So thoughtful. I must pack."

Goodrick grunted. She took it for a question.

"I understand that you wish to do good in secret," she went on comfortingly. "So I will simply say that my Own Good Angel brought my hundred dollars back to me, which will be true."

Goodrick kept silent for a while. Then he said, "You wouldn't know the truth. . . . Why should I give you the money when you're no good to me? Now try again. Did you hear J speak the name 'Willing'? Or the name 'Barkis'?"

Marietta concentrated. "A long time ago? In some novel?"

"You're crazy," said Goodrick.

He stopped the car a block away from J's house and dumped her. Marietta's rosy face, however, turned to him.

"Bless you," she began, "and may your Own Good Angel—"

A shudder rippled down the man's back. "Listen," he said, "just let me alone, will you?"

Goodrick fled.

Tony said, "Why can't you get him to meet you somewhere?"

Annette said, "He wouldn't come."

"Why not?"

"What are you going to do with him if he does come?" she countered.

"Get him into my car. I'm not going to snatch him off the street or drag him out of his own car. Softly. Softly."

"Where is this deep hole?" She was glaring at him. "In a cemetery?"

"Maybe you shouldn't know," said Tony. "What's the matter with you anyway? How come you goofed the way you did, sweetheart? Wasn't a bad idea for you to get in there."

"Why should he let *me* in?"

Tony kept quiet for a moment. He felt blind. It made him uneasy not to have his own eye on. He'd hired help, but he couldn't tell the help very much. The help was, in a way, blind.

"Say," he asked, "what's the fat lady like, the mother-in-law?"

"Just a nut." Annette flung herself on her face on the bed.

"What does Goodrick want with *her*? Any idea?"

"She doesn't know anything. His wife doesn't know anything. Let him alone, Tony. Just let the clock go around."

Tony's thoughts began to go around the same old circle, looking for the lesser risk.

"You want to know what's uppermost in his mind?" she burst angrily. "His own family, period. He's so narrow, you wouldn't believe . . ."

"Let's the both of us date him for lunch. Downtown, where his family isn't."

"What's the pack of lies we're going to tell him, then?"

"Whatever he'll swallow," said Tony, "so he'll get into my car and we can put him in aforesaid mole."

"Guess what?" said Annette. "I hate you!" She began to cry.

Tony gave up. Tears bored him.

J drove home at the end of the day without looking behind him any more than the careful driver should. The house seemed remarkably quiet. Marietta was there in her favorite chair, but she hadn't much to say. Sophia was quiet; she had a headache, she said. Nanjo crept about, subdued and too contrite to be true, J feared. When he was told about the purchase of the dress (for no good reason, Sophia said), Nanjo began to beg his permission to take it back. "I don't want to look like that, Daddy," she whined. J knew from Sophia's eyebrow that the dress was going back. "Whatever you think," he said to Nanjo indifferently. (Was he getting some coals of fire to wear in his waning hair? Or had Nanjo been seriously frightened?)

He drank his cocktail. It didn't relax him. The quiet was edgy. Dinner was not tasty.

Afterward Nanjo came shyly to J's side and said she was going to study and then go to bed early. "Good night, Daddy."

"No date?" said J.

"Cary asked me, but I said No!" Her eyes begged him to praise her for this.

J did not praise her. "Good night, Nanjo."

"Daddy," Nanjo's voice went into a near whisper, "I wish I could take voice lessons. I do sound like a whiny old pig."

"We'll have to look around and see where there's a good teacher," he said. "Scoot along, Nanjo." He couldn't cope with much more humility.

But Nanjo had more groveling to do yet. "Daddy, would you apologize to that girl for me when you see her again?"

"I doubt I'll see her," said J absently. "Quite a lot of it was her fault, actually." He opened his magazine.

So Nanjo embraced her grandmother, begging forgiveness and hearing it pronounced in full flow until Sophia said crisply, "Hop it, toots," because she had had enough of this unnatural behavior, too.

Nanjo crept away. J listened to her feet dragging. He sighed and glanced at Sophia.

Sophia was looking at him in so warm and loving a way that J felt his face poised on the impulse to beam on her, too—whether he understood the wonderful lift, the lightening of the air in the room, or not.

"You know too much," she murmured, and he felt absurdly pleased.

Marietta said, "J dear, there was something I was asked to ask you."

"Yes?" J left off rejoicing to be polite.

Marietta was looking out at the darkness, her head high enough so that her chin was betraying that it had once had a clean line. "You were *not* ill, after all," she said. "What was the name of the man in the same room in the hospital?"

"I'm not sure I knew it," said J quietly. "Why did you say you're asking?"

"But you see, it takes a hundred dollars for the first week," she said, "and surely my Own Good Angel sent him."

Sophia, alerted, signaled J to leave this to her, and with long-practiced skill she extracted from Marietta a confused tale of her encounter with Goodrick. J listened, appalled.

Sophia said at last, "Mother, there are lots of things you don't understand. It's your own fault. You've stopped trying. Now, please believe me. That man was never sent by any good angel. You mustn't have anything to do with him. You must not take his money if he offers it again. You must stay right here, where I can look after you."

Marietta began to weep. She could not think evil. The man had been kind, she felt sure. "Of course, I am *happy* here," she wept, "so comfortable, and dear Nanjo. . . ."

Sophia said, "I think I'll make up the couch in J's den for you tonight. Come along and help me. You'd rather be by yourself, I'll bet."

Marietta went, protesting that she didn't wish to bother and was never really alone.

J, helpless to be of any use, heard them in the wing of the house. He knew, as Sophia did, that although forgiveness had been asked and forgiveness given, a night of peace and separation might solidify the contract between Nanjo and her grandmother.

Goodrick! Angrily J thought that the man *must* have other things in the world to do than keep prowling and prying at J's door.

He didn't *want* to think about Goodrick. He wanted to think about his children and his children's children, about Win, the father of three, about Amy, the mother of none, and about Nanjo, who must mate. About the world and time. About the fate of man. Nobody would let him think.

Sophia came back and sat down close beside him. "J, Susie Neeby says an FBI man was at her house this morning asking questions about you."

"Name of Goodrick?" said J morosely.

"Who *is* he, J?"

"I wish I knew. Cousin Annie keeps warning me. . . ." He shut his mouth and looked at her pitifully.

Sophia said to herself, *Any minute* he's going to blurt out the whole thing. Thus she was able to smile and say, "That's all right. Never mind."

But J fell silent.

So she said, "I'm afraid Nanjo's puzzling her head about what's going *on* between you and Cousin Annie."

J said, "I spanked that Annie, but hard, and chased her away. I thought I did the same with Goodrick. Damn it!"

"You have not, then," said Sophia, "fallen madly in love with another woman?"

J darted a glance at her and began to bite his lip.

"I've got to tell you something," he said, "that's too rich to keep. Can I have a guarantee you're not going to spread it around the neighborhood?"

"What makes you think *I* can't keep a secret?" she said ominously.

But J began to tell the tale of his noonday encounter with the Lily. Sophia was, at first, astonished that he had been drinking in the morning and wanted to know haughtily if he had *found* himself yet. J said, "Well, in a way, maybe," and continued. Sophia was then concerned that he had been intoxicated. And at the denouement, although she tried very hard to be worried about Amy living across the hall from a scarlet woman, it couldn't hold. Sophia muffled her mouth with both hands.

So J made his face very lugubrious and went on to recount his solemn reflections, which caused Sophia to rock helplessly, squealing and shedding tears, because it was so weird and wonderful, so absurd, so *funny*—to be an animal.

Marietta, lying uncomfortably on the narrow couch in J's den, could hear their laughter. Something about it did not seem ... pure. They sounded ... No, no, not ribald, surely. (Think no evil!) But then she seemed to see Mrs. Arriola's face painted on the darkness and hear her voice, "Oh, Miz Thomas ..." and it occurred to Marietta that it was at least somewhat heartless for them to laugh so, in the hearing of one who, lost and lonely, *was at their mercy.* The thought ripped savagely through the clouds. Marietta quickly began to beg her Own Good Angel to close the mists and bring back roses. She couldn't help reminding him how easily and quickly this could be done, for only one hundred dollars.

Nanjo, feeling glad and guilty that the other twin bed in her room was peacefully empty, could also hear the distant laughter. Her heart seemed to contract at the sounds and squeeze into a smaller, harder organ. What did *they* care? They made her sick!

CHAPTER 22

Thursday

Moving around her house on Thursday morning, Sophia found herself worrying, not about Nanjo (who was in school) and not about Marietta, who was in Nanjo's room occupied with repacking her possessions as if she were planning to move out. *Well, she can't,* thought Sophia and went on worrying about this Goodrick. J had gone to the office. She couldn't ask him (he didn't seem to know) *why* Goodrick kept poking around, talking to Susie, picking up Marietta, wanting to know the room-mate's name, when he, himself, had told Sophia about the room-mate's death. It was a mystery.

She answered the phone, midmorning, and found J's father speaking.

Grosvenor Winthrop Little III recognized her name but

seemed surprised to find her at this number. "Oh, yes, Sophia! Yes. Ah, by the way, Mr. Tobias Thomas is your relative, is he not?"

"He's my brother, Mr. Little." Sophia had never advanced to calling this man Father.

"He has been most helpful," said the old gentleman and went on to say that he wished J to call to see him at the earliest possible moment. His wish sounded exactly like his command, and Sophia found herself in rebellion.

"J is very busy, Mr. Little. Is it anything someone else could do? Could I?"

"No, no, no." The old gentleman seemed horrified. "I simply wish J to go to my bank for me. I have come to a decision. He has access to my safe-deposit box, as you may know."

"Yes, I know," said Sophia. "But so does Win, doesn't he?"

"I beg your pardon?"

"So does your grandson, Grosvenor Winthrop Little the Fifth," she said, speaking distinctly.

"Of course. Of course. Ah, that may be the solution."

"Have you Win's number?"

"Ah, yes, I must, mustn't I?"

"I'll give it to you again if you like." She recited Win's office number.

As she hung up, feeling that she had been properly protective, Sophia herself was attacked. Marietta appeared to talk about the strength of her feelings in regard to the Retreat. Did Sophia think Marietta had understood about the hundred dollars? And Sophia thought in rebellion, Why should I have to stand between my mother and the consequences of her own acts? "You *gave away* the hundred dollars," she said sternly. "So now you *haven't got* the hundred dollars. Do you see?" She was thinking, Darned if there wasn't something to J's talk about being in the middle. "And anyway, you can't go there until I've looked it over," she added, and there she was in the middle again.

Sophia put the big boxes from the store into her car and set forth to return the dresses.

In half an hour Marietta left the house and began to walk downhill toward the bus stop several blocks away. A car

came up the hill, U-turned behind her, and came back down
to stop beside her.

"Can I give you a lift today, Mrs. Thomas?"

"Oh, no, no. I would be taking you out of your way, Mr.
Goodrick."

"Come on. Get in," said Goodrick. "You're looking worried."

"Oh, no," she said at once. "I *never* worry."

"Listen," Goodrick looked sour, "I have had orders."

"You were sent?" breathed Marietta.

"That's right. There's a man I know, would like to meet
you. Maybe he can help you. Let me take you to his hotel.
Come on. Nobody's going to hurt you." He had the car door
open.

"Of course not," she sighed and got in. "I think," she said,
"you must take the Ventura Freeway. My grandson has such
a beautiful large home, Mr. Goodrick, and three adorable
children."

Goodrick's teeth came out of hiding. "Is that so?" he said.

Only this morning he had said to Mr. Jones, "She's crazy."

Mr. Jones had replied coldly, "Before I accept your conclu-
sions I, myself, would like to see this woman. Why didn't you
bribe her?"

"She'd take money," growled Goodrick, "but she's crazy.
And the man Little must be crazy. He *won't* take money."

"Aren't you confused?" said Mr. Jones.

"I think he's suspicious," said Goodrick.

"Ah, suspicion is itself suspicious," Mr. Jones had pronounced loftily.

Now Goodrick decided that the more he knew about the
family the better. So Marietta did the directing and babbled
rapturously all the way, but Goodrick didn't say much. When
he pulled up before Win and Marion's house, he didn't listen
to her thanks but got out on his side, and when she rang the
doorbell, he stood close beside her. He had spotted the play
yard and the equipment there.

Win opened the door. Marietta seemed to notice nothing
odd about this on a weekday. She entered, exuding as usual,
and presented Goodrick as a friend of dear J's, who had been
so good, and so on. Win shook hands but seemed distraught.
He asked no questions. When Marion came into the room to
greet them, she seemed absentminded.

So small talk fell flat, and Marietta was obliged to come to her point. "It came to me, Marion dear, that I might possibly be of help to you. I have no roots, you see, for three more weeks. I am not really needed at Sophia's. Do you think I could be useful here? The dear children, so fond. . . ."

"Oh," said Marion. "Well." She glanced quickly at her husband.

"Nice of you to offer, Marietta," said Win, "but we're in a bit of an uproar, and I don't think you'd be comfortable." There was something adamant about his speech.

While Marietta sought to turn it around and make good news of it, somehow, Win turned to be polite to Goodrick.

"Nice of you to drive her," he said. "You know my Dad, do you?"

"I came across him in Chicago," said Goodrick. "Quite an adventure he had, eh?"

"It was a miracle," said Marietta. "Ah, darlings. . . ."

The Little kids had come pouring into the room to greet their great-grandmother. Goodrick's eyes slipped around to look them over.

Win said sharply, "You mean his accident?"

The cold eyes came back. "Do I?" said Goodrick slyly. "Do you know a gal named Annette Woods? Good-looking silver blonde, young—"

Win said, "I don't think so. Who is she?"

"That's something I am trying to find out," said Goodrick.

"I never heard of her."

"So she's no cousin, eh?"

Win said, "What do you mean?"

"Isn't it obvious to you that your father has something on his mind? Didn't he tell you about it?"

Win stood up. He said, genial enough on the surface, "I don't discuss my Dad, behind his back, particularly. Excuse me." He turned. "Marietta, please, would you excuse us? We have just listed this house for sale, and we have a whole lot of decisions to make, what else to sell, and so on. We are in an uproar, as I said."

"How much do you want?" said Goodrick, rising.

"I beg pardon," said Win, who didn't like the man. "Do you mean the asking price on this place?"

"I meant money." He was grinning like a pumpkin.

Marietta said, "Oh, Mr. Goodrick is so generous. He has

offered me a hundred dollars. I am not to take it, but it was good of him."

Win looked from one to the other.

"We are all here to help one another," said Goodrick. "I think a giver pays the gift tax? That's if you can help me. Could we talk?"

Win said, "This is a bad time. I doubt there'll be a good time. Do you mind if we are a little bit rude and put you out?" He stirred himself to do just that, with charm, but firmly.

When they had gone, Win said explosively, "Now where the devil did he come from? I'd sooner do business with a rattlesnake. Why is he running around with Marietta? If Ma doesn't know about this, she'd better."

Marion was keeping the Little kids close by her side. She hadn't liked that man's cold eyes on them. He had made her very nervous.

Nobody answered the phone at Win's parents' number.

"I don't understand," said Marion, "why your grandmother can't sense there's something wrong about that man."

"You should know by now," said Win. "Marietta makes things over to suit herself. Well, better get on with the job. Which car are we taking to the lot, yours or mine?"

"I don't care," said Marion bracing her shoulders. "What about the sterling?"

"We won't need it for a while, I imagine."

"Darlings, go play in your room. Not outside for a while. Because Mommy would rather."

Win was staring at the telephone. Two phone calls this day had crashed the roof in on his head. He had made the first one himself.

Mr. Faulkner's secretary had said, "Oh, Mr. Little, I am so glad you called. I was supposed to call you this very morning to say that Mr. and Mrs. Faulkner had to rush off to South America. They have already gone to the airport. I was asked to say, first, how sorry they are not to be able to come to supper on Sunday."

"Well, I'm sorry, too," Win had said. "How long do they expect to be gone?" (South America!)

"That's rather indefinite," she had said, "and by the way, I believe Mr. Faulkner also had a business appointment for Tuesday?"

"Yes."

"Then I must break that, too," she had said. "Obviously, since he will be in Rio."

"Wants to postpone it, does he?" Win had said easily "Did he suggest an alternative date?"

"Why, no, sir, he didn't."

"I see. Then, I suppose, when he does get back—"

Her voice had changed slightly, "Have you seen the business section of the morning paper, Mr. Little?"

"No. Why?"

"I'm sorry," she had said in quite a human way and hung up.

So Win had looked. Small paragraph. "Faulkner Manufacturing has awarded its two-million-dollar account to Ad Agency Jimson, Briar, and Carmichael."

And there it went, glimmering. Without even the courtesy of a personal word. You get the bad news in the paper. Where else?

When the phone had rung on the heels of this, Win had picked it up in a daze of indifference.

"Winthrop?" his grandfather had said. "Will you do an errand for me, my boy? I wish you to go to my bank and bring me from my safe-deposit box your grandmother's bonds."

"Pardon!"

"Oh, yes—you see . . . Now I believe you must know who Mr. Tobias Thomas is?"

"My *Uncle* Tobias!"

"A very clever man, is he not? Yes, he has been in session with Mr. Pudney and has succeeded in improving the terms so remarkably that I feel I ought not to let the opportunity pass. Now, I had resolved never to touch dear Alice's property for myself. But what bonds remain she had destined for Winnie, you see, and Mr. Pudney assures me that dear Alice, and Winnie, too, would both be most anxious to see my work published. If they were here, that is exactly what they would say. Do you agree?"

"Well, I . . . How much . . . Do you want them *all* turned into cash, Grandfather?"

"Oh, yes. Yes, I suppose so. Mr. Thomas says that he will be glad to attend to that for me. You need only fetch them. Will you do that?"

"How soon?" Win had said.

"Oh, as soon as possible," the old gentleman had said. "I am quite elated." He'd laughed; it was a rusty braying. "I daresay it will take a day or two. Shall we say Monday?"

"All right, Grandfather," Win had promised quietly and hung up and looked around at ruin.

"I'll call and see if they can send for a car," Win said, the children having gone. "I had better be here. The realtor is coming. Maybe the man about the paintings. I don't want *you* dealing with them. It's going to be a battle of bluffs."

"I'm not very good at that," she said.

So Win walked to his favorite spot for staring out the big window and spoke in a monotone. "With Faulkner out of the picture I've got to cut back and scramble for new business. But I'll make it. In the meantime we've got to unload around here, get the cash, pay off that loan, and deliver those bonds to my grandfather."

Marion said nothing.

"I'll tell you once more," said Win in the same dull way, "He gave me permission to use them for collateral, over the phone. I wish I'd had it recorded."

"I still don't see why," said Marion, "you don't simply remind him."

"Because I said that I needed them for only thirty days," said Win. "But the truth now is that in thirty days or a hundred I won't be able to get the money in any other way than by unloading."

"I don't mind that, you know," she said in a moment.

"Yes, you do," said Win. "Shall I ask your father to help me?"

"It's possible I *would* mind," she said, "my father thinking I had married a failure. He wouldn't understand. You could ask yours."

"I won't do that," snapped Win.

"*I* don't understand you," she wailed. "What you did wasn't dishonest. Your *father* will believe you, of all people in the world. Your grandfather will just have to believe you, although he forgets."

Win didn't seem to hear. "Grandfather won't be fussing until Monday," he said. "We've got the weekend. Anything can happen in three days."

As they drove on, Goodrick asked questions about Win

and Marion and the Little kids and sought in the flood for something useful. Win so clever, Marion so charming, children so good, so handsome, so loving and beloved.

"*You* love children, don't you, Mr. Goodrick?" she added confidently.

Goodrick made a sound.

"What did you say? I'm sorry."

"I said you didn't know what you're talking about at *any* time," he snapped.

Marietta trilled out laughter. "Dear Mr. Goodrick, you forget I have a Good Angel of my own, who sees the inside of your heart. Why, you could barely take your eyes from the dear little people."

Goodrick sank into a glum silence.

After a while he said, "This daughter we're going to see now, she's got kids, too?"

"No, no. Dear Amy. But I'm sure, in her prayers.   "

He said, "I'm on to *you*."

"Why whatever . . ."

"Never mind," he said. "I'm on to you. You're a liar."

Marietta turned her china-blue eyes. "You are sensitive to the truth," she said gently. "What have I said, I wonder, that has touched you so deeply?"

Goodrick had never met a person before whom he couldn't insult. "Listen," he said desperately, "listen, kindly stop talking for a while, will you please?"

Avery opened the apartment door. He was not in the least cordial. Amy wasn't here. He had a headache; nothing else interested him in the least.

But Marietta drew joyous breath and went, at once, into action. Goodrick looked sourly around at the decor while Marietta seated Avery on a cushion and knelt on her plump knees behind him and put her little pink hands on his brow. She began to plead earnestly for a healing. Goodrick began to snoop nervously through the other rooms.

When there was a knock at the door, it was apparent that Marietta had no intention of interrupting her treatment, or whatever it was, so Goodrick found himself forced to do the honors.

The blowsy blond woman said, "Hi. How's Avery?" Goodrick stepped back, and she came in. "I guess he don't feel too good, eh?"

Marietta said, "Nonsense. He is feeling better every moment, aren't you, dear Avery?"

"Yeah?" said Lily. "Listen, I almost forgot I said I'd check on him while Amy's on the job. Don't tell her I was so late. Okay? Hey, he ought to go to the doctor's That's what I say "

"Pain is unreal," said Marietta.

Lily blinked and glanced at Goodrick with the intention of communicating. Some kind of nut? was on her tongue.

"Glad you came by," said Goodrick, all toothy.

Lily saw something in his face that caused her to shrink away. "Well, so long as he's got company."

"Where do you live, dear?" the man said.

"Forget it," said Lily and went across the hall and locked herself in.

But Marietta's spell had been broken. Avery, who had for a time seemed to relax, now wrenched himself out from under her hands. "Let me alone. Don't touch. Pain is pain."

Marietta's face became bewildered.

Goodrick said, "*I* think we better get the hell out . . ."

Feet clattered outside; the door opened. "Oh," said Amy. "Marietta? Hi." She brushed past Goodrick. "How is he?"

Avery was coiled on the cushion in a fetal position

"*Sssssss!*" Amy pulled breath in through her teeth.

"Amy, dear," said Marietta, "I'll stay! I'll be so glad to help. As long as I am needed."

"We've got no bed for you," said Amy, not even looking at her. "Is it bad, Avery?"

"Make her go away," said Avery. "It's *bad*, and she'd better believe it!"

"*I* believe it," said Amy softly. She rose, tall, and looked at Goodrick

"I happen to be a friend of your father's," he said "Drove her down."

"Then would you please," Amy's fine eyes flicked over his face, "take my grandmother home again? I'm sorry."

"I'd like to ask you if you know what your father was told in Chicago," began Goodrick loudly.

"No idea," said Amy, "and I *will not have loud talk in here*. Just go. Please."

Marietta said in a whisper, "Dear Amy—"

She went out the door and down the stairs, stumbling a

little. Goodrick followed. In the car he said, "Well, how come no angel showed? You sure poured it on, old lady."

"Did you not see and hear the angel?" said Marietta tremulously.

Goodrick trod on the accelerator. "About time I took you to see the devil," he said in a mumble.

Marietta did not, of course, hear what he said.

Lily had listened to them leave; she came out of her burrow. "Listen, hon," said Lily, shuffling in at Amy's door, "you get that boy to a doctor, but quick, hear?"

"I know," said Amy. "I've got to. I can't go back to the office. Lily, would you sit with him while I go and phone? I don't know what you could *do*. . . ."

"I don't, either," said Lily realistically. "I'll stick around, though. So long as that fellow with the fat lady ain't coming back. Who's he?"

"How should I know?" said Amy, rummaging for money in her purse. She hadn't much. She did have change for the phone. "Said he was a friend of Pops'."

"Naw," said Lily, "not that son of a bitch. Your Pops wouldn't have nothing to do with that character."

"What?"

"Listen, I happen to've met your Pops."

"I know," said Amy.

"Man, was he stoned the other day," said Lily. "Had a real crying jag on. Real nice, though, I thought He gimme twenty bucks."

"Cheap enough," said Amy lightly.

"Not for just a coupla cups of coffee," said Lily

Amy stared at her.

"You take *this* bird," said Lily. "He'd pry the gold outa your teeth and kick in what's left of 'em. Listen, go ahead. Call somebody."

"Lily, can you lend me some dough?"

"Nope, for the reason I ain't got it "

"I'll call the eye man," said Amy. "He's got to see Avery before next week."

"That's for sure," said Lily. "Listen, while you're out, why don't you call your Pops? Could be you need him, honey.'

Amy ran down the stairs, her quick feet not needing the use of her eyes. She might have to call somebody besides the doctor. She didn't feel like calling her Pops right now.

The car stopped in front of the Retreat.

"Okay," said Goodrick, prodding his passenger. "Go on in. You got the hundred dollars."

Marietta got out of the car and hesitated on the sidewalk. She had two fifty-dollar bills in her hand. She was looking blank.

"Listen, you told Mr. Jones all about the heavenly revelation and the angels and all that. And he gave you the hundred dollars. So what's wrong?"

"I don't know." Her lips were moving.

"Look, old lady," he said, "you been all day looking for someplace that would take you in. So now you *got* it! What's the matter with that?"

Marietta said in anguish, "I'm *asking.*"

Goodrick hit the steering wheel with his fist. "Best bargain you ever made," he raved. "A C-note for nothing."

"It was cheating," said Marietta solemnly. She looked down at the money. "I must give it back, then." She held it out.

Goodrick said, "I wouldn't touch ... Take your eye off me, old woman!"

He tore away. By his own standards he must be crazy!

J, having been so busy all day long that he had stopped incoming calls and lunched at his desk, drove home at the usual hour with no idea that he was being escorted. The hired help who rode his tail saw no sign of Goodrick and Co.

When J came in, Nanjo was on the phone. She greeted him, cut her call short, and scuttled to her own room. J's spirits sank.

Sophia seemed normal. As she reported the day to him, Sophia forgot to mention his father's call. She was full of other news. The woman who ran the Retreat had called just a while ago. Marietta was there, begging to be admitted. The woman wanted to know whether her daughter understood the way the place was run. It was a retreat yes, and also a home, not necessarily for the aged, the woman had explained in a calm and sensible voice, but for certain people who needed to "retire" from shocks and alarms. Nothing fancy was provided, but there were costs—food, maintenance, and so on; the place was financed as many retirement homes are. Those entering permanently (in the event they were accepted, that is) assigned what income they had for the common use. Now, the woman insisted upon a week's trial. Too many people, it seemed, thought this was going to be the life they needed. A week helped sort them out, but for this the woman had to ask a fee of one hundred dollars.

She then explained that she was not *selling.* She did not *need* another resident. She was, on the contrary, besieged. She could take in only about thirty. Therefore, she would not negotiate with an individual without having everything put clearly before those in connection with that person, who might not approve, or might even suspect that she ran some kind of racket.

Sophia had replied in the same tone, thanked her gravely, asked her to put Marietta into a cab, and said that she herself would come there, perhaps tomorrow, when it could all be discussed in a businesslike way.

"But where Marietta got the hundred dollars is what bothers *me*," Sophia cried.

J was rubbing his forehead. He looked so ghastly all of a sudden that Sophia was sorry she had poured all this out. "J, you're tired," she said. "Don't you worry about this. She's *my* mother. That woman was pretty smooth, but I don't have a brother Tobias for nothing."

"Thirty people, did you say? Not enough, either," he muttered.

"For heaven's sake," said Sophia tartly, "rest your bones. Have a drink. Have two. You look as if the whole world were sitting on your neck."

"Just call me Atlas," sighed J. "Maybe that's who I am."

He fixed himself a cocktail, knowing that Sophia's eye was on every sag of his spirits. It was just that Nanjo was apart from him, and Amy, too, and J was lonely and unsure and bumbling around in the dark, and yes, he *was* tired.

The phone rang; Sophia flew to it.

Win said, "Ma? How are you? How's Dad?"

"He's had a rough day," said Sophia. "How are you?"

"I was thinking about running over to talk to him. Marion thinks I should. I'm afraid there's some bother. . . . "

Sophia's mind discarded the thought of illness in a flash, and she said sharply, "Bother for your *father?*"

"Ma, it's a bit of a mess. Faulkner, by the way, is not giving me his business. He's taken off for South America."

"Well, I'm sorry," she said, "if that's bad."

"Well," said Win, "I won't say it's not a blow, but I can stagger along. However, we are selling the house."

"Oh?"

"And at least one car and the silver and the mink and the paintings (if anybody will give us anything for them) *and* the piano, I imagine."

"For heaven's sakes!" said Sophia.

"So you could say I'm retracting," Win said grimly. "It's not so much that. There's a matter of timing."

"Why time?"

"It takes time to sell a house," Win's nerves snapped.

"Naturally," Sophia was turning cold. "Hadn't you realized?"

"Ma?"

"You want to come and dump all this on your father, tonight?"

"I think I'd better."

"I think you'd better *not*," she said fiercely. "The man is tired. His father's after him. Did *he* call you, by the way?"

"Oh, yes, he called me."

"Okay, you take that over. I'll see to *my* mother. It's time some things were off your father's back. You're a big boy now."

"I may be," said Win wryly, "a fairly small man."

"Call me in the morning," said Sophia, softening. "I'll see how he feels then. I will *not* have him disturbed tonight. Here comes Marietta. I'm going to hang up, dear. Good luck. I'll have to say I'm glad that you're cutting back to a size you can manage. But if that's what you're doing, shouldn't you just *do* it?"

"It seems so," said Win. "You're right, Ma. As usual."

"Give my love to Marion."

"Yes."

"And the Little kids."

"Yes, and Ma, don't speak to Dad about any of this? *I'd* rather do that some other time."

"All right, dear."

Sophia paid the cab and bustled her mother into the house, not scolding too hard, but demanding to know about the money. Marietta was in tears; she said she feared she had cheated it out of the devil. So Sophia took it away (wondering what on earth she was going to do with it) and warned

Marietta very sternly that she herself would look into this
Retreat, but *J* was not to hear one word about it. Not one
word! Not *tonight*. She then relented and said that Marietta
would be moved, either to the Retreat or to the Wimple, as
soon as Sophia could arrange to do this, and she was *promising,* so would Marietta kindly cheer up and look on the
bright side?

Then Sophia went into Nanjo's room and admonished Nanjo, "Your father is very tired. I wlll *not* have him bothered.
So can you, for once, leave off stewing around in your own
little frenzies and pay some attention to *his* peace of mind?"

"Well, sure," whined Nanjo. "Mother, what's the matter
with Daddy?"

"None of your business *what,*" snapped Sophia. "Your
father happens to need, as human beings often do, some
peace and quiet and tender loving care. And he is going to
get it if *I* have to declare war on the entire rest of the
population."

So J had quiet and a kind of peace. All was more or less
well, he guessed. He was caught up at the office. There would
be no more than the normal number of crises tomorrow. All
was more or less serene here at home. Everyone thought of
his comfort. He appreciated Marietta's silence and Nanjo's
soft deference (he guessed he did) and Sophia's calm. He
appreciated the tender loving care. (Of course he did.) He
appreciated the good food, the lazy table talk which Sophia
conducted, being gently amusing, saying nothing to upset anybody. Nothing at all.

After dinner Marietta, of all things, went into his den to
watch television. Nanjo went to her room to study, or so she
said. Sophia began to knot on her ribbon costume in smiling
peace. The phone did *not* ring.

J settled down with a news magazine. It was as if the
spider had left off spinning and rested on his web. Resting on
my laurels? thought J with a pang.

He began to read about ghettos and urban decay, about
war and riot, crime and credibility gaps, alienated generations,
fads, drugs, violence, vandalism. And then he got to read a
piece all about the prospect of man building on the moon
pretty soon. Pretty soon.

CHAPTER 23

Friday Morning

It was a half an hour into Friday, half after midnight, and Tony Thees was watching the clock go around.

He was lolling in a chair in Annette's room, passing the time. "Had a run in with the old fella, didn't you?" (He might as well tease her a little bit. Anyhow he was curious.) "What'd he do? Call you a painted Jezebel?"

"Where did *you* ever hear of Jezebel?"

"I saw the movie," Tony laughed. "Come on, tell Papa. What happened?"

"Nothing's happened all day?" she said challengingly.

"Goodrick didn't dog him around *today*," said Tony. "I'll give you that."

"Then just let him alone. I'm telling you, Tony, if you up and hide Mr. Little someplace, they'll just beat up his family."

"And you'd rather they beat him up, eh?"

"Maybe I would," she said angrily.

"You know, sweetheart, I don't think I follow you."

"I told his wife you *were* following me," she said. "How do you like that for a pack of lies?"

"I followed you, eh? That's why I'm out here? Not bad. Calmed her jealous twitches, did it?"

"Oh, shut up, Tony! Go away. Go to bed. Elsewhere."

"Well," said Tony, "I'll certainly have to tell our beloved leader how cooperative you've been."

"Just kindly vanish," said Annette. "I'm so cross I could spit."

Tony proceeded to "vanish," using the fire stairs turning toward a back way out of the lobby. Damn, he never knew where he was with that ornery female! He batted the door with his shoulder. As it swung outward, it hit somebody.

"Sorry," said Tony, pushing out.

"Sorry," said Goodrick, baring his teeth and going in.

But in five minutes Goodrick pushed out again.

An hour later Mr. Jones said, "I am unwilling to believe in Tony Thees as a lovesick swain! Very well, he knows the girl. What does that mean? What has the man Little got to do with it?"

Goodrick shrugged. "Maybe the girl is his cousin."

"The old lady says so."

"She's crazy," said Goodrick sullenly. "The son never heard of the girl. It still could be." Goodrick didn't seem to care.

"Pressures?" said Mr. Jones restlessly. "What about the teenager?"

"Deal me out," said Goodrick. "*Them* I don't tangle with. At any price."

Mr. Jones winced slightly. "What about the grandchildren? I can hire you some help."

"I don't like them odds," said Goodrick. "No good, anyway. He'd tell, all right, for ransom. He'd crawl on his knees to tell. So? They'd call off the meeting."

"Halliwell Bryce holds no valid passport at this time," purred Mr. Jones, looking sly.

Goodrick rolled his eyes and waited.

"It is my conclusion that the rendezvous must be in this country. I have acted. The plane is here and ready."

Goodrick raised his brows.

"Listen to me," said Mr. Jones. "Leave out Asia, Africa, the Middle East, Scandinavia, and the U.S.S.R. Benet is not in France. It is said he is in Egypt. Conover is not in Australia. They say New York. Andrews is not in Scotland. Paccinetti is not in Italy. Lord Mumpson is not in England. They say Baumholtz is in Tokyo; he is not in Tokyo. But Halliwell Bryce is still at the university."

"Well, well," said Goodrick.

"I've got a watch on *him* night and day," said Mr. Jones. "He is our one remaining chance. Unless we have a second chance here with the man Little."

"It's boiled down to that, eh?" said Goodrick. "You think the meeting is on soon?"

"Don't you think so? And in this country? What do you think?"

"I think that if that's so, and the man Little knows where they are, Thees isn't going to let me get within ten feet of him."

"Test it," urged Mr. Jones. "Keep after him. See what Thees does then. I'll hire someone to follow Thees. Watch the girl. Money doesn't matter."

Goodrick said rather heavily, "Everybody must be crazy."

At 3 A.M. Mr. Smith said sharply to Tony Thees on the long distance telephone, "What's up, there?"

"Not much, sir. Had him dogged all day and no sign of the enemy. He's home safe with a guard on the house."

Mr. Smith made a noise like a geyser. "Hell's to pay. Everything was fine. All our misdirections worked perfectly. I got H.B. there myself tonight. Slick as butter. And guess who crashed the party, courtesy of the host, damn it. One bishop, Protestant. One cardinal, Catholic. One Evangelist, you wouldn't believe who! Two swamis, or something. And one rabbi, on the top of it!"

"Oh, oh!"

"You said it! Brains are valuable, but these characters are *popular!* I'm scared to get big help. Scares me—some innocent pilot minding his business, he's shot down. So then they know, eh? I'm warning you, your Little man ... You think he's safe?"

"So far," said Tony. "Can I get big help and put him away?"

"Don't *you* open that can of worms! No, no. Play it by ear, Tony, and God help us all if your ear's not good enough!"

Mr. Smith had lost his cool! Tony hung up and took a good grasp on his own.

On Friday morning J slipped into his smooth and well-worn groove, expecting that it would, as usual, be roughened here and there by small surprises. At ten o'clock there was a big surprise.

Bringgold called him into his office, offered him a cigar, which J took although he didn't want it, and then Bringgold confided that poor Tom must go. J didn't argue. In fact, he agreed. He knew that the wheels—the dark-blue wheels—must roll.

The thought of Amy crossed his mind. Was J coldhearted?

Well, he didn't know about that. There's more than one person in a business. If one man's very temperament constitutes sand in the gears, should even a warm heart let the whole machine grind to a halt? Probably J's heart was somewhere in the middle, neither cold nor warm.

But to J's astonishment Bringgold began to praise his handling of the late emergency. "You're damn good at this," the boss said, "and it ain't easy, as I should know."

"I guess it's in how you look at it," said J, who was feeling rather uncomfortable. "My gardener tells me all I do is sit on my fat can and get rich."

"Oh-ho, bo-hoy!" said Bringgold, looking startled. He was a man who never quite sat in a chair but used its seat as a base upon which to bounce slightly. Bringgold now suddenly acquired weight. "I'll tell you, J," he said, "my wife wants to travel. She's got a few shekels tucked away." He touched his glasses. "A man gets tired," he said, "and you wonder. . . ."

"Yes." said J (to his surprise) affectionately.

"Well, you're in line for this position. You can handle it, eh? You think so, don't you?"

"I am inclined to think so," said J slowly and judiciously.

"Self-confidence," said Bringgold heartily. "Doesn't scare *you*, eh? Well, we'll have to get Tom replaced. I think," said Bringgold, returning to his normal bouncing tension, "you ought to get better acquainted with the Partners in the next few weeks."

J rose and said, "I would enjoy that, sir."

Back at his own desk J was glad he had not said a jubilant "Herman," and also that his "sir" had not been too humble. What J really felt, he decided, was amusement. Bringgold's job didn't scare him. J was pretty sure he had been doing it for years. He would just be in the same middle, with a slightly different title and more salary. Humph!

The other side of the middle now approached.

"Sit down, Tom," said J, reading by his face that the young man had had the bad news. "I don't think," said J kindly, "you have ever really enjoyed this kind of work. Isn't that so?"

"There's too much in-fighting," Tom said. "I don't like disharmony. I'm too sensitive and aware," he blurted. "I haven't got your sangfroid."

"My what?" said J. (Ah, yes, the cold heart.)

"Well, *I* can't just ignore other people's feelings," said Tom.

"I was going to hint around," said J, "and suggest you look for a kind of work that suited you better."

"And you could care less that I got the ax," Tom said, all hot-eyed and hurt.

"You know what my sangfroid is asking me right now?" said J, leaning back. "Why in hell (it wants to know) should a man like you work where he feels so damned miserable day in and day out? You've got advantages. Some people may be trapped, but you mean to tell me you're not free to go do something else for a living? What do you lack? The nerve?"

Tom swallowed. "I'm pretty upset right now. I'm sorry. I mean you have always been a decent ... I'm sorry, Mr. Little." Tom rose and fled.

J practiced raising only one eyebrow. He did feel sorry for Tom, although not because he had been fired. J couldn't think offhand of a job where you'd *never* run into other people's feelings. Yes, he could! How about Avery's job?

His thought veered away, turned back, swooped in on this. Okay, what if you cut off the horizontal, left off trying to relate to your contemporaries, and went inside? All alone, hard and deep. What if some men could do that? (J *bet* it wasn't easy! Himself, he never got anywhere but all mixed up trying *that*). But supposing a man could, should he not? Without thought of selling his work to other men, because he was doing it out of himself, vertically, alone? Yet might he not be speaking, whether he would or not, to men of the depths of a man?

I'll be damned, thought J. Am I understanding Avery?

"Is this Sophia?" said the old gentleman on the phone with his usual air of surprise to find that his son's wife lived in his son's house. "May I speak to J, please?"

"Why he's at his office, Mr. Little. Is anything wrong?" Sophia had heard a trembling urgency in the voice.

"I'm afraid so. I'm afraid so. Tell J that I *must* see him."

"But what's the trouble?"

"I am in a dilemma. I am at a loss as to what I ought to do."

"I'm sure J will help if he can," said Sophia. "I know he is very, very busy. But I could come. Or could Win? He might help you, Mr. Little."

"No, no. It's a moral dilemma, you see. I would very much like to talk to J. Fairly soon. Perhaps not today."

"You don't feel ill?" (Sophia imagined herself hurrying down there.)

"Oh, no, no, no. I see, I realize that I *must* compose myself. Do you think J could come tomorrow?"

"Why, of course, if you need him."

"I wish that he would come," said the old gentleman pathetically. He hung up. He had a son J, did he not? Had the woman said "Winnie"? But Winnie was dead, or so he believed. His son Willy? No, Willy was gone. He thought he would have a sip of sherry and lie down for a bit. Alice was gone.

Cary caught Nanjo in the high school corridor. "Hey, how about tonight?"

"Oh, gosh, Cary. I can't."

"I want to talk. Why *not* tonight?"

"Well, my folks . . . I'm not supposed to go out."

Cary made a rude noise. His hand tightened on her arm.

"Cary, you're *hurting* me!"

"So what?" he said. "Come on, Nanjo. You can get out if you want."

Bells rang. They both began automatically to obey, moving toward their classrooms. Nanjo kept her head down. She had not pulled away from his hand and took note that he had slackened his grip.

"Gosh, Cary, I don't know what I can do. My—my Dad doesn't want me to date for a while. So what can I—"

Cary let her go. His hand came back to slap and sting her forearm.

"Ouch!" she said. "Hey!"

"Date *me,* eh? Your old man, yah! You should've seen what I saw, him and his girlfriend! Sure, he don't want you going out with *me.* So what?"

"I don't believe . . ." Nanjo was rigid.

"Tell him you're going over to Debby's. If I don't see you on the way, I'll honk my horn in front of your house and get some other guys and we'll all honk and your old man's going to love it." Cary walked swiftly on, leaving her behind.

Nanjo pulled wisdom out of her store.

"It isn't right not to *listen,*" she told herself (and her friend Debby, who had heard some of this). "You should always be willing to listen. Well, I'm not going out with him because I don't want to, but it's only fair to listen."

The truth was what Nanjo did not want was *listening*. For instance, J listening to Cary, who had been taught to believe that Nanjo kept in with her folks, quite cynically, because she was smart enough to know where profit was. And she didn't want Cary listening to J, who'd been taught to believe that Nanjo was no snob, but such as Cary didn't mean a thing in her real life, of course.

"There's the masculine ego, too," Debby said wisely.

"I don't want to *hurt* Cary," said Nanjo, wondering if she really could.

Marion was showing the man and his wife and the realtor around her house. "The view," she said, "is really marvelous."

"Was that *black* algae in your pool?" the woman said.

"The pool boy hasn't been this week," said Marion. "It's a fairly new pool."

"You can see that by the planting," said the man sourly. "I don't like kidney shapes, myself."

"You can see by the walls that children have lived here," the woman said.

Marion said softly, "They have loved it, but they do grow. Excuse me?"

As Marion fell behind, she heard the realtor say, "Definitely a prestige area."

The man in the living room, who had come to appraise the big painting that Avery had been about to throw away, said, "Mrs. Little, this artist, who is he? Not very well-known."

"We are sure," she said dreamily, "that he will be."

"Maybe you'd better hold it for an investment," he said contemptuously.

"I would like very much to keep it," said Marion quietly. "But it needs a huge wall. I suppose a private person can't hope, really . . ."

He glanced at her sharply and then back at the painting.

Marion thought, I'm doing this quite well.

Mrs. Arriola, leaning on her mop, said, "Oh, Miz Neeby, there's bad trouble over there. As plain as plain to me."

"I heard they fired the gardener," said Susie carelessly.

"Oh, Miz Neeby, that Nancy Jo, she didn't ought to go

around the way she goes. She's going to break her mama's heart one of these days. And poor Mr. Little, he ain't feeling *right*. Something happened to that man! Oh, something's preying on him, all right! Oh, Miz Neeby, this fancy-looking girl, she turns up for lunch, and oh, Miz Neeby, I'm telling you—Miz Little, *she* wasn't so crazy about *her*."

"I thought she was a cousin of Mr. Little's."

"Oh, I dunno about that," said Mrs. Arriola with dark looks. "You know Miz Thomas? Now, Miz Thomas, she don't never want to face life. But oh, Miz Neeby, she seen something!"

"What did she see?" said Susie helplessly.

"I dunno what she seen," said Mrs. Arriola, "but, oh, Miz Neeby, it was nothing good, I can tell you that."

The ghost of Marietta's voice took brief possession.

"But it's a lovely home," said Mrs. Arriola. "And a real nice family."

CHAPTER 24

Friday Afternoon

At one o'clock, as J had decreed on the telephone, they came, and J had them shown into his office.

"This is Tony Thees, Mr. Little," the girl said. "How are you, sir?"

Gone was the turned-on allure, the little girl lost in the jungle of romance, the mischievous con woman. But J didn't care who she was being today.

"Miss Woods. Mr. Thees," he said in his business voice, "sit down. Mr. Thees, mind telling me what you said to me on the phone the other night?"

"I said I hadn't seen you since Noah built the Ark," said the young man quickly. "That's pretty good, sir."

J said, "Don't patronize me, please. Answer my questions."

"Sir, I—uh—don't think we should be here long. Goodrick is downstairs right now. He'll be wondering."

"I don't give a damn what he's wondering," said J. "I am not going to lunch with you two unless and until I get some answers."

Annette opened her mouth. Tony said, "I'll talk." Then, to J, "All I can tell you, Mr. Little, is that you may be in physical danger."

"Is that so?" drawled J.

"Tony—" the girl began.

"Be quiet," said Tony. "Mr. Little, I realize you are naturally bewildered. But it will soon be over. There's a time limit. Only let us protect you for a few more days."

"Days? And the danger will be over?"

"That's right. And also, any need for you to keep your promise."

(Indulgence, condescension, comfort from the wise?)

"How many days?" snapped J. (A week is only seven days, and what's a day?)

"Not many," the wise young man evaded.

"I'll be released from my promise?"

"That's right."

"*You* will release me?"

"That I will."

"But not now?"

"Not now."

Annette said, "Mr. Little, please consider kind of ... getting lost? Tony could fix it. It would be so much safer for you."

"Would my family know where I was, and why?" J was asking Tony.

"They would not," Tony said. "We'd tell them something, of course."

"Nothing doing," said J.

"But I would go to stay in your house," said Annette. "I'm trained, sir. I could protect. . . ."

J ignored her completely. (As if she's a babbling infant, bothering grown-ups, Tony thought, amused.)

"Tell me this," said J, smiling because he and the young man were at least being crisp. "Is it true that some men are building an ark to go to the moon?"

Tony hesitated. "That may be an allegorical way to put it," he said. "Please listen. Goodrick is only going on some kind of very slim hunch. All he's got is this. He heard you promise Doctor Willing, by way of quotation, wasn't it? that you would be *silent*. Is that so?"

"Yes," said J, feeling hit. "Yes, I guess that's so."

"Doctor Willing told me about that," said Tony. "You couldn't have known, of course, who Goodrick . . ."

"Don't comfort me, please," said J. "Who *is* Goodrick?" Tony shook his head. "Dangerous," he said. "We hoped that his interest would fizzle out, but he's still dogging you. Right now."

"What can he do to me?"

Annette said, "We don't want him to do anything! That's the—"

Tony stepped on her sentence with one of his own. "If you will just stay close to your own home, sir? In fact, stay right there over the weekend as well as this evening? That may be good enough. As long as Goodrick has nothing but a hunch, he may not risk . . . well . . . violence."

J said, "But *I* do it blind? I don't even know the secret I'm supposed to be keeping. Do I?" He pounced.

Tony said, "Believe in the danger. I'll have someone riding your tail home tonight, as I have had since Monday. Believe we are on *your* side, Mr. Little."

"Mine and who else's?" said J.

Annette said, "You don't understand, Tony."

Tony said, "Just a minute. *I* have a question. Do I take it that if Goodrick asks . . . in any uncomfortable way—you intend to answer?" He looked thoughtful.

J said, "This is what I *intend*. It so happens that we have a bridge game on tonight at home. It so happens that I have yard work tomorrow, in my own yard. Now, I *intend* to keep my promise to the man I knew as Barkis. But I am promising *you* nothing. I'm giving you my schedule. What I think, you kids have been making this whole affair into something a lot sillier than it ever had to be."

"That may be true," said Tony, seeming to be hit. "Thank you, Mr. Little."

Annette said, "Mr. Little, I think you are . . . I think you are being . . ."

She seemed to be struggling for words of praise, so J said, "Some hero, *I* am! Not everybody is damn fool enough to keep a secret—he doesn't even know what it is. But *you* know?" He looked at Tony steadily.

Tony looked steadily back but didn't answer.

"And *she* knows, eh?" growled J. "How come Goodrick is bothering about a fellow like me when here's a frail little female he could take and torture anytime he'd want?"

Annette said quickly, "He doesn't know I am connected."

"Watching me with blindfolds on, eh?" said J. "You say he's downstairs? He knows *now*, doesn't he?"

"She doesn't know a very important factor," said Tony.

"Ah," said J, "but *she* knows that *I* do?"

He saw the blood departing from under Tony's tan.

"Let's go to lunch," said Annette, becoming extremely practical. "Goodrick will listen in if he can, and he probably can. So Tony and I have this big act we can put on. It would muddle him, at least. Please, Mr. Little? Cousin J?"

J, still looking steadily at Tony, said, "All right, Cousin Annie. You owe me a lunch, I guess."

He was thinking that this Tony seemed to believe in the danger. J wasn't altogether sure that *he* did, yet. But the affair was certainly interesting; in fact, bizarre. It had cheered him up to hear that there was a time limit on it.

In the lobby Tony argued for an excellent place he knew; he had a car. But J flatly said he hadn't the time to go so far, and there was a fair place right across the street that would have to do. He sensed a faint air of dismay about the young people as they crossed over. He couldn't figure why.

The maître d' came, bustling and bowing and calling J by name, to find them a table immediately. After all, J thought, amused, a regular customer is a valuable asset, and her looks don't hurt, either. Their table was set into a semi-circle of soft bench.

"Why don't you," said Annette prettily, "sit in the middle, Cousin J?"

"Where else?" said J cheerfully and slid along the leather.

The maître d' inquired about cocktails. "Damn right," said J.

Tony said easily, "You'll have the usual, sweetheart? What's your fancy, Mr. Little?"

J named his fancy and picked up the menu. Tony gave the drink orders. Annette had her lipstick out and was painting her mouth.

Tony said, "At last, I've met the famous Cousin J!"

"He's going to be snide, Cousin J," said Annette, being very feminine and coy. "He was all wrong about you, and that makes him furious." She was testing her lipstick on a doily. No, she was printing.

"I was saying I'm glad to meet him," Tony protested. "What's snide about that?"

J looked at the fat red letters on the doily. *G can hear. Follow cues.*

J's head began to come up, but she put her hand on his arm and said, "Please, Cousin J? You are going to help us?"

"I don't know," said J in a bewildered mumble. He sat back and looked at the room and, sure enough, there was Goodrick, way over against the other wall.

"After all," Tony was saying in a voice that was not very loud but had some carrying quality, "I had a hard time believing in your existence, Mr. Little. Here's my girl. I ask her to marry me. She says No, she won't, and then and there she takes off for California. Can you blame me if I want to know what's going on out here?"

J said feebly, "That ain't the way *I* heered it." (How could Goodrick hear, from where he was?)

"What kind of yarn have you been telling him?" Tony was demanding.

"I just said I was confused about you," said Annette, "and if that isn't the truth, let lightning strike me down." Her eyes caressed him.

"Wait, wait," said Tony. "She loves me," he said to J, "with all her pore little heart. So she should marry me. Obvious?"

"It's not *that* simple," said Annette.

And Tony said at the same time, "It's as simple as that."

"Hey, hey," said J. "If I'm supposed to be the referee, give me one side at a time." The drinks had come, and he sipped his gladly. There were devices, he guessed, for listening from afar. He'd seen them advertised.

The young people put on quite a show, J thought, as they proceeded to have a lovers' quarrel, making no sense whatsoever in a most realistic way. He even began to suspect there must be a grain or two of truth underneath.

Goodrick was listening to this stuff?

"I think you're afraid of marriage," Tony said disdainfully. "You won't even try. Cousin J, she says she doesn't want to move her furniture. What the . . ."

"You heard him say try," she cried. "That's the way he thinks, Cousin J."

J was taking the opportunity to study this young man. He rather liked Tony's looks, as looks go. The eyes were intelligent; the face was clean. If his manner and his tone were slightly scoffing, as if to say, Nobody fools *me*, that was the style among men of his age. Win could behave just so.

J kept playing benevolent bewilderment, and they kept carrying on. Food came. J ate heartily.

This wasn't getting *him* anywhere. He had only agreed to the appointment to try getting something out of this Tony. But he had not. Not much. J felt he might as well take nourishment, anyhow.

But after a while he realized that he wasn't contributing a lot to the act, and why shouldn't he have some fun?

He rapped on the table. "Okay, you kids. Okay. Now, listen to wisdom."

"She's asking for a guarantee I'm not going to give her," said Tony angrily.

"Nobody ought to marry anybody for a long weekend," the girl said. "Cousin J knows what I mean."

"I do not think that you should marry him at all," said J pompously.

"You don't?" she said, not sounding joyous.

"And you," said J to Tony, "shouldn't marry her, either."

"Why not?" said Tony belligerently.

"Because," said J, "I am going to tell you both exactly what to do instead. Cousin Annie," he shook his coffee spoon at her, "you go home."

"What?"

"Get yourself on some airplane, quick, and go home, wherever that is. And maybe get a job that keeps you out of mischief. And find a man who bores you *sometimes*. You need a rest, child. And you, Tony.... On vacation, are you?"

"Things are a little slow right now," said Tony. "Why?"

"Okay then, *you* stick around out here. Put this girl out of your mind. Stay a couple of weeks. Make the scene. You don't want to marry her."

"I don't?"

"Because she's right, and you're wrong about marriage. But her trouble is, with all her fascinating moods and switches, she's practicing to *be* a weekend woman."

They were both slightly stunned. They couldn't know he had his clown face on.

"The two of you come around, dragging me into this, begging my advice—I'll tell you something you may not have thought of. Believe me," said J, "on Mondays, Tuesdays, Wednesdays, and Thursdays a man needs a woman he can get used to. And maybe vice versa."

He pushed against Tony, who was forced to get up and let him out.

"I've got to get back to the office," J said. "Thanks for the lunch. And you're welcome for the wisdom. So long, children."

He went briskly away, threading diagonally between tables, not looking at Goodrick, although he was tempted.

Tony thumped back into his seat and, keeping to the role, growled, "Well?"

"Oh, listen, Tony," she said, "I *am* going home. Don't follow me. Please don't?"

"I'll do what I feel like doing," said Tony. "He's not *my* fuddy-duddy old cousin. Now, don't bawl!"

Annette took the cue and began to cry into her table napkin.

A man at the table just behind them put the small tape recorder into his pocket and got up. Across the room Goodrick got his signal, covered his teeth, and called for the check.

In Tony's car Tony said after a while, "No Goodrick after *us.*"

"Is that good?" she said dully.

"They can't get him in his office. Better make a reservation, sweetheart."

"I'll make it for Monday," she said defiantly.

"Check out," he snapped, "at four this afternoon. Pay the extra day. Meet me at Travel Town, Griffith Park. That's an order."

"Yes, sir. What are you going to do?"

"Find you a hidey hole. And keep the guard on him. But no face Goodrick connects. Damn it," he added under his breath.

She sighed. They were on the Santa Monica Freeway. She took the doily out of her purse, tore it to pieces, and held the pieces to the rush of air outside the speeding car until they were torn, one by one, from her fingers.

She said fiercely, "You'd *better* guard that old fuddy-duddy."

"I'll have to," said Tony.

He wished he could call in the Army, the Navy, and the Air-Force. He thought there was no other sure way. *Nothing* was sure about this job. Unless it was that everything had narrowed in on one Little man. The brains were gathered; all of them had made it successfully. Even the religious contingent had slipped through into danger and had aroused no publicity. The only loose end was a Little man who did not know what he knew. Nor did Goodrick and Co. yet know *for sure* that J M. Little knew anything at all. So Tony must guard him while not seeming to guard, and all these uncertainties sucked power out of him.

Tony recognized the added feature, that he ought to keep the Little man from harm for the man's own sake. Tony was afraid he had made a mistake again. Should he have told the Little man the whole truth? Maybe he had played it too smart, taken the risk in the wrong direction.

The girl put both hands to her face suddenly.

"I'll admit he wasn't exactly what I expected," said Tony, feeling funny. He beat this down as sentimentality.

The tape from the restaurant having been played to him, Mr. Jones cried, "Lovers!" His head trembled. He looked as if he would like to do away with any and all lovers, they being the nuisance they were to serious men. "We have lost Halliwell Bryce," he mourned. "Do you realize this was all we had? And now you say that Thees was following the man Little because he was a *jealous lover!*" Mr. Jones might weep at any moment.

"Shall I pay off the help?" asked Goodrick in a practical way. "Here comes Clooney."

Another man entered the hotel room. "Thees dropped her at her hotel. Went on to his own," he reported.

"May as well take the man off the hotels, eh?" said Goodrick to his boss.

"Where? Where? All I want is the target. Will there be another target?" Jones said brightly, trying not to cry.

"She threw this out of the car on the freeway," Clooney said, "I only got this one piece. Had to stop on the shoulder, and a man could get killed."

Goodrick took the piece of paper. "Lipstick, eh?" He read

the four large letters. "*CUES*. What the devil English word has got that combination?"

Mr. Jones was looking over his shoulder. "I'm surprised at you, Barry," he chided softly. "That *is* an English word, is it not?"

Goodrick's upper teeth met his lower set, but not in a smile.

CHAPTER 25

Friday Evening

When the Neebys appeared at a quarter of eight, J had the bridge table and chairs already set up in the family room. They settled down amid chirps and twitters from the females. The draperies were open. The glass wall on the back of the house, as seen from the depths of the garden, framed a bright stage.

It was dark out there. The moon had not yet risen. A man, who was trying to make himself comfortable on the cold grass behind the heaps of elm boughs, could not see the shape that came prowling from the far side of the garage, turned the corner, and slipped along the deep shadow of the garage itself, where a jutting forth of the kitchen wing let no house light fall.

On stage J was doing his story about the mishap in Chicago, the dowager, the traffic jam, cops and ambulance, the trouser-napping, and his pitiable plight in the hospital. Gladstone Neeby was a big man with a deep laugh, but when the tale had been told, he wanted to know if J had got any damages out of the deal. "Seven hundred and fifty bucks," J told him. Susie looked enlightenment at Sophia, and Sophia winked.

Goodrick had found the back door from kitchen to yard. It was not locked.

Tony's man, nesting in the elm boughs, pricked up his ears. What was that click?

They were paired off, a man and the other man's wife, as usual. Susie dealt, chattering on about that gorgeous gown. Sophia said she'd changed her mind and taken it back. Couldn't face the upkeep. Susie cried woe.

Nanjo came out of the bedroom wing with a long white sweater over her cotton frock. She greeted and was greeted and said she was going to run over to Debby's for a little while.

"Don't be too late," said Sophia, as usual.

"It's not a school night."

"Have fun," said J, as usual—thinking that her peers might help her more than he could.

"On foot after dark?" frowned Susie when Nanjo had gone.

"It's two blocks," said Sophia. "Some boy will see her home. One club."

J, at her left, said, "Pass." (And thought he guessed he *did*.)

Glad said, "Two no trump," in a firm and manly voice.

Susie wrinkled her brow and began to count her points again.

"Say," said Glad in the interim, "how come they're checking up on you, J? I didn't realize you had to have clearance."

"What you don't know won't hurt you," said J blandly. (He did *not* believe this, he realized with a pang. It wasn't true.)

"That so?" said Glad cheerfully.

Goodrick was moving silently across the dim kitchen.

Win answered their phone.

"Win? Amy," said his sister. "Hey, I need some money. Bad."

"Ow! So do I, little sister. What's wrong now?"

"I've had Avery here in the hospital all day," she told him, "and it's not good. They're going to operate first thing in the morning."

"Gosh, I'm sorry. What is it?"

"Oh, Lord," his sister said, "it's something back of his *eyes*. It's going to be a long, hard thing they'll have to do. It's going to cost like hell. And I'm supposed to put down something for the hospital right away."

"How much?"

"They say a hundred dollars, and they won't kick him out into the street." Her voice was tight.

"I'll get it to you," said Win. "We're in a mess, selling the house and most of the stuff. But I'll get that much to you. Don't worry."

"Oh, Amy!" said Marion on the other phone. "What's the matter?" Amy told her. "Couldn't you call your father?" Marion said. "Does *he* know about this?"

"No, and I'd kind of rather not—ask him for *money*. But if it's too much on you guys, I can do that."

"No, no," said Win. "Don't bother Dad. I'll be right down." When he hung up, he said to Marion, "Leave my father out of this. Will you do that?"

"Win, you can't afford it. And besides, I don't like being left . . ."

"I don't give a damn whether I can afford it or not," he said furiously.

After he left the house, Marion locked all the doors very carefully.

The man behind the elm boughs saw Goodrick's shadow cross the pale kitchen window, and he whistled like a bird.

"Where is your mother tonight, Sophia?" asked Susie Neeby. "She hasn't left, has she?"

"No, no. She's off hobnobbing with some friends in Hollywood."

"Hollywood?" Susie was ready to be amused if this would sit well with her friend.

"They live in a hotel called the Wimple," Sophia explained, "and Mother likes to go there."

"Why?" said Susie innocently.

"Because they're a pack of nuts," said Sophia calmly.

"Down one, partner," said Glad woefully. "Couldn't do a thing with it."

Sophia felt a ripple in her shoulder blades. "Does anybody feel a draft?" she asked.

"Not me," said Susie. "My deal?"

"Nothing's open," said J, putting down the score. "Thirty on, partner. We didn't get wiped out, remember."

"Say J," said Susie, "I saw you with a pretty snazzy blonde the other day."

"Lemme see," said J, "which day was it I saw the blonde? Tuesday was the redhead." Everybody knew this was absurd.

Cary Bruce had his foot on the accelerator; he played with it. The engine muttered, raced, fell to a purr, according to his mood.

"If you're going to keep on telling stupid lies . . ." he growled.

"I am not!" said Nanjo.

"Yah! Your Mom already bought the damned dress. You *had* it. Sure you did! But you don't want it. So she takes it back. What kind of crappo. . . ."

Nanjo hugged her bare arms. She'd left her sweater in Debby's front hall. She'd walked the two blocks nervously and had seen no Cary. But almost before she had greeted Debby, they had heard him honking.

Nanjo felt she really ought to try to help him. "Listen, Cary, never mind about the dress. Don't you get in a big mess. Don't *do* it. If you got caught, you'd have it on your back, and it's not worth it."

Cary swore from sheer misery. He had just now heard that somebody else had hit the gas station last night. This was an outrage. He and his pals had even driven *by* the place, casing the job. The effort was wasted? He'd braced himself up to the daring deed to no purpose? He hadn't told Nanjo this part. He wanted her to talk him out of it, and so acquire merit, somewhere. She was firmly in her posture of being a kind of Uncle Tom among squares. "It's stupid," she argued.

"And you're smart, eh?" Cary wasn't going to succumb too soon on the basis of cowardly common sense.

Nanjo switched her attack. "Okay, if you have to show off," she said. "But don't you ever say you did it for *me*. I don't want to get messed up. I've got better things . . ."

"Yah!" he growled. *"You!"* His motor raced. "Don't want me to do it for you," he mocked. His motor roared and subsided.

"You didn't think it through, anyhow," Nanjo announced. "How could I wear the dress in the parade if you gave me the money?"

"Why not?"

"Because my folks would want to know where I got it. What could I—"

"Why should they have to know?"

"Stupid! They'll *be* there, of course."

Cary, whose folks never came near anywhere that he was on display, said, "How come you're so scared of your folks all of a sudden?"

"I'm not scared all of a sudden. And my Mom *did* buy the dress."

"Hey! Hey! I get it," pounced Cary. "This bird you dated Tuesday, *he* gave you the money. So *you* were the stupid one. So your folks took it back, and they grounded you. Yah! I get it." He laughed raucously. "What did you do for *him?*"

"I am getting right out of this car!"

He yanked the lever. The car leaped.

"Cary, I told you! I can't go anywhere . . ."

"So jump," he said, accelerating.

Life was too much for Cary this evening. He was furious with the whole universe, and for revenge only Nanjo Little was handy. Prolly she'll think I did it *last night*, he thought. "Call the fuzz," he jeered. "Baby, you know too much."

Nanjo drew into her corner and sat very still. This was the way you handled them. Don't react. If they want to scare you, don't be scared. The car hurtled on. It screamed on the corners. Nanjo was a little bit scared. She was afraid the police might pick them up. But she knew she had better not say so, or they would.

"Some people don't understand money *a*-tall," J was proclaiming.

"What do you mean by that?" Glad wanted to know.

"I mean they don't see it as I see it," said J, "and *I* am absolutely right, naturally."

"Blood of trade, eh?" said Glad Neeby casually.

"You've got it. Listen, if they abolished money, they'd just have to go ahead and reinvent it."

"That's what they do," said Neeby. "Cigarettes? Chocolate? Three hearts."

Susie passed. Sophia said, "Four hearts. What can I lose?"

J passed and began to chuckle. "I had this nutty idea. I was thinking about all us folks in the middle . . . do the work . . . pay the taxes. . . ."

"Not this, again," said Sophia in mock dismay as she laid out the dummy.

"What's all this, J? Darned right, we pay taxes," said Susie.

"What if we got to vote our *money?*"

"Huh?"

"Sure," said J. "Cast it, see? Let them take a pie-shaped ballot. You know those pies. And send it out at income tax time. Everybody gets to assign a percentage of his tax, *whatever* that is, the way *he* wants the government to spend it." J began to heave with mirth. "Can you imagine sitting up all night to listen to the tax returns? Talk about suspense!"

"That's pink, I think," said Glad. "Or else it's fascist. Hey, partner, not bad!" He began to play rapidly with concentration. Everybody had to keep up with him. "Game," he said, "so take your ace of clubs."

"Oh, boy," said J, taking his ace of clubs. "Every damn bureau would have to put on a campaign to justify itself. But nobody would vote them the money to *do* that. Imagine the post office, shaking in its sacks? All those invisible men? Betcha some tax day people would forget, and we wouldn't *have* any mail!" J heaved.

Glad Neeby said mildly, "What about people who've got no money, got no tax, got no vote?"

"Oh, we'd all get to vote for the President and all that, just as we do now."

"What difference would that make when you got the country run by the millionaires?" Glad's voice kept lazy, but his eye was narrowing.

"I do?" said J. "I thought there was more money in the hands of widows than anybody else."

"Hey," said Susie, "maybe he's got something. No *woman* is going to vote umpteen billion dollars to kill people. Especially boys!"

"Well, I don't know," drawled Sophia. "If you could get rid of a few catty females for, say, four ninety-five—"

"Oh, if it was on sale," said Susie solemnly.

J kept on chuckling. "Want to bet the American people wouldn't have the most pampered cats and dogs in history?" He was tickled by his fancy, which was absurd. But not too much more absurd than anything else. How could it be?

Tony said explosively on the phone, "What's he doing in the house?"

"Nothing, so far. Hummel's got a gun on him. At what point should he shoot. Or should we bust in right away?"

"Don't let Little be *taken*," said Tony. "Hold it as long as you can. I'm coming."

"It wouldn't work, pal," said Neeby. "The people, for Pete's sake, can't understand everything the government is doing. I'll bet no one man, in government or out, understands it all right now. Got to depend on somebody else to give you the gist. You try and keep track of the whole blooming thing *yourself*—In the first place you *can't,* and in the second place you're not going to get any work done. Who's hexing these cards?"

"Our name is Legion," sighed J. (Some revelations I get, he thought. Here's Glad Neeby—knew them all the time.)

"Whose name is Legion?" Glad inquired.

"Oh, the ones in the middle, slogging along. . . ."

"Everybody's in the middle if you ask me." Glad was arranging his hand briskly. "If you're not, man, you're in trouble."

"Okay, okay," said J, to whom his friend's remark was perfectly lucid. "But how many really want to go?"

"Go where?"

"Oh, to the moon. You want to go?"

"Not me," said Glad. "I've got high blood pressure. Four spades."

"Hex, he says!" said Susie. "Pass."

Sophia said, "I know what that means, but I forget what I need to say."

Goodrick, whose head was beginning to ache, could make no sense out of *any* of this. He wished the Neebys would go home.

Outside the glass wall a man was prone in the azaleas watching, on a diagonal past the card table, the door from the family room into the kitchen. He had a gun in his hand.

Win stood with his sister in the doorway to the darkened hospital room. "It'll be okay," she whispered. "Go on home, Win."

He put his arm around her and squeezed. "Marion's nervous," he said. "We'll both be holding our thumbs for Avery."

"*Sssh*—I'm going to stay right by him. The doctor said I could."

"Want me to call Ma and Dad? Tell them what's happening?"

"What could they do, tonight?" she said stupidly. "Avery wouldn't want them and I . . . well, I have to be with him. I'll see, in the morning. . . ."

Win squeezed her again and went away.

"I don't want to go in there," said Nanjo.

Cary had parked in front of a tavern, a blank door that did not, she knew it could not, in this part of town, conceal anything but a dive.

Cary swore. He said, "What's the matter with you? You been telling me stupid lies the whole damn night. Come on, we're going in and have a beer, so what's bugging you?"

"I don't want to," Nanjo said. He clutched her arm hard and breathed on her cheek.

"Afterward," he said, "I know where we can go."

"I want to go home," whined Nanjo.

"Well, listen at that!" Cary let go and began to get out at his side. Nanjo grabbed for the latch, tumbled out on her side, and began to run.

Cary yelled after her. He yelled terrible things. But he did not follow.

"Seven hundred rubber," said Glad Neeby. "Off your game tonight, aren't you, J?"

"Listen," said Susie indignantly, "if you don't get the tickets . . ."

"Game of skill. Absolutely," said her husband. "Am I right, partner?"

Sophia was on edge. She couldn't pull the required cliché out of her mouth. She only smiled.

J said, "There just ain't enough tickets to go around." He was looking at his wife. What is it? his eyes asked.

Her eyes answered, I don't know.

Nanjo had some notion where she was. She was on low ground in a shabby section of a shabby business street, but she knew where the high ground lay. She had never been on foot on a street like this one; she had better get off of it. But it was at least better lighted than the side streets that lay, somehow bleak, in shadow.

She tried to guess where the nearest bus line would be. Up the slope a way, surely. And up higher she might find a place to telephone. She could ask Daddy to come. She didn't want to do that. She'd rather manage to get home by herself.

Then she saw, ahead on her present course, three men standing under the streetlight at the next corner. They were all looking her way; they must have heard Cary yelling. Well, she would just stiffen into brisk decisive behavior, just as if she were fine, thank you, and knew exactly what she was doing.

So she crossed in the middle of the block to the other side of this avenue. Traffic was light. Nanjo was nimble. Now she could double back and turn uphill on a side street. When she came to the turning point, she glanced to her left. One of the men had detached himself from the corner group and was coming along the avenue in her direction. Nanjo set her legs to driving hard.

The side street was residential, she guessed. But the dwellings were mean, and Nanjo didn't know what kind of people lived in such places. Didn't *know*. She had always thought of herself as above any snobbery. But the truth was, she did not really know people who must manage on very much less of an income than her parents. She must get home, that's all. Back to what she understood.

And she'd better not get silly and begin to imagine there was a man following her. And she'd better not run. No, no. Steady and fast, up the slope to the next well-lighted cross street. How many blocks was that? Three? Four?

At the next intersection she paused to look both ways for traffic and for any sign of a drugstore, for instance, lighted, still open, safe. No, no, the cross street was dreary and deserted. But now, under the lamp that hung above this intersection, she was able to see the man. He was right over there on the corner opposite. He was looking at her. He *had* followed her.

He was Cal, the gardener.

Nanjo's heart bounced up and seemed to choke her. It thumped down. She set her face to be looking straight ahead, to give no encouragement, no sign, no signal. She crossed and walked, as fast as she could without running, on up the slope. But she was breathing as if she were running a race.

The neighborhood *must* get better. What did she mean by better? She meant more like her *own* neighborhood? She meant houses that were smarter, neater, more expensive? She meant something familiar, that she could trust because it *was* familiar? But the houses were almost all dark. She didn't *know*. She didn't want to go pounding frantically on any of these doors. She didn't want to make a big deal out of this, anyway. She wanted to get herself home, independently, quietly, secretly. So keep going—just another block or two. He wouldn't—

She knew when Cal crossed over to her side of the street; she thought she heard him call her name too close behind.

Oh, God! Oh, no! *Please!* Panic came in.

She saw the church. It was on the next corner, a plain structure of stucco with blank walls. Where was the door? At the corner? Around the corner? Would it be locked? Oh, would this be sanctuary? Would Cal follow her in and rape her on a pew? No. Yes. What difference would it make if she were in a church if he wanted to *do* it!

Nanjo began to run. He called again. The church was blank, dark, lifeless. Nobody was there. No person. So what good ... Then she saw that on the downhill side of the church there was, below the sidewalk level, a paved yard, a kind of Sunday-school playground, perhaps. The church had a lower story, and there was a door down there.

Nanjo didn't know where the main door was. Anyway, it would be locked. And so would that door down there (into the nursery, maybe?). But maybe she could hide! Just vanish. Hide in the dark. Stop breathing. Fool him. Escape him. Get away, free.

She was in shadow as she came to the flight of concrete steps that led down. Ah, they were not a solid block. She could hide *under* them. Quick as a cat she put her hand on the iron rail, slipped under it, and jumped lightly down. She felt strong and clever. She was *young*. She could do anything! She wasn't going to get messed up. She was going to get out of this, escape, *get home!*

She crept under the slant of the steps. There might be spiders, snakes. She didn't know. But above her there was a more dangerous creature.

She began to be able to hear his breathing. She had

stopped her own. Her lungs were bursting, but her wits raced. Did he know where she had gone? Was he coming down after her? Well, if he did, she could crawl through to the other side (or not, depending upon how he turned), and she would whisk up the steps before he knew it. What was he doing? Her ears were beginning to ring.

Now she could hear his voice. Oh, it was Cal, the gardener. He had an impediment. He was speaking less intelligibly than ever. She couldn't make out . . . oh! He was *drunk! He was drunk!* So he wouldn't care. He wouldn't think of stopping to think. He had lost his job because of her. He wouldn't care *what* he did to Nancy Jo Little!

She *had* to breathe. She made a sound, a gasp. She couldn't help it. She heard his boots scrape.

Nanjo had time to wonder who it was, kneeling on hurting knees in the dirt and the dark, where no one on earth—no one but Cal, the gardener—knew where she was. What girl was this?

Above her he yipped, soprano, and then like a muted explosion he crashed, and she heard him come thudding and softly tumbling down. And now there was no sound at all.

Goodrick, in the shadowed kitchen, was feeling for the flash in his pocket. It had a handy shape. He didn't carry guns. He didn't believe in them. Unnecessary. *They,* having no guns, either, were thoroughly trained to believe in them, and the illusion would do. Speed and surprise. He'd herd them into a corner. He'd threaten the women. He'd get it out of Little and shut them all up with more threats. Goodrick was tired of waiting around. They'd never go home.

At the back, outside, the man flat among the azaleas was wishing he knew the floor plan of the house. He wasn't sure how many ways he ought to be watching.

At the front, outside, Marietta toddled up the path and touched the doorbell.

Sophia pushed back her chair quickly. She was very glad to move. Must be her mother, she said to the rest. J suggested they all needed refills; he went behind the bar. Goodrick drew back deeper into the kitchen. The man in the azaleas was cursing to himself. Too much movement in there.

Marietta, conducted to the family room by her daughter, did not respond to greetings with normal effusions. She had been, in some desperation, at the movies with a friend from the Wimple, and the picture had terrified her. She had never seen such a world!

When Susie asked, sacrificially, whether Marietta would like to take her hand, Marietta said No, she wouldn't for the world interrupt their pleasure. (Meantime Glad Neeby was fanning and folding and refanning his cards, because she had.) There was a kind of social impasse; J announced that the ice was melted.

Marietta, at once, waddled over and snatched up the ice bucket. "Oh, let me!" she cried. "I can fetch some ice. I can do *that*." She started for the kitchen.

Something in her cry made Susie seek Sophia's eye, but Sophia wouldn't look. Sophia sat down at the card table stiffly. J was putting mixings into the glasses. Glad put his hand of cards facedown and sighed.

As Marietta was still feeling for the kitchen light switch beside the doorjamb, Goodrick caught her from the other side with his left arm over her chin. "Keep quiet," he said into her ear. "You want to die?" But Marietta's finger, dragging down the wall in terror, turned the light on.

As the kitchen light bloomed, it cast a bright band out across the planting of azaleas. The man there flattened himself. Marietta could not scream, but Goodrick felt a ripple of alarm. He glanced out the window. He dragged the old lady deeper into the kitchen. "How do I get *out?*" he said into her ear. "Garage? Where's the door?"

She still had the ice bucket by its handle. She lifted her arm and tried to point.

Goodrick saw the door. "Keep quiet," he growled, "or I'll take you with me all the way to hell." He gave her a shove that sent her staggering to lean on the counter. The ice bucket fell with a clatter. "Death," she said in a low, hoarse voice. But he was across and out the door that led through a short passage to the garage. The big overhead door to the driveway was open and hung high. Goodrick slunk down the aisle between the two cars, slipped quickly to his left, and was lost in the shrubbery. He'd seen a gun in the azaleas; this house and garden were no place for him. "Death?" Her and her angels! What did *he* know? He shuddered.

"What was that?" Sophia said. Her cards went splattering. She got up.

"Just a minute," said J, warning her not to move farther. His house. He would go and see.

The Neebys sat paralyzed, staring toward the kitchen. So the man in the azaleas crawled like a huge, lively worm out of the light.

But Goodrick was racing across the Neeby's lawn. A car started to life. It was moving as he leaped aboard.

J said, "What happened, Marietta?"

Still leaning on the counter, she turned her head. "The angel of darkness," she whimpered. "The angel of death."

"Where?" said J, coming to hold onto her. His question struck him as absurd. So did her answer.

"Garage," she said.

But Glad Neeby was now standing belligerently just inside the kitchen door. "What's the matter?" he said sternly and sensibly.

"I don't know," said J.

The stout woman was balanced on her feet now and turning ponderously. Sophia came running. "Mother, what happened?"

"Death," said Marietta. "Warning."

"Something's scared her," said Susie Neeby sensibly.

Sophia embraced her mother and began to croon comfort.

As the women took over, J entered the way to the garage. "Take it easy, boy," said Glad Neeby. "I'm right behind you." So they both peered into the dimness, seeing only the cars standing cold and silent, smelling as cars do smell. J put on the rather sickly garage light, one bulb overhead.

"Nobody," said Glad.

Susie now said, behind them, "Glad, be careful. I thought ... I don't know ... corner of my eye ... something moved out in the back."

"We better check around back then," said Glad Neeby in a matter-of-fact way.

The woman put Marietta down in a chair in the family room; she seemed to have no voice now. Sophia stood close to her, watching through the glass wall the moving shadows as J and Glad Neeby crossed and recrossed the backyard.

Susie said, "Of course, last week Mrs. Arriola was carrying on about this house being ..."

"Shush," said Sophia. "Wait."

(Her mother didn't have to know that Mrs. Arriola thought the house was haunted. On the other hand, if she had already been told so, this might explain the whole incident.)

The men circled the house and came in. J reached for the cord and shut the draperies. "Doors all locked, now," said Glad. "Nobody's out there."

Sophia bent and put her arm across her mother's shoulders. "Mother, did something upset you this evening?"

"I don't understand—" wept Marietta.

"Come along to bed. At least, lie down. I'll go with you. And J is going to look under *all* the beds."

The Neebys sat down at the card table and lifted their eyebrows at each other. Susie leaned and said in a whisper, "Mrs. Arriola probably told her the house was haunted."

"Nuts!" said Glad. "Damn it, I had a hundred and fifty honors."

CHAPTER 26

Friday Night

When Sophia heard a car pull to a stop out in the street, she thought, Ah, good! Somebody's bringing Nanjo home. She petted her mother down into the bed and went back to where J and the guests were drinking their drinks and chatting.

"I may *be* a rat at heart," J was saying. "I was saying to somebody not so long ago, I'm in a rut. Okay. It's a darned nice rut, and it suits me." He looked too somber for the words.

"Well," said Glad, "I guess I'm stuck in mine until retirement age. Of course, the world will probably blow up before I reach it."

"It could," said J. "Any day. Any night."

"Is she all right?" asked Susie of Sophia, who was eyeing her husband intently.

"Oh, I think so," said Sophia soothingly. "I don't know

what happened. Nothing, I bet. She's been talking about moving into some religiously inclined Home. It could be a cult of some sort. I'll have to investigate and see if they've been upsetting her."

"Ah," said Susie sympathetically.

Sophia was noticing that Nanjo had not come into the house. Still, that was natural. There were always farewell ceremonies, as Sophia knew. Nanjo wasn't alone out there, where nobody was.

Out there a man standing with Tony Thees beside Tony's car was saying, "Goodrick's gone with the wind."

"And Little is okay?" said Tony tensely.

"So far. Playing bridge. They got company, see. Maybe Goodrick was waiting for them to go home. I guess whatever Goodrick had in mind, when the fat lady came, she must have scared hell out of him. Little and his friend took a look around. We had to lie low. But believe me, nobody else is around now."

Tony stood with his hands in his pockets and watched the moon coming up.

At last he said, "I want a man on every corner of the house. I don't want a *fly* to get in there."

"The girl's still out someplace."

"What girl?"

"I guess it's the daughter."

"Well, let *her* in," said Tony.

He thought, So when the bridge game breaks up and the company goes home, that still leaves four people in the house, and three of them female and, naturally, noisy. He could see no course without its danger. So let *time* waste? That might still be the safest way. (Although an airplane can get you anywhere on earth in just one day. If you know where to go.)

But he smiled to himself. Oh, they wouldn't get it in time. *Whatever* happened would *take* time. A pitched battle on the grounds of the house would take time, too, if that's what they wanted.

Now that the moon was up Nanjo, whose eyes ached from their fight for sight, could see only the moon-made shadow of the church roof against the downhill wall.

She crept on all fours out of her hiding place because she

just could not stand it anymore. He was probably gone. He must be gone, as a dream is banished. But Cal, the gardener, was still there, crumpled on a slant on the concrete steps with his head down, moonlight on his boots, face in shadow, and *still*. It didn't take long for Nanjo to know what his stillness was.

She didn't scream.

She sprang up the steps, avoiding him with nimble feet. Once on the sidewalk she started up the hill again. She did not walk too fast. She couldn't. Her heart hurt too terribly. She was filthy. She knew that her knees were bleeding. Her dress was torn. She had to get home, had to get home, had to get back, get back to being Nancy Jo Little. Had to get back to where she had been.

And she could not tell, would never tell anybody, ever, about this terrible detour. Nobody would ever have to know.

At the next cross street there was, mercifully, a bus stop. And a bus coming. The bus was not very full. The sleepy people didn't pay much attention to the young girl who got on quietly, a cool mantle of control around her shoulders, a mien that said, Don't look at me. Don't worry about me. I know what I'm doing. I do this all the time.

Nanjo went to the very back and took off her ruined stockings and spit on one and wiped at her knees. She spit on it again and scrubbed at her face, took out her compact, and powdered herself well.

Luck! This bus would take her within half a mile of her house. She wouldn't stop at Debby's for her sweater, no. She'd just get in. She'd get in *somehow*, back to her own room, safe to her old self.

It wasn't her fault what had happened to that man. (It was—Oh, God—*terrible!* But it wasn't her fault!) And she felt bad enough without having to hear that she shouldn't have done this or that. They'd be wild! She'd rather take it by herself. She could take it. She just *would*, that's all.

Since Sophia had pleaded a natural lack of interest in any more cards, refreshments were served, and then the Neebys finally went home. They trotted down the walk, calling pleasantries and J, leaving the door open behind him, stepped out on the stoop to look at the moonlit night and the peace and quiet of his neighborhood.

He felt grateful for Glad Neeby. Grateful for that man, his

friend, his kind. But J was ashamed that his friend had heard him, even while clowning, putting his own-kind-only in fanciful control. That was the human temptation, all right. But J was *civilized*. He knew that he didn't hold the whole thing up. Legions did that. And of those legions, legions held up (each man) more than J. And legions, outside the pattern of earn and pay, held up (for all J knew) something of value. Hadn't he known at the very beginning that seven seats to salvation were worse than none at all?

He jumped when Tony spoke up quietly from the shadows. "Don't worry, Mr. Little. They've gone. We'll be keeping watch over you and your family."

Sophia called from within, "J?"

He turned and, without even answering Tony, went blindly into his cave. Over me and mine? he thought. That's not enough. That's not good enough. *That* won't save me!

Sophia said, "Isn't there a car out there? I thought I heard Nanjo a long time ago."

"No," he said, "no."

"Where the dickens is she, then? I know they get to yakking, and she'll be mortified if I phone. But I don't like this."

"She's being watched over," said J.

"Watched!"

"She's mine." J went slowly into the family room to his chair.

Sophia came slowly after him. "J, you don't go along with my theory, then? You do think there was somebody?"

He didn't answer.

"You *look* like it's the end of the world," said Sophia angrily. "Listen, J, *please!* How can I help if I don't *know?*"

"That's the trouble," he said.

"J, what can I do?"

He looked up at her. "Listen?" he said. "I'm sorry about my word of honor and all that, but I can't stand it anymore if you're not in it with me."

"Here I am," she said, feeling immediately calm and strong. "Let's go into our room."

It was in her mind that Nanjo would be coming in, and this wasn't a child's business. She left one light and followed her husband's dragging feet, feeling not frightened but filled with joy.

So J sat on the edge of his bed and told her in a low voice the whole thing from the very beginning.

Outside, from time to time, a bird called peacefully.

Elsewhere Goodrick was saying, "Can't do it by night. Neighbors too close. Street too quiet. House too full of people. You stir up that wasp's nest, middle of the night ... *Shoop. Shoop.* What can he know, anyway? Res*cues.* Barbe*cues.*" Goodrick grated his teeth.

"You make no sense," said Mr. Jones coldly. "What *is* your thought?"

"I make more sense than any of *them,*" Goodrick muttered. He took his thumb from his mouth and said coldly, "The practical thing is to get him tomorrow when he leaves alone."

"You may be right," said Mr. Jones. "Especially if, as you say, you saw no sign of anyone on guard?" Mr. Jones tried to face facts without crying.

"Nothing," lied Goodrick.

The crazy old woman had some kind of power? Goodrick didn't understand it, but a curse was a curse, and death he didn't yearn for.

Sophia was, as J had anticipated, furious.

"Well, of all the runarounds! They're using you, J! Whatever they think they're doing, they've got no business putting you on such a spot! *Sssh. . . .*"

There was a padding of feet along the hall outside their door.

"Nanjo?" called Sophia.

"Night, Mom," said their daughter. "Sorry it's so late."

"Well, get to bed," her mother said, relieved that Nanjo was safely home, but with most of her mind on J, his possible danger, on her own outrage, on all this nonsense! Seven seats to the moon!

Marietta, who was not asleep, heard Nanjo come creeping in. She lay still, expecting light, but none came. In the dark Nanjo crept out again, going into the bathroom.

In a little while Nanjo came creeping back, still in the dark, and Marietta heard her bed receive her weight. In a moment she could hear the muffled sound of weeping. But such weeping!

She sat up and turned on the bedside lamp. In the other bed there was the hump in the covers, a tousled shock of hair, and a sudden, very deep, rejecting silence.

Marietta struggled to her feet and went her way to the bathroom. She didn't know what to do. She had been told, she remembered, she had been *told* to get out. In the mirror her own blue eyes dismayed her. She closed them, but then the lids flew up, and she turned to the hamper, whose lid was not quite fitting down. She bent to adjust it and there were some stockings lying on top, within, torn and bloodied. There was a cotton dress, its skirt torn and dirty. Skirt? Torn? Dirty?

Evil! Evil! Sin and terror! Secret! Dirt and darkness!

With a silent scream Marietta held her own throat and felt the pulse pounding.

In a while she stepped as softly as she could into Nanjo's room. She clicked the lamp out. No sound came from the girl in the other bed. No sound. No loving comfort asked for? None to be given. Marietta tweaked at the quilt on the top of her bed and, dragging it behind her, crept out of the room and into J's den. Alone, but not alone—where her private angel would be comfort, for *he* knew that only loving kindness dwelt in Marietta's heart. Only. Only.

Nanjo lay trembling. She must remember to wash her stockings and whisk her dress into better hiding early tomorrow. Her mother wouldn't go into that bathroom, at least not early. Nanjo would have to work around her grandmother, but Marietta was easy to fool. Nanjo would be "washing her hair."

All traces would be erased. Nobody would know. There was proof (in her sweater) of where Nanjo had been. Debby would lie for her peer, of course. Cary didn't even *know*. He didn't care, she thought. He let her walk away by herself in that awful part of town. Didn't care, never would, didn't know *how* to care . . . Oh, why had she ever . . .

Her knees were stinging and smarting. She'd wear capri's tomorrow. Thank God it was Saturday.

Oh, what if Cal had *not* fallen?

She was shivering uncontrollably. Oh, she was glad her grandmother had got out of here. She couldn't *stand* her grandmother. She didn't know that she could stand *anything*, anymore!

Well, she'd *have* to. Couldn't tell Mom and Daddy. She'd lied to them. Dated Cary, after all. No. But oh ... Should never have got into his car. Oh, what a fool. . . .

Oh, God, Cal, the gardener, was dead! He would never move again. Or *do anything!* HE WAS DEAD!

Down in the tavern things were getting rough, and somebody called the cops.

Glad Neeby, wiggling in the freedom of his pajamas, said, "The old lady's getting senile, I guess."

"Well," yawned Susie, "she never had far to go, you know. Oh, they've got problems."

"J was talking funny talk tonight, at that," Glad murmured, vaguely distressed.

"Good old Mrs. Arriola could have something this time," Susie went on. "Oh, well, maybe it's only Nanjo's got herself pregnant. Egads, that kid! You should have seen her in that dress. *Whoo! Whoo!* Or, of course, old J could have had some kind of fling with that platinum blonde in Chicago, and Sophia's going to live it down."

"Such is life, eh?" said Glad heavily. "You take old J, though. . . ."

"Listen," said Susie. "I think the world of those people. I'd do anything in the world! But if they don't tell you, what can you do?" She crashed down on her bed.

Gladstone Neeby crawled between his earned white sheets and put his head on his own clean pillow. "Not a thing," he mourned. "Well, when you come down to it, what could old J do for me?"

"Why should he do anything?" said his wife. "What's the matter with *you?*"

"You never know," said Neeby. "We lead a sheltered life," he added. "We're kind of out of it, actually."

"What is *out?*" said Susie indignantly. "We're human!"

Her husband didn't deny it. He thought his spindly, spiky, spunky little wife was about as human as they come. He'd take care, naturally. Oh, he worried, sometimes. Often.

Sophia held J's head to her breast and said resolutely, "Nothing's happened yet. All right, then. So we'll go about our business. But if anybody or anything bothers us, for one second, *anymore,* we'll just call the police."

J thought, Ah, wouldn't it be nice, wouldn't it be loverly if this was a world where everybody could go about his business, do his work, raise his children, enjoy his friends, and the dew on the rose, and all things dear and mild, and if anything *bothered,* just call the police, who would come bringing justice and mercy.

But that kind of world it is not and never was. He wondered if it ever would be. He was wondering with his eyes wide open, his ear listening to Sophia's heart. He felt drained. He knew, of course, that *he* wouldn't like such a world. Man had to keep on making rules, trying to get along with himself, but justice was rough and mercy uncertain. And had to be. You better not clamp down absolutely. There had to be room. You didn't want to take the zing out of it. God knows who man is! *Man* doesn't know who he is, yet.

J thought sleepily that (if he knew how) he'd like to remind God that He had a nice dramatic thing going in this corner of the universe—a human life. "Listen," he argued, "*I* don't ask for the moon.

"I don't want to be Noah, Sophia," he murmured. "I haven't got what it takes to do what he did."

Sophia said, "What a terrible thing that was to ask a man to do."

CHAPTER 27

Saturday Morning

About five o'clock on Saturday morning Goodrick's phone rang. "Listen," a man said, "when do I get any relief? Seventeen hours is a hell of a stretch."

"Aw, go home," said Goodrick. "Jones took you off long ago. You're watching nothing. I checked, and she's checked out."

"So what else is new?" said the man indignantly. "Sure, she

checked out. I'm back of her motel right now. Nobody told me I was took off."

"Is that so?" said Goodrick thoughtfully.

The morning light was still shut away from Nanjo's room when Sophia went in, put her hand on the mound that was her daughter, and said, "Wake up, Nanjo. I want to know what happened last night? Why"—Sophia raced right on—"did your grandmother move into the den? Did you fight with her again? Did you say something to hurt her feeings?"

Nanjo heaved. "I did not!" she said shrilly. "I just sneaked in, trying not to wake her up, but she got up, and she went. I didn't say one single word. Not one word! She didn't say anything, either. What's she saying *now*?"

"She seems to be leaving us," said Sophia.

"Well, I don't know anything about it." Nanjo burrowed deeper into the bedcovers until only the top of her head was showing. "Gosh, Mother, it's Saturday! Am I supposed to get up and say good-bye or what?"

"No," said Sophia. "No, I don't think so."

When she had gone, Nanjo's heart kept on thumping so hard she thought the bed must be shaking. Scared about to death when her mother had wanted to know *what happened last night*. Nanjo had only just escaped blurting out the whole thing, had been saved by the time it takes to draw a breath. Only that!

Sophia found that the taxi had come, the man was loading Marietta's suitcases in. J was out there on the sidewalk. Sophia didn't think this was wise, but before she could say so, her mother appeared, encumbered by small bags and bundles but moving rather swiftly. Sophia received a kiss and a tear in passing, but as J helped Marietta into the cab, he received (Sophia noticed) a more lingering embrace.

So there went Marietta, and Sophia was glad of it.

First thing this morning Marietta had announced that she was, after all, going back to her boardinghouse.

Sophia had been shocked! Marietta's O. G. A. had never, that she remembered, changed his mind before.

Her mother had gone on to say that they had been so kind, and they were so very good to her, but she could not—she just knew that she *must* not—stay on! She would suffer out the waiting until her funds resumed, when she would definitely move into the Retreat because, she had said tearfully, "It's the only place . . . the only place for me."

That was when Sophia had telephoned the woman there and given her mother a hundred dollars.

It had come to her that her mother would be safe at least from some worldly angels of darkness.

But on Sophia's mind, at the moment, was not her mother's departure, but danger to J, who still stood out there on the lawn, seeming to brood over the view of the valley that swam in the morning haze below.

Sophia forcefully hailed him inside.

They went back to the dinette for another cup of coffee. It was good to be alone together. (Let Nanjo sleep on. Nanjo was safe.)

Sophia said that there was probably no real danger, but at least her mother was safe for a week. And J wondered aloud, with a blink of alarm, if "they" had been bothering his father.

Sophia said she doubted that. She said that *whatever* was bothering his father, J was going to stay right here, snug at home. There was no use flying in the face of advice (even if you didn't quite believe in the danger). J was not to go anywhere at all. Not today and not tomorrow. And on Monday Sophia would see.

So J, feeling as if he had a tiger beside him, agreed that he would telephone his father later on. Perhaps a moral dilemma could be dealt with over the phone. Meantime, he had better get out in the yard and do something about that cockeyed tree. Trim the rest of it to balance and dispose of the lopped branches in some orderly fashion.

Sophia agreed that he might be permitted to do so, since she would be keeping an eye on.

They had Annette tied down in such a manner that she could not break away from her many connections to the machine. Goodrick presided over the polygraph as a competent witch might preside over her daily cauldron, quite sure of the ingredients, quite sure of the results. No need to cackle or carry on.

Mr. Jones had already done some cackling meant to frighten and had slapped Annette a stinging crack on her face when she had said she would not answer questions. He seemed to favor pain and fear over a machine. But Goodrick had coldly explained that she *would* answer, whether she opened her mouth or not.

He asked the questions, and whether her response was silence or nonsense, she knew the pen points danced on the paper, putting down the truth her body was telling in spite of her.

Meantime, Mr. Jones hissed in the corner.

Mr. Goodrick was relentlessly patient. He tested again and again, even after she had gone limp in a dreary conviction of helplessness. She'd been sure it was Tony, opened the door, what a fool. . . .

"Where are they meeting?"

"I don't know."

J didn't know whether he was going to hang around the house because he had planned to do so or because he was at least a coward and perhaps a fool. Maybe Tony Thees and Cousin Annie were only fooling him, the second time around, to keep him in line. All J's guiding lights were faded and blurred now that he had broken his word, pooped out, weakened, and told Sophia. There was no longer any question of his honor or integrity or any of that stuff to help him.

Worse than this, during the course of telling Sophia again this morning, J had found out what it was that he knew. Sophia was a thorough kind of person. Sophia could narrow in on a problem. She had this power of passionate concentration. She had quickly seen that whatever J knew that he shouldn't have known must have been said aloud during the time he had lurked in the lavatory eavesdropping. And not afterward. Under the pressure of her resolute concern they had gone over it bit by bit.

Might it be, she had asked, the fact that the visitor (whom J had never seen) was he who must replace (somewhere) the man who was so ill?

J had said if so, that was strange. "Looks like *I* was going to replace him."

But Sophia was not to be diverted to worrying about the moon at this time.

Perhaps, she had gone on, it was the visitor's name? *Bright,* was it? Something like that? Still, the visitor had walked into the hospital and must have been seen by somebody in the process. How could the secret be his identity?

Well, then, was it something scientific—as a formula? To this J replied (getting into the mood of a game here) that he didn't imagine they'd have repeated a formula out loud. Formulae were always, according to J's notions, written down in mysterious symbols which J was not at all sure *could* be pronounced aloud on the human tongue.

J had been relaxed at the moment, feeling a tender amusement, and that was when the secret of the secret had sprung into his mind. Okay, he knew. He knew *exactly* what Goodrick wanted to know and what Tony Thees wished J not to tell him.

But J had kept himself from telling Sophia, although she, of course, knew at once that it had come to him. She had agreed, with remarkable control, that perhaps it would be better if she did not know, exactly. "Well," J told her, "it's not that I can figure out the *meaning* of it." (It had sounded like a language they'd use someplace like the moon!)

It was that string of syllables "the race must get used to." It was *Poonacootamoowa.* The "very top," hadn't Barkis said of it?

J was quite sure, because he now remembered that he had repeated that string of syllables during his talk with Barkis. "Poonacootamoowa to the moon," J had said and called it gibberish. And right then, *thereafter,* on the top of that, Barkis had pulled out of his brilliant, anxious brain that crazy offer of seven seats to the moon.

Not only that, but J could put together, now, some other things. Poonacootamoowa could be—what? The name of something? But there was a time connected. Goodrick asking about a date? Tony saying a few more days. Barkis mentioning a week and trying to throw J off this notion? *A week ago today,* J had heard the secret. A *time! A place?*

Well, J had already made up his mind to stay home today. He had to work on the damned elm, didn't he? (The forbidden syllables had risen like cream to the very top of his thought, all ready to be skimmed off.) He had better get busy. Turn his mind. He was already wearing a flannel shirt and his old working pants. He got up.

Sophia was holding the ticket to the moon in both hands, studying it. J felt sure no scratch on the metal anywhere had escaped Sophia's dark, inquiring eye. Now she sighed and said, "I suppose we'd better hide this? Here. *You* hide it."

But J, knowing it wasn't this that Goodrick wanted, put it

in his shirt pocket and buttoned down the flap. He went out to unlock his tool cupboard and get on with his homely task.

Sophia sat still, listening to the house. It was quiet. She rose and went all around, looking out all the windows except Nanjo's. She saw nothing unusual. A panel truck parked across the street. Some repairman? Nothing dangerous. Nobody.

Nanjo could hear her mother moving in the house and lay low. She had early skipped out and washed the stockings and the skirt of her dress. They hung behind the closed door of her closet now. Nanjo's scraped kneecaps were scabbing over. She'd put some flesh-colored adhesive patches on. Her capris lay ready for her to jump into. She'd brushed her hair, hard.

But she knew she had better stay in bed as long as she possibly could, because the concealing of the physical evidence was easy. But to paste some calm-colored patches over the wounds in her mind and memory and imagination—that was harder. Nanjo lay, willing iron into her soul. She would not tell them. She wouldn't *do* it! They'd be so upset, so hurt. But she was *young!* She was stronger and cooler than they. She could take it!

Amy had been sitting in the hospital's waiting room since six thirty in the morning. No news had come to her. Nothing. Time dragged on. When she was paged, at last, it was her brother calling. She had to tell him that, as far as she knew, Avery was still on the operating table. Win said, "Are you all alone? Somebody should be there!"

"Oh, no," said Amy, "I don't want anybody. I'd rather wait by myself." She went back and sat down and put her head very low, as low as she could, and let it spin. Before somebody else, Amy might have to bear up.

As Win hung up, Marion said, "I'll go if you could watch the Little kids. It's too *awful!* She mustn't be alone! *Nobody* should!"

Win heard (in the way he had) the cry she didn't utter: *Don't ever leave me!* He put his arms around her. "If Amy says she doesn't want us, that's what Amy means. She's a character who doesn't kid herself very much." He was wondering, Do I?

Marion pulled away in a moment. "My mother isn't a happy person," she said in a monotone. "Her house is never hers. Church people always in and out. She has to ... serve my father's profession and never be anything but kind and sweet. I guess I've despised her for not being *happy*. I thought it was easy."

Win listened carefully, didn't understand, but said intuitively, "Who told her how she always had to be?"

"She did," said Marion. "I'm sorry."

Goodrick was finished. One of the other men had carefully put the machine away, as they had found it, in what must be a rented office. Annette was free of any bonds, free, at least, to sit there. The men behaved as if she were a thing wrung out and of no further use to them.

Goodrick was giving Mr. Jones the results. Yes, the meeting was taking place right now. It had been in session since Thursday. It would break up on Sunday evening. They had so many hours.

"Enough," purred Mr. Jones. "Go on."

But the girl did *not* know the all-important fact. *Where?* This was the truth. Annette Woods did not know the place. And neither (at least to this girl's knowledge) did Tony Thees.

Mr. Jones seemed to be going into some kind of convulsion. But Goodrick continued in the same cool way. However, J Middleton Little did, indeed, know the place. The girl believed that, feared that, *knew* that. Goodrick believed that, too. All they had to do, therefore, was get it out of the man Little. Now they could be sure. He had in his head the one fact they needed.

All the men moved to an outer office where Mr. Jones definitely went through a seizure of some kind. At last they were gone. Silence roared in her ears. She stood up, trembling, and reached for the telephone.

What weathermen call an early morning high cloudiness was breaking up; the day was turning out bright and fine. The foliage sparkled. Only the elm was a ludicrous sight. Industriously J dragged branches into a heap back of the garage and attacked the remaining limbs as best he could, not caring so much for the health of the tree (about which he understood very little) but trying to restore to it some of the decent symmetry, the beauty it was born to. Sophia was helping him by sighting at the shape of things and directing him where to place the cutting blade of the awkward device on the end of the pole, and when to pull hard on the string.

They heard the phone ringing. It kept on. (Nanjo must not be awake.) J said, "I suppose that's my father."

Sophia thought, Maybe it's Win. She let him go into the house to answer and drifted to inspect some iris, thinking, I was too hard on Win. I'm a bossy woman. Something, help me?

It was neither J's father nor J's son on the phone. It was Annette.

"Good morning, Mr. Noah," she said in a high voice, terribly gay. "This is your girl guide calling. We are having a little practice launch. Just a trial run. Don't prepare. Go on doing what you're doing, but when the Ark comes up the river, go with it?"

"Where would I be going?" said J sourly.

"There is news for you," she sang out, still too gay. "My boyfriend now agrees with me. Just get aboard, and you will hear all about it."

"Why not now?"

"No, no, not on the phone. Pixies could be listening in!"

"I am getting pretty goddamned sick and tired of this whole idiotic *bit*," J exploded. "All I know is, I am not going to leave my wife and daughter and go anywhere on any Ark or anything else, and you can just take that and—and *like* it!"

"Don't hang up," she cried, her voice ready to crack. "Bring them, too. Please? Help us?"

"I may, and I may not," snapped J and hung up.

Annette, resting her head on one hand, dialed again, spoke for the second time to Tony. "Okay. I did what you said. If it's bugged, I doubt I did very well. But I think he'll go along."

"Damn right, he'll go."

"If you take his females, too."

"All right. There'll be room."

"Hurry?" she said. "If they did have his line bugged, *they'll* hurry."

"The car will be bullet proof, at least. Not that they'd

shoot him. Can you make it back to your room, sweetheart?"

"I'm all right. *I* don't know, so they don't want me. They don't want you, either."

"So I'm safe. And it's all laid on for our Little man," Tony said soothingly. "I'm going ahead to scout it out, right now."

He hung up, and the girl said, "I didn't say you were *safe*." She went wobbling to the hallway and down and out of the building, squinting at the street signs to find out where she was.

Nobody was watching her.

At J's house the phone rang again and he, having been standing right next to it (unwilling to move, resenting cryptic orders), picked it up.

"Oh, Mr. Little, I don't know if you heard. Oh, Mr. Little, that boy, he's in jail. Oh, *I* knew . . ."

"What boy is this, Mrs. Arriola?"

Sophia had come into the house. "Let me. I'm used to her." J mutely handed her the phone.

"Oh, Miz Little, is that you? Oh, I knew something bad was going to happen to that boy. Oh, poor Miss Nancy, how's she feeling about this?"

J drifted off to his bedroom. Something told him he wasn't going to do any more work on the elm today. He began to change his trousers. What did she mean, trial launching? Why couldn't she say what she meant? Did she mean that somebody listened in on his telephone? Well, if the Ark is *going*, he thought irrationally on another level, they can't put me off with three instead of seven. I was promised.

Sophia poked her head in. "Cary Bruce," she said grimly. "Arrested last night in some brawl in a beer joint. Does Nanjo know about this?"

J turned. "She was pretty late," he said alertly.

"I'll see," said Sophia with retrospective intuitions.

But the phone rang. J got it this time, right here in the bedroom.

His daughter Amy said, "Pops? I've got some news that isn't very good."

"Shoot, Amy," he said, bracing, so that Sophia flew to his side to listen in.

"They operated on Avery this morning. It took hours. He's out of it now, but it's not so good, Pops. He's probably going to be almost totally blind."

"Ohhhhhh," said J on a falling note of sorrow. "Where are you, sweetie?"

Amy told him. "And also, Pops . . ."

Sophia said briskly, "What can we do, dear?"

"Oh, Mom? Pops, are you there? I guess I need some money. Win came and gave them some last night, but now I need . . . Oh, gosh, I'm going to need . . . Could you come?"

"I sure could," said J. "I'll be there in two shakes. You hold everything. I'm on my way."

As he put down the telephone Sophia said, "Me, too! Oh, God, poor Avery! Poor man! Poor soul! Poor Amy!"

J said, "What about Nanjo?"

Sophia blinked and braced. "All right. You go to Amy. I'll deal with Nanjo and be there later."

"I'll call you," said J. He grabbed his checkbook and hurried through the family room into the kitchen, to the garage, into his car, and popped it out of the driveway, reversed, and tore away.

There seemed to be some confusion as he went.

A car coming in the opposite direction braked in shock. A second car swerved to pass the first. (J slipped between). In the first car Goodrick said, "That was him!" In the second car Tony Thees uttered suitable words.

The first car began to move, going into a U-turn. The panel truck from across the street moved and blocked it. The truck driver leaned out and said, "Can you tell me how to get to Stowe Park?"

A man came sidling around a shrub, went to the hood, unlatched it, and raised it. Mr. Jones began to scream that he had no *right!* Goodrick got out, went up to the door of the house, and rang the bell.

From Nanjo's window Sophia saw who it was. She refused to answer. "But mother . . ."

"Sssh. . . ."

"Where is everybody?" said Goodrick at the curb to one of Tony's men. "Who was in that car?"

"What car?" the man said.

Tony, who had driven around the block, passed at the corner. He was hurrying. But as he took the turn to start downhill, he realized that Goodrick and Co.'s car was loosed and after him. So Tony let J keep his long lead. He himself drove at a smart enough pace, with a deceptive air of purpose, and took a right turn up onto the Golden State (having seen that a certain speck in the distance had not). Goodrick and Co. fell into the trap and followed Tony.

But J had already raced around the entrance ramp and was down on the Ventura.

After a while Tony, having lost the hounds, stopped playing fox and found a phone booth.

"Tony," Annette said at once, "he's gone! Nobody answered the door, and his car's *gone*."

"Yep. He's gone where the wild goose goes," said Tony. "Tell the boys with the armored car to go home."

"Tony, they didn't get him?"

"Nope. Not they. They were on *my* tail. Any news?"

"Yes," she said tensely. "Old Coughdrop. Says it's all over."

"What! What happened?"

"There was a big flap," she said, speaking fast and nervously. "The religious prayed all the time, and it made the scientists nervous, and they got into a flaming row among themselves about whether or not God was dead. So they've gone home in a huff, I guess."

Tony collapsed against the wall. He couldn't help laughing hysterically. "Mission accomplished," he croaked at last.

"Tell Goodrick and Co.! Mind you do that," she said sharply.

"Right." Tony came out of the booth, wiping his eyes. No Goodrick and Co. was to be seen, of course. He had lost them two miles ago.

Their car was parked, and Mr. Jones was screaming at them all.

CHAPTER 28

Saturday Afternoon

"Does he know?" J asked his daughter Amy in that waiting room. "How's he feeling, poor kid?"

"Yes, he knows," she said. "He's not feeling much yet. I told him myself. I wouldn't let anyone else."

"Ah, good girl," said J, his heart aching.

"Pops, it wasn't curable last week or last month or even last summer."

"I see," J sighed because he had been afraid. Now he reached for his checkbook. "How much would you say ... Oh, oh!" He stared at his balance. "My checking account— humph! Never mind. I'll fatten it up first thing Monday morning."

"There's more in it than you think," said Amy. "I tore up three hundred and fifty dollars' worth the other day."

"Why?" said J, astonished.

Amy shook her weary head. "I don't feel like telling you why, Pops."

"Okay," said J promptly. "The thing for me to do is talk to them at the desk. We'll fix it."

Amy's eyes were ringed with dark smudges of fatigue. She looked utterly beautiful. Her smile was nearly too much for her father. So he began to ask brisk, practical questions. What kind of care did Avery need here? How about private nursing? How long must he stay? Where would Amy take him later on? What kind of dwelling would be best for them? Could J help her find it? Wouldn't Amy want to stay home with Avery and so give up the thought of working?

Amy said, "No. I want to keep on working, Pops. I think I'll keep this job as long as I can. I had to take yesterday off, but they were nice about it. I'll go back Monday."

"Oh ..." But J stopped himself from objecting. If she

thought she could, she must be allowed to try. Who was he to say she couldn't?

"And afterward, as soon as Avery learns how to be by himself, I'll work, of course."

"Well," said J, "we can wait and see about that."

Amy leaned back against his shoulder and sighed. He could feel her weariness, and he could feel her trust. Then she said, "Pops, you know I enjoyed it."

"What's this?"

"I darned near enjoyed it, anyhow," she said. "The job. So many kinds of people. Trying to match what they can do with what needs doing. Trying to help both sides. If that's what the job is, you know, I don't mind business."

"Well, I'll tell you," said J. "Business is not all people trying to help one another. Oh-ho, no. People in business can get into the kinds of fights that two-year-olds have got to the bottom of and abandoned."

"I'll bet." Amy cozied her dark head to his shoulder. "But then you've just got to cool them all down? Is that what you do, Pops?"

"Oh, I tell them where to head in, *I* do," said J absurdly pleased, absurdly happy.

"I'm going to be darned good at it," said Amy abruptly. "Pops, would you do one more thing for me?"

"Why, sure." His spirit coiled around her to save, but let her *be,* since otherwise he could not save her.

"I was thinking. You know, Avery has . . . this talent?"

"I was thinking about that, too," said J somberly.

"But it might be," she said, "that he could express it in music. It *might* be so! He has an excellent ear. He *sees* sound in some funny way. He's even tried to paint it. And they say there's compensation, and his hearing could get even better. So—Win is selling off a lot of stuff, he told me. The house and all. I wondered if I could possibly have their piano? Cheap?"

"Good idea," said J (concealing surprise at this news of Win). "Darned good idea! Why not? Avery's got to do what he alone can do. I know that." (Amy concealed surprise.) "A piano and a tape recorder, maybe?" J went on. "Wouldn't have to write, eh? You're darned tooting I'll see to the piano. Right away."

Amy said sleepily, "I'm glad you came."

"Can you rest?" he said quickly. (Oh, the dark road this

child must go!) "Come home, Amy. In between. When you can."

"Yes," she said. "I will. I sure will."

After having called Sophia, J took off looking neither to the right nor the left, but straight ahead, to do what more he could for Amy. He was thinking that Avery *had* to have a seat to the moon. How did the race *know* it didn't need a blind painter? Who could say what might not come out of that? Not J.

There were at least three clumps of strangers touring the long spread of the house when J arrived. The place had already acquired the subtle air of a house about to change hands. Win had long ago called the hospital for news of Avery and knew that he had survived the surgery, but he did not know, until J told him, that Avery's sight was almost gone.

Both Win and Marion were so stricken by this news that they seemed to have received a strong yank at the patterns of their anxieties. Some trifles fell away. Of course, they'd *give* Avery the piano. Win said, with heavy cheer, that he'd even have it tuned.

J told them there was no need for them to go to the hospital. Avery had to be absolutely immobile and quiet. He could not be seen. As for Amy, she was about exhausted and would soon be going to the house in Burbank. Driving herself. Wanted the old car with her. She'd make it.

"Sure, she will," her brother said. "Of course, she will," said Marion.

So J telephoned Sophia again. (She had already told him that Nanjo had confessed to being with that miserable boy. It seemed that she had been more or less blackmailed—Sophia did not say how—into meeting him last evening. But Nanjo had seen her chance to get away and had actually, in the traditional manner of good girls, "walked home." She hadn't wanted to tell her parents; she'd been ashamed; she'd known they'd be distressed and so on. Oh, how could they help Amy?)

So now J said, "How's everything?"

"Fair enough," Sophia said. "Amy called. Avery's doing as well . . . and so forth. She's on her way home, thank God."

"Good. Tell her she's got the piano."

"Good. Tell Win and flock to come here, why don't you? They'll be wanting to see Amy."

"I'll tell them. Be home soon."

"Take a little time out," Sophia said. (Everybody was tired.) "Oh, I forgot to say, before ... There was a limousine or something came looking for you. I didn't answer the door. And somebody called an hour and a half ago, wanting to know where you could be reached."

"Who was it?"

"I don't know. He didn't say. Man's voice, a kind of purring effect."

"What did you tell him?"

"Just that our son-in-law was in the hospital, and you'd been called away."

"Okay," said J. "Hold the fort," he added.

"Certainly," said Sophia merrily.

As he hung up, J did not feel in the least depressed, either. The family was acting, dealing with its affairs. J was in the middle, functioning. No point in being depressed. No time for that.

Win said they'd surely come to the house later on. "Dad, have you got a minute?"

They were in Win's den, which was on the street side of the house and was not an "area." It had an old-fashioned door that could be closed. Strange people were shuffling through the house. Win closed the door. Marion crept into the couch corner. The little kids were out in their play yard.

Win said, "First, I am definitely not getting the account I had hoped to get. So I'm cutting back my staff. I'll survive. That's maybe not so easy, but I will."

"Good enough, eh?" said J with a cheerful shrug.

"We're selling out here, as you see. I don't know why it is that I handle money in the office better than at home. I suppose I'm forced to be solid and reputable, there; I couldn't gamble at all without that basic chip. But here ... I'm over my head, all right. Which is no way to serve my profession." (J caught the communication between husband and wife.) "I've got an obligation to meet on Monday, and I just can't do it," Win went on. "Going to be short. We've got rid of one car, Marion's coat, but two paintings and the silver are on consignment, and even if we sell the house this afternoon, I can't touch any considerable cash before escrow."

"The five thousand, is it?" said J.

"It's six. There were other outstanding . . ."

"What's the missing difference?" J said steadily.

"I'm not asking you for it," said Win. "That's not the reason I'm telling you all this. You've got to know that I used Grandmother Alice's bonds from the safe-deposit for collateral."

"I see," said J. (His mother had left in her will some bonds to each son. J had had his share long ago. Willy's share had gone to his only child. But Winnie's share had reverted to his father. The old gentleman had always vowed he would never touch them. They were destined for the namesake. For Win. Someday.)

"Old Mr. Little," Marion was saying "told him that he could, Dad. For thirty days. He said so. Win didn't steal them."

"No," said J, "I wasn't thinking so. Gambled with them, did you, Win?"

"They're secured," said Win. "But the hitch is Grandfather says he wants them cashed in *now*. He's got some deal going that Uncle Tobias arranged with Mr. Pudney."

J groaned.

"So," said Win, "as soon as the rush dies down around here, I'll be going down to see Grandfather. No use stalling. Nothing is going to make up the missing difference by Monday. So I'll go down and lay it on the line."

"But Win had permission," said Marion stubbornly. "The old gentleman just forgets. You understand, don't you?" Then she realized that there was something here she did not understand and fell quiet.

Win was looking out the window. "I could repeat that phone conversation word for word," he said. "If I'd had it recorded, most people would have to believe that he did definitely give me permission."

"But?" said J.

"But you know, Dad, just as I know. My grandfather really did not understand what he was saying."

"So, no contract?" said J.

"That's right," said Win. "As good as stealing."

"No," said Marion in pain.

But Win was shaking his head. "Dad understands," he said gently. "I won't go to jail, honey. Grandfather will be—disappointed in me."

"He's already upset," said J, shaking his shoulders looser. "He wants to see me about a moral dilemma."

"Ow," said Win, and it wasn't humorous.

J got up. "Well, it so happens that I'm going down there and tell him that he is *not* selling those bonds."

"What?"

"And no more needs to be said," said J. "If he has discovered that the bonds are gone, I'll say, 'Of course they're gone. You gave Win permission, whether you knew it or not. They are secured,' I'll say. That's right?"

Win said, "That's right, but I wish you wouldn't. It's not your problem."

"I don't doubt you wish I wouldn't," said J, "but I happen to be in the middle here, and I have a problem you don't seem to understand. He's my father. And you, my son, can't see past your own nose."

Win sat down.

Marion said angrily, "Win could have pretended . . ."

J thought, she's got the fine point. He didn't say so but smiled at her with affection and said instead, "I'm getting on down there because *I* want to know what Pudney is up to, what the money is *buying,* and who conned my father into touching those bonds. And if it was Tobias, he'll hear from me."

"I may take after Uncle Tobias, somewhat," said Win painfully.

"I doubt Tobias gambles much," said J. "He's pretty careful to cheat only cheaters. Whether you are a cheat or just slightly stupid, that's up to you to figure out. What you are not seeing is this. There's such a thing as protecting the innocent. My father doesn't need you meowling." (J remembered Barkis' word.) "He needs *me.* Because there comes a day when a man's child is father to the man." (He thought, but that day hasn't come for you, my son. Not yet!)

Win looked exactly like his mother suddenly. As if he could hear, as she so often did, a body's thought.

Marion had fled J's unbearable affection and was standing at the window. She said sharply, "Win! There's a man out there! I won't *have* him watching the Little kids." She turned and with ferocious purpose opened the door and ran through the rooms to gather her children to herself.

Win was at the window. J joined him. There was a car pulled up behind J's. J said, "Oh, *that* man? He's after me."

"After *you!*" said Win, astonished. "He came here with Marietta—I meant to call Ma . . . Who is he?"

"Tell you what you do," said J. "You call the police. Tell them there's a suspicious loiterer, and you've got small children, and you don't like it."

"But why, Dad?" Win was bewildered.

"Because I've got things to do, and I can't be bothered." He looked sideways at his son. "Take a chance? Help me, blind?"

"Of course," his son said.

The strangers in the house noticed nothing of its fluster, the mother with her children, the father on the phone, the grandfather watching slyly out the window. The timing worked out well. At the first sound of the siren J went out and got quickly into his car. Win, on his heels, swiftly approached Goodrick. When the police car turned into the curve of the street (just as J turned out of it), Win was standing in front of Goodrick's car, signaling them to stop here. Here was the trouble.

J chuckled and drove on, although what he had to chuckle about he did not analyze, nor why he felt so fine.

Goodrick, having worked very hard to discover which hospital harbored Avery, and having got on to J's tracks there, was alone. He was forced to maintain that he had come to inspect a house that was for sale. Win said it was not for sale to *him,* and he did not believe that Goodrick was here for that reason. The cops, who believed nobody one way or the other, listened to both sides very conscientiously before letting Goodrick go.

J, by now, was on the San Diego Freeway heading through the hills, once more, toward Santa Monica.

At the house in Burbank Nanjo was very glad when her sister came, whom her mother must receive and surround with all the concentrated passion of her sorrowing heart. Sophia put Amy down on Sophia's own bed, fed her, cosseted, and listened to her.

So Nanjo, wearing her green capris, green blouse, and sweater, sat by the telephone, and whenever it rang told the caller, and most particularly her own cronies, that the line had to be kept open. Sorry. Could not talk. Her brother-in-law was in the hospital.

When Annette called, therefore, Nanjo told her very firmly that her father was not at home, her father was very busy, there was nowhere he could be reached, he had no time, right now, for anyone but the family.

She hung up with a brief feeling of triumph. She had, by some miraculous strength, so far kept from telling her mother all of it. However, by now, Nanjo had a doubt gnawing on her which she did not wish to examine closely and dared not expose. Nanjo tried not to think too much. If she were going to keep on successfully in this course, she had better not think about Cal, the gardener, at all.

As for Cary Bruce, Nanjo didn't care where *he* was. If he was in jail, so much the better. Her mother had wanted to know if Nanjo wanted to go and see him. But that was ridiculous! Nanjo never wanted to see him again. He was guilty, wasn't he? (Oh, was she?)

"Ah, J," said his father. "When I came upon this, I was very much shaken. Look at this verse. Ben Jonson wrote it to be placed opposite the Droueshout engraving in the First Folio."

J looked, lying low, waiting and listening.

"Now, you have heard that Baconians, in particular, keep finding ciphers in the works. They are never valid. They are not true ciphers. Those who pretend to find them are rightfully despised as brainless wishful thinkers." His father's voice was quavering. "Oxfordians have also been known to find such ciphers. I do not believe in ciphers. Have *never!* Yet, in that verse, I have found a perfectly valid cipher message which may say that the Earl of Oxford wrote the plays. But it cannot be *so!*" The old gentleman pounded his desk. "That—that arrogant *ninny!*" Grosvenor Winthrop Little III steadied himself.

"I do not, for instance, believe," he went on with less heat, "that he was ever called Ver! Edward de Vere, the Earl of Oxford? He signed himself Edward Oxenford. But Ver is a designation that suits the wishful idiots. It can be said to mean true, you see, or green or spring. And even the common word 'ever' becomes loaded with ridiculous double meanings. I don't believe it!"

The old gentleman was very much upest.

"Just where do you see this—uh—cipher, Father?" J asked gently.

"You know what a poetic foot is? Here. Slash those lines into feet. Four to a line. Here. I've done it."

J looked at the paper on which his father had done it.

> This Fig / ure that / thou here / seest put, /
>   It was / for gen / tle Shake / speare cut; /
> Wherein / the Gra / ver had / a strife /
>   With Nat / ure, to / out-doo / the life; /
> O, could / he but / have drawne / his wit /
>   As well / in brasse, / as he / hath hit /
> His face; / the Print / would then / surpasse /
>   All, that / was e / ver writ / in brasse. /
> But, since / he can / not, Read / er, looke /
>   Not on / his Pict / ure, but / his Booke.
>
>   B. I.

"Now," said his father, pointing to the signature, "*B* is the second letter in the alphabet. *I* and *J* (in those times interchangeable) make the ninth letter. Nine and two add up to eleven, you will agree?

"So count to the eleventh foot. Extract it. From that, count to the ninth foot following. Extract it. Count eleven more. Then nine. It is not," his father mourned, "to be attacked as an improper cipher. Reason tells me so."

J did what he had been told to do and read off the result. *'Ver had his wit, Ver writ his Booke.* Well, well," J was impressed.

"How can I honestly omit this from any account of my researches?" his father said passionately. "Is it not my moral duty to reveal it, although it will give my enemies ammunition against me? As far as I know, no one has noticed this before. I could simply keep quiet. But would that be *right*, J? You see my dilemma?"

J felt an astonished relief. No thought of Win or the bonds was in his father's mind. J began to feel touched and fond. The old-fashioned code, he thought, the delicate conscience, the fine point—lost in the shuffle of modern mores, yet existing. Yet handed down to haunt the young, although they knew not whence it came.

But J roused to stop meowling to himself and say something helpful. The matter needed more study, he suggested. Perhaps there was another meaning in this. His father was dubious about the meaning of those three letters *V E R?*

Then might they have a meaning not yet correctly interpreted? Could not, for instance, the syllables be just the *two* letters, the *E* and the *R?*

His father listened and was comforted. "Not Elizabeth Regina." he said scornfully. "Yet, I believe you are right, J. I should take the middle course, here. Neither suppress this discovery nor announce it with fanfares until I, myself, thoroughly understand it. Yes. Well. Telephone, would you, J, to Mr. Thomas at this number, and say to him that I fear the book must be delayed, pending a great deal more work on my part?"

"I'll be glad to, Father. There's one more thing. You do know that Win has used my mother's bonds temporarily?"

"What's that? Oh, yes, I suppose ... Young Winthrop did call, I believe. By the way, J, would you mind telling young Winthrop that he need not fetch the bonds to me after all?"

"I'll be glad to, Father," J said gently. He called the number that was on the piece of paper.

Tobias said that he was very glad to know that J kept some kind of watch over the old gentleman's affairs. It was a scandal, in Tobias' opinion, how vulnerable J's father was to unscrupulous people. *Naturally,* Tobias himself had volunteered to take charge of those bonds. Did J think he was going to let them into *Pudney's* hands? About the book, Pudney would be glad to be off the hook, since Tobias had persuaded him into a deal that was of very slight profit to Pudney. None to Tobias. A favor. He'd be glad to do it. Himself, Tobias, was off (he said not when or where), and how was his mother?

J told him where his mother was, and Tobias bristled immediately. Well, he washed his hands! He had Done His Share! If Marietta was to be allowed to let some rackety, religious phonies get her funds into their clutches, that was Sophia's or J's responsibility. Tobias was no such fool!

J agreed with this cheerfully, hung up, saw that his father was already at his desk making tiny marks on paper with a sharp pencil, his white head bent, his face quiet—gone away from present trouble, safe in the turmoils of the past.

J phoned Sophia. Amy was there, was resting. Avery was doing as well as could be expected. (Sleeping was what Avery was doing.) Yes, Nanjo was all right, being helpful.

Win and Marion were coming. All was as well within the fort as could be expected.

So J said to tell Win he had news that was quite surprisingly mild, and he told Sophia that he thought he might stop by that Retreat on his way home. J thought he ought to check up on Marietta.

Sophia said fondly, "You're right, dear. We ought to. So you do it."

Thus it happened that as Sophia hung up, Annette, calling yet again, got Sophia this time.

"Mrs. Little, could I please speak to Mr. Little? Is he there?"

"No, he isn't," said Sophia without rancor. "He's had things to do today."

"If you know where he is, don't tell me on the telephone!"

"I have no intention of telling you on the telephone or otherwise," said Sophia calmly. "We have enough on our minds. . . ."

"Did he think it was wise to—go away by himself?"

"I am afraid," said Sophia, "that neither of us has had any time . . ."

"Mrs. Little," said Annette in a loud clear voice, "I know you have no idea what this is all about. But will you give him this message? The danger is over. He is perfectly free to tell anyone anything he likes. There is nothing to worry about now."

"How nice of you to call and say so," said Sophia acidly and broke the connection. She was furious! Nothing to worry about? *Nothing, eh?* Just life, that's all. Just life!

Tony had come into the motel room to stand behind Annette. "Smart, aren't you?" he said.

"Elementary," she said. "You think they may have his phone bugged. Okay, then, that was the quickest way to let them know they've lost the war."

Tony sighed and sat down. "I'm going to get you fired. You're no good at this kind of work."

"We don't know where Mr. Little is. We don't know where *they* are, either. How else can we tell them they've lost? You want to put it in tomorrow morning's paper?"

"Not me," said Tony. "But it now seems that 'people in responsible places' have decided that Mr. Jones has got to go. But where is he? Not at the Biltmore. Well, he has got to go just the same, and his toy with him, and it would be very handy to smoke him out and also catch him in an illegal act, such as a kidnapping. *Right away*."

Annette turned on him. "You want to make my Mr. Little *bait?*" she howled at him. "Then, you're damn right I'm no good at this kind of work!"

Tony said, "You've got to see it in proportion."

"I do not!" she howled. "I'll see it the way *I* see it. Let the Army and the Navy and the Air Force do their stuff, damn them! Mr. Little isn't going to be kidnapped. They don't want him anymore. I just told them so."

"Still and all," said Tony, "maybe the line isn't bugged, you see? Too bad, if you're so upset about him, you weren't smart enough to find out where he went."

She threw the motel's Bible at him. Tony ducked it and got the phone. He dialed J's number.

"Mrs. Little?"

"Yes."

"Is Mr. Little there, please?" Tony's voice was pleasant.

"No, I'm sorry. He isn't."

"This is Simon Gottschalk from his office. Can he be reached anywhere?"

"I doubt it, Mr. Gottschalk."

"Then when do you expect him, please?"

"Why, I expect him for supper," said Sophia.

"Then will you tell him I may ring him later? Thank you very much."

Sophia hung up, wondering about that name. She had never heard it. Still, she did know that Tom Pollack had been fired. He may have been replaced.

Annette said with a glittering eye, "*When* is supper? Didn't think to ask, eh?"

"You are the poorest damn sport I ever met in my life," said Tony. "Shut up and let me think."

"I think," she said, "*I'll* drop in for supper."

"No, you won't."

"*I resign!*" she howled. "Listen, they can't make him say a *word*, a place-name, that they don't *know*, by using the machine. They can't ask him a hundred million names of places to find out when they guess right. Don't you see? You weren't there. You don't know Mr. Jones like I know him."

"Cool it, why don't you, sweetheart?" said Tony. "Watch

those guilt feelings. If they've got him, *she* doesn't know it."

Annette made a mighty effort and became very calm indeed. She sat down and said, "Think, then."

"You know where the machine is. You think they rented. Maybe Goodrick gave an address. Suppose we could find them? If they have our Little man, *voilà!*"

"And if we find them, and they haven't got him," she said, agreeing on their course with perfect antagonism as to their goal, "then they'll *never!*"

CHAPTER 29

Saturday Evening

The woman who ran the Retreat received J in her very businesslike office, of which he found himself approving. She was a middle-aged person, very respectably gotten-up. Her name was Mrs. Langdon.

She told J that Mrs. Thomas was just getting acquainted. No judgment could be made now in the matter of Marietta's residence becoming permanent. "We are not a cult," she explained. "We have a chapel and services every day. Visiting speakers from many sources, religious, yes. But if we are fanatics about anything, it is cleanliness. Our people do their daily chores. They are supervised and so protected. The living here is very plain. What we accomplish is a tremendous simplification. People who can cope," she added, "wouldn't like it here, at all."

"How did you get into this work?" he asked her, interested.

She didn't quite know. But here she was, and the work was needed by people who were, to her mind, cripples of a sort.

"You do the coping?"

She smiled at him. (She liked him very much.) "Perhaps I do. It isn't always easy. I have to hold down the ecstasies and keep a firm grasp on the earth or we might all vanish in a cloud of incense." She had a nice laugh. "But you must see, Mr. Little, that I can't take everyone. Some people, when there are no longer any worldly excitements to resist, discover that they have fed on that resistance; they can't do without it. You might be surprised to know in what petty ways some 'religious' people can find 'evil.' "

This sounded darned shrewd to J. He said he guessed he wasn't very religious himself. He'd got as far as to think that something had put him here, all right. But he never had gotten his mind all the way around it.

She smiled and said that she had come to believe that, by definition, no creature could. "Well, sir, we shall see how your mother-in-law fits in here. Shall I tell you where to find Mrs. Thomas? She would like, I imagine, to show you around."

J thanked her. He liked her very much, darned if he didn't.

The building had a kind of inner garden court. There he came upon Marietta, seated on a wooden bench in the waning sunshine. Her round pink face did not look ecstatic to him.

J sat down and explained that he had just been talking to Mrs. Langdon and thought she was very nice. He and Sophia would be coming along later in the week to be sure that Marietta was happy.

"Do you like it?" he asked.

"I can't *bear* it!" she said and began to weep.

"Oh, now, come on," said I. "Then I'll take you home right now."

"No, no," she sobbed. "I can't bear to think of what I did. Oh, J, I was frightened and selfish. I ran away. I don't understand too many things. Poor child. Poor child. It's such a weight on my heart. It's such oppression. Poor little Nanjo!"

"What's this about Nanjo?" said J sharply.

"Oh, to come creeping in, so battered and so torn, and crying. I could *hear* her heart breaking and her terror. But I don't know what evils there are in the dark. I don't understand the world anymore. J, I don't know where she had been, or what evil she met in the dark world, the nighttime. . . ."

"Now, now," J soothed. "Nanjo's okay. Her boyfriend did

get into a little trouble. He's in jail. Was that what made her cry?"

"Oh, was poor Nanjo running away?" wept Marietta. "Oh, did she fall, that her stockings were bloody and her skirt ... her skirt all bloody and torn?"

"I don't know," said J quietly. He got up.

"J," she said, reaching out and grasping his jacket, *"you* understand the world."

"Oh, no, no, I don't," he said. "But I'll see to Nanjo. Don't you worry."

"Oh, I never ..." began Marietta mechanically and shut her mouth.

"Well, I'm pretty good at it," said J. "I'll do the worrying." But he found he could not simply walk away. "Don't sell your Good Angel short, now," he said kindly. "Get in touch, why don't you, and see if he'll put in a word for our side?"

"J," she said, "Avery is very, very ill. In dreadful pain. He should see a good doctor."

"I know," said J. "He has. Ask for Avery to be included. Tell your angel he could use a song?" J bent and kissed her cheek and went off tasting salt.

He was *worrying,* all right. *He was scared!*

He had no idea, as he whipped his car into the garage, whether anybody noticed. It was getting on to be late in the day. J had had no lunch. But no thought of food was in his mind. Sophia said, hushing him, "Amy's asleep. J, that Cousin Annie called and says it is all over. The danger. She says you're free to tell."

"Oh?" said J indifferently. "Where is Nanjo?"

"On the phone. She's been taking calls all day, like a good child." Sophia read his mood. *"What?"*

"We'll have to see," said J.

Nanjo was talking to Bobby James. Bobby's admiration was soothing; his attention to her every word relaxed her. She looked around and saw her father's face and his gesture that summoned her.

"Oh, Bobby, Daddy wants me for something."

"Well, sure," said Bobby. "But listen, I'll see you then?"

"Of course," said Nanjo. "That'll be fun. Thank you for asking me."

As her parents wordlessly directed, she walked into the family room. She knew this was ominous; her father had heard something. She sat down, but he did not. He said, "Nanjo, why were your stockings bloody and your skirt torn? And why were you crying in your bed?"

"Who told you?" she said angrily in a last effort to be what she thought was strong.

But J shook his head. "The only thing that counts, right now, is what hurt you. I have to know."

He wasn't angry. He spoke the truth. He was her father. He had to know. Nanjo bent over and said without wailing, "He was dead, Daddy, and I never meant for him to be dead."

Sophia, controlling her knees with great care, sat down. J kept asking quiet questions; they both kept listening, without comment, to the answers.

In the car Mr. Jones was saying to Goodrick, "Transparent! Don't you understand human motivations? *Why,* if the meeting is over, should *they* care what happens to the man Little? The girl gave it away. They *wish* us to think that the meeting is over. And why so urgently? Ah, because the meeting is *not* over! I am encouraged," he added. "We still have twenty-four hours."

Goodrick made a strange sound with lips and breath, *"Shoop. Shoop."*

"They were *lying,* I say," shouted Mr. Jones. "I don't need a machine to tell me that. And I'll handle him *my* way."

"Better play it cool," said Goodrick. "Noise in that neighborhood, and you won't get him. Slow down. Let it get dark."

Dusk was brief in this latitude. Win and Marion and the children came in the last light.

While the Little kids were being fed, Amy woke and stretched and rose and washed, and Nanjo, curled in her mother's chair, kept silent, listening to her father tell her brother (first) what the old gentleman, her grandfather thought was *his* moral dilemma. She saw Win blow out his breath, look sheepish, and shake his head.

J dropped the subject. He went on to tell Win—and Marion and Amy, now—Nanjo's story. He told it more quickly than she had.

A family session, a conference, simply developed.

Sophia put the Little kids snug to the television in the den. Amy reclined on the sofa in the family room. Win and

Marion sat side by side. Sophia was in her own chair, beside Nanjo, who now curled on the floor, red-eyed and silent, although her heart was surging along in rhythm, already comforted.

As for J, who by some instinct had drawn the draperies against the evening—he sat in the middle of his web. (He had heard Sophia tell him that the danger was over. He didn't understand how the danger could be *over*. He didn't know what it had ever been. But he put it out of his mind.) There was something, here, to be decided. He asked his family, How should Nanjo be advised?

Win thought it was a bad risk for Nanjo to keep silent. Cal's body must have been found; questions must have been asked on that block. Best she were not found out by detective work on the part of the police. Best she volunteered. She was wrong to have kept silent all day.

Marion said that to tell the truth was right, of course, but she hated to think of the consequences. Couldn't they protect Nanjo?

Sophia said, "I know what you mean, Marion. She's in for bad punishment. Not many will say she exactly caused Cal's death. But most will want to know what she was doing in that part of town, at all—suspecting the worst while they're at it. And the fact remains, if he was drunk enough to fall—" Sophia shook her head and was silent.

Amy finished for her. "He *might* have fallen anyhow? Sure, and if Nanjo gets into it, her peers are going to call her a bit of a jackass, so she'd sooner be dead, herself. And her elders are going to wonder if she asked for it. Of course . . ." She paused.

J said, "Go on, Amy."

Amy said, "What *I* wonder is, did he really have rape in mind?"

"That's what I wonder, too," Nanjo said without whimpering. "I don't know. I don't *know now*."

J said, with a brooding air, as if he thought out loud, "I'm thinking about Cal's people. Say we put forth to the public Nanjo's panic and Cal's behavior. I don't know as I care to imagine his children insisting for the rest of their lives that he wasn't that kind of man, that he must have simply seen a young girl (whose family he knew) alone and in distress, and he was only going to see her safely home."

Amy looked stricken. Nanjo began to cry again.

Win said, "We don't *know* that."

Sophia said, "We don't know otherwise. Nanjo had Cal down as a menace in her mind. Her judgment was impaired, remember. And that's a part of the truth, too."

Amy said, "We're not ever going to know, remember?"

"So what's the answer?" said Win. "Nanjo's got to get clear, somehow. I mean, *clear.*"

"What shall we do, Dad?" said Marion.

"It's a tough one," said Amy promptly. "Pops, you say."

J said, "It comes to me there could be a middle way. I'd suggest that Nanjo and I (and her mother, naturally) might go to see Judge Carroll. He knows us. He's an elder with experience in this kind of thing. We really don't know much about it. We'd ask him what authority we could go to and tell the truth we know, and our doubts besides, but first—*in private.* I don't believe sane people want the young punished all the rest of their lives. Anybody's young. Punishment isn't the point at all. I think he would certainly be able to advise us where to go and warn us what's probably going to happen when we do."

"Yes," said Sophia with a sigh.

"On the other hand," J went right on, "I, having been Cal's employer for a long time, will naturally go to see his people, wherever I can find them. They'll have to have the truth, all of it, including how Nanjo, if she was mistaken, came to make that mistake. And what they'll do, they'll do. But I should think *we* would have done the best we could."

Amy said, "See?"

Win said, "It's risky, but what isn't? I agree, Dad."

"Yes," said Marion.

"What about Nanjo?" said Nanjo's mother.

"Do you agree, Nanjo?" said her father.

"Yes, I do," his youngest said. She had the funniest feeling that if Cal had people, they would be real people, and this made *Cal* real, and everything was different. Because, although it was going to be awful (what she had to do), it was going to be *real,* and it was the only way to undo the nightmare.

Sophia said cheerfully, "J, you'll call Judge Carroll, then? But for heaven's sakes, let's have some supper. Everybody must be starving." Nanjo moved to let her mother rise. She looked as if she were about to crawl across the floor to where her father sat. Amy rolled slightly and came, with a spring, to her feet. "Stand up, Nanjo. The least you can do is set the table."

"Let me," said Marion.

Sophia said, "I'm putting everything that's in the icebox out. But I don't think there's enough bread."

"I'll go for bread," said Win. A double howl rose up in the den. "In a minute," said Win crisply and started toward the problem.

J, having watched his youngest stand up, went to the phone and spoke to Judge Carroll, who most courteously agreed to an appointment at his house for eight o'clock.

J went back into the family room, listening to this house, his daughters in the kitchen and the dining room, handmaidens to Sophia, his son's voice busy with some fathering.

J felt worried, but *happy*. Okay, if anybody wanted to make something out of it(happiness was not a matter of the absence of problems. It was not being perfectly comfortable and never had been. What the devil had *comfort* got to do with it?

But he did not sit down in his comfortable chair; he veered toward the kitchen, where he told the feminine flock that he'd just as soon go for the bread, and waited to receive the news that the coffee was low and he had better bring some, but the cream (they felt) was adequate.

So . . . in his mind still testing all his threads for strength and tension . . . J opened the door to the garage and went through the short passage, not bothering with the lights.

J had no sooner left the kitchen when the front doorbell rang. The females looked at one another, but they could hear Win going to answer.

"Excuse me," said the girl at the door in a breathless manner, "I'm Annette Woods. Could I please see Mr. Little?"

"I seem to have heard that name somewhere," said the good-looking young man. "Come in. I'm his son, Win."

She preceded him to the family room, which was empty. Nanjo came out of the dining room. "Oh," she said. "Hello."

Sophia, in the kitchen, lifted her head and said sharply, "Who's that?"

Amy heard a slate-colored crack, outside, in the evening. She stepped into the family room, thinking of Avery, and said, diverted at once, "Hey, you're the girl I saw at the beach. With my father." She raked Annette up and down with her smudged and beautiful eyes.

Annette seemed overwhelmed by the presence of all these young people. She said, "I just want one word with him. It's awfully important or I wouldn't . . ."

But now Sophia had come to see what was happening.

"Oh, Mrs. Little," cried Annette in a kind of relief. "Please may I . . ."

"I'm afraid," said Sophia coolly, "we can't ask you to stay."

"Oh, listen, please." Annette began to pour out a tale. "Tony and I found them. There was a meeting, our side and their side. We told them it was all over. We swore to them. We offered any proof they'd want. We *begged* them to test us. But one of them is *mad!* He pretended to believe us, finally. But he took off with Goodrick and two others, and we're afraid. He may think we were bluffing, just trying to trick him. . . ."

"Fancy," said Sophia distantly.

"Tony's outside, making sure. Where is Mr. Little? It would be terrible if *now* . . ."

"He's just gone for a loaf of bread," Sophia said.

"You . . . *fool!*" said Annette.

"Now, wait a minute!" said Win. He wasn't having his mother called a fool. He was braced for his mother to blast off immediately, but Sophia did not.

She said, "Outside? *Now?*"

It was Marion who said sensibly, "I don't think Dad's gone yet. I haven't heard the car go out."

Because of his mother's face, Win strode past her and began to cross the kitchen. Annette ran after him, caught up to him, said to him peremptorily, "I've got a gun. Get out of the way."

He had the door to the garage open, and he blocked her with his shoulder and snatched the gun out of her hand. Sophia and the girls were all crowding into the kitchen.

Amy said, "I heard what could have been a gunshot."

"Oh, J—" said Sophia faintly.

"Call the police," said Win. "One of you. Hurry!"

"I will," said Nanjo stoutly, and she ran.

Marion began to run; Win knew where she was going. To the Little kids, of course. She always would.

He started cautiously along the way to the garage. The strange girl was right behind him, twitching at his coattail.

"No lights," she warned. "No lights."

The garage door was up. Both cars were there. There was some light out on the driveway. There was some heap, some lumpish thing, some *body* out there on the concrete.

"Dad?" said Win. The whole world was falling, heavy, heavy on his shoulders. He could not move for the weight. Then a car started, somewhere in the neighborhood, and the spell was broken. Win went swiftly along the garage wall and into the open. The light was poor. All he could see was an outline of a fallen body. It was not his father's. The strange girl came skittering past him, went down on her knees, and said, "Oh, no! Oh, Tony!"

Breath came sweeping into Win's lungs; the garage light went on behind him. He turned. He saw, down on the floor, between the cars, another heap, another silent heap.

Amy, who had turned on the light, came along the rear wall to that slot, and he saw her freeze. The girl at his feet said, "Listen! Listen!"

Win turned his head; he had sensed his mother's impending presence, and he did not want to see. There was a whispering and then a crashing of branches.

Gladstone Neeby burst out of the dividing shrubbery. "What's going on?" he said. "Did somebody fire a shot? Who's that?"

Then Nanjo's young voice calling, "They're coming. Should I call anybody else?"

"Call an ambulance, that's a good kid," said Amy strongly.

Win looked. His sister was standing, and as he looked, Amy put her folded arms on the roof of J's car and her head down on her arms in an exhausted way.

Sophia was standing in the very center of the garage, and the wan light fell on her head and shoulders. She was looking down. Her right hand came up slowly, and she began to rub it against the bodice of her dress, as if to cleanse it.

Neeby said, "Oh, my God! Sophia!" He began to move.

Win said, "Get out of the way," and began to run.

His mother's head came up, and she took a step backward. The light made her face into a mask.

"He's dead," she said. "But where is J? Does anybody know where J is?"

A police car came. An ambulance came. Goodrick was DOA. The police searched all the shrubbery, the whole block, and came at last to say, "No. Nothing."

Nobody knew where J was.

CHAPTER 30

Saturday Night

At 9 P.M. the Little kids were asleep in Nanjo's room. Left in the family room were Sophia, her three children, Marion, the Neebys, and apart in the corner, Annette Woods and Tony Thees, whose damaged ear was bandaged under a white cap.

All the officials had gone away. A search was on. Over the city, over the state, men looked for J Middleton Little, "Male, Caucasian," and so on.

Everyone had heard everything. They were beginning to go around again.

Gladstone Neeby said, "I saw a car, all right. Sedan, dark color; that's just about all I can say. I heard a shot or what might be a shot. So I looked out. Didn't seem to be anything going on out front. I looked out the side. Nothing. So I looked out the front again, and two men were helping (I thought) another man into the back. I couldn't see who they were. They took off slow and easy. I let them go. I don't know what I could have done. I damn well wish I'd done it."

Susie said, "They'll find him. They *will*. They'll *have* to." (Everybody knew this was desirable, but not necessarily so.)

Amy got up and said, "Well, I've got to go. I have a husband. But just once—tell us again, Mr. Thees?"

So Tony went over it again. How he had thought he heard feet scraping on the garage side of the house, had sent Annette inside and drawn his gun, and gone very cautiously to see. He had seen, although very dimly, what he had taken to be two figures in the slot between the cars, deep within the garage. So he had gone softly and said softly, "Hold it!"

There had been silence and no movement, and he had taken one more step when there had come simultaneously a shot and a blow. He had fallen, banged his head (he thought, now), blacked out, and had heard no more. His own gun had not been fired. Whoever had sent a bullet through the flange of Tony's right ear may have sent that same bullet into Barry Goodrick's brain.

Tony was pretty well convinced that it had been this man they knew as Mr. Jones. There was a determined search on for him. Jones must soon be found, Tony said (knowing that this was desirable, but not necessarily so).

"What would he do with Pops?" Amy was blunt.

Tony said, "We don't know." (Amy's eyes said, Never mind. I know.)

"Mother," said Amy, "I have to go to Avery now."

"I know you do, dear," Sophia said.

So Amy left them. She said not a word to the girl, Annette, whose eyes, ruined now, all the paint smeared, watched her go.

Glad Neeby said, "And the damned meeting really was over, eh? And *where,* did you say?"

"A place called Poonacootamoowa," Tony repeated patiently. "It's an estate, a very rich man's country place. Any librarian could have found out whose and where. It's in the mountains, isolated. Pretty vulnerable from the air, you see."

"And old J, he knew that," Glad sighed. "But he thought he had seven seats to the moon. Seven, eh?"

"As long as it always was just a yarn," said Susie Neeby angrily, "not to say a big fat lie—why didn't you tell him he had enough to go around?"

"Ah, hush, Susie," said Sophia. "They meant it to be cruel. But J wasn't so foolish."

The tenses of the verbs began to linger on the air. Glad said quickly, "So what did the big brains decide? The world is doomed or what?"

Tony said, "I guess it's not that simple."

Susie used her handkerchief.

Win got up and said, "Ma, will you be okay if Nanjo and I go and attend to that matter? Judge Carroll said he'd wait until nine thirty. And it's nearly."

"Of course. Yes, you'd better do that. But I . . . won't go at this time."

"I'll be fine," said Nanjo. "Win will help me." She sprang up, ready.

"Listen, can't *I* go, wherever it is?" Glad said.

"Thanks," said Win, "but this is where I take over."

"Why, sure," said Susie brightly, "until your Dad gets back."

Her husband touched her.

When Win and Nanjo had gone, Sophia said to her friends, "You don't have to stay with me, Susie and Glad. I've been pretty thankful for you both ... but now, I can't keep on talking."

"Come on, Susie," said Glad Neeby promptly. "Just remember, Sophia, we're right next door."

"I'll be here," said Marion.

So there was another exodus. Neeby said sternly to Tony and Annette, "Hadn't you better go someplace else, too?"

"In a minute," Tony promised.

The Neebys left quickly, because Susie was absolutely going to cry.

Annette was crying. She wasn't making any noise, but the tears were slipping out of her eye corners. "Oh, please," she said to Sophia, quivering to be punished.

Sophia said, "I understand, I suppose, that you did according to your lights, but don't ask any more of me right now. *"Who,"* she flared up suddenly, "did you think he *was* anyway?" She turned her back.

"I think you'd just better go," said Marion fiercely.

The phone rang.

"Shall I?" said Tony quickly, and Sophia, white and ready to fall, said, "Yes, quick!"

"This Thees?" the voice said. "Well, we got this fellow Jones, or whoever he is. And from the papers on him we've got the location of the plane and so forth. So that's under control."

Tony kept himself from saying Good. He said, "What about the car?"

"We got the car, too. Did I say Jones had a gun on him and maybe we had a hot suspect for the killing of Goodrick? Trouble is, right away they had to put him in a straitjacket and then he ... I don't know what ... I guess he had like a stroke. He won't be telling us much. Neither does the car. Somebody lost a little blood, not ... uh ... necessarily significant."

"Where was the car?"

"In an alley. Industrial section. Practically deserted by night. No watchman saw or heard a damn thing."

"The other two men?"

"No sign of them. We found this Jones, laughing like a maniac, on a bus bench on Wilshire Boulevard. Looks like his men dumped him there, drove off, and then ditched the car."

Tony said nothing.

"And as for your friend Little," the voice went on, "we haven't got a thing. Don't tell his wife, but the chances are they panicked and just dumped his body in some out of the way place. It figures. That Jones would murder as soon as pick his teeth, the shape he was in. Oh, we'll find it. But I don't think before morning. If then."

Tony now gave over the phone to Sophia, who chose to hear for herself, and the voice gave her a somewhat less blunt account of these developments.

She hung up and stood—the tall woman, the aging woman, the agonized woman. Tony swallowed and said, "I wish you'd let me stay and take your calls." (Cushion them, he meant.)

Sophia said, "No, I don't want you around. I have many things to think about." Color came into her face. Her dark eyes flashed to life with her temper. "Better things than how you two behaved."

"We should have—" Tony began.

"I'll tell you what you should have done," Sophia cried, magnificent in anger. "You should have caught J in Chicago and told him the truth. What do you know about people like us? Did you think we had been such fools all our lives that you could fake up a foolish tale and tempt us to save our simple-minded selves ... while you, in your wisdom, sneaked around behind our backs *playing God?* Oh, go away," she cried. "It is not right for me to talk like this. It is not *seemly,*" said Sophia, and then quietly, "I think you had better leave me. I'll take my own calls, thank you."

Tony drove. His ear hurt like hell. Beside him Annette was carrying on, sobbing and twisting. "Oh, God," he could hear her saying, "I want to go home. I've got no home. I only want to go *home! Somewhere?*"

Tony had glimpses of what she meant. Sure, maybe he'd

like to go home, too. To the womb, that meant, of course. No problems, eh? Well, you can't do that.

He wouldn't have thought *she'd* crack up like this. He couldn't—he hadn't—he had never (he guessed) really wanted to tie himself to anybody. So better not think about the crazy idea of getting married, having a pack of kids, and *making* a home. That was nothing he'd quite had in mind. Who needs, he thought, to get so involved, so *used to,* so dependent on somebody else ... that you got to go through suffering like that woman's? Why should you let yourself in for *that?*

"Grow up," he said aloud. "You can't go home again."

So copping out? Ah, but you don't have to wonder if you're selling your soul for comfort. All you have to do is say, "There is no soul." And play it cool.

And miss the whole thing?

"Look, sweetheart," he said after a while.

Marion, having checked on the Little kids once more, came out into the hall of the bedroom wing, glanced into the family room, drew back, and flattened herself against the wall. She could comfort the children, but she could help Sophia only by being here. So she waited in the middle. Being there was all.

Sophia, by herself in the family room, had crossed over to J's chair. She hadn't switched on his reading lamp. She had gone down on her knees, because she needed the sense of being closer to the earth. Her hands were clasped on the leather of his chair's arm.

She was not weeping. If she was praying, she didn't know it.

She knew she must take on the elders if J never came home. She must watch out for his father and catch that moment when he could no longer live alone. She must watch out for Marietta. And she must do for her children whatever she now could and accept what they would increasingly be doing for her. She must live out her span, taking all things in order.

Through the glass wall she could see some of her garden now that the moon was up. She thought, And if J is translated, now, into something like moonlight, I must try to think that it is beautiful? (Someday she would weep for her desolation, but not now.) Be brave? she mused. Remember him? That's pretty bleak. But still it's necessary. *Because I mustn't blame J!* He wouldn't leave the rest of us behind if he could help it. He wasn't tired enough, not yet. J loved being alive. Nobody knew that so well as I. Did nobody else know it at all?

Forty miles away to the south, in the city, two police officers were speaking together in low voices.

"Can't talk, hardly. Makes no sense. So a John Doe?"

"*He* dunno who he is. That's what the doctor said. Look at the description. Average. Average. Scars? Naw! Nothing you can see. And no prints off of *them* hands." The speaker glanced at the great puffs of bandages on the two hands of the man in the hospital bed. "And with his jaw broke and wired up, the teeth we don't get at so good, either. He musta had a partial denture, they say, but it ain't there now."

"Nothing on him to help us. That hunk of stainless, or whatever it is, won't do any good for us, eh?"

"Listen, we don't even know it's got anything to do with him. What is it, anyway? Some junky souvenir from a million gift shops. So it was lying there in the weeds. And so was he. So what? Forget it."

"And who the hell threw him there—beat up, out of his head, and naked as the day? We got nothing on *that*, and we're not goinna."

"Well, put him on the list. Move him to Big County tomorrow. Maybe somebody will come looking, although how his own mother . . . C'mon. Better tell the nurse she can give him another shot now if she wants."

They went out of the room.

"In a way, you know," said one of the officers on the other side of the door, "too bad he's not going to die. Some world, right?"

In the silent hospital room the blackened eyes of the man in the bed near the window were open. After a while he began to moan.

His room-mate, a man named Robinson, who had had an appendectomy (which is nothing, these days) wished the nurse would hurry up and put the poor fellow out of his misery again. The other man began to move the great mittens on his hands in a restless way, as if he were weaving or something.

Mr. Robinson, who was feeling terrible (although not, himself, in pain), said, "Listen, try and take it easy. Okay?"

The other man could hear, had heard; his head turned.

"Listen," said Mr. Robinson, "it's got to be pretty rough, not knowing who you are. But you don't want ... I mean ... you don't want to give up or anything. I mean, I don't think you ought to worry *too* much about who you are, anyhow," said Mr. Robinson, who ran a delicatessen in an ordinary way and was no genius, no angel, and not even a psychiatrist, but who just wanted in an ordinary human way to stop the other's suffering if he could. "The thing of it is," he said, "your connections, once they show up, they're the ones will let you know who you are, believe me."

The other man lay very still.

"At least you're not alone," his room-mate said. "For tonight, anyway, there's me, whoever I am."

"Sssso ... Sssso ..." The other man made sound through his wired jaws, and the sound blurred off to a kind of buzz.

"What's that you're trying to say? *So?* Is that it? *So?*"

The other's head rolled, despairingly. "Oonacoota ... oom ... oo ... ah. "Oonacoota ... oom ... oo ... ah ..."

"Now wait, " said Mr. Robinson. He reached for the pad and pencil he had handy. "I'm writing that down. You said that *before.* Those cops, seemed to me, kept egging you. But they didn't believe you's meaning anything. Gimme that again."

"Oonacoota ... oom ... oo ... ah ..."

"That's what you said before. So it's got to mean something. Well, what *I* mean ... you never know. So why don't you go ahead, say what comes in your mind. I'm listening."

The other man wasn't moaning anymore. His attention seemed caught. Mr. Robinson was glad.

After a long silence, the man said, "Oom ... id ... ul ..."

"Yah, I'm listening. Ooom ... id ... *Middle,* you mean, maybe?"

"Oom ... iddleton ... lil ... lil ... lit ... ul...." The head turned. A hope seemed to spring up and tighten that neck to the tension of life.

"Gotcha," said Mr. Robinson, scribbling. "Go on."